CIVALIA

SCOTT MORTON

First Edition.

What if...
IDEATION
PUBLISHING
DESIGN

Editor: Catherine Cattrello
Managing Editor: Robin Shukle
Design and Production: Liz Mrofka

Bruck Illustration by: Shannon Watts - Art & Design
Portico LPE & Sean's Sculpture by: Pauline Verbest
John's Mind Illustration by: Eve Margo Withrow–www.evemargowithrow.com
Flammarion: Public Domain
Other Illustrations by: Scott Morton
Front Cover Image by: Liz Mrofka, Doc Thissen–docthissen.com, and
  NASA: Blue Marble, Sky image by Sergey Nivens
Back Cover image by: Stocksnapper

Printed by: Kindle Direct Publishing

 John Tantivy Press

ISBN: 9781671962545

TABLE OF CONTENTS

PREFACE

On April 21, 1969, Ian McHarg, a landscape architect, recorded a radio program entitled, *Is Man a Planetary Disease?* Two years later he answered his question when he gave the 1971, B. Y. Morrison Memorial Lecture for the Department of Agriculture, Agricultural Research Service, entitled *Man: Planetary Disease.*

My friend Stellan King and I agreed with Mr. McHarg then, and we have only seen the disease worsen with the Earth experiencing spreading lesions on its epidermis, ever deepening puncture wounds, severe burns, skin rashes, lacerations, abrasions, wasting away of its vital organs and systems, an ever increasing fever, and an exponentially increasing number of disease organisms; we humans.

Examining these disease symptoms thoroughly, and applying our engineering knowledge, Stellan and I diagnosed the cause of the Earth's ailment to be a buildup of waste energy, quantifiable as entropy. After lengthy study, investigation, learning, and soul searching, we arrived at what we consider to be a humane and reasonable treatment for this malady. The time came when we sought to implement our cure, and this is a record of our journey and our efforts.

DECLARATION OF LIFE

LIFE, being the fundamental, moral postulate,
is an unalienable right.

Because life of indeterminate length can only
be sustained by domains of such size and
composition only energy need cross the
boundaries, a PERSONAL DOMAIN,
the individual and the domain comprising an
indivisible entity, is also an unalienable right.

To maintain the integrity of an entity, it is
essential the person consent to any alteration
of the mass and energy fluxes by others.
Therefore, the MORAL OBLIGATIONS
of each individual are to make no unauthorized
alteration of another's entity and to effect
faithful stewardship of their own.

Recognizing the truth of this declaration,
we commit ourselves to a life based on
this moral code.

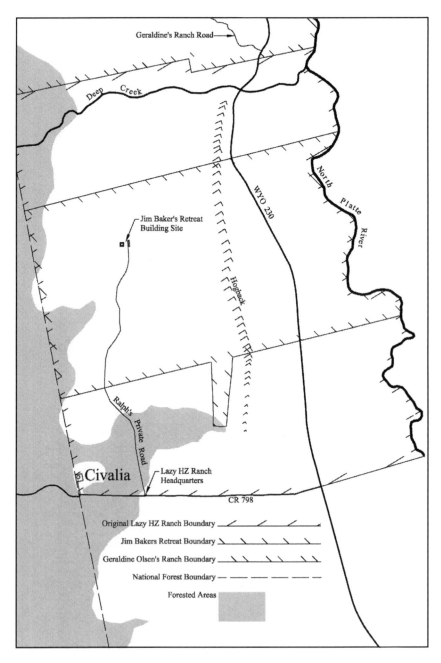

Geraldine's Ranch Road

Deep Creek

North Platte River

WYO 230

Jim Baker's Retreat
Building Site

Hogback

Ralph's Private Road

Civalia

Lazy HZ Ranch
Headquarters

CR 798

Original Lazy HZ Ranch Boundary

Jim Bakers Retreat Boundary

Geraldine Olsen's Ranch Boundary

National Forest Boundary

Forested Areas

LOCATION OF CIVALIA

PART I

THE CONCEPTION
OF CIVALIA

CHAPTER 1

S ome friends and I had embarked on the development of plans for Civalia, an intentional community designed to maximize our satisfaction in life and to address the root cause of the major, interlocking, environmental problems appearing worldwide. These problems include heating of the oceans, climate change, buildup of garbage and trash, annually occurring dead spots in the oceans, air pollution, overpopulation, and loss of topsoil to name a few.

I was looking for a building site for Civalia in the Upper North Platte River Valley when I met Ralph Hertell. Ralph had a ranch, the Lazy HZ, just north of the Colorado border in south central Wyoming, and through my developing friendship with Ralph, we not only found a building site, but I began my career as a bank robber. Over the next several years I stole, perhaps I should say legally "extracted" or "wrested" more than 370 million dollars from the banking industry to finance our efforts to build and promote Civalia.

Some people call me Seeker, but my birth name is John Tantivy. At the time I met Ralph, I was in my mid-sixties, as was my friend Stellan King, whom I had met when we both studied engineering in college. Slightly shorter than my six-foot height and slightly stockier than me, Stellan was raised on a farm in eastern Wyoming and dressed accordingly: jeans, plaid shirts, and boots, the same as I did. We also shared blue eyes and light brown hair, which we both allowed to seek its innate arrangement, as we were always too busy deliberating, experimenting, and building to bother with hair styling. I don't know about mine, but Stellan's eyes would sparkle as we followed trains of thought through the thickets, swamps, deserts, mountain ranges, oceans, and prairies of thinking; places I know I could never have traveled alone.

Where our travels took us was an understanding of our situation on Earth, which Geraldine Olsen, Ralph's friend and neighbor, articulated in a down-to-earth, comprehensible way. A paraphrase of her analogy is this:

> You are in your cottage, and the cottage is sealed on the outside, so no air, water, or solids come in or go out. There are food and water bottles in the pantry, sunlight streams through the windows, and heat travels in and out through the outside walls. How long can you survive?

When I was a child, I actually experienced a scenario somewhat like this. My family was living in a remote Forest Service ranger station without inside plumbing during the blizzard of 1949. The upwind two sides of the house were completely frozen over with ice, and the whole house became buried in snow up past the eves. During the three days the blizzard raged and another couple of days it took my parents to dig out, we could not use our outhouse. We did have plenty of food and water, but sometime in the second day we had to put out the fire in our wood stove. There was not enough ventilation to supply oxygen for both us and the fire. Mom and Dad worried about us all being asphyxiated.

The odors from our bathroom wastes became unbearable, and the air had become smoky and stuffy from the fizzling fire in the stove. Although we had plenty of food and water, we were miserable. This was not exactly like Geraldine's scenario, because there was no sunshine, and there was a little air exchange; unlike her analogy where there was full sunshine and zero air exchange. Still, I can say from personal experience, no one could last long in Geraldine's hypothetical cottage. You'd die of waste buildup long before you ran out of food, and it wouldn't take long. There'd still be food on the table when you were gone.

Geraldine's analogy continued:

> Suppose some plants are added to the cottage. Now some of the air is regenerated by the plants, using the sunlight as energy to accomplish this task. In the process, they restore some of your waste products to usable, primary materials while creating waste energy in the form of heat. All of this waste energy, plus the waste heat generated by both you and the plants in the normal course of living, either goes out through the sealed walls of the cottage, or, if it can't get out, raises the temperature inside. If there are enough plants in the cottage, all of the air is regenerated and all of your wastes are used by the plants. However, plants cannot exist all by themselves. They need bees, wasps, flies, and other insects and creatures to pollinate them; birds, bats, squirrels, and other creatures to spread their seeds; and worms, fungi, microbial decomposers, and other living things in the soil to help them obtain the nutrients they require. So, all of these other living things need to be in the cottage with you, requiring even more plants to restore all of the wastes generated by all of these creatures.

Although Geraldine did not specifically mention this fact in her analogy, the cottage has to be larger than an actual cottage in order to contain all of this biological activity; much larger, and if you are going to survive indefinitely, the plants also have to become the base of your food chain. The zinger in her analogy came when she pointed out:

> The Earth really is just one big cottage, and we're all living inside it, and here we are burning all the furniture and all the old dead plant material, meaning fossil fuels, tearing up the plants, making more and more people inside the cottage, piling up our wastes and garbage everywhere, and killing off a lot of the other living things the plants rely on.

Geraldine allowed these actions don't make much sense, and she questioned whether we deserve the moniker of *Homo sapiens*, since we don't seem to be very wise about what we're doing. Some other harmful things we're doing she didn't mention in her list are stripping the topsoil, making lots of materials that plants cannot change back to primary materials, and changing the reflectivity, absorptivity, emisivity, and insulation of the Earth.

The road I traveled to meet Ralph and Geraldine was long and winding. After Stellan and I graduated from college, we drifted apart as we pursued our separate careers; Stellan on a more conventional engineering path, and me into following further the road on my quest. In my early childhood, at least as far back as I can remember, I'd been seeking to understand the basic meaning and functioning of myself and the world; searching for that definitive paradigm of life.

Every person acquires a paradigm within their first few years. The Jesuits are thought to have said, "Give me a child until he is seven and I will give you the man." Few, if any, of us have a clear understanding of where and how our early paradigms are learned, but learn them we do! They appear to osmose into our brains from the myriad of experiences we have in those first few years. Once established, paradigms are terribly difficult to change, and most people take theirs to the grave with little modification. I have found this to be true for the vast majority of people I have encountered in my now more than eight decades of life. Few of us ever change them.

Mine changed over time, but not without a tremendous amount of mental anguish and upheaval. The paradigm I now hold bears little resemblance to my childhood one and little resemblance to those of my fellow citizens in the USA. I am also not aware of any similar worldview in other cultures or countries. I believe the genesis for the changes in my paradigm is to be found in an early awakening of an intense curiosity about most everything, a series of experiences calling into question the major foundation blocks of the culture in which I live, and the recognition that my childhood paradigm was inconsistent.

Memories of my early paradigm are difficult for me to organize. Whenever I try to recall what it was like, I find my mind wandering from bit to bit, somewhat like wandering through a junk yard with no organization to the bits of wreckage and debris scattered about. These bits of rubbish generally appear as injunctions of various intensities, often contradictory. An early example was when I spied some leftover cake on the kitchen counter. The injunction "God helps those who help themselves" came to mind, so I did. Later when my sister was crying for a piece of the cake I had consumed, my mother forcefully reminded me of the injunction "share with your sisters," and I was stricken with remorse and guilt. Another one was "eat everything on your plate; remember those starving children in China," so I did. I was then smitten with a bad case of indigestion and ended up vomiting, reminding me of my parent's injunction "gluttony is a sin," and I was fearful of going to hell.

I held hundreds, maybe thousands, perhaps even more, of these injunctions in my paradigm; a chaotic, seething mess. When any of these conflicted, the one foremost in my mind became dominant. Later, when a rival injunction surfaced and became foremost, I would experience guilt, fear, remorse, regret, or some other negative emotion for having violated this now dominant, conflicting injunction.

At some point, I can't say exactly when, I began to recognize these inconsistencies and conflicts. I think this process started with the word **STOP**.

My parents gave me a set of wooden American Bricks, the progenitor of the plastic Lego® blocks of today. I built houses, bridges, roads, cars, and even stop signs, hand lettering the word STOP on pieces of cardboard. I was two years old and do not remember these actions. I was told of them years later by friends and former colleagues of my parents who expressed amazement one so young could print words. The American Bricks proved to be crucial in my life, because a few years later they became the basis for the first step in my journey to overhaul my paradigm.

American Bricks came in only three forms and two colors; a full brick, a half brick, and half-sized roofing brick, some yellow and some red. With such a limited variety of bricks, not everything

I tried to build was possible, or if possible, not very realistic or satisfying. The solution to these problems came in the form of another gift my parents gave me, for which I will be forever grateful.

This second gift was a child's tool box. It contained not the useless plastic replicas of tools given to children today, but fully functional ones; a hammer, hand saw, coping saw, screwdriver, square, pliers, chisel, hand drill and bits, and a folding rule. I began damaging my toys. I cut the full bricks into two lengthwise pieces, drilled holes for string, wire, and rubber bands, and cut notches in various locations. These modifications vastly increased the utility and flexibility of the toy bricks. I will admit some of them did not survive my surgeries.

From that time forward I tended to either modify my toys to suit my own imagination or manufacture my own toys from various materials and castoffs I found. Sometimes the results were very satisfying and instructive, and sometimes they were disappointing, but also instructive. The net result was I stopped living according to the injunction given to me by my parents, "do not damage your toys." This was probably my first step in becoming the seeker of a better paradigm; a better way to interact with the world around me and a better way to understand how the world really works.

Digging in the dirt, building roads for toy cars, climbing trees, mowing the lawn in a city street pattern, taking things apart, attempting to put things back together, or repairing broken things, all built up an intuitive knowledge of how things work; the beginnings of my engineering education in statics and dynamics. One memorable lesson was when I built a boat with a four-layer superstructure from scrap boards, nailing spools on the top board to represent funnels. I was immensely proud of my wooden boat creation and filled the bathtub to launch it for the first time. The boat did float, of course, since it was wood, but only on its side, because it was very top heavy. From this I began to learn about buoyancy and centers of gravity.

Over time my boats became more sophisticated, eventually even motorized. My thirst for understanding the physical world grew, and eventually I graduated to automobiles, then tractors and other heavy machinery. I was on my way to becoming the engineer I eventually became and to gaining empirical and theoretical knowledge of how the world works. Along the way I **stopped** living by the injunction, "if you don't know anything about it, leave it alone." I loved to know how things worked.

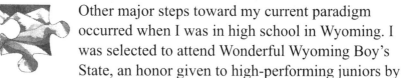Other major steps toward my current paradigm occurred when I was in high school in Wyoming. I was selected to attend Wonderful Wyoming Boy's State, an honor given to high-performing juniors by the American Legion. The goal of the program was, and still is, to give boys from across the state a week of activities to teach them about the State of Wyoming, its governmental structure, and its law-making processes. Boy's State was then held on the Wyoming State Fairgrounds, and we were housed in four large dormitory rooms, each dorm room being a city.

My first lesson on the American version of democracy occurred when the Wyoming Legion Department Commander roused us out of the dormitory at daybreak on the first morning we were there. My memory of this event is as fresh as the day it happened.

> The Commander lines us up in ranks outside the dorm, and tells us what to expect for the week. His lieutenants make certain we are lined up in straight rows and columns and standing at attention. The Commander begins his lecture, "You are going to learn about Democracy. Now, drop and do pushups."
>
> The young man to my right has been straddling a gift left by an errant horse wandering through the fairgrounds during the night. To avoid doing pushups directly over the pile, he moves to the side.
>
> "Get in Line," the Commander bellows.
>
> "But, sir . . . ," the youth begins an explanation.
>
> "I said, get in line!" he interrupts.
>
> My neighbor reluctantly moves back over the pile and proceeds to do very shallow pushups.

After the more scholarly among us, me included, were humiliated by the jocks, who were able to do a hundred or more pushups without breaking a sweat, the Commander praised them and then dismissed all of us to return and police our cities for inspection. No city did very well that first day; the beds were not made to military standards, the floors were dirty, our belongings were messy, and so on. I couldn't understand why democracy required military regimentation, inspections, and hospital corners on beds. I **stopped** believing the injunction, "democracy is the best form of government to provide freedom and equality for all."

 My second lesson occurred later that day when elections were held for the various mock state, county, and local offices. The highest offices, Governor, State Legislators, Secretary of State, etc., went to popular kids, usually athletes who had played against other schools and therefore had some name recognition throughout the State. I ended up being a local prosecuting attorney and was elected Mayor of my city, probably because I was a reasonably friendly, outgoing person. I knew some of the kids elected to higher offices, and knew for a fact some of them were less than upstanding citizens. I had crossed paths with one boy in particular over such issues as plagiarism, lack of integrity, lying, and sloth. I knew some of the other boys, elected to much lower offices, were more knowledgeable, ethical, and honest. I **stopped** believing in the injunction, "work diligently and hard and you will be suitably rewarded."

 As the week wore on, the imaginary court case, for which I was the prosecuting attorney, took shape. The defendant, one of the least popular Boy's State delegates, was charged with reckless driving after going off the road and injuring a bystander. In the resulting mock trial, I railroaded him into a conviction by the use of invented testimony, taking advantage of the bumbling defense attorney, and surprise witnesses. I was praised by the Legionnaires running this part of Boy's State. I learned my third lesson on democracy, and I **stopped** believing the injunction, "the rule of law is the best way to achieve justice for all." I am not proud of what I did, and I am glad Boy's State was not real.

The least popular and unathletic delegates to Boy's State had gravitated to the city where I was Mayor. After some posturing and scuffling for positions, the more popular boys banded together in hierarchical structures in the other three cities. We all got along well in our city and decided we would cooperate to win the daily inspections. And we did, after the first day when no city won, right up until the last morning.

The Wyoming Legion Department Commander, whom we had not seen since our first morning lecture, performed the last inspection. He entered our city, swiped his hand across the cinder block wall, and then found sand on the floor. He approached one of the bunk beds, surreptitiously pulled out one of the perfect hospital corners, and dinged us for poor bed making. We lost the last inspection. All of us were incensed, but rationalized our loss by deciding the Legion had determined our city could not be allowed to win all of the inspections. I **stopped** believing the injunction, "all of those in positions of authority are benevolent, trustworthy, ethical people." I was looking forward to going home the next morning.

 That last night our city was awakened by sounds in the hallway. One of our city's residents discovered a group from one or more of the other cities approaching with buckets of water and sand. We quickly surmised they were going to trash our city, so we barricaded the door. They attacked, pouring sand near the door and washing it under with water. We plugged the gap under the door with towels to minimize the damage, but some got through. I recognized the voice of the less than model plagiarist, whom I mentioned previously. I'm certain some of the other attackers were his buddies. Some of them went outside and began throwing rocks at our windows. We were on the second floor, so the rocks were thrown fairly hard to get to our level. A window broke.

I slipped out and went for help. By the time a couple of Legionnaires managed to get up, get dressed, and get outside, making considerable noise in the process, the night had quieted down. The attackers had gone back to bed, pretending to be asleep. Even though the evidence clearly showed our city was attacked from without, we were blamed for the damage. I **stopped** believing the injunction, "the truth will always triumph." I was thankful the ordeal was over.

When I became aware of these small pieces of my paradigm (plus a myriad of others), examined them, found incompatibilities as well as downright violations of reality, and assembled them into a whole, the picture that emerged appeared similar to the lithographs, *Waterfall* and *Belvedere*, by M. C. Escher; small pieces of which appear consistent and coherent, but when taken as a whole, become impossible. An artist friend of mine, Eve Margo Withrow, coming to know me well, created a lithograph she called John's Mind, showing clearly the jumbled, chaotic, contradictory, nature of my mind.

I came to understand almost all people also have such confused, disorganized, unworkable, paradigms, but they, as I had, live with these bewildering, muddled, scrambled, mental messes by compartmentalizing thoughts and beliefs. This describes how a professed religious/political leader such as Jim Jones, who claimed to be the reincarnation of Jesus Christ, can perpetuate such a horror as the Jonestown Massacre. Had I lived out my life with my childhood paradigm would I have become another Jim Jones or even something worse? I would like to think not, but I can't be certain.

As it is, even though I have forged a much more coherent paradigm, I have become a bank robber, albeit a legal one. Let me tell you how the transformation of my paradigm and my metamorphosis into a legal bank robber came about.

As I have noted, my childhood paradigm, primarily based on the injunction, "work hard and you will be suitably rewarded," began to exhibit inconsistencies from my earliest childhood. But these were minor, soon forgotten, and I was able to ignore them by compartmentalizing my thoughts. My Wonderful Wyoming Boy's State experiences were a turning point when I combined those experiences with Solomon's writings in Ecclesiastes 9:11 (KJV), ". . . the race is not to the swift, nor the battle to the strong, neither yet bread to the wise, nor yet riches to men of understanding, nor yet favor to men of skill; but time and chance happeneth to them all."

My subsequent experiences changed this first inkling into a certainty and exposed a major raison d'être for many of these inequalities. This culprit? Hierarchies. Hierarchies of all kinds; governmental, business, civic, and even religious and philanthropic hierarchies. Hierarchies may ostensibly claim to have some great and noble purposes, but almost universally those claims prove secondary at best, and are usually even lower down the priority ladder. The primary purpose of hierarchies appears to be funneling money and power, these two things being essentially equivalent, from a broad base of those at the bottom of the hierarchical pyramid to a few at the apex. One has only to be a member near the bottom of a few of these organizations to experience this first hand.

Having stumbled upon this serious disconnect with hierarchies, I tried to figure out if some religion might prove to be an exception. I immersed myself in a pilgrimage to find a coherent paradigm through religious studies.

I was raised in a protestant household. Every Sunday was church and Sunday school, and I was so steeped in my religious heritage that, when I went to college, my intention was to obtain a liberal arts degree and then go to seminary to become a religious leader of some sort; yes, probably to head some sort of hierarchy.

My freshman year in college I was away from home, where I attended a church with a much larger membership than I was accustomed to. This congregation had a new church building with rather dreadful architecture, the building looking like a capsized ship. Every Sunday the pastor asked for more money to pay for this monstrosity with its leaking roof. The odd geometry of the building, even though it was new, seemed to make the leaks irreparable. A multitude of questions began bubbling up in my mind.

Should our monies go into buildings and real estate? Where is it written we are supposed to build these large edifices for worship? Doesn't the Bible quote Jesus as saying "wherever two or three of you are gathered together in my name, there I will be also?" Could our monies be better spent to feed the hungry or clothe the poor?

I sought better answers than I was getting from my fellow congregants and the hierarchical leaders. I tried other brands of religion, finding some more satisfying than others, and finding some downright scary. I remember one Sunday attending a worship service at a church I'd never been to before. The minister, a man with a terribly grim visage, the corners of his mouth turned down at least three quarters of an inch, his brow furrowed with deep frown lines, and his voice sounding as if he was sentencing us to eternal damnation, vehemently exhorted us, "You must have Christian joy!" If Christian joy was that grim, I decided I wanted nothing to do with it. In the end, regardless of the religious brand name, I always asked too many questions. As a result, I either drifted away because of dissatisfaction with the answers, or as was more common, I was more actively excommunicated.

The end of organized religion in my life came in a flash of insight. One day I was driving down a street musing on the workings of the human mind. I'd been introduced to computers and integrated electronics in my college work, and the analogy of the human mind being the equivalent to a powerful computer was taking over as the dominant model of the human mind. However, problems exist with this analogy.

Computers, when their memory is damaged, usually become non-functional. Memory repair is very limited and check-sums are mainly good for detecting when it has been damaged, not for repairing it. Backups are generally needed to repair the damaged computer memory.

I read Michael Talbot's book, *The Holographic Universe*, where the author presents the hypothesis that mind exists not within the cellular structure of the brain, but in the fluctuating, three-dimensional, electro-magnetic field generated by the electrical currents within the brain. This seemed to me to be a better model of the human mind. After all, we do have varying brain waves, which are associated with thinking.

Furthermore, one of the features of holograms produced from holographic films is this: damage to the film does not delete specific parts of the resulting hologram. Instead, the resolution of the hologram is decreased. This more closely matches what happens when a human brain is damaged. Often when afflicted with strokes or physical damage, a person's memory is not erased in discrete blocks, but becomes porous. As physical brain damage heals, a person's thinking and memory may regenerate to a remarkable degree. This never happens with computer memory. Thus, Talbot's suggestion that mind consists of these three-dimensional, electromagnetic holograms, produced by approximately 23 Watts of electrical activity in the neural network of the brain, rang true to me. The brain structure is then both the generator and the receiver of the holographic mind.

A flash of insight came when the question, "Do brain cells have to be connected to make a holographic mind?" exploded in my brain.

The answer was a thunderbolt. "No!" Electrical activity can take place in any conductive medium, and living cells contain and often exist within such media. My mind took flight. Most of the attributes of deities in a wide variety of religions could be applied to a mind based on populations of single cell organisms.

Consider, for example, "you are the temple of the living God." Yes, we have about a cup full of micro flora and fauna living in our gut with biological activity approximately equivalent to our own. "God is all powerful." There is a single species of algae in the Dead Sea, a body of water not noted for its bio-mass, having a power flow of over one billion Watts, an unfathomable power compared to our measly 23 Watts. "The voice of God is a still, small voice." While the total power flow of such a mind could be astronomically high, the power density is low and diffuse compared to our more compact, connected-cell, brain structure. "We are created in the image of God." Yes, we are made with a cellular structure.

Because the hologram of these proposed god minds, immensely powerful compared to our minds, would have very low power density compared to ours, we could never fathom a god mind in its entirety. Our minds would be similar to birds flying through the air. The wind can experience everything about the bird, but the bird cannot experience everything about the wind. Just so, "God knows all of our thoughts," because our mind hologram would be immersed within the god mind, allowing the god mind to read every facet of our hologram.

Yet we would only be able to experience a very small fraction of the god mind, and even that would be difficult for us, because the low power density of the god mind would likely be in the noise range of our much higher power-density minds. To overcome this last difficulty traditionally we often find places of worship located in or near regions of relatively high biological activity; glades, stream banks, and lake or ocean shores to name a few. We also find people try to alter their mental states, mediating or doing other activities to quiet their own thoughts, in order to hear that "still, small voice of God."

Of particular significance to me was the Biblical story in Genesis 15:7-17 of Abram, who wished to speak with God. He took a heifer, a doeling, a ram, a turtledove, and a pigeon butchering the larger animals into pieces, laying all the parts on the ground, and leaving only the birds whole. He then waited, driving away the scavengers. Given the region, the weather must have been warm to hot, reinforced by the observation he was there well into the night. The logical conclusion is the meat, starting out warm from the body temperature of the animals coupled with the obviously less than sanitary conditions, began to rot. The biological activity in the meat may have doubled many times over given the time span of this incident. Eventually, after sunset, ". . . a smoking furnace and a burning lamp passed between those pieces." God then spoke with Abram. So, was a mind based on single cell organisms the source of the message?

I don't know if this concept of human and god minds is valid, but I don't know of any reason why it could not be true. I do know this concept twisted my traditional religious views to the point they shattered.

Two of the major pillars of my childhood paradigm, faith in the social structure in which I lived and faith in the religion in which I was raised, were gone. A floodgate of thought about all manner of subjects, previously circumscribed and excluded by my childhood paradigm, opened. My thoughts exploded. I felt like the shepherd in the Flammarion engraving, lifting up the edge of

the familiar world to see new universes. I began to think and read with a critical mind about philosophy, religion, economics, sociology, psychology, physiology, geology, geophysics, physics, chemistry, astrophysics, biology, anthropology, and thermodynamics to name some of the areas of my wanderings. The list of authors I read is too extensive to list, but one characteristic was of paramount importance to me in my reading adventures; new ideas.

All of the new ideas I garnered by my reading spotlighted the extent of my ignorance and how fragmented my paradigm really was. Over the next few years, I patched together and tested several new paradigms out of bits and pieces gleaned from my readings and from paradigms offered by others. I was not successful. Upon close scrutiny, all of these paradigms I borrowed or assembled failed to emerge as coherent; some were better than others, but all failed.

I was in my early 30's around the time I was engaged in searching for a definitive paradigm, and I was fortunate to re-cross paths with Stellan. He had earned a graduate degree in engineering and then partnered in an electronic design firm. I sought him out for his expertise and the resources of his company for one of my projects. We had much to talk about with our common engineering interests, but eventually, because it was such a major effort in my life at that time, I introduced Stellan to my struggles.

He was intrigued, and we began the process of trying to craft a coherent paradigm. Stellan had not been raised in a religious family, so he did not have to overcome the assertions from that source. Additionally, being raised on a farm had brought him close to nature and the realities of rural life. These factors helped him to easily discard many of the paradigms I had struggled to jettison. I was envious, but also excited by his companionship on my journey.

Our mental travels and engineering studies brought us to the field of energy, and together we began to build a paradigm based on the physical reality that energy plays in our lives. We discussed how absolutely nothing occurs without an energy transformation taking place; not a single jot or tittle. Therefore, adequate energy sources are absolutely necessary for life. We were in good company. There were, and are, a multitude of others who subscribed to an energy source paradigm. Indeed, an energy paradigm was, and still is, the dominant paradigm of the State of Wyoming, where I then lived and still do. Wyoming proudly advertises itself as an energy producing state. It is that, mining nearly half of the coal used in the United States, plus a significant amount of the natural gas and oil, and some uranium. Wyoming also has some of the premier wind energy resources.

We recognized the bulk of engineering thought is based on energy transformations of all kinds, and our advancing studies demolished the last tatters of my mystic, religion-based, childhood paradigm, substituting maximizing energy sources as a new foundation. The energy-source paradigm also appeared to be a dominate paradigm of the United States and other developed nations, as evidenced by voluminous writings and statements on energy. Energy production was, and is, touted as the basis of economic health. I eagerly looked forward to the two of us forming a more coherent paradigm on the basis of energy sources.

As Stellan and I explored this realm, I was comforted and excited to learn that as United States citizens, we each have somewhere between 200 and 8,000 energy servant-equivalents catering to our every whim; available around the clock without needing to be fed, clothed, housed, given coffee breaks, or paid living wages. We would, of course, have to pay for the energy. While we might need to pay an average service worker about $30,000 for working a full year, 40 hours per week for 50 weeks (we magnanimously gave them two weeks of vacation), Stellan and I calculated the cost of purchasing electricity to supply the equivalent physical energy of this human service worker to be worth only about $15.

We also found engineering jobs abounded in the energy sector, and the salaries were some of the highest in any industry. Significant growth was predicted into the foreseeable future, and even higher rates of energy consumption were predicted in order for all Americans to increase the luxury, convenience, freedom of movement, and amusement in their lives. All of this was not only true for the United States, but the whole world was chomping at the bit to catch up with and even surpass the United States in all areas. A veritable energy orgy was envisioned.

However, deeper investigation of energy sources began to raise some red flags. Our current energy use pattern on this planet Earth is limited; limited not in geologic time, but in the much shorter anthropologic time. The finite fossil fuel energy sources we are now transforming at prodigious rates will end. There is much debate on the actual end date, but no one is claiming they will last for even 500 more years, a mere 0.26% of the time Homo sapiens have been on the Earth.

There is reason to think fossil fuels will be economically exhausted well before they are physically exhausted; perhaps well before the end of the 21st Century, a run of less than 250 years. The evidence for this is the little-known fact that energy cost for these energy sources has been steadily increasing over time. When the first oil well, the Drake Well, was drilled in the United States in 1859 near Titusville, Pennsylvania, the energy cost of energy was about 1/30th to $1/40^{th}$, that is 30 to 40 units of energy were available for every unit of energy expended in the process of obtaining that energy. Now the cost is probably somewhere about ½, only two units of energy available for every one put into the process.

Since a 2:1 return is the approximate energy cost of renewable energy, renewable energy is now becoming increasingly economical. However, do not rejoice too quickly, because the energy cost of renewable energy is also increasing as they are being developed. The best locations for harvesting energy are utilized first, and increasingly more difficult, remote, and less economical locations must then be developed to expand renewable energy capture. Whether we use fossil fuels or renewable energy, we will be forced to work harder and harder to supply our energy appetite as time passes.

Are you wondering why it seems harder to keep our infrastructure repaired, educate our children, deal with civil problems, and find items of similar quality to those manufactured several decades ago? It is harder. The total amount of supplemental energy required for most everything we do is steadily increasing.

Replacement energies for fossil fuels are few in number and

fraught with difficulties and dangers. Only three of these have sufficient capacity to fill the void that will exist with the demise of fossil fuels. These are nuclear, solar, and wind. All three of these have low energy return on energy investment. Some, such as nuclear, may well have negative cradle-to-grave energy return. All will require immense effort and cost to replace fossil fuels. Therefore, a paradigm based on maximizing energy sources leads to some obvious contradictions.

Can a modified energy paradigm be formulated? Stellan and I tried. What if some sort of limit was included; a set point if you will? We could find no rational way for arbitrarily setting a limit, and more importantly, we could not conceive of a way to enforce such a limit. Within our societies on this Earth, some individuals use prodigious amounts of energy transformations, and others do not have enough for even the minimal creature comforts. How could an energy paradigm be tailored to equitably distribute energy transformations? Our efforts stalled.

The situation became worse when we confronted the unimaginable large web of energy transformations possible from a single energy source. Take oil for example. Oil can be turned into fuels, plastics, fertilizer, medicines, toiletries, construction materials, and the list goes on and on. There are thousands, perhaps millions, of products made from oil. When viewed from the perspective of energy sources, a nearly infinite number of pathways away from a source are possible, an enormous spider web of energy transformations.

Some pathways are highly desirable; food production, shelter construction, and clothing manufacture for example. But some are highly undesirable; roadside bombs, chemical warfare stocks, trichloroethylene in the ground water, to name a few. Not only that, but each pathway can branch with products being used for both good and bad purposes. Explosives can be used to build homes, roads, bridges, and other structures, but they can also be used to destroy those same structures. How can an energy paradigm differentiate? Stellan and I tried mightily, but we were unable to develop a coherent energy paradigm encompassing all of these possibilities. We decided to retrace our steps and look deeper into the physics of energy.

CHAPTER 2

I'm in the kitchen of my family home. I hear a noise at the back door, which opens out onto a landing above three steps leading down to the floor of the garage. I open the door to investigate. The family cat, a tuxedo cat which has been missing for over two weeks, is at the back door. She is emaciated, but looks alert and moves easily as she comes into the kitchen. I can't imagine where the cat has been, since there is no cat door to the outside of the garage. I know of only one place she could have been for two weeks; the storage cupboard under the stairs.

I walk down the stairs and discover the doors to the cupboard are tightly closed and latched. Puzzled, I look around and happen to glance up. In the open rafters under the roof of the garage there is a strange, black rectangle. This is not an ordinary black; it is somehow infinitely black; a hole into an immense volume with absolutely no light. I realize our cat has been on the other side of this opening into another . . . space? world? dimension? I don't have a name for it, but I know, with an unshakable certainly, I am going to investigate what is on the other side of this black opening. If our cat has survived the trip, so can I.

I awoke, feeling profound disappointment that the black rectangle in the roof of the garage was only a dream. At the time of the dream I had not lived in that house for a number of years, and when I did, my family did not have a cat. Yet the feeling remained that unknown realms exist, realms which I longed to investigate. Since Stellan and I were planning on studying energy and energy transformations in much greater depth, I viewed this dream as spurring us to delve more deeply into these subjects.

At first, we didn't give the nature of energy transformations much thought. Sure, we transform some energy when we drive our car to the mountains for a picnic, just one of the myriad of energy transformations we make every day. So what?

I began to seriously think about "so what" when one evening a friend of mine frantically called me with a cry for help. The main sewer in his neighborhood was plugged and sewage was backing up into his basement. Could I help him? I slipped on my rubber boots, loaded my two wet/dry vacuums, and rushed to his house. Normally, the sewer is out of sight and out of mind, but not that evening. There was an inch of stinking brown sludge on his basement floor and it was slowly rising. We located the source, a floor drain in his laundry room. A plastic garbage pail filled with water for weight, fitted neatly over the floor drain and stopped the sewage inflow.

My friend rigged a fan to give us at least a modicum of fresh air, and for hours we vacuumed the sludge, carried the filled vacuums out and dumped them down an open manhole the city sewer department had opened as they worked to unclog the main sewer line. I can only image the cleanup efforts my friend still had to go through after we at least got down to bare floors again.

This incident caused me to think about our wastes, not just feces, but everything. What are they? Do they still contain energy? They must, because zillions of microbes and even some large creatures live on our feces. For obvious reasons we consider them lower on the food chain. But what does that mean? Is there an end to the chain, and if so, where does it start?

Stellan and I discussed the food chain, and found ourselves generalizing into all ilks, kinds, of energy transformation chains. We recognized these chains are governed by the First Law of Thermodynamics, which states **energy cannot be created or destroyed; only transformed**. So, after every energy transformation, there is just as much energy as before, but it has changed form.

But energy transformations always have a direction. They go from an energy form with higher potential, the source, to one or more forms with lower potential, the sinks; rocks roll downhill, cups of coffee cool, gasoline burns into combustion products and heat, food people eat turns into the sewage in my friend's basement. Chains of transformations result in energy moving to ever lower potentials.

Stellan and I consider the question of whether these energy transformation chains have an end, and we discovered, yes they do. While varying potentials of energy are contained in various compositions and positions of matter and in radiant energy, an end of the line does exist. All energy transformations in our neck of the Universe eventually arrive at a single end, the background, long-wave, cosmic radiation at a temperature of 2.7 degrees Kelvin, the ultimate energy sink. Probably in the far, far distant galactic future, this background temperature will decline even further toward absolute zero, pushing the galactic entropy toward infinity. For now no other transformations are possible from that potential, the energy has become totally unavailable, the entropy is maximized.

I realized I was wrong. The black rectangular opening in the roof of our garage in my dream was not just an opening into some other dimension, it was a view of the ultimate energy sink, and from this bedrock of the ultimate energy sink, the functioning of the Earth and our beings can be understood. This is the pathway of the entropy paradigm.

This reality of all energy transformations in toto proceeding toward this end point of the ultimate energy sink is expressed in the Second Law of Thermodynamics, which states **the sum of entropies in energy sources and sinks will increase with any energy transformation.**

My friend's predicament with the backed up sewer points out another reality. If unavailable energy, entropy, builds up in an area, the results can be dire, and if allowed to build up too much, fatal. In his case lots of work—energy transformations—had to be performed by him, with my help, to get the sewage out of his house and remove all traces of it. In the process we made additional entropy, mainly waste heat from our bodies and the oxygen depleted air laced with CO_2 we breathed out plus the entropy associated with the electrical energy used. Besides the sewage this additional entropy had to be removed from his house. This was done by ventilation, which carried the heat and depleted air outdoors. Much of the entropy from the electrical equipment was released elsewhere.

Stellan and I, having located the end of the energy transformation chains, considered the implications of what we'd learned. If we remove produced entropy out of our houses, where does it then go? Obviously, it ends up in the air, water, and soil. Yet these are also our sources of food, oxygen, and water, the basic low entropy substances we need to remain alive. So somehow the entropy must be taken from these and moved elsewhere, but where and how?

We know there is negligible mass entering and leaving the Earth system, so the entropy cannot be removed as we did with my friend's house, exporting high entropy mass and importing low entropy mass. Instead, low entropy radiant energy, sunlight, enters the Earth system, and autotrophs, plants are the most familiar of these to us, use this energy to convert our high entropy wastes back into low entropy mass, primarily oxygen and carbohydrates. In the process they turn the entropy we produced plus the generous amount of entropy they themselves produce by their conversion activities into long-wave radiant heat energy. Yes, plants do produce heat. This heat is radiated into outer space, carrying with it about 20 times the entropy of the incoming solar radiation. Heat from all the other inanimate processes on Earth is also radiated out, and in the long run the total heat energy out must equal the incoming shortwave solar radiation energy. Otherwise the Earth will either heat or cool.

Entropy buildup can also affect the temperature of the Earth. Since the industrial revolution began about 1760, we have done six major things to create entropy buildup in our environment, and today we are experiencing the results. The first of these six things is transforming internal stored energy, which increases the entropy load in the Earth environment. The second is decimating the plant kingdom over large areas, which decreases the conversion of the entropy in our wastes into heat for export into space. The third is increasing the human population on the Earth, which requires an ever-increasing magnitude of energy transformations. The fourth is appropriating more than 40 percent of net photosynthetic production for human consumption or use, thus increasing the extinction rate between 3 and 4 orders of magnitude. The fifth is generating many new materials, such as plastics, the entropy from which autotrophs cannot convert. The sixth is learning how individuals can transform orders of magnitude more energy in their daily lives compared to our ancestors before the Industrial Revolution, thereby increasing human entropy production several times over.

Having discovered the underlying cause of these problems threatening to destroy life on Earth, Stellan and I began weaving this knowledge into a new paradigm of life; a paradigm to guide how individuals should conduct their lives, and how societies of humans should be organized. The basic tenets became striving for optimum entropy states in our lives and minimizing our entropy footprint on the planet.

Suppose a Little Princess, much like Antoine de Saint-Exupéry's *Little Prince*, lived on her own house sized asteroid, but unlike the Little Prince with his three volcanoes and a few plants, she has enough plants to balance her entropy rejection into the intermediate sinks of the air, water, and soil on her asteroid. The plants supply all of her sustenance and transport all of her entropy, as well as that produced by any other animal life on her asteroid, and even the entropy produced by the plants themselves, into outer space by long wave heat radiation. All of these processes whereby the plants eventually export all of the produced entropy on her asteroid are what are called environmental services. More simply put, her environment would have to function with no external exchange of mass with the environment of space.

Now suppose a second person, a Little Prince, who requires exactly the same environmental services, is added to her asteroid. If the environment is the same as before, the intermediate sinks, the air, water, and soil, will degrade, as will the lives of the two of them and every other living thing on the asteroid including the plants. All of the plant life, and the asteroid base which supports the plant life, that is the environmental services, must be doubled in order to support both of them. If others are added, the environmental services must be increased sufficiently for all to be able to exist as if each has their own asteroid.

I do not claim to have arrived at this understanding by myself. My friend, Stellan, and I spent many hours considering thermodynamic systems, how we are such a system, and how we relate to other systems around us. Based on the postulate, "life is an unalienable right," as asserted by the United States Declaration of Independence, we arrived at an inescapable conclusion. This postulate requires that all environmental services necessary for maintaining the quality of our lives must also be an unalienable right. We wrote these concepts into a statement, our *Declaration of Life*.

DECLARATION OF LIFE

LIFE, being the fundamental, moral postulate, is an unalienable right.

Because life of indeterminate length can only be sustained by domains of such size and composition only energy need cross the boundaries, a PERSONAL DOMAIN, the individual and the domain comprising an indivisible entity, is also an unalienable right.

To maintain the integrity of an entity, it is essential the person consent to any alteration of the mass and energy fluxes by others. Therefore, the MORAL OBLIGATIONS of each individual are to make no unauthorized alteration of another's entity and to effect faithful stewardship of their own.

Recognizing the truth of this declaration, we commit ourselves to a life based on this moral code.

We then had a concise rendering of our new, coherent, paradigm of life based on entropy. The implications of this declaration were staggering. If a personal domain is an unalienable right, there can be no such thing as property rights as we currently know them. A domain by right cannot be purchased or sold or given away or taken away or seized or rented or leased or taxed. Perhaps a domain could be traded, so humans would not be anchored to a specific location. Because a domain is of such size and composition a person can live within such a domain without depending on any other person, a domain can be viewed as a sanctuary, a Thoreau's *Walden*.

This concept makes a great leveler of all people. A person, regardless of their race, ethnicity, gender, sexual orientation, age, or beliefs, could retreat into their domain and be able to meet all of their basic needs by their own efforts. No king or lord or boss or dictator or ruler or tyrant or autocrat or landlord could hold them in a privation grip. The individuals would differ, the domains would differ, but each would have, by right, the environmental services to support their life.

Stellan and I were eager to explore all of the ramifications of our *Declaration of Life*. We met many times and discussed our future courses of action. We broached the subject of attempting to establish experimental domains somewhere, although we were both a little hesitant to do so. We recognized we had more to learn about entropy and energy transformations, and we had considerably less experience than Antoine de Saint-Exupéry's *Little Prince* at living in an environmental services domain. Nevertheless, we agreed we had entered a new phase; a definite project.

After Stellan left one day, my mind turned to the subject of what to call our project. The easiest would be the acronym DOLP for *Declaration of Life* Project. My mind rebelled. DOLP would simply be lost in the clutter of acronyms in the English language. There could be hundreds of them, maybe millions. I abandoned any name likely to be shortened into an acronym.

I tried some other names; Stellan's Paradise; The Seekers' Retreat, Utopia, Eden, Nirvana; The Back to Nature Community.

I gave up and decided to wait and take up this issue with Stellan.

A few days later, Stellan came over along with his 14-year-old son, Gyan. I began by telling Stellan about my struggles to come up with a name for our project.

He mulled this problem over for a few moments and then spoke hesitantly, "The best trade names are two syllable adjectives with the emphasis on the first syllable, like Kleenex®. Since entropy plays a prominent role in our project, why don't we try using the first or the last syllable of entropy as part of the name?" Stellan tried a couple of variations. "EnCom, ComTropy. Oh, that last one is three syllables."

I had to admit Stellan's efforts were better than mine, but I was still left cold by these names.

Gyan spoke up. "I like to read science fiction, and Dad has told me about your project. He let me read your *Declaration of Life*, but he had to explain it to me. What I think you and Dad are doing is trying to make an alien civilization, a 'Civalien' project."

We were speechless. Our project had been named. Stellan finally found his voice. "The Civalien Project." It fits, and it doesn't matter if Civalien does have more than two syllables"

Stellan had to take Gyan to a music lesson, but after he returned, it took us a while to settle down and continue our investigation of domains. "Just what would these domains be and how large should they be?" I asked.

Thinking about this for what seemed like hours, but was really less than a minute, Stellan replied, "For the sake of visualization, consider a theoretical pyramidal shape with the apex at the center of the Earth and the base at the outer edge of the atmosphere. If the pyramid was somehow enclosed with a boundary transmitting radiant energy but not mass or work, a person could exist without limits other than the natural biological ones, so the pyramid's volume would then define a domain."

"I get it. It would be an equivalent domain or a virtual domain or an implicit domain."

"I like the word 'virtual' best." Stellan said and then continued. "Somewhere through the body of the pyramid, the surface of the Earth would intersect, defining a land area where most of the activities of life exist in a very thin film on the surface of the Earth. That land area then defines the domain."

"Your conceptual definition of a domain will work well," I said, "because we currently use land area as a measure, so most everyone has some sense of what it means." My mind was racing. "Of course, the required area will depend on what's in it. A domain in Antarctica would have to be enormous, if even one is possible on that continent. In the Amazon rainforest, domains would be fairly small. The main determinant is the amount of permanent biological activity in the area, specifically plant activity. And, of course, the area would not really have to be square."

"Of course," Stellan said with exaggerated emphasis. "Some generalizations and averages may give an idea of the extent of domains. So, let's take a shot at estimating how large a domain should be. I think we should base it on the average area needed to supply the energy flux necessary for life."

I looked up a reference I had been reading about net photosynthetic production, NPP, on the Earth. "NPP on the Earth is about 67 terawatts," I said as I thumbed through another reference to find the surface area of the Earth. I made a calculation. "The average per square meter is then about 0.13 Watts." I looked up data on human food consumption and made some more calculations. "An adult human takes in about 2,700 kcal of food per day, and this converts to about 130 Watts energy flux. So, to supply just their daily food, a human needs about 1000 square meters, that's 0.1 hectares or 0.25 acres. That's about 11,000 square feet on the average."

"That's assuming they consume 100% of all the net photosynthetic production," Stellan added. "That assumption is, of course, unrealistic. For a domain to be viable, it has to also support the varied plant and animal life making it robust and alive. Besides, I'd go crazy if all I had was food and nothing else. Also, if something went wrong for even a short time, I'd be dead."

"On your last point," I said, "There have been studies on life satisfaction and happiness versus energy consumption. The curve is an asymptotic curve starting at zero, rising steeply, going over a 'knee' at energy consumption of about 1200 Watts. The curve then levels out with diminishing returns as energy consumption increases. If we increase the human power consumption to 1200 Watts, the required average area increases to. . ." I made some more calculations. "9,100 square meters, that's 0.91 hectares or 2.25 acres. What do you suppose we are consuming now in the USA?"

"I don't know. Let me check." Stellan spent some time paging through his reference books and finally looked up. "It looks like US citizens consume about 11,000 Watts on the average."

I made some more calculations. "Power consumption of that magnitude would require 83,700 square meters, which is 8.4 hectares or 21 acres, and I haven't allowed anything for all the other animals yet. I'm just figuring all the net photosynthetic energy is allocated for humans."

"Yes," Stellan said, "and we've already established using fossil fuels for our energy consumption above what's required for basic sustenance cannot be done without increasing the entropy load on the environment."

I thought about these supplemental energy sources. "What about using solar energy or a derivative like wind for our supplemental energy?"

"Let's look at solar voltaic panels," Stellan said.

I cracked my reference books again. For the next hour or so, Stellan and I perused our books, looking for information.

I broke the sounds of turning pages. "From what I can gather, the energies going into the manufacture of the panels, if all of the overhead and energy expended in setting up the manufacturing facilities is considered, are greater than the energy produced. At best they may break even. If the panels are used to charge batteries, there's no question about the negative energy return, because batteries are so energy-intensive. Obviously, if the panels don't break even, they can only be a net producer of entropy."

"John, even if they do better than break even, they still might produce more entropy than their use can export. From what I've been reading, they use a lot of materials relying on fossil fuels; electricity, aluminum, plastics, silver, iridium, tellurium. And I couldn't find where anyone has taken into account the entropy produced to build the manufacturing plants, from all the transportation associated with their manufacture and life cycle, from the mining necessary for all the materials for both the manufacture and the installation, and if they are grid connected, for the grid itself; I don't see how they can be entropy-neutral even if they are energy-neutral or better."

I was inclined to agree with Stellan. "The biggest drawback I see," I said, "is photovoltaic panels require large-scale infrastructure to manufacture, so they are intrinsically incompatible with the concept of domains."

We both sat silently for time, slouching in our chairs.

"The same argument goes for large-scale wind," Stellan said quietly.

"It does. Large scale anything is pretty much out." I felt a distinct difficulty in adjusting my thinking to a domain basis. "Let's go back to the subject of the size of a domain, based on only solar energy capture by the biosphere."

Stellan straightened and began punching numbers into his calculator. "Well, assuming the US has average net photosynthetic production, we obviously can't supply our population with the 11,000 Watts we are currently using, since there are only about 7½ acres per person. If we all dropped back to 1,200 Watts, we would still be hogging about 30% of the NPP. I don't know for certain, but my first guess is that's too much."

"I second your guess." I had also been busy at my books and had some numbers of my own. "There are an estimated 7 million animal and insect species in the world, all depending on about 1½ million plant species. The decomposers feed on us all, and I didn't find an estimate of the number of them. What would be a reasonable percentage allowance for humans?"

We both were silent. Finally, I said, "Somewhere in the dim past I read a generalization stating the average species can be predated on by about ten percent without harmful consequences. Perhaps we can set an upper limit from this observation. Assuming humans are the only predator, the best percentage for maintaining a domain must lie somewhere less than 10%."

"Your last assumption is patently wrong, of course," Stellan said.

Stellan didn't say anything else, so finally I continued. "I'll suggest about 2½ percent, a number which still may be overly generous. Using 1,200 Watts as reasonable human energy consumption and an allowance of 2½ percent, I calculate an average domain size of 364,000 square meters; that's 36.4 hectares or 90 acres. I'd round it to 100 acres."

Stellan was busy at his books and calculator, and after a while he spoke up. "Estimates of the population of North American prior to colonization by Europeans range from about 2 million to 18 million, and the indigenous peoples used primarily net photosynthetic energy fluxes. Given the 24.7 million square kilometers of North America, the area per person would have been somewhere between 3,040 acres and 340 acres. So, your 100-acre estimate is probably at least within an order of magnitude of the per capita area for a population of 18 million in 1492, but this information indicates you are still too generous."

"Maybe so," I answered, "but the estimates you found for the North American indigenous peoples might be based on an inflated value of NPP energy consumption. I'm willing to bet those people had no formal understanding of energy and entropy fluxes, and we know they had practices inconsistent with the energy and entropy laws. One example I can think of in Wyoming is the Vore Buffalo Jump, where they slaughtered large numbers of bison, way more than they could use, by driving them into a sinkhole. Other buffalo jumps have been identified in Montana and Alberta. Another example might be the use of fire by the indigenous people to alter the landscape and hunt animals."

Stellan still looked skeptical. "Maybe, but I'm still thinking more area may be needed.

Over the next few weeks Stellan and I spent quite a bit of time arguing back and forth about the average size of a domain, but we were unable to come to a firm agreement. We finally agreed to use my 100-acre number unless we found better information.

I am working in the basement of my home, finishing installing a new, four-inch, water line into my home. The line terminates

at an oversized valve above the utility sink. I am satisfied I will now have plenty of water supply for my kitchen sink, dishwasher, washing machine, three showers, two bath tubs, several toilets, an oversized aquarium, swimming pool, hot tub, flower garden, garden fountain, garden hoses, and my automatic pet watering station.

I turn on the valve, pleased with the substantial water flow. My wife and children look on with unfeigned admiration as I turn and walk toward them. Behind them our family dog is sniffing at the floor drain and cocking his head to listen intently to the drain. Suddenly, fetid dark water begins to spout from the drain and the dog jumps back with a yipe. I whirl around as I hear splashing behind me. The utility sink is overflowing. I attempt to get back to the sink, but the water is rapidly rising and I am not able to make headway against the current. I watch in helpless terror as the water level rises over my childrens' heads.

I awoke with terror lingering in my emotions. I actually didn't have such a family, house, or pet dog. What could this dream mean? If looked at in the light of energy sources and sinks, it began to make sense. Our culture's approach to some of the most egregious pollution problems identified to date has been to apply even more energy to the problem to "remove" the offending high entropy chemical substances. This approach is analogous to the bigger water line in my dream. But does this work? Not any better than in my dream. The entropy may be moved, redistributed, or converted into other forms with the associated extra entropy production, but the increased application of energy transformations ensures an overall entropy increase.

More energy transformations mean even more entropy rejected into the intermediate sinks of the air, water, and soil; ergo, the buildup of water in my basement in the dream. Because the ultimate entropy sink, long-wave radiation into outer space, the drain in my dream, is not handling our increased entropy production, we are experiencing ever increasing problems.

Stellan and I were alarmed by our insights into the issues associated with entropy production and flows within the Earth system.

We tried discussing these concerns with our friends and colleagues, emphasizing our understanding of the need for domains to truly have the right to life.

Most of our friends and colleagues, but not quite all, agreed with us up to the point where we discussed the number of possible domains in North America, about 82 million, falling far short of the population, about 360 million. When we reached this point in our discussion, they would turn away, stop listening, perhaps change the subject, or say God will take care of it. None of them offered a rebuttal or pointed out an error in our thinking. Some did point out the population was much greater than we claimed it should be, and since we were all still alive and flourishing, we couldn't possibly be right.

Stellan and I thought the reason behind this incongruity was simple; human societies are eating oil. We supplement solar radiation with fossil fuel energy, because we use fossil fuel to power agricultural and transportation equipment, pump water, make and apply fertilizer, and make and apply pesticides and herbicides. The consumption of fossil fuel energy in North America exceeds the entire net photosynthetic energy flux by about 14%. This fact means even if the entire net photosynthetic production of plant life in North America could be 100% devoted to the task, it would not be capable of exporting the entropy from our current fossil fuel use into outer space.

Pointing out our dependence on a finite supply of stored fossil energy and the discrepancy between the associated entropy production and the Earth's export mechanisms, compounded by issues of human overpopulation, did not faze our disbelieving friends and colleagues. We were greeted with incredulity, indifference, and disbelief, the most common comeback being, "Somebody will figure out a way to fix those problems." I felt as if I was living in my dream where the water was gushing into my basement from an oversized source, and I was struggling against the current to try to help my friends, family, and strangers. Stellan and I were having difficulty making any headway against the current of existing societal paradigms.

*I am standing at the edge of a low, rocky, desert-like ridge
with very little vegetation. There are a few low growing plants,
maybe one or two per square yard. There is little soil, and what is
there is very coarse and colored much like the protruding rocks.
Next to me is another person. I don't know who, but I do know I
am very comfortable with this person and I value their contribution to my life. In fact, I know my companion is responsible for
bringing me here to this place looking out over the landscape.*

*The day is fairly warm and my dark western long sleeve shirt
and my Levi® 501 blue jeans are soaking up sunlight. I am beginning to feel hot. In the distance, probably about 300 yards,
judging by the apparent size of the people visible, work is ongoing
on some sort of structure. It has somewhat the appearance of a
stadium except the sides, sloping out and downwards, appear to
be earthen berms.*

*There are people on the top of the structure who are building
a gently curved roof. Other people are climbing and descending
the earthen berms carrying various articles, some of which look
like window frames but must be roof panels, because they are
being laid down flat. The base of this structure is below the crest
of a ridge in front of us, so we cannot see what is going on around
the base. The structure is large, seemingly oval or round. From
the size of the people, I would estimate it to be somewhere in the
vicinity of 500 or 600 feet in diameter. A person has appeared
on the far side of the ridge, walking directly toward us from the
direction of the left side of the structure.*

*I continue to study the building activities, somehow excited
about them and the possibilities the structure might hold. Since
I'm an engineer, and I have identified earth-sheltered structures
as being potentially very energy efficient, this one interests me
greatly. The person coming toward us has crested the ridge and is
clearer now. The trail of his footsteps is visible across the grainy
soil. I can now see he is an elderly man, somewhat stooped and
grizzled. He is wearing a light-colored plaid shirt, gray pants,
and he is bare headed. He still has a full head of light brown hair,*

although both his hair and his beard are shot through with white. His eyes are a penetrating blue, and he is looking directly at my companion and me. As he comes closer, I realize there is some-thing familiar about him, and when he gets within about 20 feet I realize—HE IS THE FUTURE ME.

I awoke with a riot of feelings, the first one being I couldn't imagine myself wearing gray pants. I had been a faithful Levi® 501 blue jean wearer since high school. The second was I couldn't imagine being as old as I was in my dream, since I was a fairly young man then in my middle 30s. The third was I couldn't pic-ture myself walking away from a project like an earth-sheltered building. I loved to be in the thick of projects, and walking away from one under construction did not, and does not, fit with my MO. The fourth was a feeling something I passionately desired was pretty far in the future.

Stellan and I had no idea how a project implementing domains could be accomplished in the face of existing, socially accepted paradigms. We also had no idea how the transition between the existing human population of the Earth and the far smaller popula-tion dictated by the entropy paradigm could conceivably happen, except, perhaps by the Four Horsemen of the Apocalypse. Financ-ing a demonstration project consistent with our new paradigm and *Declaration of Life* was far beyond our economic means. Our enthusiasm sputtered, and then our nascent project seemed to die as we both went elsewhere to jobs more than 2,000 miles apart.

CHAPTER 3

I look down from the third-floor dormer window. A line of seven men is about two and half blocks away, advancing on the diagonal street to my right, guns drawn and at the ready. The late afternoon sun glints off their guns and the sheriff's badge. The stupid pigs are all lined up like a shooting gallery. The sheriff is in the middle of the street. I ease the top window sash down slowly so as to not attract their attention. The sash slides down easily, since the construction is new, but the scraping sounds loud to me in the still air. The pigs don't seem to have heard. The dormer isn't finished yet, and some sawdust, wood shavings, and plaster crumbs are on the floor.

My accomplice moves to the window to my right, looks out, and gasps, "Oh, God!" I've had it with that deadbeat. He's losing his nerve. Two and half blocks is a long shot for my pistol, but I draw down on the sheriff, making certain the muzzle of my gun is far enough inside the window to keep the smoke from giving away my position. His badge makes a lovely target, right over his heart. I fire.

The line of men scatters like autumn leaves in the wind. Success! The sheriff falls backward, but then he scrambles up, holding his shoulder, and runs for shelter at the side of the street. I track him with my gun, but don't think I can hit him again at this range with him moving so fast and erratically. Damn the luck! My accomplice backs away from his window, gibbering and moaning. The only thing I clearly hear him saying is "They're going to hang us." I swing my revolver to the right and shoot him in the heart. I smile at the shocked surprise on his face as he falls back and the life drains from his eyes. At least that shot was true.

Getting rid of him is like a weight lifted from my shoulders, like discarding a pile of garbage. But my smile changes to a frown when I look out and see my pursuers dodging from shelter to shelter to advance even more rapidly up the street. I'll have to work quickly to escape.

I holster my gun, pick up the sack of gold, and step to the dormer window on the back side of the room. I open the window, stick my head out, and look around. I'm in luck. A white drain pipe, which looks stout enough to support my weight, runs down the back of the building, and I can reach it from the window. It looks easy to slide down. I'm glad my slob of a partner is dead, because he's probably too heavy for the pipe. A quick shake of the pipe confirms it is firmly attached. I start to climb out the window, but stop and think for a moment. If I leave now, the vigilantes moving up on the front of the building will be here shortly, see the open window, and give chase. I won't have much of a head start, and they might catch me. I climb back inside.

I move back to the front window, glance out, and see the middle of the street is still empty, but I see one of my pursuers dodge from a doorway to shelter behind the corner of the next building. They are still coming. I hold the substantial sack of gold from our bank robbery in both hands. I so want to open the sack and feast my eyes on that golden hoard, but I refrain and look for a hiding place. I find it in a narrow space between a raised portion of the floor and the ceiling of the rooms below. It is a tight fit, but I manage to wiggle in feet first, pulling the sack of gold in with me and then down by my left side. The space is a little dusty, so I pull my bandana up over my nose and wait.

The sack of gold makes a satisfying, if hard, lump. My revolver is pointed toward the entrance to my dark hiding hole in case anyone does happen to look in and spot me. They will pay with their life for their error. I am slight of build and my clothes are uniformly dark and made darker and less visible by the dirt they've picked up by crawling into this space. I'm reasonably certain no one will spot me.

The pigs do find the attic eventually, and I listen to them examining my dead partner and surmising I had gone out the open back window and slid down the drain pipe. A little dust filters down from their clumping around over my head, and I have to suppress a cough. I'm thankful for the bandana over my nose. Those bastards don't have anything good to say about me, and I can barely restrain myself from firing up through the floor to kill at least one of them. I'd like to kill them all. I console myself with the thought of what is really important; the sack of gold right here by my side. An even more satisfying thought is this gold is now all mine.

The pigs leave after a while to continue looking for me out back. I smile to myself as I imagine them searching the neighborhood in back of the building for non-existent leads. They drag the garbage, my dead accomplice's body, down the stairs with them. I listen with satisfaction to his boots thumping on the stairs as they descend. Quiet returns, but I do not move. I wait till after dark before crawling quietly from my hiding place, lashing the bag of gold to my belt with my bandana, easing across to the open rear window, and reaching for the drain pipe.

I awoke from this dream with the experiences reverberating through my brain and the emotions of that evil, cold-blooded, ruthless, killer, who had robbed a bank, slowly fading from my consciousness. I had never in my life had such a dream, at least not that I could remember. In my dream I WAS that killer. I felt the disappointment when I did not kill the sheriff. I felt the satisfaction I got from putting a bullet through my accomplice's heart and knowing the gold from our robbery was now mine alone. I experienced the cunning as I staged a scene to make the pursuers believe I had escaped from the back of the building. And I experienced the effort it took to not only suppress the cough threatening to reveal my hiding place, but also to refrain from shooting through the floor to try to kill some of those looking for me.

The detail was tremendous; far greater than in my usual dreams. The setting was in an eastern city in the United States. I believe it was Philadelphia, but I am not entirely certain. The date was sometime in the second half of the 19th century. The streets were dirt, not at all smooth, but rutted and potholed from horse, wagon, and carriage traffic. The building was in the Federal style; not yet occupied on the third floor. The dormer windows were double hung with the window sills only about 20 inches from the floor, and as was the standard for the time, the dormer windows were far shorter than the main windows on the lower floors; hence the need for me to lower the upper sash to shoot out of the window. The floors were hickory planks, not yet finished, even slightly splintery.

The space between the raised floor of the attic and the ceiling of the room below was relatively clean, having not had time to accumulate a thick layer of dust, but there was some. There were no cobwebs, which would normally accumulate in such a space within months.

The weather was fair, not cold, since no one was wearing a coat, but not too hot as I was not sweating. My accomplice was sweating heavily, but I think his sweat came from fear and anxiety. The wind was not blowing. The time was initially late afternoon, four or five o'clock maybe, with light haze, but no clouds.

My accomplice was a stocky man with a round face, probably in his early 30's. He had brown hair, rather unruly, a bushy mustache, and 5 o'clock stubble. His shirt was light colored, but rather dingy, long-sleeved. His pants were dark, perhaps black, mottled with dust, dirt, soot, and food. Somehow, I knew he often used his pants to wipe his hands, and he smelled. I did not like to be too close to him.

I, on the other hand, prided myself in my appearance, had much cleaner clothes, and I know I bathed regularly. I have no idea what my facial features looked like, but I was clean shaven. My shirt was long-sleeved and navy blue, as were my pants, but of a darker shade than my shirt. Neither of us was wearing a hat. The pursuers were all wearing hats, so perhaps we had lost ours during our flight from the bank. Hats were the furthest thing from my mind at the time. Although I am certain we both had names, that particular detail was also far from my mind during the dream.

A friend who is familiar with antique guns told me my gun was probably a Colt® army six-shot percussion revolver when I described it to him. If this is so, it places the time frame some-time after 1860 when the gun was first manufactured. Since my gun was well-used and the brown, walnut grip was worn, the date was probably sometime later than 1860. The revolver seemed an extension of my hand and arm, and I am certain I had used it on other humans without hesitation or remorse prior to the events in my dream. I was a fit and strong man, since handling both the gun and the sack of approximately 20 to 25 pounds of gold coins seemed effortless.

My use of the word "pigs" to describe lawmen seemed out of place, since I was familiar with that word being used for the same purpose during the 1960s. However, an investigation into the origins of this word to describe lawmen revealed it was in use during the 1860s and 70s.

Being self-aware in my dreams prior to this one was not at all unusual, nor has it been unusual in subsequent years. What was unusual was my totally foreign personality in the dream. Awake and outside of the dream, I was approaching 40 years old at the time; single, working on a ranch located north of Laramie, Wyoming. About two decades prior, during the Vietnam War, I had applied to be a Conscientious Objector with my local draft board, only the second in the county to do so, and my application had been granted. I had never owned a firearm before having this dream, and I have not owned one since. My father was an avid hunter and fisherman, and he was very disappointed when, even though I had tried, I did not share his enthusiasm for these sports. I had no prior interactions with the Law except for one minor traffic ticket. Overall, my emotions and thoughts in my dream were the antithesis of my life at the time.

I was at a loss to explain or understand this dream in any way, and it haunted me throughout the day, intruding into my thoughts with unwelcome frequency. By bedtime I was no closer to making sense of it than when I first awakened. At various times during the day I thought maybe I had experienced some sort of past-life regression, but I did not believe we have past lives and had seen little credible evidence they exist. I thought it might be some sort of vision, but if so, the meaning of it escaped me completely. I thought it might be a replay of something I had read or seen, but if so, I had no memory of any such experience, and that explanation is not consistent with the vivid details. Much of my thinking was simply, "I don't know what this crazy dream means." When I went to bed, it took me some time to go to sleep.

I'm exhausted. Weeks on the trail have taken their toll on both me and my horse. As I push my way through the swinging batwing doors of the saloon with my saddlebags slung over my shoulder, I'm thinking maybe here, Laramie, Wyoming, is a place to end my journey. It is a raw frontier town, a railroad town, where nothing is very old. No family here is a multiple generation family. Strangers are common. The recently completed coast-to-coast railroad is injecting money into the city, and opportunities for a sharp operator like me should abound. The bar is located on the south side of Thornburgh Street between 1st, sometimes called Front Street by the locals, and 2nd Streets.

I look around the room and see only one other customer, a derelict looking fellow well into his cups, sitting on the left end of the bar. His head is resting on the bar, and a half empty glass of whiskey sits in front of him. The bar odors of stale beer and tobacco smoke are welcome, as is the dim lighting. The bartender, standing behind the bar near the center and wiping a glass on a dingy towel, is a heavy-set man with dark hair and a moustache. He reminds me vaguely of the partner I had killed several weeks before. I drift to the bar about halfway between the bartender and the right end of the bar.

When the barman asks what I want, I set a 2-bit coin on the bar, order a whiskey, and lean on the bar with both hands. The barman sets the glass he had been polishing on the bar, picks up a bottle of whiskey, and pours a generous shot in the glass. He steps toward me, sets the glass in front of me, picks up the coin, and steps back to his post, continuing to gaze at me. I continue leaning on my hands for a moment and consider putting down the saddle bags. They feel almost too heavy to hold up. But then I recall what they contain and straighten, wipe my hand across my face, tip my hat back a bit, and reach for the glass, the sharp whiskey smell giving me a jolt of energy.

At that moment a thump and a squeak announce someone is coming into the bar through the batwing doors. My mind is seared with the conviction the person entering is a pig coming to arrest me. I whirl around, drawing my gun as I twist. I fire and the man falls back outside through the swinging doors.

Suddenly, instead of being that murderer, I am a disembodied being watching him from a location slightly to the right of where he had been standing. I watch as he runs from the bar room, leaping over the body of the man he just shot, and disappears as he angles east on Thornburgh Street. I know, but I don't know the source of my knowledge, the man he has shot is dead, and the dead man was not a lawman.

I am a raptor, a rough-legged hawk, floating on the thermals high above the foothills of the Laramie Range northeast of Laramie. An intense thunderstorm is moving in from the northwest with gusty winds leading the storm core. The storm darkens the land-scape as it advances, and I am buffeted by the gusts being generated by the leading edge of the storm. The turbulence flexes and ruffles the flight feathers of my wings, and I continually adjust my tail and wings to maintain my flight path. The slanted, opaque gray column of rain is lit from within almost continually by lightning flashes and the thunder claps pound against my body.

My attention is drawn to a horse and rider angling to the northeast up the increasingly steeper slope of the mountain range. The man, leaning low over his foam flecked horse, is flogging the horse to greater effort as if all the hounds of hell are in pursuit. I know with a certainty the man is insane. The horse and rider are on a collision course with the rain column, and just before they reach the edge of the column, the horse collapses, falling on its right side, the uphill side. With a certainty I again cannot explain, I know the horse is dead.

The man struggles to get out from under his dead mount, and when he is free, he struggles to pull the saddlebags out from under the horse. He lost his hat during the fall, but he seems oblivious to the fact. This seems unusual, because during his struggles, the rain began to assault him in sheets driven by the wind. A hat might provide at least a little protection. By the time the saddle-bags are free, he is soaking wet, and water is running in streams from strands of his hair plastered to his skull. Having freed the saddlebags, he begins struggling through the rapidly deepening mud up the slope. The rain and darkness from the storm progressively obscure the scene until even the lightning flashes reveal no trace of the man. Only his irregular, sliding tracks in the mud remain, and even those tracks are being quickly washed away.

I am no longer the raptor. I do not have a corporal body, but I am seeing a bright, sunlit scene. The sun is warm, and a slight breeze blowing. Ahead of me, looking uphill and to the east, is a mountain swale with brushy foliage, the bright green of spring on the right, new grass covering the bottom, and on the left an earthen bank. The smells of the new grass and the sounds of insects and birds fill the air. Sometime in the past, probably within the past two or three years, the bank eroded to a vertical wall about three feet high. However, by this time a talus deposit covers approximately the lower half and has about a forty-five-degree angle of repose. The vertical part of the bank is still raw earth, but the talus is covered with a scraggly mixture of low grass and broad-leaf plants.

As I watch, spurts of loose soil come irregularly from a hole about two-thirds of the way up the sloped bank. Then the spurts stop and the head of a ground squirrel pops out of the hole. The bright-eyed animal looks around and then, satisfied no danger lurks, turns and disappears back down the hole. The digging resumes with the skritch'-scratch' sounds of the animal's digging, and the soil again flies from the hole. After a short time, the ground squirrel repeats its survey of the area. But this time, when it goes back to digging, a gold coin flies out of the hole along with the soil and lands shining in the sunlight on the tailing pile of the squirrel's excavation.

I awoke. A dream with a sequel the next night? I had never had such an experience before, and it has never happened to me since. I was again the evil, cold-blooded, ruthless, killer, of my dream the previous night. I felt the intense weariness of weeks, if not months, of riding the 1,750 miles from Philadelphia to Laramie, the need for a drink of whiskey, and the desire to find a place to stop and begin a new life. And then there was the complete psychotic break resulting in me shooting an undoubtedly innocent person. Madness! I experienced it.

Again, the details were astounding. As the killer, I was wearing black wool pants, and the countless hours in the saddle had turned the seat and the inside of the pant legs smooth and shiny. I didn't understand this, but one of my friends, familiar with wool fabrics, told me this does happen to wool in contact with hard smooth objects, such as saddles. I had never before experienced this phenomenon personally.

The smells, lighting, ambiance, and fixtures of the bar seemed authentic to me, but I have no reference for those sensory experiences, since I do not drink, and at that time in my life had only been in a bar once or twice. All I can say about the experience of becoming psychotic is I hope to never have such an experience again either in a dream or in reality.

What can I say about being a raptor? I don't think my cognition about the mental state of the rider is normal processing for a bird, but I do know I could feel the wind gusts move me about, much as I have since experienced in small aircraft. I could also feel the wind ruffle my flight feathers, and my muscles compensating and correcting for the pushes and tugs of the wind. The buffeting from the thunderclaps was also clear. Even though I was a few thousand feet above the tableau below me, my vision was sharp. I could easily see the dust being kicked up by the horse's hooves as it galloped across the terrain. The rivulets of sweat foam sliding along its hide and then being carried away in its wake were also clearly visible.

Even the dust devils kicked up by the advancing rainstorm and then moving away and dying were clear. The tableau of the downed horse, dead by the time it impacted the ground, pinning the momentarily stunned man's leg to the ground, was exceedingly clear and burned itself into my memory. And then the man struggling with superhuman strength to first shift the dead horse enough to free his leg and then repeating the feat to free the saddlebags was astounding.

The swale seemed real, even though I did not seem to have a corporal body. The scene reminded me somewhat of a movie, but that is not a totally accurate analogy. Unlike a movie the sunshine was warm and the smells of a warm spring day drifted with the slight breeze. How could these happen when I had no corporal body? I don't know. What does it all mean? I didn't know then, and I don't know for certain now. But I do know these dreams, or events seemly connected to them, have had a profound influence on my life.

CHAPTER 4

Over the next three decades I became interested in the economic world; banking, finance, and money. Thoughts about my dreams of being a bank robber arose occasionally as I discovered some disquieting things about the flow of money through our economy and the markets of the world. There is a strong correlation between money and energy transformations, which leads to massive production of entropy. Other troubling issues were the nature of banking loans, the underpinnings of the profit motive, and the role of advertising in our society.

This new knowledge led me to have diminishing respect for the existing economic system and to view it as exploitive, unfair, and damaging to our environment and the human pursuit of happiness. Then when I reunited with Stellan and heard his thoughts on our system of the "Rule of Law," I thought even more about my dream of being a bank robber.

Our reunion came about like this:

Stellan and I had both pursued engineering careers, having little contact with each other for many years. I retired at age 67, but Stellan, a couple of years younger than me, was still working. Whether it was coincidence or fate, his work brought him back to Laramie. We began spending time with each other again, and I came to realize how parched my intellectual life had been and how much I had missed the repartee we had enjoyed together.

We admitted to each other our earlier investigations into entropy and our *Declaration of Life* had changed the course of our lives and had permanently changed our world views. Neither of us had learned or experienced anything invalidating our original thoughts and understandings. If anything, the intervening years had demonstrated ever more clearly the accuracy of the entropy paradigm and our *Declaration of Life*.

Our views had distanced us to some degree from our fellow travelers in the United States, and probably most everywhere else on the Earth. Naturally we began to re-explore our insights of so long ago, tentatively at first, but soon we were plowing new ground and thinking of revitalizing the Civalien Project. In our years apart we had discovered two more major implications of the entropy paradigm. I had found the incompatibility of our economic system, and Stellan had discovered the incompatibility of our legal system. These new revelations came out in our discussions on how to proceed with our project.

"Stellan," I said, "do you remember how we could not figure out a way to humanely introduce the concept of domains into the world and bring the human population down?"

"Do I ever. I don't think I'll ever forget your suggestion we should have about three worldwide lotteries with half of the people eating the other half each time to deal with the problem of all the bodies accumulating, and getting the world population to about one billion in three months. I think you suggested the eaters would get the property of the eatees each time, so it would also be a redistribution of the wealth of the world. Talk about a hair brained idea!"

"You know I wasn't serious, but I now do have a serious idea. Would you agree a child born without a domain, even if they live a frugal life, will degrade the biosphere to some degree, effectively displacing the equivalent of another person?"

"Let me think about that for a minute." Stellan looked thoughtful and was silent for a time. "If I understand what you are saying, a person born without a domain damages multiple people a little, and the total is equivalent to displacing, in other words killing, one other person. Is that right?

"Yes, so I maintain having a child without a domain available for them is morally wrong."

"Boy! Are you ever going to get pushback on that," Stellan told me emphatically.

"I'm sure you're right, but it is the logical truth, isn't it?"

"It seems so, but it is a hard truth, and one most people, at least the ones I know, won't accept easily. It also occurs to me if lots of people have children without domains for them, the biosphere could degrade, which would decrease the number of domains available in a given region. In those circumstances, the ratio of equivalent deaths would be greater than one to one. So, where does all this lead us?"

"Prevention is essential," I told Stellan. "To prevent children without domains from being born, careful education, easy access to birth control, and intensive research into safe and effective birth control for both males and females are all a must."

"Good luck! You are going to find that road tough going. How does it get us closer to a society based on domains?"

"I envision establishing domains in some sparsely inhabited regions where there is room for additional domains at a later time. The initial populations of these domains should be a mixture of ages and skills, and they need to begin learning how to live and thrive on net photosynthetic energy."

Stellan interrupted, "This initial population would have to be a community of some sort to survive. Few, if any, people could live entirely on NPP by themselves."

"That I grant you," I said. "The crux of this plan is those without domains would retreat to existing cities, using some of the remaining fossil fuels and the existing infrastructure to live out the remainder of their lives. Obviously, without domains for offspring, they could not have children."

"What do you think they would do, play tidily winks?"

I could tell Stellan wasn't thinking too highly of my idea. "No. I think the city dwellers would have five main missions. The first would be to research procedures and technologies compatible with individual domains."

"The second would be to invent new compatible technologies for exporting entropy into outer space using only incoming solar energy. The purpose of such work would be to export the entropy which has already built up in the intermediate sinks from the prior use of internal stored energy and to mitigate the entropy from their own use of internal stored energy."

"Third, they should work on decreasing their own energy consumption while living in the city environment and try to reduce their dependence on fossil fuels."

"Fourth, those with domains will have to learn how to care for them. City dwellers could help them learn and help them care for their domains."

"Finally, as the populations of the cities decline over time from the deaths of the residents, the remaining inhabitants would need to reclaim land from abandoned infrastructure within and without the city, returning land to biological productivity and making more land available for domains."

Stellan had begun to look less skeptical and more interested. "You've put a lot of thought into this, haven't you? At least in theory, I think your plan could work."

I confessed to Stellan, "I've only thought of this fairly recently. For a lot of years, I despaired finding any path from the entropic mess current societies are making to an individual domain society. I didn't think any ways existed except violent ones, essentially the Four Horsemen of the Apocalypse. I don't know why I didn't think of this years ago, and I will admit there might be better ways, but what this thought has done for me is to give me hope and enthusiasm to again try to actually organize and establish a Civalien Project."

Having discovered at least one way forward, coupled with being older, hopefully wiser, and more experienced, Stellan and I eagerly took up the task of envisioning and attempting to build a domain-based community. We decided to call our nascent community Civalia, again a name with more than two syllables, but a name easily derived from our Civalien Project name and one which readily rolled off the tongue. Our intervening engineering experience would certainly help us design the community, but financing was a looming hurdle.

"Years ago, we calculated an average domain size would be

about 100 acres. Have we learned anything new or has anything happened to change that number?" I asked Stellan.

"Not that I know of," he answered. "But if we wait much longer, the global NPP may be reduced by roads, housing, and shopping centers being built on arable land."

"I think wild fires might be more likely to reduce it by burning over some impressively large areas."

"Fires only temporarily take land out of production; development is permanent." Stellan, with his agricultural background, was highly sensitive to and knowledgeable about agricultural issues.

I changed the subject. "If I did have a domain, how could I maintain it and keep from making unauthorized alterations to others' domains?"

Stellan gazed thoughtfully up and to his left. "I suppose you would necessarily have to consider the entropy implications of all of your actions. Could you cut down a tree? Probably, but it would depend on how the tree interacted with the rest of your domain. If that particular tree was providing shade both for you and your neighbor, you couldn't cut it down without their authorization."

"I probably couldn't clear-cut my domain either," I laughed.

"Probably not," Stellan responded. "The environmental effects of clear-cutting extend well beyond the that area, including increased runoff and erosion, displacement or destruction of various bird and animal species habitat, the encouragement of various weedy plant species, the alteration of the subsoil biome, changes to the insect population, and so on. The main principle of the *Declaration of Life* is at least to try to maintain, but preferably increase, the biological activity and diversity of your domain."

"That's a far cry from the principles the vast majority of the societies on Earth currently use," I added.

"Why don't any societies operate according to the principles of the *Declaration of Life*?" Stellan asked.

After thinking about his question for a few moments, I began my answer by bringing up my insights into the incompatibility of our economic system with the entropy paradigm and our *Declaration of Life*. "It seems to me, today's societies view the

Earth and all the living things in and on it as an inexhaustible supply of resources and energy sources for exploitation, use, and discard, limited only by human imagination and the cost. I've come to think the problem is money, or rather the desire for money; the profit motive."

"How so?" Stellan asked.

I asked in return, "Would you agree the profit motive underlies most of the economic structures in societies around the world?"

Stellan got a thoughtful look. "I suppose I would agree the majority rely on the profit motive, but not all people do."

"I'll buy that. Would it be fair to paraphrase the profit motive as the maximum money in the minimum time?"

Stellan nodded. "Sounds reasonable. If I made a million dollars and it took me 50 years, I wouldn't say it was a good profit, but if it took me 50 minutes, I'd be ecstatic. If it was 10 million, I'd be even more ecstatic."

"Right. So, are you aware money highly correlates with energy transformations?"

Stellan was startled. "I've never looked at it that way, but yes; I can see how it's true. Aircraft carriers cost more than destroyers, and destroyers cost more than a 28-foot sailboat, and metal paper clips cost more than plastic ones."

"It's not a perfect correlation, because sometimes people buy things like an art work or other rare object and pay far more than what the energy transformations in its creation dictate."

"Yes," Stellan said, reflectively, "and sometimes people pay far, far, less than the energy transformations would dictate. I'm thinking about a car restoration project a friend of mine did and then was forced to sell for only about one sixth of what he had put into the project."

I delivered the coup de grâce. "The profit motive then pushes for the maximum energy transformations in the minimum time, and since every energy transformation produces some entropy, the profit motive tends to maximize entropy production."

"No shit! I mean lots of shit." Stellan was obviously slightly rattled. "How did you come up with these concepts?"

"You know, I don't really remember when these thoughts

occurred to me. I think it might have started a number of years ago when I saw a graph of money transactions versus energy expenditures. I doubt I could find that reference again. I'm quite certain it is valid, because I have seen the effects of maximizing energy transformations within my life time."

Again, Stellan asked me, "How so?"

"When I was young, I walked a morning paper route six days a week. The morning weather varied, but a brisk morning walk was always a nice way to start the day. Once in while I would spot something on the ground, and often it was something of value, a lost Parker ballpoint pen one time, a useable barrette which I gave to my sister, a comb in perfect condition, sometimes a coin, and occasionally it was just trash dropped by a careless passerby. But there was not much trash. That is not true anymore. Now a walk finds the streets and sidewalks littered with trash, candy and gum wrappers, merchandise packaging and plastic shopping bags, cigarette butts and cartons, beer cans. The other day I saw a shattered smart phone. Sometimes there are car parts, oh, and a lot of unidentifiable plastic shards."

Stellan nodded in understanding. "I've seen pictures of vast stretches of the ocean covered in trash, most of it plastic. A lot of this trash comes from the efforts of advertisers urging us to consume more and more things we don't need for activities which are often damaging to our health in pursuit of happiness, which becomes more and more elusive, so we can end our days shunted off into an institutional setting where the last of our money can be extracted from us by the so called health care system."

"Whoa, get off your soapbox!" I said to Stellan. "There are some caring people who work diligently to help us when we are sick." Stellan was a little sensitive on this subject since one of his uncles had lost his farm when he had been gravely ill, and the mounting medical bills had impoverished him.

"I know there are, but I fault the system that turns every misfortune into an opportunity to make a profit. Enough!" Stellan said. "My preaching; it is probably to the choir anyway, since you've undoubtedly experienced the health care system firsthand."

"Yes, more so now since I've hit retirement age. There is

more," I told Stellan. "I discovered advertising attempts to make people unhappy because happy people make poor consumers; unhappy with their looks, envious of what other have or do, and so on. Another characteristic of our economic system doesn't make sense, but no one seems to notice."

"What might that be?"

"The basis of our economic system is the gross domestic product, GDP," I asserted. "At least it is the measuring tool for how well the economy is functioning. But everything goes into the GDP. When I had an accident with my car last year, I totaled it, and the towing, the insurance settlement, what I had to pay for a different car, the sales tax, the licensing fee, and the new insurance policy all went right into the GDP, but my life was not more orderly or happy. Instead of working on things I wanted to work on, I had to deal with my wrecked car. Even a year later, I am still dealing with the disruption that auto accident caused in my life. That incident created a lot of entropy, and it was all part of the GDP."

"If you really want something to increase GDP, along with lots of entropy increase, try war." Stellan said heatedly. Stellan was in the military for a time, and did not recall his stint fondly. "When the effects of war are examined, the picture's terrible. War destroys indiscriminately, people, infrastructure, fields, equipment, life of all species, and everything orderly in its path. It is the ultimate creator of entropy. Yet it adds to the GDP as we not only construct the instruments of destruction and wipe out everything, but also when we have to recover and try to rebuild from the destruction."

"You are right," I told Stellan. "War is one of the primary tools to rev up an economy and get it going after it has taken a nose dive. The gargantuan energy transformations of a war get the economy moving in high gear and growing."

The word "growing" seemed to spark some thoughts for Stellan. "Growing. We always have to have the economy growing. Unchecked growths in our bodies are called cancers, and when uncheck growth of other organisms happens, we often refer to those as cancerous. Cancers, no matter where, cause sickness and death. Isn't continuous growth in an economic system the same thing? And isn't it causing sickness and death in innumerable ways? Why do we allow it? No wonder large swatches of the biosphere are sickening and dying!"

I was somewhat taken back by the vehemence Stellan showed in his last outburst. Maybe he still had feelings about his father's death from non-Hodgkin lymphoma about nineteen or twenty years prior. His Dad was a farmer, and his exposure to pesticides likely contributed to his cancer.

"I venture to guess you've never heard a politician say we need to shrink the economy and the GDP. Have you ever asked yourself why?" I ask somewhat mildly.

"Not really," Stellan said, regaining his composure, "but it's an interesting question."

I marshaled my thoughts and picked up a pad of paper and pencil. "Stripped of investments, taxation, government spending, imports and exports, and actions of such entities as the Federal Reserve, the current GDP model for this country and most of the rest of the world, is of the form. . ." I wrote the equation $\$=C/(1-MPC)$ on the pad.

"I've never seen a GDP equation that looks like that," Stellan told me. "Are you sure you have it correct? Where did you get it?"

"I'm not surprised you haven't seen it in this form. When I went looking for GDP equations, I found a basic equation which looked simple and straight forward. But when I got into it, the GDP term appeared on both sides of the equation. The book I got the equation from gave the method of solving the equation as multiple iterations. You know me; I had to see if I could simplify it. When I did, I finally arrived at the form of the equation I've written down, or I should say the expanded version with the investments, taxation, and other terms included. I extracted some of the confounding terms to get to the essence of the equation."

"Are you sure it's right?" Stellan asked me.

"Yes. I tested it against the iteration method, and got the same results."

"So, what do you have to tell me about it?"

"In this equation $\$$ is money; it was GDP in the original equation, but I changed it to money because it's obviously not

GDP anymore with all those other factors removed. C is the rock bottom necessary consumption, the energy transformations necessary to survive, and MPC is the marginal propensity to consume ranging in value from 0 to 1. If any excess money exists above rock bottom necessity, the MPC represents how much of the excess is consumed. Increases in money tend to lead to increases in the MPC, which lead to further increases in money. Similarly decreases in money lead to decreases in the MPC, which lead to further decreases in money." I paused. "This is a classic positive feedback system," I said dramatically.

"I'd never looked at it in quite that way before." Stellan looked thoughtful. "So that explains why irrational exuberance tends to lead to bubbles and downturns lead to crashes, recessions, and depressions. This is the same thing as the loud screech you often hear in an auditorium when a person steps up to the microphone. Noise from the person is amplified, issues from the speakers, impinges on the microphone, is amplified again, issues from the speakers with even more volume, and so forth."

"Yes." I was off in my professorial mode. "The screech is generated when both the highs and lows of the sound waves are amplified through positive feedback. The economic system responds in the same way. I think the Federal Reserve was instituted in an effort to control the wild behavior of the positive feedback financial system by trying to control the MPC. Balancing at exactly zero growth is nearly impossible, because any perturbation of the system, either up or down, will send it careening even farther out of balance, either up or down, depending on which direction it is changing. Data indicates recovering from a down is more difficult than recovering from an up. Obviously, balancing on the negative side of growth would be disastrous, since eventually the economy would be driven as low as it could go."

"So probably," Stellan said, "the goal of the Federal Reserve has been to keep the economy growing at a low rate, leaving room for some variation in the growth rate while avoiding wild plunges associated with excursions into the negative regions."

"Right," I said. "The Federal Reserve tries to maintain about a two percent growth rate." I was heartened by how quickly Stellan picked up on my ideas and even began to carry them further.

"Sometimes it works and sometimes it doesn't," Stellan said, and then went on, "but continuous growth is guaranteed to be disastrous in the long run, if it isn't disastrous already. The very structure of a positive feedback system will drive everything to extremes, which is bound to produce problems. Why do we put up with this?"

"I don't know," I told Stellan. "What I do know is maintaining the integrity of a domain has to intrinsically be a negative feed-back activity, so the economic system, a word derived from the Greek meaning household management, should also be a negative feedback system. A positive feedback system will not work for personal domains any more than it would work for driving your car. Imagine if your car began drifting to the left, you turn your steering wheel to the left and as the car turns even harder to the left, you turn the steering wheel even more to the left."

"I wouldn't even get out of the garage!" Stellan said emphat-ically. "How about a positive feedback thermostat? The house is too warm, so the thermostat turns on the furnace. If house is too cold, the furnace goes off, and the air conditioner turns on. Wouldn't that be uncomfortable?" Stellan frowned. "Yes, indeed, what we need is an economic system with negative feedback, a system generating a countering force to push the system back toward equilibrium whenever there is a disturbance. The world seems to be filled with all kinds of negative feedback systems, but is a negative feedback economic system possible?"

To answer Stellan's question I reminded him of a simple positive feedback system. "Have you ever played with in inverted pendulum?" I asked.

"What's that?"

"Hold the end of a broom handle in the palm of your hand with the head of the broom up, and try to keep it balanced. That's an inverted pendulum."

"Oh, I tried that when I was a kid, but I didn't realize that's what it's called. It takes practice to keep it upright very long."

"Well, it's an example of positive feedback. When the broom starts to tip, gravity makes it tip more, and if you don't correct the tip, it'll fall to the floor. This is analogous to the adjustments the Federal Reserve Bank makes to our economic system to prevent it from crashing."

"I get it," Stellan says. "If you turn it over with the head down, it becomes a regular pendulum with negative feedback."

"If the negative feedback pendulum is pushed to the side, gravity pushes it back toward the equilibrium position," I added.

"So, what do pendulums have to do with an economic system?"

"Interestingly enough, the only difference between the force equation for an unstable inverted pendulum and the force equation for a stable regular pendulum is a sign change. So, the question then is whether a stable economic system can be established with a sign change somewhere in the system? Suppose in the GDP equation, the minus sign in front of the MPC factor is changed to a plus sign and the MPC factor is fixed at a set value, the set point for the economy." I took up the pad of paper and the pencil again and wrote the equation $\$=C/(1+MPC)$. "In this case, if the $\$$ value is perturbed by some random event, say it increases, which in turn increases the MPC factor, the result would be to decrease the $\$$, a negative feedback to bring the $\$$ back to the set point. Conversely, if the $\$$ decreased, decreasing the MPC factor, the $\$$ would be increased; again, a negative feedback."

Stellan looked puzzled. "I can see how the equation is a negative feedback system, but how can it be translated into an actual economic system?"

"One way I have considered is to make money what it really is. If you examine a dollar bill," I pulled out my wallet and handed Stellan a bill, "you will see it is a Federal Reserve Note, and a note is a debt instrument. In the current system, transactions occur when some object or service offered by a person, the seller, is of value to another person, the buyer. Currently, the buyer gives money to the seller. Money is considered to have value, but it actually has no intrinsic value. What if the transaction is reversed? Now the buyer, I'd prefer to call him the receiver, wishing to acquire the goods or services from the seller, let's call her the giver, must agree to accept debt from the giver along with the goods or services. The receiver is now holding debt. If a person is holding debt, any other person may call that debt and demand something from them in the way of goods or services then taking debt off of their hands."

Stellan shuddered and said, "I'd not like holding debt under those circumstances."

"Neither would I, but that's just the point. Debt is not desirable so the MPC factor would reverse in sign. Natural limits would likely exist in such a system, since the more debt an able-bodied person held, the less likely another person would be willing to give them goods or services and transfer even more debt to them. Such a deadbeat would be unlikely to have or do anything anyone else valued."

"Your system would require complete transparency and a way to ensure no one could cook the books," Stellan said.

"True," I said, "but I also think it would encourage individuals to acquire skills which are in demand and discourage free loading, because who would want to give more debt to a heavily debt-laden person? Such an act would only decrease the amount of debt available for calling in among more productive individuals. Unproductive people acquiring lots of debt would make desirable goods and services more difficult to obtain over all. I have no idea whether this economic system would actually work, but it might be worth a try."

"We'd have to find a way to test your proposal," Stellan said. "I'd hate to deploy such a system without some testing."

"I wholeheartedly agree," I said. "Perhaps, someone else can devise a much better negative feedback economic system, and if they did, I would be one of the first in line to sign on."

"At first, I thought this discussion was a digression, but now I see it's not," Stellan ruminated. "A personal domain is not possible within the existing economic system. Suppose my domain was forested, and my neighbor offered me a million dollars for one of my trees to cut up for lumber, a handsome profit. I would be sorely tempted. Just one tree, I would tell myself. No problem. What if it then became two trees? Three trees? A dozen trees? Would I know where to stop? I'm doubtful I'd know. This may seem like an extreme example, but I'll be willing to bet almost everyone can come up with examples of their own, and perhaps most people have, at some time, crossed some line for the sake of money, a crossing they later regretted. I know I have."

Years before, I had realized the implications of the *Declaration of Life* were staggering. Now they seemed even more so. Stellan and I had established internal stored energy (fossil fuel, nuclear, and geothermal energy) cannot be used to export entropy out of the closed Earth system; reasoned the extant social and economic system had overwhelmed the natural biosphere's ability to export entropy into outer space; determined a right to life exists, and therefore a right to a closed-system-equivalent domain in the biosphere would also have to exist; recognized the population levels in North America, and the rest of the world, were significantly greater than could be accommodated by reasonably sized domains; reasoned the current economic systems are positive feedback systems and unworkable for maintaining the integrity of individuals' domains; and postulated a negative feedback economic system could be developed. All these certainly indicated a shakeup of the status quo was needed. Was there more?

Yes, there was. Stellan brought up the legal system.

"John, have you thought about the legal system in relation to domains?"

"It has crossed my mind, but I've not given it any deep thought. Mostly, I've thought about the impact of building codes on domain structures. What do you have in mind?"

Stellan flipped open his computer and brought up a web page. "Throughout history, terrible oppressions and violations of individuals' rights and their beings have been, and are being, written into law. It is not difficult to find examples."

Stellan showed me a list on a web page.

- The legal institution of hereditary, chattel, slavery as applied to persons of African ancestry in many nations of the world and in the USA from the early 1600s till 1865.

- Civil asset forfeiture laws allowing police to seize personal assets if they are suspected to be proceeds from a crime without having to prove the crime.

- Laws restricting the vote in the USA, first to only white, land-owning males, and then extending the vote to all males in 1865, and finally including females in 1920.

"Blue" laws enforcing religious standards on all persons regardless of religious or non-religious beliefs.

- Up until 2018, imprisoning women who were caught driving a car in Saudi Arabia.

- A Wyoming law including the weight of the container with the weight of an illicit drug, so if a person is arrested with 2mg of marijuana in a 20 pound contain, they can be charged with possession of 20 pounds of marijuana, a felony instead of a misdemeanor.

- As late as 1945 the state of Wyoming passed a miscegenation statute stating marriages of whites to Negroes, mulattoes, Mongolians, Malayans was void. Penalty: $100 to $1,000 and/or one to five years imprisonment.

- All states have Eminent Domain laws allowing the state or subunits or even some corporations to take property for purposes of the "public good." Since a 2005 US Supreme Court decision (Kelo v. City of New London, 545 U.S. 46d9), some states allow the unwilling transfer of property from one private owner to another for the purposes of economic development.

- In all states in the USA, failure to pay property taxes results in seizure and resale of the property for back taxes.

Stellan said, "These last two examples show clearly a personal domain cannot be an unalienable right under the legal system of laws existing in this country. I think this can be generalized to any governmental unit operating under a system of laws, because the laws can be changed by persons of power and by legal procedures not under the control of the domain holder. Laws can take a domain away, which means they can take a life away. As the lawyers say, 'I rest my case.'"

"What could possibly take the place of a legal system of laws?" I asked. "Some of the alternatives aren't very appealing; a tyrant, a clergy, an aristocracy, oligarchies." I thought about this some more. "The *Declaration of Life* is a good start; somewhat like the Declaration of Independence. Could the *Declaration of Life* be embodied in a constitution and set of laws?"

"I don't see how," Stellan answered. "You would come right back to the problem of law making and enforcement. How could the making of laws and the enforcement of laws be accomplished without making unauthorized alterations of another's domain?"

I thought about this issue some more. "There are some interesting passages in the *Bible* which may shed some light on this issue. In . . . ah. . . I think it's the book of Judges. Just a minute, let me look it up. Here it is; Judges 17:6. 'In those days there was no king in Israel, but every man did that which was right in his own eyes.' This passage is repeated in Judges 21:21."

Stellan asked me, "I thought you'd given up on religion. How come you're quoting the *Bible*?"

"I did give up religion as a basis for my paradigm, but the *Bible* is not devoid of wisdom. After all, I did read it and study it zealously in my younger days. Such knowledge doesn't just go away. Actually, there are all kinds of interesting ideas in the *Bible*. I'm sure other religious books like the *Torah, Quran, Vedas*, and *Bhagavad Gita* also contain a lot of wisdom, but I didn't study those texts."

"So, what does your quote tell us?"

"Well, Israel had judges during the period in question, and it is said of these men they 'sat in the gate.' Apparently, these judges, also known as elders, would be stationed somewhere near the gates to the city and people with disputes would come to them, present their stories, and these judges would render their opinions based on the underlying principles of their culture. I don't think we want to have people who are designated judges, but the way they operated could be used. Suppose we had some kind of deliberative group . . ."

"Like a jury?" Stellan interrupted. "A jury is the basis for a possible system I've considered. The jury would be selected by lot and hear the evidence. Then they would have to decide whether an entity had been altered without permission. If so, the jury would then have to decide what just recompense would be appropriate. The principles for making these decisions would be those set forth in the *Declaration of Life* and in the First and Second Laws of Thermodynamics."

"That might work," I said, "but it could take a lot of time. How would those involved be compensated for their time?"

"If the jury decides in favor of the plaintiff, the defendant has to reimburse all the others for their time, but if the defendant prevails, the plaintiff has to reimburse everyone else. That might give people an incentive to negotiate settlements with their neighbors rather than invoke more drastic measures."

"Would you have lawyers?" I asked.

Stellan looked askance at me without saying anything.

"Oh, right. Breaking old habits of thought is difficult. No laws, no lawyers. But what does happen if a person is not able to present their case?"

"If a person is incapable of initiating and carrying through the judicial process," Stellan said, "some other person would have to be able to start the process on their behalf. I'd call them an advocate."

"Do you think your system could work?" I asked. "What would you call it?"

"Of course, I'm not sure such a system would work. We'd have to test it. To answer you second question, I'd call it a system of principles and procedures. Ideally, it would rarely be used."

I moved on. "Ok, so we don't have laws, only principles and procedures, but how do the daily things get done in Civalia? Who decides the who, what, why, when, where, and how?"

"Are you asking about the governance of Civalia?" Stellan asked. "Are you talking about a community level governance, regional governance, or national governance?"

"I'm talking about community level first, and then maybe regional," I answered. "I've already written off national. I have essentially zero ability to affect national issues, and I don't think anyone 1,500 miles away can know diddly about what is going on right here in my home and yours in Laramie. On a community level, we have some control, on a regional level much less."

Stellan thought about this for a moment and then continued. "I assume in a community like Civalia, the situation would often be something like a work place. We would need to cooperate to get certain things done, and since many of them would be for our basic survival, I would guess we'd all appreciate harmonious relationships, ones providing satisfying social ties. I think we can automatically rule out despotic systems of governance."

"You are undoubtedly right about despots," I said. "I've been in some reasonably good working relationship and some really bad ones, generally stemming from despotic bosses. I remember one project I was on; it was a disorganized mess. I tried to get it straightened out, but couldn't do it in the end. There were too many bosses, each one considering himself king, each giving conflicting orders right and left, and not enough workers. To make matters worse, the institutional inertia was huge. What about a democratic system of majority rule?"

Stellan answered my question with a snort, and then he said, "Our heritage tells us the majority rule system is the best, but the best at what? We have so many examples of the majority of people being wrong, I don't know where to start. Perhaps, the best example I can give you is the one you brought up earlier, the idea most people seem to subscribe to, growing the economy forever."

"Ouch." I said. "You really know how to cut a person down, don't you?

"Most organizational systems seem to be hierarchical," Stellan said. "Are there problems with hierarchies?"

I looked at him with incredulity. "Do you have to ask that after your experiences working for hierarchical companies or organizations? Don't you read Dilbert?"

"Well, I guess what I am trying to ask is whether there is anything intrinsically wrong with hierarchies, because most every activity or project has some sort of leader and . . ."

"You just said the magic word, Stellan, leader. A leader is a person with knowledge or skills applicable to the task at hand. Most of the leaders, I hesitate to call them leaders, perhaps heads of hierarchies, are dictators, and a lot of them don't seem to know much about what is going on. I think most of them seem to be in it mainly for the power. Did you know about one in a hundred persons in the general population are psychopaths, but one in five CEOs are psychopaths?"

"No kidding?" He was shocked.

"That's right. They don't stick to their areas of knowledge and skills, but they do stick it to others in the hierarchy. Oh, and to give you some perspective on this issue, about one in five prison inmates are psychopaths. Yes, I do think there is something intrinsically wrong with hierarchies. I have come to think the main purpose of hierarchies is to funnel money and/or power from a broad base of people at the bottom to a few at the top, there really being little difference between money and power. Some people have said they think it is a good thing for some CEOs to be psychopaths, because they can readily downsize a company to improve the profit to the shareholders. The fact they wreck the lives of thousands of workers does not cause them to lose any sleep."

Stellan put up a weak argument. "Sometimes I have worked on projects with a group of my co-works and had a very productive, cooperative, enjoyable time."

I didn't cut him any slack. "I'd be willing to bet the experiences you are talking about were just with co-workers. There were natural leaders among your group, who moved the project along by their knowledge and skills. Those leaders were on the same level of the hierarchy as you and didn't have power over you. Did the high ups contribute?"

"Well, not really, most of the time we had to fly under the radar to get things done." He ventured an observation, "I suppose you think corporations won't work then, since they are hierarchies."

"Let me count the ways," I said and began ticking them off on my fingers. "Most corporations are for-profit organizations, even the supposed non-profit ones, since they are mainly restricted on how they spend their money. Oh, and restricted a little on how they make their money; it has to be related to their purpose. Corporations are hierarchies. Corporations are legal constructs; remember we aren't going to have laws? Corporations are considered persons in the eyes of the law. For-profit corporations are charged by law to make money for their shareholders, so they value profits over health and safety; the emotional and physical wellbeing of employees, customers, and the general public; the wellbeing of plants and animal; entropy reduction and export, and even in lot of cases, legal responsibilities. So, no, I don't think a corporate structure will work for Civalia, and I don't think you do either."

Stellan sighed, "You are right. I've experienced most of the points you made with corporations I worked for. One I remember clearly was an instance of your last point, legal responsibilities. A company where I was employed had some produced wastewater which should have been tested and disposed of according to the Department of Environmental Quality directives. Instead, it was sprayed on some county roads by order of the company president. Fortunately, it was not another Times Beach, Missouri. Another one I remember was some software our group developed to improve the efficiency of our work. It was flat out sabotaged by the company CEO; I think because he could not work a computer well enough to use it."

"I remember you telling me about the first incident a lot of years ago," I said, "but the second one is new to me. I'd add sometimes, however, even the statutory objective for shareholder profit is lost to an insidious drive by those at the top of the hierarchy for personal gain of power, money, or status. Look at Ken Lay of Enron. I'm sure there are a lot more of these; after all, remember one in five of these characters are psychopaths."

Recalling an experience I had a number of years ago, I also offered, "I've had some personal experience in a corporate setting with a person with psychopathic characteristics. I was on the board of directors of a non-profit, and the board was taken over by a board member just after I left it. He installed himself as director and milked the company dry; giving himself and a henchman huge salaries. It only lasted two years after he took over. The real losers there were the people the non-profit was serving. The non-profit used taxpayers' money, no less."

Having conceded my point, Stellan asked, "Ok, but how do you keep a cooperative endeavor from turning into a hierarchy?"

"I don't know for certain, but I do know being a permanent head honcho can bring out the worst in some people. One job I had was as a plant engineer for a project. I had six plant operators under my supervision, and I needed to appoint one of them as a shift supervisor, since at that point in time we were running continuously for 48 to 72 hours. The budget to hire someone directly was not available, so I just had these six operators rotate through the supervisory position two weeks at a time. Had the money been available, the operator I would have chosen to be the supervisor turned out to be totally unsuited for the position. He lorded it over the others and tried to micromanage them. Fortunately, it was only for two weeks. I have never been so relieved to have a two-week period over in my life."

"I understand what you are saying," Stellan told me, "but I'm not sure we can come up with a workable solution to this problem. We are both engineers, and if there is any truth in some of the jokes about engineers, our social skills may not be the best. I think we may need to get some help in some of these areas. What do you think?"

"I agree with you. To tell you the truth, I don't think I really do know the best way to organize Civalia. I just do know I don't want it to be like most of the jobs I have had."

Both Stellan and I felt relieved, deciding to offer responsibility for this area to someone else.

I was not quite ready to let this topic go. "Stellan, I think you and I can probably agree aggression, violence, and warfare are antithetical to the *Declaration of Life*, can't we?"

"Certainly. What are you getting at?"

"Well, just think for a moment about a person, alone in the middle of their domain. There is no one to tell them what to do; their every action must be self-directed. Isn't that so?"

"Of course, but what difference does it make?"

"I've described the technical definition of anarchy," I told Stellan.

"What? Are we going to be a bunch of bomb-throwing terrorists?" Stellan looked taken aback.

"What you are talking about is the popular definition of anarchy, but it is not the technical definition. Technically, anarchy is the rejection of hierarchies. Perhaps Civalia can be an anarchy. I've already told you the Israelites had anarchy during the period of the Judges. What happened to end it is also interesting."

"What happened to them?" Stellan asked.

"The people wanted a king, so the judge at the time, Samuel, asked the Lord about the situation, and the Lord told him to give them a king, but to tell them what was going to happen. It is pretty graphic. Let me read it to you."

I found the passage, 1 Samuel 8:11-18, in my *King James Bible*:

> 11And he said, This will be the manner of the king that shall reign over you: He will take your sons and appoint them for himself, for his chariots and to be his horsemen; and some shall run before his chariots.
>
> 12And he will appoint him captains over thousands, and captains over fifties; and will set them to ear his ground, and to reap his harvest, and to make his instruments of war, and instruments of his chariots.
>
> 13And he will take your daughters to be confectionaries, and to be cooks, and to be bakers.
>
> 14And he will take your fields, and your vineyards, and your olive yards, even the best of them, and give them to his servants.
>
> 15And he will take the tenth of your seed, and of your vine-yards, and give to his officers, and to his servants.
>
> 16And he will take your menservants, and your maidser-vants, and your goodliest young men, and your asses, and put them to his work.
>
> 17He will take the tenth of your sheep: and ye shall be his servants.
>
> 18And ye shall cry out in that day because of your king which ye shall have chosen you; and the LORD will not hear you in that day.

"Wow!" Stellan said. "The writer certainly got it right, except I think the 'king' is getting a lot more than a tenth these days. I think the overall average is now around 30 percent in the USA."

"The point is," I said, "anarchy was the governance of choice prior to the king. Perhaps we could make an anarchy work; subject, of course, to the First and Second Laws of Thermodynamics and the *Declaration of Life*. Anarchy would require concurrence from all the members of Civalia."

"I'd have to think about it, John. I do, however, think we've drifted around quite a bit on this topic without reaching any really strong conclusions. We've covered a wide range of governance possibilities from the micro- to the macroscopic without even a clear-cut direction. I'm feeling like an autumn leaf in the wind."

I was a might taken back by Stellan's statement. "I'm surprised to hear you say that. You were very adamant about several issues, such as the legal one."

"I suppose I was, and I do have some strong feelings about some of these areas. I guess what I don't have is a sense of is whether we have a strong, workable plan for how Civalia can be governed. You mentioned earlier about finding someone to help us with these issues. I'd like to see that happen. Are you going to work on it?"

"Yes, I will. However, I have another issue I need to discuss with you."

"What is it?" Stellan asked, a bit of wariness in his voice.

"I hesitate somewhat to bring this up with you because of my strong stand against corporations, but there may be a problem with Civalia where a corporation could be helpful."

"So now you're going to do an about face?" Stellan asked.

"Not exactly," I said and launched into an explanation. "In our society and legal structure, land is not a right, but is an economic good. To make Civalia work, we can't have the individuals own the property, because laws can take it away, and when a person dies, inheritance laws determine what happens to the land. Furthermore, an individual's land is taxed, and can be seized. It just won't work."

Stellan still looked skeptical. "So how is a corporation going to help?"

"I think we may need to form a non-profit corporation, maybe a 501(c)(3) charitable organization or a 501(c)(4) social welfare organization to be the legal landholder. But the individual could still be a domain holder, probably by an unwritten agreement. The corporation can exist in perpetuity, and we may have some tax advantages, a not inconsequential thing, since we will be trying to operate outside the existing economic system."

Stellan began looking a little more thoughtful. "I can see what you're saying, but everyone would have to have a lot of faith in the board of directors of such a corporation. A LOT of faith! The same thing that happened to the non-profit you mentioned earlier could easily happen in this case. The temptation to rip off the corporation might be very strong with the amount of land involved."

"I'm aware of that," I told Stellan, "but I haven't been able to think of any other way to start up Civalia. Eventually, I dream of the whole country changing to the Civalia model and all of these issues going away, but in the short term, these problems exist and won't go away. We have to deal with them."

Stellan and I called it quits for a while, and I stepped up my search for someone to help us with the personal interaction issues in Civalia.

PART II

THE BIRTH
OF CIVALIA

CHAPTER 5

S tellan and I put our engineering background to work by establishing formal project goals. I started this effort by saying, "Our *Declaration of Life* is certainly a basis for our project, but it seems to lack guiding principles."

"What do you mean by that?" Stellan asked

Suppose," I said, "I claimed the whole state of Wyoming as my domain, and you claimed the whole state of Montana. Even though we'd be living right next door, so to speak, with that much area I'm sure we could both do all kinds of environmental mayhem within our domains, and as long as we did it far enough away from our common border, neither of us would be making any unauthorized alteration of the other's domain. We could drive the biggest, baddest trucks, build palatial homes, dig, blast, kill, and burn all kinds of fossil fuels."

"I see what you mean. So, we need an explicit way to state what we have been taking for granted all along; our domain sizes should be minimized. Of course, we need a reasonable factor of safety." Stellan stared into space.

"Right. So how can we say that?"

"Let's see." Stellan thought for a while. "At the current time, environmentalists urge people to minimize their carbon footprint."

"That's all well and good," I said, "but carbon emissions are only one form of entropy." A thought struck me. "Hey, that's it! We need to minimize our entropy footprint, and reduce the entropy of our domains, if possible."

"I like that," Stellan said. It is direct and simple. Well, maybe not so simple to calculate, but in principle it's simple."

After long hours of argument, and using the principle of minimizing or reducing our entropy footprint, we arrived at a list of goals for Civalia, our first community within the Civalien Project.

Civalia Design Goals

- Community — Self-sustaining, diverse, cooperative, egalitarian, permanent
- Domains — Adequately sized
- Water — Adequate supply, appropriate quality for designated uses
- Food — Adequate quantity, high quality, age appropriate
- Solid waste — Unrecyclable wastes minimized, low environmental impact
- Structural materials — Local, durable, environmentally benign
- Embodied energy — Minimized, low entropy footprint
- Supplemental energy — local source, low entropy footprint
- Transportation — Minimize energy usage & entropy production
- Factors of Safety — Appropriate in all realms
- Satisfaction — Goal of Maslow's self-actualization

With these goals in mind Stellan and I tackled one of the next major steps in an engineering project, site selection. I caught him as he was walking by my desk to get to the kitchen. "Where should we locate Civalia?" I began.

Stellan paused. "This is obviously a topic that's going to take a while. Let me finish getting some coffee." He continued on to the kitchen, but was back shortly with a steaming cup and sat down by my desk. "Well, the middle of any city is clearly out of the question. For that matter any location with high population density is out."

"Sounds like a rural location."

"Right. Then there is the issue of zoning. Any heavily zoned area will be unsuitable, because zoning puts limits on what we can do. And land prices will be an issue, as will taxes."

"Unless my idea of using a 501(c)(4) works to avoid taxes." I added. "Overall, you are describing a low population area, or some deserted island. Wouldn't we also need a reasonably long growing season, so we could garden?"

Stellan thought about my question. He cracked a mischievous

smile and posed a question for me, "That would certainly make Civalia easier to do, but what do you think a reasonably average domain, which has about average NPP, looks like? It goes without saying that it would be in a low population density area"

"I assume by NPP you mean net primary production. I don't know. Maybe some prairie land in central Kansas?"

"I think you nailed the average NPP land, long grass prairie regions. But you missed low population density. Have you ever looked at a map of Kansas? The road network looks like a chain link fence. The average population density in Kansas is about 60 per square mile."

"Alaska?"

"Now you have really low population density, but the NPP sucks."

"Why don't you just tell me?"

"Okay. I've been studying this question, because I think we ought to at least try to set up our experiment on some land somewhere near or somewhat below the NPP average of the world. Then if we succeed, we'll know at least half the Earth can become domains. With some experience and innovation, probably a lot more of it could be utilized. When I looked into this, I found the short grass prairie states, like Wyoming, are about 80% to 85% of the world NPP, and believe it or not, overall the state of Wyoming is about 72% of the world average."

"What? I'm not sure I believe you. Wyoming seems rather barren. There's just mile after mile of sage brush and shrubs. Let me see your numbers."

Stellan pulled out a well-thumbed, dog-eared, notebook and paged through to find his notes. "Okay. Wyoming is about 44% desert or semi-desert, 25% temperate grasslands, 23% temperate evergreen forests, 7% the equivalent of temperate grasslands, and 1% swamp and wet lands. These five land types have mean NPPs of 90, 600, 1300, 650, and 600 grams per square meter per year respectively. From this data, the average NPP is about 554 grams per square meter per year. The world average is 773 for all lands."

I shook my head. "I never thought we'd be that close to the world average."

Stellan said, "I think Wyoming would be a good place to experiment with domains, not just because it's near average, but also the population density's low. The population is estimated at about 600,000, and the land area is a little over 62 million acres. That gives about 100 acres per person, close to the land area we calculated years ago for an average domain size. We've got at least an outside chance at making a domain community work."

"On the down side, the growing season's short," I said. I did a quick internet search and found a map of the days between killing frosts. "Wyoming varies from 80 to 160 frost free days. That's not very long." I found another map which showed the average annual extreme minimum temperatures in Wyoming. "Look at this," I said. "It gets cold. The best places in the state have lows ranging from -10 to -15 degrees Fahrenheit. The worst go from -35 to -40."

Stellan waited patiently for me to finish. "I am aware of those problems. I don't think a domain community can work in Wyoming without using greenhouses to extend the growing season. I think greenhouses would also give us a leg up on dealing with other issues in the community. Why don't you give it some thought, and we can work on it again later. I've got to get back to the house before 3 pm." Stellan looked at his watch. "Damn, I'm going to be late. I've got to get back to meet Gyan."

"Right," I said. "I think you told me he was coming for a two-week visit."

After Stellan literally ran out the door, I started thinking seriously about what he proposed. It actually made a lot of sense. I decided to investigate Wyoming for myself, and went looking for some maps. My thoughts drifted to Gyan as I began poking around my house to find what maps I had available. I hadn't visited with Gyan since the time Stellan and I had first conceived of the Civalien project, and he had named it for us. I realized I had almost no current knowledge of him, and I looked forward to catching up on the twists and turns his life had taken.

I eventually found a road map of Wyoming with topographic

features, and on the internet I found a map of land status in Wyoming. I printed that map. For a long time I looked at those two maps, evaluating the major regions. I was looking for areas with significant private land, away from major transportation corridors, having low population density, and containing some agricultural land, although preferably not irrigated agriculture.

I had been in the Red Desert, the Great Divide Basin, and the Big Horn Basin regions, and I knew life in any of these could be very harsh. In particular, water would be a major issue; if not the quantity, then the quality. The Great Divide Basin is one of the world's largest playas, about 3,960 square miles. The Red Desert is about three to four times bigger, and the Big Horn Basin, looked to be about two times bigger than the Red Desert, so obviously sufficient area was available. The scarcity of major roads, another indication of the harshness, helped me consider the risk too great to start our experiment in any of these three regions. Another factor bolstering my decision was the fact a large percentage of these lands, situated mostly in the western half of Wyoming, was either state or federal government owned. These large tracts of government land limited the possibilities for expansion despite there being some private land scattered throughout.

I considered the Wind River Indian Reservation in central Wyoming. In truth, I had thought of approaching these Indian tribes with the concept of domains because their cultures are traditionally much closer to the *Declaration of Life* than the profit motive driven society in the rest of the state. The prospect of trying to learn and adapt to another culture, as well as developing the expertise to make Civalia work, was daunting. I decided tackling the Indian Reservation should wait for a later time.

Next, I considered the mountainous forested areas. A large percentage of forested land is national forest, national park, state park, or national monument land. What is not government land is generally well used for recreational purposes, making it expensive, crowded, and jealously protected. I rejected those areas.

The interstate and major US highway corridors were also not appealing for many reasons. Among them are exposure to the traffic pollutants, the possibility of eminent domain seizure, the vagaries of the profit motive economic system, and the unknown intentions and motives of the many people traveling these roadways. The Interstate 80 corridor also has the drawback of the Railroad checkerboard ownership pattern that had been generated by the Pacific Railroad Act of 1862 and the amendment of 1864. The Central Pacific and Union Pacific Railroads were granted the odd numbered sections of land, 640 acres each, from 10 to 20 miles on each side of their right-of-way, and I-80 generally follows the railroad.

I had lived in the Powder River Basin area, and I was not impressed. A large number of coal mines and fossil fuel extraction facilities were very negative factors. I easily rejected that region.

The northeast corner of Wyoming had fairly low population density. That was attractive, but the downsides were the Interstate 90 corridor, the presence of a high-profile national monument, Devil's Tower, indicating a lot of tourist traffic, and the close proximity of some populated areas in South Dakota.

I dismissed the northwest corner of the state almost out of hand because of Yellowstone National Park. With peak visitation of nearly one million tourists a month and an average of about 3.7 million visitors a year, the area is flooded with humanity. Land prices in the region are also astronomically high.

One relatively small region in central Wyoming, between the Laramie Mountains and Interstate 80, the Shirley Basin, interested me. Although that region is similar to and could have easily been included with the Red Desert, it does have significant private land on the south eastern side. For that reason and the isolation of this region, I didn't rule it out.

I found two other regions interesting; the first being east central Wyoming comprising northern Goshen, Niobrara, and southern Weston Counties, and the second the Upper North Platte River Valley. Stellan was raised in eastern Wyoming, so I figured he would be the logical person to assess that area. I had some familiarity with the Upper North Platte River Valley, having lived near that region as a teenager, and I planned to investigate it further.

I decided to generate a list of location factors important to establishing Civalia. I wrote down these factors, and added my notes to explain my thinking.

Three days later, Stellan and Gyan stopped by for a visit. Since I hadn't seen Gyan since he was fourteen, I don't know that I could have recognized the man with Stellan as him. Gyan was both taller and heavier than his dad. He had his dad's round face, but his mother had given him her brown eyes. Unlike Stellan, Gyan had a deep tan with squint-lines around his eyes. I assumed his tan and squint came from spending a significant amount of time outdoors with his agricultural research. Like both his dad and me, Gyan dressed in western jeans, boots, and a long sleeved plaid shirt.

We spent an hour or so touring my shop and looking at my antique cars before settling down to catch up on where our lives had taken us. The talk immediate focused on Gyan's position on the faculty of Texas A&M where he was researching field crops. I was interested to know if his research had any relevance to Civalia.

Location Factors Page 1

Land availability—A minimum of about eight (8) square miles, assuming 50 residents, is required. Additional lands should be available for expansion of Civalia and the Civalien Project and to provide a buffer with neighboring land owners.

Low population density—100 acres per capita or greater in the region is desirable.

Reasonable land cost—Since Civalia must be initiated within the existing for-profit, economic system, the land must be purchased; a major factor for the project.

Climate—Extreme climate locations should be avoided. However, Wyoming will be a cool climate regardless of where Civalia is situated.

Water availability—Local sources of potable water must be available.

Water quality—Generally poor water quality in a region will make it much more difficult to build and maintain Civalia.

Water rights—Civalia should own all water rights within their jurisdiction.

Accessibility—Accessibility to some aspects of the existing region would be positive. These include community fire and emergency services, libraries, and schools.

Resource availability—Sustainable, local resources for construction and some types of cottage industry will be needed.

Slope—Some slopes, for example south facing ones, may be useful. Extremely steep slopes should be avoided.

Woodlands—Because woodland biomes have significant diversity and wood products are useful in many ways, some established woodland or the potential for establishing some woodland is desirable.

Growing season—Since the growing season essentially defines net photosynthetic production (NPP), the growing season will be the dominate factor in determining the size of individual domains.

Net solar insolation—Solar factors, such as cloudiness, terrain, vegetation, and atmospheric aerosols, must be carefully evaluated, since solar energy must be the primary energy source for Civalia.

"Gyan, we are thinking we will need greenhouses to make Civalia functional in Wyoming. Do you have any expertise in greenhouse production?"

"Most of my background has been in field crops, but I had some indirect experience when I got the greenhouse guys to do some controlled experiments with some row-crop varieties for me. So I've learned a little about them."

"Well," I said, "this is an area where we need help. Do you think you have enough knowledge to help out?" I asked Gyan.

"I think so. I've been studying permaculture, and I think that can help us. . ."

Stellan had picked up on something, and interrupted our dialog. "What's with this 'us' thing?"

Gyan looked at his dad. "I've been associated with the Civalien Project ever since I was a kid. Right? It has given me a different outlook on life. I've felt like Heinlein's *Stranger in a Strange Land* most of the time I've been in Texas. Since you and John are moving toward realizing your dreams, I want to be a part of them. I want to belong, and I want to live and raise my daughter, Cindy, in a society that is not so. . . so warped. That's part of the reason I'm here." He turned back to me. "I'll make it my business to learn what's needed to make greenhouses work for Civalia."

An emotional scene between Stellan and his son followed. After they settled down a little, Stellan asked his son, "What about Nancy?" Nancy was Gyan's wife.

"Dad, the other reason for this visit is to tell you we're splitting. She feels like she needs to find herself and is planning on moving to Italy. I'm not sure why she decided to go there, but that's her plan."

"Will she be taking Cindy?" I asked.

"No, Cindy is staying with me, but I came to Laramie by myself since Nancy wanted some time alone with Cindy before she takes off for Italy."

I could tell these revelations were hard on Stellan and Gyan, so I suggested we postpone talking about Civalia for a couple of days, giving them a chance to become reacquainted with this new reality and come to terms with the changes in both of their lives these events portended.

Later that day, a friend of mine at the University where I had been making inquiries about someone to help us with relationship issues for our Civalien Project gave me a book on intentional communities. He told me the author just happened to be located in

Laramie, and I finished reading the book before the day was out. The author seemed like just the person we needed to give us advice about organizing Civalia to minimize problems with personal interactions. I contacted her.

On Friday, Stellan and Gyan stopped by my place for a short visit. I could see that the bond between them had deepened. After some small talk, we gathered around my table. "Are you going to move to Laramie?" I asked Gyan.

Stellan answered instead. "Yes, he and Cindy are going to initially move in with me."

Gyan laughed. "We'll drive the old man crazy."

"Are you going to look for a job?" I was being my usual nosy self.

"I've already started," Gyan answered. "I've checked out openings in the UW College of Agriculture, and there's an open lecturer position I think I more than qualify for. I plan to submit my application on Monday."

"I'm sure you'll qualify for the lecturer position. Aren't you shooting a little low for your skills and education?"

Gyan looked me in the eye and said, "Intentionally so. I don't want to get into the 'publish or perish' grind again. I want to have time for developing Civalia. I think, no I know, I need a job to keep body and soul together; and, of course, to support Cindy until we can get our own place or Civalia is up and running. I don't want a long-term commitment."

"You're really serious then," I responded.

Gyan had a determined look, "You bet." Stellan looked on with a pleased smile.

"Hey," I changed the subject. "Do you remember we need to find someone to help with the demographics, interpersonal, and organizational stuff?"

"Yes, what, er-r, I mean who have you found?" Stellan asked.

"A woman who has written about intentional communities plus lived in several of them. She's living here in Laramie now and is willing to help us with community issues. I've made arrangements for her to stop by next Tuesday at 1:00. Are you two available then?"

"I'm very free, being unemployed at the moment," Gyan said.

Stellan consulted his schedule. "I have something scheduled for then, but I think I can move it to later in the afternoon. Count me in. What is this woman's name?"

"Cassandra Martine. She goes by Cass," I told them

"I'll look forward to meeting her," Stellan said.

"Me too," Gyan added.

Stellan and Gyan left, and I tried to think of other subjects to curb my impatience. I was only marginally successful, so I was anxiously waiting on Tuesday when first Stellan and then Gyan arrived shortly after 1:00. I ushered them into my dining room. A short time later, the doorbell rang again and Cass was at the door. I was pleased to see she was dressed similarly to rest of us, Wyoming causal; it went well with her strong face, devoid of makeup, but featuring a wide, welcoming, smile. Her brown hair had some of the free will tendencies of Stellan's and mine, but I have to admit it was not quite so unruly. She was only slightly shorter than Stellan. I invited her in and led her into the dining room.

"Cass, this is Stellan King, and his son Gyan. Stellan and Gyan, this is Cassandra Martine."

"Pleased to meet you," Stellan responded. He shook hands with Cass.

Gyan, somewhat shyly, also shook hands with her, and Stellan indicated a chair for her at the table. To make room for her notebook, I pushed aside some of the papers and books we'd strewn around the table getting ready for our work session. With the basic introductions out of the way, we began getting acquainted and talking about Civalia.

"As I discussed with you, Cass, the three of us are attempting to design a community based on our *Declaration of Life*. I gave you a copy of it, when I talked with you last Saturday. Would you like to tell us a little about yourself, and give us some of your thoughts and impressions about what we are trying to do? And I'd like to hear what you think about our *Declaration of Life*."

"First off, I'll have to say that some of your project I don't understand. I'm not strong on equations. However, I do think a lot of what I've been working for in my own life, my goals, are similar, if not the same as yours. I've been working to reduce my personal energy consumption to about a tenth of the average for Americans, and the best way I've found to do that is through intentional, consensus communities. My work now includes nonprofit, administrative, and activist work to promote cooperative culture, sustainability, positive group dynamics, and consensus relations. My educational background covers anthropology, sociology, multicultural studies, community counseling, environmental education, and a few other topics related to community living."

"That's impressive," I said, "and it sounds like you will be able to help us with aspects of the Civalien Project with which none of us are adept. I've already told you some of my background, a stereotypical engineer, but Stellan and Gyan can tell you a little about themselves before we get down to the brass tacks. Gyan?"

"I've been associated with the Civalien Project for about 30 years."

"I understand you named the project," Cass said.

"That's true. It just came to me that day when Dad and John were trying to come up with a name. My real passion in life is agriculture, farming in particular. I may have gotten some of that from my grandfather. He had a farm, you know, and I spent a fair amount of time when I was young on the farm with Grandpa. I went to college at UN—Lincoln in the Agricultural Science and Natural Resource College."

"Is that the University of Nebraska?" Cass asked.

"Sorry. Yes, it is. I studied field crop production and I'm now on the faculty of Texas A&M. I'm planning on moving to Laramie to contribute to the Civalien Project."

Cass asked, "What is your field crop specialty?"

"I started out dealing mainly with corn, sugar beets, beans, and potatoes. In the last few years I've gotten interested in permaculture."

"You mentioned that before," I said, "but I'm not familiar with it. What is it?"

"Most of our field crops are annuals, so we plow, plant, and harvest every year. However, soils are very complex and there is a tremendous amount of life in the upper few feet of soil. Annual crops and pesticides destroy that biome and make the soil less productive. That is one reason we have to use so much fertilizer to produce crops. Permaculture is planting perennial crops and decreasing the amount of tillage, fertilizer, and pesticides needed."

"I wasn't aware of that soil dynamic," I told him.

"Neither was I," added Cass.

"Stellan, why don't you tell Cass a little about yourself?" I said.

"As John has probably already told you, I'm also an engineer, and although I have degrees in agricultural engineering, I consider myself a generalist."

"He's a renaissance man," I interjected.

"I've worked in a lot of areas, but probably electronics has been the largest chunk. I met John when we were in school, and we started dreaming up projects together. He initially started us on the road to the Civalien Project, and it's changed the course of all of our lives. I don't know if there is a lot more to say. I'm approaching retirement, and I would like to do so in Civalia."

Cass asked him, "Do you have a specialty?"

"I guess I'm like John, my specialty is having no specialty. I suppose in relation to the Civalien Project, John and I are the ones interested in making the physical plant as convenient, workable, low cost, and low entropy as possible. John has invited you here because when we were in school, there was a quote on the wall which read, 'Human beings are not infinitely malleable and, hence, a dynamically negligible part of the system.' Neither John nor I, nor Gyan, falls in the category of being good at figuring out how people work. I know this is one area where I'm lacking."

"Me too," I added. Gyan nodded. I continued, "Right now, we're trying to figure out where we should locate Civalia. Stellan made a good argument for locating it in Wyoming, so I've started considering where we might begin looking for a suitable site."

"Well then, let me get started helping you." Cass leaned forward and rested her arms on the table. "Where are you considering locating Civalia here in Wyoming?"

Stellan surprised me by taking over the discussion. I was not aware he had also been considering this question in depth.

"I've looked at the map of Wyoming, Cass, and I think there are perhaps three regions that we should consider." Stellan pulled out a road map of Wyoming he had brought with him and spread it out on the table. "I boiled it down to and investigated three regions of Wyoming. The first is Sheridan County because it is one of the lowest spots in the State and is protected by the Big Horn Mountains. These factors give it a better climate than most of the rest of the State. However, Interstate 90 runs through the western part of the county, and the area per person is about 55 acres. The land prices are high, since it is somewhat of a playground for wealthy people. Rock bottom price for ranch land is in the $1,500 per acre range. Small acreages may be as high as $60,000. So, Sheridan is on the bottom of my list."

Stellan indicated an area on the eastern border of Wyoming. "The next one is Niobrara County, although some of the surrounding counties may also be possible. This county has the highest number of acres per person, more than 640. Land prices are a lot more reasonable too, somewhere around $500 per acre for ranch land and maybe around $2,000 per acre for small acreages. There are also no interstate highways running through the county; hardly any major highways at all. The county is largely agricultural, but it is pretty dry, getting only about 14 inches of precipitation per year, so most of the agriculture is ranching. The terrain is mostly short grass prairie. This is certainly a place where Civalia could be located."

"The third region I have considered is here." Stellan pointed to an area near the border with Colorado where the Platte River enters Wyoming from Colorado. "This region is in Carbon County, the Wyoming county with the second highest per capita land area, about 325 acres per person. The Upper North Platte River Valley lies between the Snowy Range and the Sierra Madre mountain ranges. Much of these mountains are covered by the Medicine Bow National Forest, which becomes the Roosevelt and Route National Forests on the Colorado side of the border. The river valley is predominantly private land used for ranching and it is fairly dry, about 10 inches of precipitation annually. There is, however, more surface water runoff from the mountains on either side. Land prices are about double those of Niobrara County, but still less than Sheridan County."

"Regardless of where we locate Civalia, the climate will be relatively cool and dry. For example, the Upper North Platte River Valley is about 7,000 feet and Niobrara County is a little less than 5,000 feet in the southern end and drops to around 4,200 feet toward the northern end. The county seat of Niobrara county, Lusk, gets about 16½ inches of precipitation annually, and has an annual average high temperature of 58 degrees Fahrenheit, monthly averages of 83 max and 44 min, and an average low of 30 degrees, with monthly averages of 52 max and 10 min. Saratoga, Wyoming, in the heart of the Upper North Platte River Valley, has about 10 ¼ inches of precipitation annually with an average high temperature of 57 degrees, monthly averages of 82 max and 33 min, and an average low temperature of 29 degrees, 50 max and 10 min."

"In my estimation these are the most likely areas for locating Civalia," he continued. "Do any of you have thoughts on these or other regions where Civalia could be located?"

"Wow, Stellan!" I exclaimed. "I came up with almost the same list, but I rejected the Sheridan area because of the interstate highway, and I included the western slope of the Laramie Mountain Range, the eastern part of the Shirley Basin. I mentally ranked the Shirley Basin region at the bottom of my list."

"I haven't given it much thought at this point," Gyan said. "I'll defer to you two on this issue, but since you both agree on east central Wyoming and the Upper North Platte River Valley, can we agree to focus on those two areas?"

Cass looked bemused. "Obviously, I've not had the opportunity to consider this question in detail. What sort of criteria do you have for selecting an area and a site?"

"I've been thinking about all the factors we should be considering when we select a site, so I've made up a list." I handed out copies.

Cass read through my list and said, "Not bad, but I think you've left out a few things, mainly issues that deal with the relationships between other people in the community and the region. I'd have a least two additions to your list."

Cass began writing more factors on the bottom of her list. "The types of neighbors in a region can make a huge difference," she said. "Some of the feuds that can get going are brutal." Cass then dictated and I wrote down, "Neighbors. When a final location is being considered, research into the temperament and proclivities of the nearest neighbors should be conducted." She paused while I caught up. "Community assessment. Community acceptance of Civalia must be evaluated."

We all discussed Cass's additions, and then Stellan said, "Another factor I don't see on your list is just how isolated we should be."

"I've covered that in the section on accessibility," I protested. "We want to be as much a part of the community as possible."

"I was thinking of isolation in a different way," Stellan countered. "We don't want to be living next to an interstate highway or right next door to the city of Denver, or next door to the Belle Ayr Coal Mine, or to Denver International Airport."

I couldn't disagree with Stellan, so I added isolation to the list. However, I made certain we included a disclaimer about not being isolated from the immediate community.

"You don't have anything on your list about the actual terrain," Gyan noted. "That can have a lot of effect on how Civalia is organized and how it functions." I agreed. We added terrain to my list.

Gyan checked back over the list. "You also haven't included anything about the agricultural possibilities. That can make a huge difference on whether we are agriculturalist or become hunter gatherers."

"I thought we'd agreed we'd have to grow food in greenhouses," I half-heartedly protested, knowing that I had indeed overlooked the agricultural possibilities.

"We did, but that doesn't mean that there won't be any agricultural endeavors. What about a milk cow, or sheep for wool? If the local soil is not good for growing much of anything, we wouldn't have those options. Just look at the Red Desert and Hell's Half Acre. Now there are two places that even if you add water, not much will happen."

I conceded and added two more items to the list, one covering the agricultural potential for the region and the other specifically addressing the soil quality.

Stellan frowned. "You have the sun on your list but not the wind. What gives?"

"Well, I just didn't think it would make sense to use wind energy." I had worked quite a lot with small wind systems, and my general opinion about them in Wyoming was they are more trouble than they are worth. "The winds are too variable," I said. "Few small wind systems survive for any length of time. I've never seen one live out its design life."

Stellan parried. "Just the wind constantly blowing can be wearing on people's psyche. There is some evidence hot dry winds increase murder and suicide rates. Some people have claimed the suicide rate in eastern Colorado increased markedly during the Dust Bowl."

"All right," I gave up. "We'll put wind on the list. I'll even concede that it might be a source of energy. Maybe someone smarter than I am will figure out how to harness wind energy reliably."

"You also haven't said anything about wastes," Stellan looked stern. "Here you are preaching about the intermediate sinks, and you haven't addressed those in your list."

"Okay, Okay." I add waste handling and recycling to the list.

"I can think of a real biggy you're missing: geologic and environmental hazards," Cass said.

As soon as she said this, I was chagrinned that I had not included this on my list. It is so obvious! Civalia should not be located in a flood plain, at the mouth of a draw that is prone to snow slides or flash flooding, under a cliff that is likely to break off and fall, where landslides can occur, where the ground is unstable or expansive, where tornados are likely, or where other hazards exist. Without saying a word, I added hazards to the list of considerations.

"You also don't have anything about the potential for generating income in the area," Cass said. "How are you going to make a living?"

I was silent, because the subject of the economic system we were envisioning for Civalia seemed like an overwhelming topic to broach at that moment. Stellan and Gyan were also quiet. I looked to Stellan for help and he just shrugged. Cass looked puzzled and then a little alarmed as she shifted her glance from one to another of us.

Gyan finally broke the silence. "Cass, that's a very complicated subject. It took my dad a couple of hours to explain it to me. Perhaps we can get together sometime later and I'll try to pass on what I've learned to you."

"Okay," she said, sounding a little doubtful.

"I can't think of anything more right now," Stellan said. Cass and Gyan nodded agreement

I printed these updates to the location factors list and handed out these copies to the group.

Using the new list, we discussed places to locate Civalia. After a while, when it seemed we weren't making much progress, I asked, "Why don't we each rank Niobrara County and the Upper North Platte River Valley on a scale of 1 to 10 for each of these factors? Then when we sum the results, we'll have a numerical value to go on."

"Okay," Gyan responded. The other two just started marking their lists.

Since I had been thinking of this for some time, I finished first, added up my numbers on the calculator, and then watched Stellan tapping his fingers on the table as he considered each factor before writing down a number. When he finished, I slid the calculator over to him and waited while he totaled his numbers. Cass finished and waited for Stellan to finish with the calculator and pass it to her.

When Gyan finished, I burst out, "I have the Upper North Platte River Valley by 30% over Niobrara County."

Stellan looked thoughtful. "I have Niobrara County by 8% over the Upper North Platte River Valley."

"For all practical purposes, I'm split evenly," Gyan told us.

"We all looked at Cass. "Well," she said, "I prefer the mountains, and that's how it came out on my list."

"Then we'll go with the Upper North Platte River Valley, since more of us are in favor of there rather than Niobrara County," I said.

Stellan grinned, "What a crock. I marked the Upper North

Location Factors Page 2

Neighbors—When a final location is being considered, research into the temperament and proclivities of the nearest neighbors should be conducted.

Community assessment—Community acceptance of Civalia must be evaluated.

Isolation—High-entropic infrastructure must be avoided, but contact with existing communities should be maintained.

Terrain—The terrain surrounding Civalia must be considered to minimize energy requirements, and maximize residents' satisfaction.

Agricultural potential—Uses of the surrounding land for appropriately sized agricultural endeavors must be evaluated.

Soil quality—Soil quality will be important not only for agricultural ventures, but also for domain size and maintenance requirements.

Wind—Winds in the region must be considered for both potential wind energy conversion and also for potential habitat and human psyche interactions.

Solid waste—The potentials for adequately disposing of solid wastes, the presence of existing solid wastes, and the potential for recycling solid wastes must be evaluated.

Geologic and environmental hazards—The potential for catastrophic events, acts of nature, must be evaluated and minimized.

Platte River Valley down because we'd have a lot of trouble getting a block of land big enough for Civalia there. It'd cost a bundle because we'd have to buy a lot of small acreages to put it together."

"We could try," I countered.

"Yes, we could, and it might take us several decades. Do you have several decades?"

"No," I admitted, "but Niobrara County is so—so desolate. It's just that I think the area around Saratoga is lovely and would be a wonderful place to live."

Stellan retorted "You along with a zillion other people. Why do you think the Old Baldy Club is located in Saratoga?"

"What's the Old Baldy Club?" Cass asked

"It's a high prestige club where new members have to be sponsored by existing members," Stellan answered.

"So, it's the Upper North Platte River Valley. Right?" I said.

Cass spoke. "John, you're working at violating one of the principles I think is essential for small communities; consensus."

We were all silent for some time. I was thinking about how Cass was correct, and how I sometimes had difficulty with personal relationships, because maybe I sometimes steamrolled over others.

Then Stellan roused himself. "I'll tell you what. Since the climates of these two places are very similar, and we think we'll probably have to include greenhouse facilities for food regardless of where Civalia is located, why don't we design with the idea Civalia can be located in either of these locations? If we can achieve that goal, Civalia or Civalia-clones can be located in a lot of other places in Wyoming, or even in other States with low population density."

I was grateful to be let off the hook. "Hear, hear. I'm on board with that idea."

Cass murmured her assent, and Gyan agreed.

Stellan and Gyan began making preparations to leave. "What's your hurry?" I asked.

"Dad and I are going to pick up Cindy," Gyan answered, "and move all of our stuff to Laramie. We have to get ready to take off early tomorrow."

Gyan and Stellan left, but Cass stayed for a while and asked me more about the Civalien Project. I found myself frustrated in trying to explain entropy and the *Declaration of Life* in greater detail. The gap between the knowledge base Stellan and I were operating from and Cass's was significant. Eventually, the afternoon grew late and Cass had to leave. I thanked her for her insights and made certain she would at least give us one more opportunity to tap her knowledge and experience. I spent some time thinking about how we could make the entropy paradigm clearer and more accessible to someone like Cass.

CHAPTER 6

The next day, I still felt restless, and I was as excited as I had been the day before when we were beginning to conjure the Civalien Project and Civalia out of the mists. But it was still indistinct, and since I didn't have any immediate tasks on my plate, I decided to go for a walk. As I strolled the streets of Laramie, my thoughts continued to dwell on the Civalien Project and Civalia. I wandered for some time, my thoughts weaving in and out of the promises and problems associated with our project.

Eventually I found myself outside a book store. I love books, so I went in. Near the front of the store was a sale rack, and because I also love bargains, I perused the books. There it was, the book, *Monopoly® The World's Most Famous Game & How It got That Way*, by Philip E. Orbanes, for only $2. How could I resist? I spent the rest of the day reading. I was startled to learn Monopoly® evolved from an earlier game, *The Landlord's Game*, invented and patented by a fascinating woman named Elisabeth Magie Phillips. I was even more startled to learn *The Landlord's Game* had been invented to demonstrate the evils of land monopolies and the benefits of a single tax, called a land value tax (LVT).

"That's a far cry from modern Monopoly®, where the goal is to bankrupt all of your competitors," I thought.

Elisabeth was a contemporary of Professor Scott Nearing, who used The Landlord's Game in his Economics classes. It seemed like a small world, and this coincidence ignited the thought, "Could a game be developed to explain the reasoning foundation of the Civalien Project and Civalia?"

Sleep was slow in coming to me that night, as thoughts of games churned through my mind. I awoke early, with these thoughts still stirring my brain. I decided working on anything else would be a waste of time, so I gathered a few coins to use as tokens, some dice, notepaper, and raided a Monopoly® set lurking in my closest for the houses and hotels. I began experimenting.

My goals were to illustrate the closed cycle of the Earth, the open cycles of all living things on the Earth, and how our human economic systems interact with these physical systems. First, I wanted to show how the entropy produced by energy transformations ends up in the intermediate sinks of the air, water, and soil, and then must ultimately be converted into radiant heat and exported into outer space by long wave radiation. Second, I wanted to show how plants use incoming solar radiation to convert the high entropy mass in the intermediate sinks into low entropy mass and long-wave radiant heat; making animal life possible. Finally, I wanted to show how transforming internal stored energy results in entropy buildup in these intermediate sinks with deleterious results. Could these goals be met in a game, which was fun, absorbing, and perhaps addicting? I set out to discover if it was possible.

I lost track of my experimental games after 137 trials over the next couple of days. Some were very short, proving to be unworkable, and some went for quite some time. As the hours went by, the games generally become longer and more intricate. Somewhere early in the second day, I determined I was really trying to develop at least two games, maybe three. One game was necessary to demonstrate the actions of physical laws in the absence of human interactions. Then games with economic rules would be required to show the effects of both our current economic system and the Civalien economic rules. My strategy then became to first develop a basic game demonstrating physical laws, the rules of the universe, and then include the interactions of economic factors with the physical laws as practiced by humans. At the end of that second day, I was close to what I thought might be a workable game.

I spent another day ginning up a game board, making prototype game pieces, and writing three sets of rules. The first one illustrated the underlying physics; the case without humans. The second added the operation of our capitalistic economic system, and the third added the Civalien economic system to the underlying physics.

———∞∞∞———

On Thursday morning I was ready to get feedback on my game, so I loaded my prototype game into the car and headed over to Stellan's. He was not home. I castigated myself for not calling him first, but my self-reproach did not make him appear. I went back to my car and sat for a while trying to decide what I should do. I was really energized with the development of the game, keyed up, and ready to charge forward. I knew if I went home, I'd get little or nothing done, and probably would either spend the morning eating everything in sight or pacing my apartment and shop, maybe both. I decided to do something entirely different.

I'd been thinking off and on about the location for Civalia, and since the day was young, the weather fair, and I was already out of the house and in my car, one of my antique cars, a 1984 Cadillac Seville, why not take a drive and look at the Upper North Platte River Valley? I'd been through there numerous times in the past, but never with an eye toward establishing Civalia. My dashboard clock read 9:47 AM; plenty of time for a reconnaissance expedition. I set out on highway WY-230, driving through Woods Landing, Mountain Home, ducking down into Colorado on highway CO-127, and then turning onto CO-125. Finally, I ended up back in Wyoming on the west section of WY-230. Once in Wyoming, I slowed considerably and began looking carefully at the landscape.

From consulting maps of the area, I knew the Medicine Bow National Forest boundary and BLM boundaries were very close to the northeast side of the road, the right side. On the left side, the forest boundary angled away with some BLM land having state School Sections interleaved.

A car with a Colorado license plate passed me, headed somewhere north at high speed. Otherwise the roads were nearly deserted. A local rancher, identifiable by the dog in the back of his pickup and the gun rack in his rear window, passed me traveling south, probably going to Walden or headed for Laramie. I noticed a County Road, CR-798, heading west, and I turned on to it. CR-798 was an unimproved road, but it was reasonably smooth. I took it easy anyway, since my antique Cadillac was not exactly an off-road vehicle. Having driven two or three miles in, and climbing a couple of hundred feet up, I stopped, got out, and looked around.

The terrain was grazing land, some of it looked as if it had been subject to "improvement," meaning the woody plants had been destroyed and non-native grasses planted. The area north of the road appeared to be reasonably original and had obviously not been overgrazed. This land generally sloped down to the northeast toward the river. Several drainages were visible, some with brush and a tree or two. In contrast, the land south of the road had been cleared, leveled, and planted to crested wheatgrass, a grass introduced in the early 1900s.

I was looking over the land on the north side of the road and picturing a Civalia structure in such a setting, when a rancher came down the road and pulled in on the wrong side, nose to nose with my car.

"Howdy," the man said as he climbed out of his truck.

"Hello," I answered, feeling like an interloping voyeur and somewhat guilty.

"This here yer car?" he asked me.

"Yes, it is. Am I blocking something by parking here?"

"Naw. I just had one uh these here a lot uh years ago. Kind uh liked it. Boy, it had a smooth ride. Drove the shit out uh it. I think it gave up with over 200,000 miles on it." He started walking around my car, looking it over. "This thing's in good condition. Looks like it's right off the showroom floor. Did ya fix it up?"

"Just some minor repairs, no body work except for gluing one of the headlight bezels back together." I held out my hand and said, "By the way, my name's John Tantivy." In an attempt to assuage my vague feelings of guilt, I volunteered, "I'm from Laramie and just out for a drive today."

"Name is Ralph, Ralph Hertell. Pleased ta meet ya." Ralph took my outstretched hand and shook it.

His hand was rough and felt arthritic. I'm not good at guessing peoples ages, but Ralph looked like he was in his late seventies or maybe even his early eighties. He was slightly bowlegged, and his gait was slightly lurching, as if his right leg was a little stiff. Most of his hair was hidden underneath his Stetson, but what did show was light iron gray. He sported a much lighter gray handlebar moustache on his well-tanned, leathery, lined face. His eyes were faded blue, set off by squint lines.

Not really knowing Ralph and feeling just a trifle uncomfortable, I waved a hand out toward the land I had been looking at and said, "This looks just like it may have looked back in the early 1800s."

"Ya thinks so?" Ralph asked, looking at me a little more sharply.

"Yes," I answered. "That land on the other side of the road," I indicated the field on the far side of the fence to the south of the road, "has been tilled and planted with crested wheatgrass, and it looks like it has been overgrazed." I immediately cursed myself for not keeping my mouth shut. What if that field belonged to Ralph? I would certainly have stuck my foot in my mouth if it did.

"Well, young feller, you're right on both counts." Ralph turned to look out over the land to the south. "That's my neighbor Tom's place. I call it Tom's foolery. He done that back in 1958 or nine, I don't remember which. Grazes the hell out uh it every year, or I should say his kid, Marvin, does now." Ralph looked out over Tom's pasture with an unseeing gaze. Then he shook his head and turned back toward the north. "This here's my land."

"Have you lived here since the 1950s?" I asked.

"Yup, sure have. I was borned on this place; spent my whole life here. Ya 'pears ta know somethin' 'bout land. Ya live on a ranch?"

"No," I said, "I worked on a ranch up near Glendevey, Colorado, and another one in the Centennial Valley when I was in high school. Then I worked on a couple more during my college days."

"Who'd ya work for up by Glendevey? I knowed a couple a guys up there."

"It was a rancher by the name of Charlie Jensen."

"Jensen. . . Jensen. . .Did 'e have two ranches, one up in them there trees an' another along the river?"

"Yes, he did."

"He was a nice guy; careful rancher too." Ralph looked my way. "Why didn't ya' get into the business?"

"I would have liked to be a rancher," I told him, "but I couldn't afford the land." I indicated his land with a tilt of my head. "Why is your land so different from your neighbor Tom's? And by the way, I'm not such a young feller. I hit sixty-seven my last birthday."

"No shit! Ya don't look it. But yer still a young fella to me. I've got a few years on ya."

I wanted to ask how many, but was afraid to. "Tell me how your land came to be preserved," I urged.

"Well, young fella," Ralph emphasized the 'young fella,' "I'm on my way ta check on some livestock, and tellin' ya about this land would take more time than I've got. So, if ya ain't got anything real pressin', ya can ride along with me, and I'll tell ya about it."

Ralph was beginning to intrigue me, and I had no deadlines, so I climbed into his truck. He backed up and we took off down the road towards the highway. I was surprised to find Ralph's truck clean and neat inside. The cabs of pickups driven by most ranchers I'd known were pig styes. I wondered what else about Ralph would surprise me. He began telling me some of his history.

"My granddad an' his brother hit Laramie in 1868 along with the railroad. They was fixin' ta set up in Laramie with a hardware store, but Granddad's brother was killed. He walked into a bar one day, an' some stranger shot 'im."

A chill went down my spine. 'My god!' I thought. 'We may have a connection!' "Did . . . did they ever catch the killer?" I asked.

"Na. Granddad told me a couple uh people had seen a guy

riding north out uh town like a bat out uh hell. A couple uh months later, a cowboy came across remains uh a horse an' tack that could uh been the guy's on a hillside northeast uh town, but nobody ever laid eyes on the guy again. Nobody'd seen the guy before, either."

I felt a little weak, so I leaned against the truck door and kept quiet. Ralph continued his story.

"Granddad was shook up real bad, so he packed a little grub, saddled his horse, an' struck out west from Laramie. He told me he didn't have no place in mind when 'e went, 'e just wanted ta get away. He never tol' me 'xactly how long 'e wandered, but eventually 'e ended up camped in this here valley near what's now Saratoga Inn. Folks called it Warm Springs then. There was some other guys around, so Granddad drifted south, built a cabin, staked out some land. He liked the hot springs and went there sometimes. That's where 'e met Grandma."

I didn't know if I could trust my voice, but I tried anyway, "So, your land dates back to your grandfather?"

"Some uh it. Dad an' me added quite a bit ta it."

"How come you didn't uh—uh develop it?" I asked.

Ralph hawked and spat out the window. "Land developers! Land despoilers I calls 'em."

"An oxymoron," I said.

Ralph looked over at me, "A what?"

"An oxymoron; contradictory words put together, such as a sanitary landfill."

Ralph looked back at the road, and said, "I like that; oxymoron. Oxymoron. I really like the moron part, and a landfill's anything but sanitary. I like that one too."

Ralph turned off the county road and pulled up to a wire gate. He started to get out, but I hopped out and opened it for him. I closed it after he was through and then got back in the truck. "I'd forgotten ya' probably know how ta work a gate," he said. Before he started driving again, he looked around and pointed to some cup-shaped white flowers off to the right. "You ever seen those flowers before?" he asked.

"Mariposa lilies," I said. "They're beautiful, aren't they?

I think the ones I've seen in this region are some of the best in the world, with the deep, royal purple flecked with yellow in the bottom of the cup." I had noticed the flowers when I walked from the gate to get back in the truck.

Ralph gave me a long look. "Son, me an' you seem ta have a few things in common. Why did ya drive up that there road today?"

"Ralph," I said. "You probably don't have time to hear all of the reasons I was on that road today, but the short answer is I'm looking for a home."

"One uh them there little ranchette thingies?" Ralph asked.

"Not at all," I said. "You see, I've come to understand we, every person, need some land with plants and living things on it to keep us alive. It's not something just nice to have, it's necessary."

"And how much land do ya think ya need?"

"That, of course, depends on how much plant life there is on the land, but we calculated we need somewhere around 100 acres on average."

Ralph rubbed his chin and thought for moment. "That's somewhere near right, a cow-calf pair in this country needs 25 acres, but that's with us humans makin' sure they get most all the grass in the summer and supplyin' 'em with hay in the winter. Who's this 'we', an' how many are there?"

"Some friends and I have started a project to see if we can put some of our ideas into practice. There're just four of us now, but we think we might end up with somewhere between 25 and 50."

"Ya know, the two uh us might have some things ta talk over." Ralph put the truck in gear and headed down the two-track road. "You hungry?" he asked.

"Sure," I answered. I'd been thinking Ralph was a person I definitely wanted to get to know better, so I told him a little white lie. "I was going to suggest I take you into Riverside or Encampment and see if we can't find a restaurant."

"No need for that, I've got grub at the house."

About that time we crested a little hill. Below us was a stock tank with a few cows, some goats, some sheep, and a couple of mule deer in attendance. The domestic animals came running as the truck rolled down the hill. The mule deer did not behave as I expected; they didn't bolt the opposite direction, but just turned their heads and looked at us as we drove over the hill and down towards the tank. Then they simply turned back and continued browsing on some small shrubs growing downstream where they were being watered by the tank overflow. The shrubs looked green and succulent.

Ralph climbed out of the truck and I followed suit. When I hit the ground, the mule deer took off and the domestic animals on my side of the truck backed away. Clearly, Ralph was well known, but I was a dangerous stranger. Ralph grabbed what looked like a very fine fish net from the back of his truck and went to the tank. I followed.

"I like ta keep the algae in check," he said as he began sweeping the net around the inside of the tank. "Helps keep the water fresher." He emptied his net into a trough a ways away from the tank and went back for more sweeps. "After this here algae dries out, at least some, the critters love ta chow down on it. There's a mixture uh algae in this here tank, an' it supplies 'em with some extra nutrients." He finished sweeping the tank and cleaned the net in the clear water streaming from a pipe emerging from the hillside above the tank. I figured the water must come from a spring. His animals remained crowded around him, seemingly vying for his attention. He petted them, roughhoused with some, examined them all carefully, and when he was done with that, he put the net back into the truck and pulled out a small sack. The animals became more insistent and excited as he began distributing treats to them. "They're my family," Ralph explained.

We drove back to my car, and I followed Ralph to his home. It was a modest ranch house, well maintained; not at all flashy, very utilitarian. There were a few outbuildings, but not nearly as many as I had expected. The drive to the house, fairly wide and well used, continued straight past his house and the outbuildings. The road continued on around a low hill. I figured Ralph's ranch must not be very large, based on the size and number of buildings, but the thoroughfare going through his place indicated there were other buildings beyond his. Perhaps there were some other ranch buildings on the other side of the low hill.

Ralph retrieved the treats sack and the net from the truck, and we walked toward the house. A squirrel began scolding us from a nearby tree.

"Gerald don't like ya bein' here," Ralph said. He pulled a peanut out of the treat sack and went over to the tree. The squirrel, I assumed its name was Gerald, stopped scolding and came down the tree, grabbed the peanut from Ralph's hand, and retreated back to the branch it had been sitting on. Gerald made short work of the peanut, and came back down the tree as Ralph and I headed for the door. Gerald followed us up the steps onto the porch, but kept his distance, scooting away when I turned to look. "Good thing you're here," Ralph said. "I have trouble keepin' that little rascal out uh the house when I'm alone."

We stepped into Ralph's kitchen. It was as neat as his truck. "Do you live alone?" I asked.

"Yup, ever since Dad died. That was back in 82." Ralph rummaged in his refrigerator and pulled out a fairly large container. "I hope ya likes stew."

"That's great," I told him. "Is there anything I can do?"

"There's some bowls in that there cupboard over there," Ralph indicated the cupboard with his chin, "and some silverware in the drawer below."

After minimal exploration, I located the bowls and silverware. Ralph had pulled a sauce pan from a cupboard, spooned some stew into the pan, and put the pan on a round, black unit about 1½-inches tall on his counter. He punched some buttons and a fan came on.

"What's that?" I asked.

"A great gadget a friend put me onto," he said. "It's a induction hot plate; heats the pan. Saves me lots uh time an' 'lectricity. Glasses're in the cupboard ta the left uh the plates. Ya'll have ta make do with water. I don't generally have lots uh company and don't keep any fancy beverages 'round."

I filed all this information away for future reference and was astonished at how quickly the stew started to bubble. The piping hot stew was not what I expected. With Ralph being a rancher, I assumed the stew would be heavy on meat and potatoes, with

114

maybe a carrot or two thrown in. I was wrong; the stew was a savory mixture of a variety of vegetables. If it had meat in it, I couldn't find it.

"What do you call this?" I asked.

"Sri Lankan stew," Ralph told me. "If ya don't like it, I can find ya something else."

"Oh, no!" I protested. "This is very good." I had seconds.

After we cleaned up and put away the lunch dishes, Ralph led me back out to the porch, and we sat in some rocking chairs. Gerald was back before we got settled.

"Just ignore 'im," Ralph told me. "He'll give up an' go away after a while. Ya asked me why my land's so different from ol' Tom's."

"Right," I said and settled in for a lengthy explanation.

It was lengthy. Ralph rocked and got a distant look in his eyes. "Granddad homesteaded the original spread an' ran his cows on the open range. In them days everyone did. The Lazy HZ; that was his brand. Still have it." Ralph indicated a brand burned into the lintel above the door. "Dad told me it would uh been Lazy HS, standin' fer Hertell and Sons, but a Z was a lot easier ta make than a S. Granddad didn't have sons when he made that brand, but he had intentions." Ralph gazed speculatively at the brand. "In some things, like that there brand, Granddad was lazy, but in others. . .." Ralph shook his head. "Granddad wanted land; was never satisfied with just a single homestead, so he got Dad an' his brother, my Uncle Irvin, ta homestead some more. Then he got some uh his cowhands ta homestead even more for 'im. Would make sure everything for provin' the homestead was done right, then when the title was issued, give 'em a bonus and have 'em sign it over. Other ranchers came and went. Most would homestead a place an' then run their cows on the open range."

Ralph shifted in his seat and started rocking again. "Everybody'd get together in the fall ta drive them cows ta the Laramie stockyards. That must uh been quite a sight." He turned to me,

"Ya ever been on a cattle drive?"

"Nothing as large as what you're talking about," I said "but I've been on small ones; moving the cattle from the home place to summer range on the forest. One day at the most."

Ralph sat back, "Dad said them there Laramie stockyards was the biggest ones in the state back then, but Cheyenne took over pretty quick. Laramie's weren't nearly as big as Cheyenne's, but it still beat drivin' them there cows over the hill by the time I was big enough ta be in the saddle. Anyway, them other ranchers came and went, depending on the cattle prices, an' when one went, Granddad'd try ta pick up their homesteads. Dad told me they all thought Granddad was crazy tyin' so much money up in land, 'cause grazing was free. Dad even told me he and Uncle Irvin thought Granddad was a little crazy; until 1890 hit an' open range ended. Granddad didn't seem so crazy then, and the Lazy HZ grew quite a bit when Grandad, Dad, and Uncle Irvin bought out them as couldn't make it. By the time I was born in 1937, the ranch was about 22,000 acres. I think when I came along, I was one uh them surprises ta my folks."

I was shocked. I had no idea the ranch was that large, and I wondered if something had happened to reduce its size, or if Ralph had started selling it off. I confess that I was also struck by the question, 'Had I found the location for Civalia?' I also did the mental math, Ralph was 83 years old.

Ralph continued. "I was the only one, and Uncle Irvin and his wife didn't even get surprised by even one. Them Hertells weren't very fruitful."

"Do you have kids?" I ventured.

"Only the four-legged variety," Ralph laughed. "Ya met some uh 'em out by the stock tank. I never married. Thought about it a few times, but it just never worked out." He was silent for a while. "I growed up spendin' a lot uh hours in the saddle, punchin' cows, and when Granddad died, he left me a third uh the ranch. That's when I got really busy. Then Uncle Irvin died. Aunt Wilma was kind uh sick uh ranchin', so she sold out ta me an' Dad. I suppose me an' Dad inherited some uh Granddad's hankerin' after land. We kept buyin' land, an' I did too after Dad died. Kept buyin' until sometime in the 60s, an' then things just changed." Ralph gazed up at the brand again.

"What changed?" I asked. I was expecting to hear how Ralph had somehow lost the ranch or decided to sell.

Ralph looked back down at me and said, "The land begun ta cry out ta me. The SCS'd been hounding me an' Dad for a long time ta 'develop' the land an' water; ta produce more an' make more money. I'd seen what my neighbors'd done, an' at first it looked good, but then I noticed the animals was leavin'; the ground squirrels, the shrews, the chipmunks, the packrats. I stopped seeing as many killdeers flopping 'round in front uh me tryin' ta lure me away from their nests as I walked 'cross the fields. I decided ta do somethin' about it. Stopped running as much livestock an' began payin' a lot more attention ta the land an' the critters."

"I think I know what you mean, about things disappearing," I said. "I called last year 'The Year without Flying Insects.' True, they do spray for mosquitoes in Laramie, but I still only saw three the whole summer. There were hardly any other bugs in my shop either. In prior years there were mayfly hatches that coated the back of my building. Nothing last summer. And then in September, I made a trip to south Denver and back. My windshield was almost bug-free when I got home."

Ralph sat forward and looked at me sharply. "I thought I was the only one noticin' that. No bees, just a few grasshoppers, butterflies way down."

"I think we're killing the Earth," I told him.

Ralph sank back in his chair and was silent for a long time, not rocking. "What can we do 'bout it?" he asked.

"You've done something," I said. "Your lands look fantastic."

"It's not much," he said. "What'd ya have in mind ta do?"

I felt a little helpless because the explanation of the Civalien Project was long, arduous, and confusing to someone without a background in engineering. I began tentatively. "Well, I think I told you I'm looking for land, about 100 acres per person."

"An' what do ya do with it?" Ralph asked. "Fill it with roads, houses, horse pastures, golf courses, an' shootin' ranges?"

"No, no, nothing like that." I thought desperately of how to convey to Ralph the physics behind domains, then the thought hit me; I had the entropy game in the car. Perhaps I could test out the game on Ralph and maybe, just maybe, give him an understanding of the Civalien Project. "Do you like to play any sort of games? Card games? Board games?"

"I don't know. It's years since I done anything like that, an' it's not clear ta me what playin' games has ta do with takin' care uh the land."

The professor in me was beginning to show. "Have you heard of the word 'entropy'?" I asked.

"Can't say as I have. Is that some new thing that's supposed ta cure everything?"

"No, no, nothing like that," I said again, "and it isn't new. It's been around a lot longer than either one of us. For that matter, it's been around a lot longer than the Earth."

Ralph frowned, "Then why haven't I heard uh it?"

"Probably because most people don't want to know about it, or even think about it. But I'd be willing to bet you've experienced it."

"You're soundin' like a salesman. Why don't ya just tell me what it is?"

I realized I was prevaricating, because I wasn't certain how to approach Ralph with this information and I didn't want to make a mistake; but prevarication itself was a mistake. I took a deep breath and said, "Whenever energy is transformed, changed, from one form to another, some of the energy becomes unavailable. Entropy is a measure of that unavailable energy."

Ralph had a blank look. "I'll have ta think 'bout that."

"The reason I asked if you like games is because I have a game with me that illustrates these concepts, and I thought if we played, it might make them clear, and um. . ." I trailed off.

"Well, it might, an' it might not." Ralph was looking at me closely. "Sounds like a big chunk ta bite off. Now I'm willing ta learn a new thing or two, I've done that before." He smiled at me at his last remark, but then he turned more serious. "But I'll warn ya, a lot uh people've tried ta pull the wool over my eyes, an' I think I can spot a con pretty well. Why don't ya drag out your game, an' we'll have a go at it."

I got my prototype game out of the car, and Ralph asked, "Where'll we play this game?"

"Inside might be better," I said, "so the breeze won't blow the game pieces around."

We went in and set up on Ralph's table, where we had eaten lunch. I explained the rules as I set up the game, and Ralph and I began to play. After a while he said, "I think I get some uh this. Ya got sunlight coming in an' that grows some plants. Course I've seen that for years, an' it varies from year to year; that's yer dice throws. What I don't get is swapping out the plants for these here dark things, and putting some uh those off your board into this here box with the moon and stars on it. What's that supposed to be?"

"The dark things are the unavailable energy, the entropy, that's produced in every energy transformation—I mean change."

"Can ya put that into layman's terms?" Ralph asked.

"I'll try," I said. "For lunch we had some of your excellent Sri Lankan stew. That is our energy source, and it gets changed in our bodies into our muscle movement, our thoughts, some heat to keep us warm, and some of it comes out in an altered form when we take a dump."

"Shit, in other words," Ralph said.

"Yes, shit," I said, feeling my face grow red with embarrassment. "That's the unavailable energy."

"Well, we'd sure not want ta eat it again," Ralph said.

"Right. Now, if we don't get the shit out of our houses, eventually they'd fill up and we couldn't live in them anymore."

"So, the stables have to be cleaned," Ralph observed.

"Right. Well, the Earth is no different. It receives energy in the form of sunlight, various energy transformations take place, and then the unavailable energy, the entropy, has to be cleaned out."

"Okay," Ralph said, "I understand that, but how does that happen? I can't think uh any way we shovel shit off the Earth."

"That's because you can't see it. The energy coming in is light from the sun; some of it is visible light, so we see that. But the sunlight gets changed into heat in various ways, and eventually the heat goes into outer space. That's the Earth's shit, long-wave heat energy; it's unavailable energy, the entropy, and it's invisible to us."

Our conversation was interrupted by the rumbling of a truck going past the house and out the driveway. Ralph had a decidedly unhappy look as the house trembled and a cloud of dust drifted past the front window. He rearranged his features and went on, "So, the Earth's like a livin' critter, it's got ta be fed an' has ta crap."

"Well, yes. You could look at it that way."

"Maybe it's really a livin' critter."

"Some people think it is," I said. "They call it Gaia."

"I've heard people call it that," Ralph said. He sat quietly for a while, looking thoughtful. "I think I'm understandin' that, but there's more goin' on in yer game. Ya've got these here black things that can be used for energy. What're these?"

"I intended for those to represent oil and coal," I told him. "I'm not a very good artist."

"Ya got it black enough," he said. "So, when I use this here coal energy, it produces shit, just like we do. Is that right?"

"That's right."

"So where do we shovel that shit?"

"That goes into the air, the soil, and the water." I pointed to some areas on the game board that represented these intermediate sinks.

"I see," Ralph said, "and how's it get over into this here space box?"

"That's where the problem comes in," I said. "The heat from burning the coal will go into that box very soon."

"That makes sense," Ralph said.

"But we aren't so fortunate with the carbon dioxide and sulfur oxides that go into the air; the particulates in the smoke, the fly ash, and the radioactive materials that. . ."

"Radioactive materials?" Ralph asked. "Are ya tryin' to tell me them coal-fired power plants're nuclur reactors?"

"Oh, no; but there are radioactive materials in coal, which either go out the stacks or are concentrated in the fly ash when the

120

coal is burned. All of these things I mentioned are the unavailable energy, entropy. The problem is, when we use the energy stored in the Earth, such as coal, a lot of the produced entropy sticks around. There aren't enough plants to handle it all, and now we're swimming in it, so to speak. There just aren't good natural ways that plants can recycle all those materials and get that entropy exported to space."

Ralph sat back, looked thoughtful, and idly fidgeted with the coal token. "I see two things here," he said. "If'n there's too much shit, like the shit piles at feed lots, the plants and land can't handle it. An' if'n Ma Nature don't have a way to handle it, like the cow shit in Australia when there weren't no dung beetles, the shit doesn't get taken care of. If'n I recall right, about a half million acres a year was goin' out uh production over there."

"Exactly," I said. I liked Ralph's dead on agricultural energy examples, but I wanted to somehow convey to him the more universal concept that transforming any internal stored energy resulted in an entropy increase in a closed system like the Earth. I eyed my game board and tried to think of a way to make that clearer.

Ralph held up the coal token and said, "There ain't no way I can use this here coal ta get rid uh the shit either. If'n I got me a steam tractor and gathered up all that there shit, all I could do was haul it away to somewhere else. Same problem, only worse, 'cause now I've burned the coal." He dropped his hand and looked thoughtfully at me. He reached out and picked up one of the sun energy tokens. "What if I burned the shit with sunlight?"

I had underestimated this man, and I had difficulty speaking around the lump in my throat. "That would be better than the coal, because the entropy from the solar transformation would all be heat that goes into outer space, but some of the entropy from the shit would still be around and you would need some plants to recycle those materials and ship the entropy into space."

"John," he said, "If you've thought about all this, ya must have some ideas about where to go from here. What might those ideas be?"

"Ralph," I said, my voice a little husky, "back in 1985 when a friend and I began thinking about energy and entropy, we put the implications of these thoughts for our lives into a short summary we called the *Declaration of Life*. I've had the *Declaration of Life* printed on some cards." I took one out of my wallet and handed it to Ralph.

Ralph read the card, holding it away from his eyes and squinting. "I'll have to think about this some." He tapped the card on the arm of his chair. "You've given me a lot uh things to think about. An' you better get on the road, so as ta miss the critters that come out at night."

I looked out the window and was startled to see that it was dusk. "Yes, I'd better get going." I stood and started to reach for my game board.

"I'd like ya ta leave that with me," Ralph said. "I notice it'll play just as well with one as with two, an' I'd like to play with it some more."

"Um-um, sure," I stammered.

"An' that'll make sure ya come back to visit an old man," he said with a grin.

I don't remember much of my drive home. I do remember patting my pocket more than once to verify I still had the slip of paper with Ralph's phone number safely tucked away. And I do remember my imagination weaving fantasies of where my contact with Ralph might go. Of one thing I was certain; I wanted to see more of and develop a close friendship with this sage man. He was certainly an unconventional rancher. I wondered what forces had molded him into the person I had met that day and what changes the forces that were unleashed by our meeting would make in both our lives in the future.

CHAPTER 7

I t was late when I got home, and even later when my mind slowed enough for me to fall asleep. The next morning, Friday morning, much earlier than etiquette dictates for calling someone, 6:30 AM, I started to dial Stellan. Before I finished dialing I remembered that Stellan had told me he was going to be gone. He went with Gyan to Texas to get Cindy and help move their household goods to Laramie. It dawned on me that was why he was not home yesterday or today, and would not be home until the middle of next week. I had been so engrossed in trying to develop the Civalien Project game, and then my meeting with Ralph, that Stellan's schedule had slipped my mind. I paced the floor like a caged bear, feeling like I was about to burst with the load of thoughts whirling around in my mind.

I tried doing some mundane tasks, my laundry, house cleaning, balancing my check book, but I kept finding myself staring into space and thinking about Ralph. I finally gave up and began searching to see if I could find any information about him on the internet. I hit pay dirt that was less than two years old.

Two years ago, a developer had targeted a large chunk of Ralph's land, 13,368 acres to be exact, for a vacation paradise project which was to include a golf course, hiking and riding trails, shooting ranges, a bird hunting area, fishing ponds, luxury accommodations, five star restaurants, old west reenactments, and the list went on. The developer claimed his resort would be not just the equivalent of, but a vast improvement over, the Old Baldy, a private club in Saratoga. He gave as the reason for this improvement the fact his resort would be open to the general public. The economic benefit to the Saratoga community was pegged at $10 million per year, provided, of course, the community gave him a tax break for the first ten years and other assistance to get his massive project underway.

I was able to locate a proposed map of the project; the developer called it Jim Baker's Retreat, referring to the early mountain man, Jim Baker, who had lived in south central Wyoming in the late 1800s. I also discovered the developer, one Harold E. Wainright, had proposed purchasing half of Ralph's ranch, taking his half out of the middle of the Lazy HZ. Ralph had turned him down. So, the enterprising Mr. Wainright had talked the Carbon County Commissioners into taking the land by eminent domain for his wonderful project, estimated to cost $126 million. Ralph fought it in court, but lost. I was able to find some newspaper articles from the *Rawlins Daily Times* describing some of the arguments in the case. At various times, Wainright, or probably Wainright's lawyer, argued that the land was unused; at other times that it was underutilized. He emphasized the increase in land values for those lands surrounding the project, and the increase in revenues in the community coming from the flow of tourists. The courts had given Ralph $200 per acre for his land, a total of $2,673,600, a low ball figure because the land was just "wasted" land.

A realtor in the area was quoted as saying, "If that land had been developed and used, it might have been worth 10 to 20 times more." Wainright, financed by the Amalgamated Bank and Trust Co. of Omaha, started construction.

I was sick for Ralph, when, late in the day, I turned off my computer in disgust. I now understood why a truck had gone by his house, and why he had reacted as he did. In fact, I was amazed he had not reacted more strongly. Ralph had appeared to be just annoyed with the traffic and the dust, but I would have been enraged if I was in his shoes. Probably if I was to ever be there again when a truck passed by, I would react more strongly than Ralph had, even though it was not my land that had been seized.

Any thoughts I had about obtaining land for Civalia through Ralph were dashed. I couldn't imagine adding to the abuse he must have experience by having his land wrenched away from him when he obviously cared so deeply about it. I debated with myself about calling Ralph, wanting to let him know I knew what had happened. I wanted to offer whatever comfort I might give him, but thought I might only be calling to vent my own rage. Yes, I think rage is the correct word; rage over what I saw as a great injustice. I stewed.

Ralph solved my dilemma for me by calling early Saturday morning.

"I've been playin' yer game and thinkin' about what ya told me," he said. "I was wondering if ya might come back over here an' tell me some more about yer project."

"I'd like that very much," I told him.

"You might bring that there Caddy uh yours too, if ya would. I'd like a ride in that there critter; for old times' sake."

"You can drive it," I said. Ralph laughed. "When and what time did you have in mind?"

"Most any time will work for me. I don't have no plans for the next couple uh days, except caring for the critters."

"How about now?" I asked.

"Well, that's okay with me. Sure I ain't puttin' ya out any?"

"Oh, no. I was just thinking of calling you," I told him. "I'll see you in a couple hours."

I scrambled to change into clothes appropriate for hiking, since I intended to get Ralph to show me what was happening to his land. I threw in a small bag with some clothes and my dopp kit, thinking I might stay over in Riverside or Encampment. As an afterthought, I added some snacks, and then went back for a few tools and some heavy-duty work clothes just in case. By 8:15 I was out the door.

I remembered even less of my trip back to the Lazy HZ on Saturday than I remembered of the trip coming home on Thursday. Lots of questions coursed through my mind, but very few, if any, answers.

I drove up to Ralph's house shortly before 9:30, parked, and was met by Gerald's scolding as I went up to the front door. Ralph opened the door before I could knock.

"Come in," he said and stepped aside as I went in. "Ya made good time."

There was so much I wanted to say to Ralph that I didn't know where to start. "It's good to see you," I said lamely.

"Sit a spell," he said. "You want any coffee? Tea?"

I sat down, "No, thanks. But if you want some, go right ahead." I felt as stiff as a board and a little idiotic. I hoped Ralph was more at ease than I was.

He sat down without getting himself anything to drink, and indicated the game board that was still on the table where we had left it on Thursday. "I think the lessons from yer game are beginin' ta sink in, but some things are still a little fuzzy. Animals livin' on this here planet I understand pretty well. They take in somethin' ta keep 'em goin', some kind uh grub an' water, an' they poop out what's left on the other end."

"And they also exhale carbon dioxide," I added.

Ralph nodded. "Plants are somethin' else. So, they take in sunshine and water. . ."

"And carbon dioxide," I added.

"Right, an' carbon dioxide, an' they poop out oxygen?"

"Yes, oxygen, carbohydrates, and heat." I said. "Actually animals put out heat also."

"So we're like dung beetles for plants," Ralph said, "living on what they poop out."

I laughed. "That's a good way of putting it. Either directly or indirectly we're dependent on plants."

"I didn't know plants put out heat," Ralph said.

"All plants do, but most don't produce enough to raise their temperatures above ambient; and they tend to produce the most heat when the sun is shining on them, driving the photosynthesis reactions. Generally, we can't really distinguish between the plants producing their own heat or being heated by the sun, but some plants, called thermogenic plants, produce lots of heat. One of the best known is skunk cabbage. It can melt its way through a light snow cover."

"Okay," Ralph said. "Where I really need some help is with the Earth. As far as I can tell, it don't take in anything but sunshine an' it don't poop out anything that I can see. So how can it be a living thing? Gaia was it?"

"Ralph, can you imagine taking one of your animals and wrapping it in a rubber film that fits right against its skin or fur or hair, or whatever it has on the outside?" I asked.

"Yes, I can. It would struggle and die right away." Ralph looked a little askance at me.

"I didn't mean to imply that we were going to kill the animal. Perhaps you can imagine that it has holes in the plastic film for air, shit, urine, and whatever else naturally goes in or out of the animal to freely go in and out. Okay?"

Ralph sat back and looked thoughtful.

"It's just an imaginary boundary," I added.

"Like a property boundary?" Ralph asked.

"Yes. That is a great analogy, except the boundary we are trying to imagine is not static like a property boundary. It can stretch and contract and change shape, but it's totally limp; it can't put any force on what's inside or outside the boundary." I collected my thoughts and moved on. "So, there are substances, air, water, and food that go through the boundary, and other substances, urine, shit, sweat, skin flakes, breath, and other stuff that go out of the boundary. Radiant energy, like the heat from your pot-bellied stove over there, can go across the boundary, and heat from your body can go out. You can experience heat going out when you hold your hand next to, but don't touch, a frosted window. Feeling the cold at a distance is the heat leaving your body."

Ralph frowned, "I think I understand that so far. Go on."

"When you have something you can surround by one of these imaginary boundaries, it can be living, non-living, or a combination of both. It's called a system, and there are three types of systems. The animal we just talked about with a boundary around it? That's called an open system. Both energy and matter cross the boundary in an open system. You and I, your animals, and all the plants on your ranch, even your entire ranch, would all be classified as open systems if we put imaginary boundaries around them. But if we imagine a boundary around the whole Earth, very, very little matter crosses that boundary, but lots of energy does; sunlight going in and heat going out. That's called a closed system. With the third type of system, an isolated system, neither matter nor energy cross the boundary."

Ralph picked up the card I had left for him on Thursday. "So, what ya describe in this here *Declaration of Life*, yer domains're closed systems. Right?"

I was astounded Ralph had made that connection so quickly. "Yes, yes, it is; but the idea is that it would be possible to make it a closed system, not that we'd want to actually make it into a real one. Does that make any sense to you?"

"I reckon it does," Ralph said. "You're not goin' ta stop the butterflies an' rabbits from comin' and goin'. But I see how if'n ya put up glass walls, ya'd be able ta live yer life in that there space, provided it was big enough. An' I think I understand what yer tryin' ta get across with yer game." Ralph again sat thoughtfully tapping the edge of the card on the arm of his chair.

I tried to gather my courage to bring up the subject of Ralph's land being taken; he again beat me to the draw. "I think I was beginin' ta think this way back in the 60s when I started cuttin' back on them cows. I'd cut back a little an' see what the land looked like after a while. Then I'd cut back a little more. I tried some uh them hardy breeds ta see how they'd overwinter. I finally came ta the conclusion that domestic cows probably can't make it on their own in this country. It'd take an elk. Nature's way."

Ralph had been kind of looking up to his right, reminiscing. He then dropped his gaze and looked at me sitting somewhat to his left. "I used to have some land that would uh been fine for tryin' what you have in mind. It got took away last year."

"Ralph," I said, "I hope you don't take this the wrong way, but you impressed me so much that I wanted to know more about you. So, I looked you up on the internet and ran into what happened to you with Harold Wainright and his project, Jim Baker's Retreat. I was really steamed for you."

"Probably not as steamed as I was," Ralph said with a trace of amusement.

"I don't know how you can be like you are right now, after what happened," I said. "I'd still have steam coming out of my ears, even if it was a year later."

"It ain't been quite a year," Ralph said, "and I guess I just decided, stayin' mad all the time don't change nothin', so I quit worryin' about it. You want ta go see this wound on the land that Wainright's makin'?"

"Yes, I would," I answered.

Ralph and I went out and got into his truck. He backed up and then headed down the road toward the low hill visible from his house.

"They tore out my front gate an' 'improved' this here road down through my pasture ta their buildin' site."

I could tell by his emphasis on the word "improved," and the sarcasm in his voice, that he really didn't think they'd improved anything.

"Was it always this wide?" I asked.

"Naw, it was just a two-track most uh the way.

"Are there a lot of trucks going by here every day?"

"Depends on the day," Ralph said. He turned left off the "improved" road and took a true two-track road that curled around the low hill. "When they're pourin' concrete, it's bumper ta bumper trucks, but most days there's just three or four comin' in ta work in the mornin' and leavin' at night."

The road we were on had climbed the hill, and as we came to the top, a vista opened up in front of us with some construction work going on about two to three miles away. Ralph stopped the truck and got out. I followed suit. We walked about fifteen feet in front of the truck and looked over Wainright's development site.

"Looks like they've set up a bunch uh forms, so they'll probably pour on Monday," Ralph observed. "Seems like they pour early in the week, so's they can strip 'em and get ready for the next one by the end uh the week."

I looked around the site and noticed there was a deep ravine beyond the construction area. The land sloped down toward the river to the east, but a rocky spine cut diagonally across the landscape, cutting off and isolating the construction area from the river and from Highway 230. The highway could be seen inter-mittently as it wound its way downstream toward Riverside and Saratoga. To the west, above the construction site, the land sloped up to a ragged tree line. From our position, the terrain undulated gently downhill to the site. The road Wainright had widened was a raw gash more or less following the land contours over to the construction disturbance.

"Where are the boundaries of your land Wainright took by eminent domain?" I asked.

Ralph gestured toward the west. "Up there the boundary goes ta the national forest line, 'bout a quarter mile up from where them trees begin. They said they needed some forest land." He pointed toward the ravine. "It pretty well follows this side uh that there ravine, 'cause it's a bugger ta cross; can't do it except on horseback. It goes clear down ta the river an' follows it. They said they needed the river for fishin'." Ralph turned to look back in the southeast direction. "It's more complicated on this side. It comes up from the river and over that hogback, an' then it heads south." Ralph turned more south. "It don't go clear south ta the county road though. Just goes far 'nough ta pick up that there spring what feeds the stock tank."

"Those bastards!" I said.

"I reckon," Ralph said with a sardonic grin. "Hopefully, it'll be a little while 'fore they divert it an' the critters have ta move. Then the line comes back this way an' sweeps around the bottom uh this here hill an' goes back up into them trees up ta the forest boundary."

"So, is this the only road in?" I asked, pointing to the raw gash of the road that ran by Ralph's house.

"The one and only fer now. Far as I know, they plan ta build a road up through the hogback, but that'll take time an' a pile uh money. I think they're plannin' on gettin' things up and runnin' 'fore they tackle that."

"Could they build a bridge or causeway across the ravine?"

"Maybe, but they'd have ta work with me if they did, 'cause they left me that there ravine an' a strip uh land on the other side. That land's hard ta get ta now. I've got ta drive around on the highway, an' I don't exactly feel like workin' with 'em. We're standing on this here hill, 'cause they don't seem ta like me none either. Told me ta stay off'n their property. Not much love lost between us."

"What's that building over there?" I asked, pointing to what looked like a finished structure a short way uphill from the main construction site.

"That there was the first thing Wainright built. Told some uh the folks in town it was going ta be the retreat headquarters, but those as has seen it thinks it's just Wainright's house. See that there Hummer sittin' out front? That's Wainright's. It's there most ever day n' night, so I'm thinkin' they're right. Rumor is Wainright's bragged that there place cost five an' a half million ta build."

I turned my attention back to the road. "Ralph, do they have an easement for that road? Was there ever an easement for the road?"

Ralph pushed back his hat and scratched his head. "I don't rightly know. I know I never gave 'em no easement. No reason ta give anyone no easement, since I owned everything out ta that there ravine, and I was the only one usin' it. I think I'm getting the drift uh yer thoughts. Let's go take a look, an' see if'n we find anything."

We drove back to Ralph's house; Gerald was there to scold us through the door. Ralph took me into his office, and I was not surprised to see a neat room with a desk and a couple of four-drawer filing cabinets. I sat down in a chair beside the desk and waited while Ralph went to the right-hand filing cabinet and pulled open the third drawer down. He riffled through some files and pulled one out, laid it on the desk, closed the drawer, and sat down in his office chair. He then pulled a sheaf of papers from the file folder.

After selecting one and looking it over carefully, he said, "I was pretty sure that were the case. The land this here house sets on was part uh my ol' Uncle Irvin's homestead. The last time a deed was filed on this here land was when I got it from 'im, an' there ain't no easements on this deed."

He handed the deed to me and began thumbing through a desk journal. I read through the deed while Ralph slowed and began to read some entries in the journal.

"Yup," he said. "There's still time."

I had seen for myself that no easements were listed on Ralph's deed. "What do you mean there is still time?" I asked.

"Well, it's like this," Ralph said. "If'n I let people cross my land without asking permission for more than a year, where they're crossin' can be declared a public road, an' I'm just shit outta luck. But if the land owner, an' that's me, closes it off an' don't let nobody go over it at least once a year, it'll stay private land. You an' me're goin' ta close down a road." Ralph's grin was broad. Then he looked startled and his grin faded. "Oh, I guess I should ask if'n ya would like ta help an old man close a road."

This time, I was the one grinning broadly. "I wouldn't miss it for the world!"

Ralph's grin returned. "We'll have ta plan this here caper carefully. If they're goin' ta pour on Monday, that'd be the day ta do 'er. Can ya stay till then?"

"I think so." I said. "I'm not well prepared in the clothes department, but I did throw in some work clothes. You never know when you might need old clothes when you drive antique cars, like I do."

"Good," Ralph said. He pulled a sheet of paper from a desk drawer and began to write a list. "We'll be needin' some barricades an' some signs. We better saddle up, an' hit the lumber yard." Ralph dropped his pen and riffled through the phone book. He picked up the phone and dialed.

"Hi Shirley, is Leonard in?" A pause. "Well, have him call me when he gets in." Another pause. "Yes, it's important. I've got ta go ta town . . .," Ralph looked at his watch, "right soon. Maybe I'll catch him when I'm in town. If'n I don't, have 'im call me this evening." Pause again. "You take care, Shirley. Bye." Ralph hung up. "I'm tryin' ta get in touch with a friend uh mine in the Saratoga Police Department, an' see if'n I can get 'im ta talk ta the County Sheriff's office. Wainright don't like ta be told no, so's we'll likely need some police backup come Monday."

We drove to Saratoga in Ralph's pickup, stopped at the lumber yard, the hardware store, and then dropped by the Police Station. Leonard was not in, so we headed back to the Lazy HZ. When we got back, we unloaded the supplies into Ralph's shop. I have to say that his was not as complete and stocked as mine, but it was neat and very functional. We set to work building barricades and making signs to go with them.

"Ralph," I said, "if you don't hear from your friend Leonard, does Saratoga have a newspaper, and if so, do you know someone at the newspaper?"

Ralph straightened up from sawing a board in two. "There's a weekly paper, the Saratoga Sun. Comes out on Wednesdays. I think I know where yer going. A little publicity wouldn't hurt, an' it might keep things from getting ugly."

"It wouldn't hurt to have a photographic record of the results of this escapade either," I said.

"Right." Ralph laid down the saw and headed for the door. "I'll see if'n I can raise someone."

I continued to paint the sign that I was working on, a "Private Road, No Trespassing" sign, and waited for Ralph to get back. When he did, I put my paint brush in a jar of water to keep the paint in the bush from drying while I listened to Ralph. I didn't want to miss anything he had to say.

"Got hold uh the Sun editor, an' he told me he'd see if'n he could rustle up a reporter or two. I asked him ta keep this under his hat, so word don't get back ta Wainright. He told me he'd keep mum, an' I think we can trust him, an' he's only got ta keep his word fer one more day. I figger we should wait till the construction crews arrive on Monday, an' try ta setup our barricades 'fore the cement trucks come. I don't want ta trap them there cement trucks and have them cleanin' 'em on the land over there. Best ta keep 'em out."

"So you're planning to trap the construction crews at the construction site?" I asked.

"Yup," Ralph answered. "Wainright lives there, so he'll be

there, an' I want ta bite his wallet as much as we can. They won't have nothin' ta do, an' no easy way ta get out."

"When do the construction crews usually get there?" I asked.

"They're usually all here by a quarter after seven, so I figger we ought ta set up between seven thirty an' eight. If'n we do stop a few uh 'em, it won't matter too much"

"When do you expect the concrete trucks?"

"They'll be comin' outta Walden, an' it'll take 'em 'bout half an hour ta get here. If they start loading at seven, the first truck'll probably get here 'round eight. We'll set up a barricade at the county road first, an' then the one down toward Wainright's."

"How do we know where to set the barricade on the boundary between your land and Wainright's?" I asked.

Ralph looked pleased, "I made Wainright survey the boundary, an' had the surveyor put pins on both sides uh the road. Didn't want Wainright getting even one inch more'n he's legally entitled ta. He's supposed ta put in a cattle guard and a fence, but 'e ain't done it yet. If'n this little legal maneuver works, maybe it won't happen at all. What ya say we clean up here an' knock off for the evenin'?"

I wanted to carry at least a little of the load of my upkeep, so I made a pitch to Ralph, "Okay. Let me take you out to dinner in Saratoga. You said you would like a ride in my Caddy, and we may not get another chance to do it before things heat up around here."

Ralph thought a moment and then agreed. "We better get a move on then," he said.

I cleaned my paint brush while Ralph swept up the saw dust. We washed up, changed out of our work clothes, and set off for Saratoga with Ralph driving. Ralph entertained me with tales of the area as we went. He had a large stock of those, having lived his whole life there. He seemed in very good spirits.

"This here Caddy's sure in nice shape," he told me, "an' it 'pears ta have all the whistles and bells. Mine was a little plainer, didn't have these leather seats, and that number speedometer. What'd ya call them things?"

"They're call digital dashes," I said, "and ones this old

usually don't work. This car is in amazingly good shape. I haven't done much of anything to the body, and I only had to make minor repairs to the drive train."

When we arrived in Saratoga, Ralph drove to the bar and restaurant where the locals hung out. As we pulled into the parking lot, he was looking intently toward the cars in the front rank. "Well, well." He said. "Ya just might get ta see the illustrious Mr. Wainright. I think that's his Hummer right over there." Ralph pointed toward a dark colored Hummer. I couldn't tell what color it was in the fading evening light, but I could read his vanity license plate, TOPDOG. "He's not exactly modest, is he?" I queried Ralph.

"No, he ain't. An' he's probably three sheets ta the wind too, 'cause he's likely been here quite a while. You don't get no parkin' space right near the door when you're as late as us. We're goin' ta be back quite a ways farther."

Ralph was right about that. He found a slot three rows back in a corner of the parking lot. When we entered the restaurant, the bar section was to the left and a loud voice dominated the conversation, the subject of which was the performance of the Denver sports teams.

"That's him," Ralph said.

I couldn't get a good look at Mr. Wainright since some hanging plants divided the bar and restaurant sections, and I was looking at him from the back. What I did see was a portly man in a garish western shirt wearing a ten-gallon hat. With a little guidance from Ralph, the hostess seated us in a booth along the wall farthest from the bar section. I was happy about that, because Mr. Wainright was way too loud for me, and I suspected Ralph wanted to be as far away from him as he could get. We had a pleasant dinner talking about our earlier life experiences, and were only occasionally aware of loud outbursts from the bar area. When we finished eating and left the restaurant, Wainright was still holding court in the bar.

"Do you want to drive back too?" I asked.

"I'd like that."

We got into the Cadillac and, after a very brief familiarization with the controls for the automatic dimming lights, Ralph pulled out of the restaurant parking lot and headed back to the Lazy HZ. On the way back he told me some more about Wainright.

"He came from somewheres around Omaha. He's got money, or access ta money, so's a lot uh the locals kowtows ta 'im. Funny thing is, he's as likely ta stiff 'em as not." Several uh the locals have been burned by 'im. Not as bad as 'e burned me, but bad enough. He's also quick with the lawyers, an' most uh the locals don't have the scratch ta keep up with his hatchet men. Somehow he got in good with Judge Kendrick, the Second Judicial District Court Judge in Rawlins, an' that's how he got that there eminent domain judgment. Kendrick's retired and gone now, an' if'n he tries anything today, the results might be different. But then again, it might not. I could've gone ta the State Supreme Court, but my lawyer told me I'd be wasting my money and time, 'cause the United States Supreme Court has already allowed such theft."

"Kelo versus City of New London in 2005," I said.

"You've looked into this?" Ralph asked.

"Since the first community planned for our project will need to have significant land area, and the domains for the citizens of the communities need to be theirs by right, we've investigated ways to keep the land from being seized by someone else. The Kelo versus City of New London decision is worrisome.

"Yes, an' I'm a poster child uh what that there law can do." Ralph was thoughtful for a time while the Cadillac hummed along the highway. "I think he's got designs on the rest uh the Lazy HZ. I suspect he wants ta develop his Jim Baker's Retreat, an' then somehow get the rest uh the ranch ta subdivide an' sell ranchettes. Makin' a big profit, uh course. He probably thinks he can outwait me; wait till I croak, an' then pick up the rest uh the ranch fer peanuts."

"Maybe what you're doing tomorrow will slow him down some," I offered.

"Maybe." Ralph was quiet again, lost in thought.

"Maybe you could close the road permanently," I said.

"I thought 'bout that, an' I'm thinkin' that just doin' it fer one day might be better. If'n it's closed permanently, Wainright'd stop all his construction work an' take ta the courts again. If'n he can still get ta his place, he might keep buildin' an' gettin' hisself deeper an' deeper in hock." Ralph looked over at me, "That might give us more leverage."

I thought about what Ralph had said, and the fact that he had used the word "us," was not lost on me. "I see what you mean. If he spends his money on construction instead of lawyers, he won't have as many options. You're right; one day is best for now."

We spent the rest of the trip honing our action plan for Sunday and Monday morning. The trip back seemed shorter than the trip to Saratoga, and we pulled into Ralph's yard with a nearly full moon lifting above the horizon.

"I saw a motel with a vacancy sign in Riverside," I said. "I'll go get a room and be back here by 7:00 tomorrow."

"You'll do nothin' uh the sort," Ralph said sternly. "I've got sleepin' quarters here."

I got my dopp kit out of the Cadillac, and we went inside; Gerald being absent and probably sound asleep. Ralph showed me the bathroom and his spare room, and then retired to his office. I heard him making a call as I performed my nightly rituals, and headed for bed.

Sunday was entirely devoted to manufacturing the barricades, and we worked until late in the evening. It was a long day; I was tired, so I fell asleep shortly after I went to bed Sunday night.

When I awoke Monday morning, breakfast smells were drifting into the room even though it was still dark outside. I looked out the window and could see the horizon beginning to lighten in the east, but a lot of stars were still visible. Without city lights bleaching out the stars, the sky was breathtaking. I dressed in my work clothes, made a morning bathroom run, and went into the kitchen. Ralph was dressed in the same work clothes as the day before, and was turning some pancakes that smelled wonderful.

"Good morning," I said, "Those smell great."

"There's a plate and some stuff ta put on them," he indicated some dishes, cutlery, and condiments on the counter. "I like ta butter these, layer 'em with applesauce, a dab uh yogurt, an' then some fruit."

"That sounds good. Why don't you show me what you do?" I asked.

Ralph flipped a couple of pancakes on my plate, and then two more on a plate for himself. "Ya butter the bottom one an' put some applesauce on it," he said, demonstrating his technique. "Then ya butter the top one an' spread some applesauce on it, too. Then add some yogurt, an' finally some fruit." Ralph spooned some raspberries on the top of the layer of yogurt. "These here are wild raspberries."

I followed Ralph's directions and when I took the first bite, I knew not only was this combination an epicurean delight, but there was something special about the pancakes. "These pancakes," I said, "how did you make these?"

"Them there are sour cream pancakes," Ralph said. "I really like that recipe."

"So do I!"

We were quiet as we finished eating, then I helped Ralph clean up the kitchen and wash the dishes. By then the day had brightened considerably and the sun was beginning to peek over the Snowy Range Mountains. We had been hearing a scattering of vehicles pass the house on their way to Jim Baker's Retreat earlier, but it had been quiet for a while. I checked my watch. 7:25.

"Shall we get started?" I asked.

"Let me brush my teeth," Ralph said.

"Good idea." I retrieved my toothbrush and brushed my teeth at the kitchen sink while Ralph was in the bathroom. By 7:32 we were dragging the barricades and signs out of the shop, setting up the ones for the junction of his road with the county road first, and then hauling the ones for the north end of the road to the boundary with the Jim Baker's Retreat land.

"Why don't you go back up to the county road?" I asked Ralph. "That's probably the first barricade anyone will hit, and it wouldn't hurt to have someone there."

"I reckon you're right about that. You sure you can handle these on yer own?"

138

I assured Ralph I could, and he drove back up the road. I finished setting up the north end barricade and stepped around it to see how it looked. We had done a professional looking job, having crossbars up to four-feet high and two signs sticking up into the air above the crossbars. One read "Private Road No Trespassing" and the other read "Road Closed No Trespassing." We had filled some sand bags and I placed these on the bases of the triangular barricade braces. I checked to make sure the barricade was entirely on Ralph's land and was far enough back that if Wainright drove right up to the barricade, he'd be trespassing. Satisfied I'd set up the barricade as well as I could, I hiked back to the house. There was another car parked along the county road a little ways past Ralph's driveway, and there were three people standing by our barricade, two men, one of them Ralph, and a woman.

Ralph introduced me when I walked up. "John, this here's Sally Kelley, owner uh the Saratoga Sun, and this here's Al Gearheart. He's a reporter. I told 'im ya was helpin' me. Al's got a camera an' is goin' ta take pictures uh what happens."

Sally smiled at me and said, "This is the most unusual thing that's happened all week; it ought to spice up Wednesday's paper a little."

About then we heard a distant roar and could see a dust cloud headed our way.

"Battle stations," Al said and winked at me. "I'm a Viet Nam vet, and this brings back a few memories."

A cement truck swung into the drive and came to an abrupt halt. The driver climbed down and came over to the barricade.

"What's up?" he asked. "Is there a problem with the road?"

"Nope," Ralph answered, "The road's fine. The problem's this here is a private road, so today ya can't drive on it. Can't ya read the signs?"

Al was busy videoing the scene, but the driver didn't seem to notice. "Well, I've got a load of concrete for the Callaway Construction Company. How am I supposed to get the concrete over there?"

Ralph had a slight smile as he informed the driver, "I don't rightly know, son. I only know ya' can't go over this here road."

"Look," the driver said, beginning to get a little heat in his voice. "I started adding water to this mix when I left 230, and if I don't get down there pretty soon, I'll have to dump this load somewhere. Now why don't you open up these barricades, and let me through."

Ralph got a sorrowful look on his face. "I just can't do that, son. It's a private road."

The driver's face really clouded over. "Don't call me 'son,' you old goat. I'm going to get in my truck and if you don't pull these barricades aside, I'm going to run over them."

"I wouldn't do that if'n I was you," Ralph said and pointed toward the road. A Carbon County Sherriff's pickup had pulled up behind the cement truck, and a pair of officers, a woman and a man, got out of the truck and strolled up toward the barricade.

The driver turned on his heel and strode out toward the officers. "Sheriff," he said, looking from one officer to the other, not certain which one to address, finally settling on the man. "This old man has blocked the road, and he refuses to let me through to do my job." He pointed emphatically back at Ralph, who was standing placidly beside the barricade.

The officers walked up to the barricade with the truck driver, clearly angry, stomping along in their wake. When the officers got to the barricade, the woman, whose name tag read Lieutenant E. Thompson, carefully and exaggeratedly sighted first to the left and then to the right along the barricade boards. She turned to the driver. "Yup," she said, "this barricade's on private land, and we have no jurisdiction to have it removed. Now if it had been in the county road right-of-way, we'd of had you on your way in no time. As it is, you are just S.O.L." She drew herself up and said with a more authoritative voice, "And you will address your comments and questions to ME, since I'm the ranking officer."

"What?" sputtered the driver. "These guys can't just block the road anytime they feel like it. We've got work to do, and . . ."

Everyone turned, looked, and waited silently as a second cement truck came over the crest of the hill to the east, drove up, and stopped behind the sheriff's truck.

The second driver got out and walked over. "What's happening?" he asked the first driver.

"These . . . These . . .," the first driver stammered,

Lieutenant Thompson broke in. "The road you have been using is a private road belonging to the Lazy HZ Ranch owned by Mr. Hertell. He can legally close down this road anytime and whenever he pleases. In fact, Mr. Hertell must close it down at least once a year to keep this a private road." The lieutenant smiled at the men. "You boys will just have to go some other way or go home."

"There isn't any other way," the second driver said. He turned to the first driver. "Jerry, we'd better call in and find out what we should do."

Jerry said, "Yah, and we better let CCC know what's happening."

The second driver said, "Let's let the boss deal with George Callaway. That guy can be a bear when he gets mad. We better get moving. There're at least two more trucks on the road." The two men walked back to the second truck, the driver of that truck got in, and I could see him talking to someone on a mobile phone.

"I suppose it's 'bout time we manned that northern barricade," Ralph said. "Won't be long till we've got us some company over there." Ralph turned to Lieutenant Thompson. "Elaine, will you an' Melvin help us out with the northern barricade?"

With Ralph's question and the officer's name tag, I now had the male officer's name, Sergeant Melvin Trujillo. I'd been feeling like a fifth wheel, but an interested fifth wheel, so I volunteered for duty at the northern barricade. "Someone will need to stay here, so why don't I go to the northern barricade?" I said.

"Okay, John, but ya' better take my truck," Ralph answered. "No vehicles but my own should be on these here roads today, just in case I've got ta defend this little caper in court," he said as he tossed me the keys.

I had wondered why the newspaper people's car was parked west of the driveway along the county road, and now I understood.

"I'll go along with John to the northern barricade," Lieutenant Thompson said, and she issued some orders to Melvin. "Have those drivers get their trucks out of the roadway, and park our pickup across the end of Ralph's driveway."

"Can I go with you to the northern barricade?" Sally asked, removing a journalist's notebook from her bag.

"Feel free," Lieutenant Thompson said. "I don't think walking is covered in the statute on private roads, but perhaps John will give us a ride."

"I'd be happy to oblige," I said.

"Let me get a camera," Sally said as she hurried toward their car. She called out to Al as she went. "Al, stay here and get anything good on film. You might get some statements from the truck drivers and Ralph if you have time." She got a camera bag out of the car and hurried back to us.

We all climbed into Ralph's truck, and I drove down to the northern barricade. Lieutenant Thompson had me turn around and back the truck onto the side road that Ralph and I had taken the day before.

"Leave the keys in the ignition," she told me. "We might need to move out of here in a hurry." She then instructed me to man the barricade, placing Sally off to the east side of the road far enough away that if someone tried to go around the barricade, she'd be out of harm's way.

"I'm going to keep out of sight here for a while. If anyone comes, I'd just like to see how they react if they don't know the police are present. Get comfortable, because this may take awhile."

She was wrong. It wasn't ten minutes later when a dust cloud swirled up from the construction site, stretching out our way. I stood toward the east end of the barricade and watched the Hummer I had seen the night before in the restaurant parking lot tearing up the hill. Wainright came to a sliding stop in front of the barricade and leaned out of his window.

"Pull that f**king barricade out of my way!" he yelled.

"No, sir," I said as mildly as I could manage with adrenaline beginning to course through my veins.

He repeated his curse, calling me a "twerp," as he started to climb out of the Hummer. He stopped abruptly when he spotted Sally with the video camera on her shoulder aimed his way. He shouted at Sally, ordering her to turn off her camera, liberally using the same curse he'd aimed at me but adding a particularly feminine one.

"Your vocabulary seems to be rather limited," I said.

Wainright turned toward me and began to advance with his fists balled.

"That's far enough, Wainright," Lieutenant Thompson commanded as she stepped out from behind Ralph's truck. "You are now trespassing on Mr. Hertell's property, and as you can clearly see, if you can read it, the sign says 'No Trespassing.' I must cite you for this infraction. If you strike Mr. Tantivy, I will arrest you for assault and battery."

"You. . . You. . ." Wainright ground his teeth and looked ready to explode.

"I'll tell you what I told the cement truck drivers," Lieutenant Thompson said in a conversational tone, but I saw her hand was not far from her weapon. "This is a private road, belonging to the Lazy HZ Ranch owned by Mr. Hertell. He can legally close this road whenever he pleases. In fact, to prevent this road from being subject to becoming a public road, Mr. Hertell must close it down at least once a year. He has chosen to do so today. I suggest you watch your language, including your body language. While you do have the first amendment right of freedom of speech, it must be done peaceably." She pulled a citation book from her pocket and began writing a citation for Wainright. She tore out the citation and handed it to me to give to Wainright. He snatched it out of my hand and whirled around, stomping off to his Hummer.

"You'll be hearing from my lawyer," he said through clenched teeth. He raced the engine, executed a dusty U-turn, and peeled out back down the road.

"I hope you don't mind me having you give the citation to him," Lieutenant Thompson said to me. "I didn't want to get close enough for him to try to grab me or try something really violent. This is probably not the last we'll hear from him,"

Sally came hurrying over and joined us. She looked excited. "I got some great footage. I think this may be front page material."

"Shall I take you back now?" I asked. "The worst of the fireworks are likely over by now. The only player who hasn't been on stage yet is the contractor, George Callaway I think his name is, and Mr. Wainright will undoubtedly tell him what is happening."

"That would be fine," Lieutenant Thompson answered, and Sally nodded, busy putting her camera back into the bag.

We drove back to the barricade at the county road. By this time, three cement trucks were parked along the road. Lieutenant Thompson got out and went to confer with Sergeant Trujillo, and Sally went over to Al. I walked over to Ralph and handed him his keys.

"Did ya' have a good time?" he asked me.

"I don't think I'm very high on Wainright's list right now." I told Ralph about our confrontation.

"Sounds like 'im," Ralph said. "It's been pretty quiet here, but the trucks haven't left. I'm guessing Wainright's trying ta figure out a way ta get 'em into the construction site. He'll have ta pay for the concrete regardless, an' if they can't get it out uh the trucks in time, there'll be hell ta pay with having ta chip it out."

A thought crossed my mind. "I wonder if Wainright will try to cut across your land to get to that finger of land he took—stole—to get control of the spring," I said.

"I thought 'bout that too," Ralph told me, "so early this morning I went down ta the tank an' shut off the pipe. Water's been backin' up an' should be runnin' down the hill by now. I don't think them trucks can cross anywhere but below the spring, an' if it's muddy. . . well, you get the picture."

I smiled. Indeed I did get the picture. My respect for Ralph's intelligence ratcheted up another couple of notches. I then heard the cement trucks start up one by one. They pulled out and headed down the road. Ralph walked over to the Sheriff's officers and I tagged along.

"Elaine, Melvin" he said, "I sure want ta' thank ya' fer comin' all the way out here for my little show this morning, an' I sure thank ya' for protectin' John from Wainright. Since, the trucks have left, there's not much sense in you sticking around, but I'd 'preciate it if you'd wait about ten, fifteen minutes before ya' leave."

Lieutenant Thompson looked puzzled. "We were just getting ready to go, but why do you want us to wait?"

"Oh," Ralph said, "I just don't want them cement truck drivers ta get any ideas if'n they see ya leavin', an' ya might check they don't dump their loads where they shouldn't."

"I get it," Sergeant Trujillo said. "That cement is probably getting pretty hot by now." He looked at his watch, then at Lieutenant Thompson. "Shall we give them ten minutes?"

"Ten minutes it is," replied Lieutenant Thompson.

Ralph winked at me and said to the officers, "How about I get ya a cool drink? I got some lemonade made."

The officers agreed, and Ralph headed for the house. Lieutenant Thompson turned to me. "Are you an old friend or a relative of Ralph's? I don't think I've seen you around here before."

"I'm a new friend of his, but it seems like I have known him for a long, long time," I said. "We have a lot in common."

"Where're you from?"

"I live in Laramie, I was an instructor at the University, but I'm retired now."

"Well, you take care of him," she said. "He's a remarkable man, and I don't want to see him hurt."

"I'm well aware how remarkable he is, and I will take care of him as best I can." I told her. I had been warned, and I understood how much the community respected Ralph.

Ralph returned with a tray of glasses, and we all had cold lemonade. The talk was of local people and happenings; people I didn't know and events I didn't know about, so I kept quiet. After ten minutes the officers walked to their pickup, got in, and drove off. Lieutenant Thompson was driving.

Ralph had a merry grin as he asked me, "Ya wana bet on how long it takes 'im ta come back here?"

"Are you thinking the truck drivers will either be trying to get to the construction site by going cross country, or will be dumping their concrete somewhere they shouldn't?"

"As I said, I'm willin' ta' bet on it." Ralph laughed. "Wainright don't think rules apply ta him. Let's go sit on the porch for a while an' see what happens."

Ralph and I hadn't been on the porch more than a couple of minutes when Gerald showed up. He scolded for a while, then shut up and began inching his way down the tree. Ralph reached into his pocket and brought out a peanut, which he laid on the porch floor in front of him.

"We'll see how brave he is with ya around," Ralph said.

We sat quietly, watching Gerald advance, retreat, dodge sideway, but slowly work his way toward the porch. When he finally raised his head above the step, seeing the peanut at eye level was too much; he couldn't resist any more. He snatched the peanut and retreated back to the step to chew it open and eat the nuts. When he was finished, he jumped onto the porch and circled around Ralph, staying as far away from me as possible. He obviously wanted more peanuts, but Ralph quietly rocked and watched Gerald's antics.

"He'll get used ta ya pretty soon; even sooner, if'n ya feed him."

We both looked up as the Sheriff's truck came back into view over the rise on the road. Ralph grinned at me. "They're right on schedule," he said. We stood up, Gerald scampered for the safety of the tree, and we walked out to the road. Lieutenant Thompson made a U-turn and stopped in front of our barricade. She leaned out the window.

"I thought you'd like to know the truck drivers went through your fence and started to head across your land. The lead truck hit some soft ground and went in up to the axles. The other two were backing up when we arrived, but they were still clearly on your land. We cited them all for trespass and called in a wrecker to extract the stuck truck. The driver of that truck was emptying his load when we arrived. Claimed he had to dump his load to keep it from hardening in the truck. We cited him for littering also. We told the other two that they had better not dump their loads anywhere we might find it, so I think they won't try to dump them until they're in Colorado. Just as a courtesy to them, we notified the Colorado HP of the situation,"

Ralph smiled at Lieutenant Thompson, "Sounds like ya handled all that just right. I assume ya' notified Harold that them there trucks was trespassin' on his land too."

"Of course," she said with a straight face. "He was mighty upset, but when I asked if he would like to have me cite them for trespass on his land, he declined. I don't think this has been a very good day for him. We'll lean on the concrete company to clean up the dumped concrete and fix your fence. I suspect that will filter back to Harold also. You were expecting this?" she asked.

"I thought it might be a possibility," Ralph answered, and grinned.

"Well," she said, "you've made our day interesting. If you need anything more, let us know. Melvin and I will be heading back now. We're pretty sure the excitement is over."

"I reckon it is," Ralph said. "I really wanna thank ya' for yer assistance today. Things might'n 'ave gone so smoothly if ya hadn't been here."

"Take care," she said and started down the road. Melvin waved through the rear window of the pickup.

Ralph and I went back to the porch and sat down again. I looked at my watch and was surprised that it was only 10:17. I felt like it should be a lot later after all that had happened.

"What do you think Wainright's next move will be?" I asked.

"I'spect he'll lawyer up," Ralph said. "He'll try ta figure out a way ta get legal access. The easiest way would be working out a easement with the Lazy HZ. He might've succeeded at that 'fore I met ya. But now I don't think so."

My mind froze for a moment when I heard what Ralph was saying, and I briefly wondered if I had heard correctly.

Ralph continued, "I'd sort uh given up, after losing such a big chunk uh the ranch an' not havin' nobody ta leave it ta anyhow. I ain't no spring chicken anymore, an' I can't care for it like I used ta. I was beginnin' ta think there weren't any other people around that thought 'bout the land like I do. I suppose I was beginnin' ta doubt myself at times. Then ya came along."

"Ralph," I said, "meeting you has really shaken up my world, too. My friend, Stellan, and I started thinking about entropy and the implications of it back in the mid 80s. But from what you have told me, you understood a lot of these things twenty years before we did. We were just wet behind the ears kids then, and you didn't have the assistance of engineering text books that we had. I've been both humbled and excited to begin learning how much you know about the land and how to live with it. The extent of your knowledge and understanding is amazing to me."

Ralph looked at me seriously and said, "Those're nice things yer sayin' 'bout me, but you've told me an' showed me things I didn't know nothin' 'bout. You're puttin' yourself down a little by sayin' all those things."

"I could disagree with you on that, Ralph, but how about if we just agree we have a lot to learn from each other?"

Ralph smiled and sat back in his chair. "Sounds good ta me. So ya' told me when we first met ya' were lookin' for some land ta set up a community. Well, I've got land, and I think we might just come ta a understandin' about ya havin' some, if'n your friends are anything like you. But if'n they're like Wainright, it just won't work out. Now, if'n I remember right, ya' said ya' might need up-wards uh 5,000 acres. I'll give ya' that if you'll let me visit once in a while."

I was choked up and my mind was whirling, "Ralph . . . Ralph, that is so generous of you." My mind began to function and a zillion thoughts flooded through my brain. Some of them began to coalesce around some negative thoughts. It was difficult for me to put some of these into words, but I had to speak out. "Ralph, I can't tell you how much your offer means to me, but I'm thinking it might not be the best thing to do at this time."

Ralph frowned, and stopped rocking. I worried I had hurt his feelings, so I hurried on. "Such a gesture might send Wainright the message he should make a grab for the rest of your ranch, since he'd view you as losing your mind, getting senile, or being duped by us."

Ralph chewed on that thought for a while. "There's some truth in what ya' say. Ya' have any thoughts on how we might work out somethin'?"

"What if we buy some land at a price well above what Wainright paid for what he took from you? We can't afford 5,000 acres, but we can buy enough to start building our community."

Ralph thought about what I had said, and I envisioned a lot just large enough to build Civalia. That was depressing to me, because it violated the basic premise of the *Declaration of Life*. But then the proverbial light bulb came on. Maybe there was a workaround.

"Doesn't some of your land border the National Forest?" I asked.

"Yes," Ralph answered. "What're ya' thinkin'?"

"If we purchased some land from you next to the National Forest, we could consider some of the National Forest land as domains for our citizens. We wouldn't own it, of course, but no one else could build on it, and it wouldn't likely get changed a whole lot. That land could serve the purpose of providing solar energy capture and entropy export into outer space, even though we wouldn't have total control of it. In time, we might be in a better position to purchase some more land from you, that is if you still think we are good neighbors. Is there heavy use of the National Forest next to your ranch?"

"Used ta' be, with grazin' allotments. I still have some an' I still turn the animals out on 'em for a while in the summer just ta keep 'em current. I don't use 'em as much as I could, and some other people're hankerin' ta take 'em from me. We might have ta make sure we keep 'em up. I like yer idea. It could make sense for both uh us. Ya' could get ta know me better, and I can get ta know all uh ya' better without ya'll havin' ta make a big investment." Ralph started rocking again. "Why don't me and you take a little tour up along the forest boundary after lunch? We'll see if any uh that there land along the forest boundary might suits ya'. And I want ta meet these friends uh yours. If they're as savvy as ya, it'll be a challenge."

"Then you better prepare yourself to be challenged," I said, "because my friends are probably savvier than I am, at least in some areas. For example, my friend Stellan's son, Gyan, named our project when he was only fourteen."

"We've talked a lot about it, but I don't recall hearin' what you've named this here project. Care ta tell me?" Ralph asked.

"It's called the Civalien Project. Gyan combined 'civilization' and 'alien' to coin that name."

"Civalien . . . Civalien. I like the sound uh that."

"We plan to call the first community we build Civalia," I said.

"I like that too," he paused. "Civalia," Ralph murmured to himself. "That's quite a feat for a fourteen-year-old."

After another delicious lunch, which further fueled my amazement at Ralph's culinary abilities, we took a drive farther up the county road. When the road appeared to dead-end into a buck and pole fence, but really made a sharp bend to the left, Ralph pulled off to the right onto a side road headed to the north, and stopped at a wire gate.

"This here's some uh my land," he said. "The buck fence's the forest boundary."

I got out and opened the gate, then closed it after Ralph drove through. I got back in, and we drove slowly along, paralleling the forest fence. The land was typical mountain meadow land with some scattered aspen groves interspersed with pine and spruce trees. We topped a barren ridge and from the top we could see an extensive, verdant, green meadow sloping away to the northeast. The meadow was approximately circular with a diameter about two to three city blocks long and sprinkled with wild flowers. The trees were denser on the forest side of the fence, with the evergreens becoming dominant.

"It's beautiful," I said.

Ralph got out of the truck and I followed suit. "I thought ya' might like this place. I come up here ta watch the wildlife graze an' soak up some sun ever once in a while." He indicated a salt block about a third of the way down the meadow. "I put out that there salt lick ta get 'em ta visit a little more often. One time, I was sittin' on that there log," he indicated a log off to our left, "an' a doe came up behind me and sniffed my ear. Like ta' scared both uh us half ta death. I jumped a mile an' so'd the doe. Think this might be a place for Civalia?"

"Ralph, I don't know what to say. I don't know if I could find a better place if I looked for a hundred years."

150

"Well, ya could just say 'yes' or 'no,'" he said quietly. "What if I sell ya 40 acres uh this here land fer a thousand an acre?"

"That's not enough, Ralph. I haven't priced land around here, but around Laramie it would be five, maybe six grand an acre for a parcel that size. How about we give you at least three?"

"I won't take a nickel more than two," Ralph said, "an' it depends on meetin' yer friends."

"Of course. . . of course," I stammered. "I'm overwhelmed."

"Well, get over it," Ralph said. "I 'spect yer work's just be-ginnin', if'n you're goin' ta' get done what yer talkin' about." He pointed to the other side of the meadow. "There's a little draw over there with a stream. It's ephemeral, but some years it's at least damp all year. It grows some nice wild strawberries, even if it dries up. They're not much bigger 'n a pea, but they're sure tasty."

"Ralph, can you wait here a minute?" I asked. "I want to check out something."

"Okay."

I'm sure Ralph was puzzled as I walked back the way we had come then back over to the other side of the barren ridge. Slowly, I turned back and looked toward the meadow. There was no earth-sheltered structure rising up in the distance, only the top of the cab of Ralph's truck, but it looked like the same ridge I'd seen in my dream.

CHAPTER 8

When I got back to Laramie on Tuesday after my weekend with Ralph, I remembered even less of my drive home than I had on my previous trips. Thankful when I arrived home safely, I had been a little worried about having, or causing, a major car crash with my inattentive driving.

I was lonely. I missed Ralph. Stellan and Gyan were not back yet. Even my shop could not console me, and I wandered around without getting much of anything done. Finally, I decided to investigate the legal issues with forming a 501(c)(4) social welfare corporation. After a brief internet search, I found a relevant IRS publication, only forty pages long, and began to read. I quickly found the publication composed primarily of legalese; it was very heavy reading. My mood lifted when I located the passage that states, "The organization must be a community movement designed to accomplish community ends". That was heartening, as was the description of the first precedent:

> An organization that purchases acreage in a stated locality, makes arrangements for water and sewage facilities, and enters into arrangements with the erection and sale of dwellings to low- and moderate-income individuals qualifies as a social welfare organization. Rev. Rul. 55-439, 1955-2 C.B. 257.

Next, I moved on to the Wyoming Nonprofit Corporation Act; one hundred nineteen pages. After several hours of reading that had me literally scratching my head and rubbing my eyes, I decided I needed the help and advice of a lawyer. Fortunately, I had a friend in the profession, and I called her office. I made an appointment to visit with her on Thursday and then thankfully closed the documents.

My next move was a visit with my financial advisor to start the process of rounding up the eighty grand I would need for purchasing the forty-acre parcel of Ralph's land. I knew from experience that shaking money loose from the financial tree took time. Nothing could be started this late in the day, but I wanted to be prepared when, and if, something happened.

Home again, I was still restless. So much had been packed into the last few days, and into my mind! I decided I needed some physical exercise; lots of physical exercise. One of my projects was just the ticket. I'd been working on a human powered truck; a pedal powered, four-wheeled, articulated vehicle that could be configured for a dump truck, a two-passenger rickshaw, a flatbed truck, an enclosed van, or whatever else a person could dream up. I called it a Bruck, a combination of bicycle and truck. Designed to carry a thousand pounds, the Bruck was geared low, and was not exactly a feather-weight vehicle to begin with. I hooked up the two-passenger rickshaw trailer and took off across town.

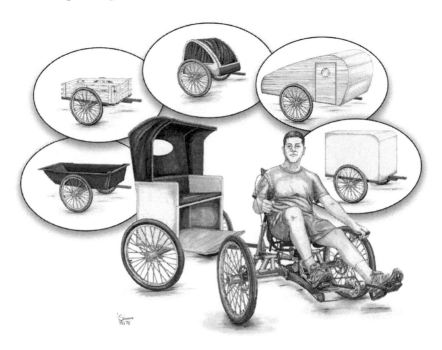

After riding aimlessly for some time, I found myself in Cass's neighborhood and decided to see if she would like to join me for a ride. I'd like to think my selecting the rickshaw and ending near Cass's was purely chance, but I had to admit to myself I really did want to talk to someone in addition to exercising. I was in luck; Cass was home and seemed intrigued with my machine.

"This would be really useful in several of the communities I've lived in," she told me. "How much will it carry?"

"It's supposed to carry about half a ton. I've had several hundred pounds on it before; I've carried between three and four hundred pounds of passengers. It can also be a dump truck; I've hauled at least that much weight in ice. I've also hauled some dirt, but I don't know how much it weighed. Climb on," I said.

Cass settled herself in one of the seats and we set out at a sedate pace, ending at a nearby park.

We toured the perimeter, drawing curious looks from adults, and open-mouthed stares from kids. I waved at a few of them, and they waved back. Cass joined into the friendly waves, and the kids shouted a few comments. I was tiring, and after about half an hour we arrived back at Cass's house.

"I'd like to talk with you a while if you have time," I said. "Could we go have a bite to eat or a cup of coffee or some ice cream? Maybe all three?"

Cass looked disappointed. "That's very nice, but I've been working on an article I have to send off this evening. Can I take a rain check on your invitation?"

I was disappointed. "That's what I get for last minute invitations, so let me make another one that's not last minute. Would you be able to go on a picnic either Thursday or Friday?"

"Would that be local or somewhere out of town?" Cass asked.

"Out of town," I said, "so you'd have to plan on a significant part of the day, leaving about 10 and getting home . . . .This reminds me of a quote from a Little Golden Book, *Mickey Mouse's Picnic*; 'We will frolic all day in the happiest way, and we won't get back home until dark.'"

"You have the most amazing memory for trivia I think I have ever encountered!" Cass said.

"Yah, lots of trivia. Stellan calls it *The Tantivy Storehouse of Useless Information.* So, can you make it?"

"Let's see." Cass opened the scheduler on her smart phone, looked at the remainder of the week. "I have something on both Thursday and Friday, but I'm pretty sure I can reschedule my Thursday appointment. I'll see if I can, and let you know one way or the other."

"That'll be fine with me," I said, and I pedaled away heading for home. The work of pedaling the Bruck had effectively tired me and quieted my mind. What little I had talked with Cass also helped, and sleep felt more likely.

Sleep finally came, but not as swiftly as I would have liked. Wednesday dawned. A new day, the day Stellan and Gyan might be back. At a relatively early hour, I tried calling Stellan. A very sleepy voice answered.

"Hello?"

"Hi, Stellan," I said.

"Do you know what time it is?" he snarled.

"It's 8:30," I said. "That's not very early, and if you're still in Texas, it's 9:30."

"It's early, if like me, you got in late last night. Oh, I should say early this morning. What do you want?"

"I want to invite you to a picnic tomorrow, leaving town about 10 o'clock."

"What!" Stellan shouted. "You got me up to invite me to a picnic?"

"It's an important picnic; Gyan and Cindy are invited, too," I said.

"Sometimes I wonder about your sanity," Stellan growled. "Because of this insanity, you'll have to come over this afternoon and help us unload. Two o'clock sharp. You can ask Gyan and Cindy yourself then. Right now I'm going back to bed."

Stellan hung up without even telling me whether he would go on the picnic or not. At least I would see him at 2:00. Maybe by then he'd have cooled down a little; at least I hoped he would. Meanwhile, I needed to make arrangements with Ralph. I called him, but he was not in, so I left a message. My next move was to head to the grocery for some picnic goodies. I spent the rest of the morning putting together picnic supplies and enough food for a small army.

I was eating lunch when I suddenly remembered I had made an appointment with my lawyer at the same time as the picnic. 'Shit,' I thought, and reached for the phone, but before dialing her number, I realized she would be out for lunch. I'd have to remember to call her sometime between 1:00 and 2:00. Reminded how badly I needed to get a grip on my exploding life, I went to work making a quick scheduling list. Ralph called back, and hearing his calm voice helped me settle down a notch or two.

"Got yer message when I came in fer lunch," he told me. "I've been out fixin' fence where them trucks went through. There's pretty deep ruts from where they dragged out that first one."

"Have you heard anything from Wainright?" I asked.

"Not directly. There's an interestin' article in the paper today, a picture uh Wainright at the barricade lookin' mighty angry. Sally called 'im fer a statement, an' he said he'd sue me for damages. I 'spect he'll try. He told Sally it'd cost 'im between twenty- an' thirty-thousand dollars, but I'll bet it cost 'im more'n that, since 'cordin' ta the article, the concrete outfit decided ta stop doin' business with 'im anymore."

"Wow," I said, "Probably the next closest place is either Rawlins or Laramie, and the unknowns of the weather, coupled with the question of whether or not you'll close the road without warning, will make it tough to get another supplier."

"I reckon it will." There was more than a trifling note of satisfaction in Ralph's voice. "I think it might've caused a problem with 'is contractor too. At least there hasn't been anyone comin' through my place in the mornin' the last couple uh days. Wainright's been through, though. 'Pears he's drivin' through fast as 'e can ta stir up dust. Makes me think 'bout closin' off the road permanently."

"Do you think he'll try to build a road out to the highway?" I asked.

"He might try, but it'll take him a while. He'll have ta get a permit from the highway department an' pay for a impact study an' he'll have ta 'ave a road design 'fore he makes the application fer the permit. I can't see that gettin' done fer a few months, an' it won't be cheap. Ya' said ya' had somethin' ta ask me, so what'd ya have on yer mind?"

"I'd like to bring my friends over on Thursday, that's tomorrow, to meet you and to have a picnic lunch in the meadow. I've checked the weather report, and it looks good, so I have two questions. First, is it okay with you if we come, and second, if it is, could you picnic with us?"

Ralph didn't hesitate. "Of course it's okay. It's practically yers anyway, an' I'd love ta meet yer friends. When do ya' think ya'll be here?"

"I'm planning on leaving here at 10:00, so we should be there about 11:30."

"Why don't ya' just go directly up ta the land, and I'll meet ya' there."

"That's fine with me. Is there anything special you'd like for the picnic?" I asked.

"Good conversation," Ralph answered. "At my age, food's less important than the company."

"You will have to excuse me for taking that with a grain of salt, judging from the food you have fed me," I told Ralph. He laughed. I continued, "I'll try to make my food relatively close to how good you'd fix it."

"I'm lookin' forward ta meetin' yer friends. I'll see ya tomorrow," Ralph said, and we ended our call.

By then, it was after 1:00, so I tried my lawyer again. She was in, and I explained my gaffe of scheduling two things for the next day, groveled a bit as I explained what I wanted to talk about, and in a moment of inspiration, asked if she'd like to go on the picnic with us. I was actually a little shocked when, after a short silence, she said that she would. I told her to meet us at my house at 9:45, and we'd all go in my car. Two o'clock was inexorably creeping up on me, so I quickly changed into my work clothes and headed for Stellan's house.

A U-Haul truck with a trailer was parked in front, so I parked across the street. When Stellan answered the door, he was sounding, and probably looking, much better than when I talked with him earlier.

"Welcome to the madhouse," Stellan said, as Gyan and then Cindy, whom I had never met before, came in from the kitchen. "Cindy, this is John."

"I've heard a lot about you," she said. "Somehow I thought you'd be bigger, you know taller and. . ." She made some horizontal widening motions with her hands.

"Sorry," Gyan said. "We probably gave her that impression from all the things we've been saying about you and the things you've thought of." He looked at his daughter, "He's more a mental giant than a physical giant."

I was embarrassed. "Actually, I'm neither," I said. "Just today I realized I'd made two mutually exclusive appointments for tomorrow, but I think I have it fixed. Are you two available for a picnic tomorrow?"

"Where's the picnic?" Cindy asked.

"Over toward Saratoga."

Cindy looked blank. "What's over there?"

"Well, some deer, a few goats, squirrels, some cows, and, oh, a hot spring."

Cindy immediately looked interested. "Can we go, Dad?"

Gyan looked at me, "Did you find some land we might be interested in?"

"Perhaps." I looked at Stellan, "Will you go along?" He nodded, and I looked back at Gyan, "How about the two of you?"

"I suppose, but we have a lot of work to get settled. I rented a house just before we left, and I've got to go back to work on Monday."

"I'll help all I can," I said. "Shall we get started?"

As we trooped out of the house, I asked Cindy, "How old are you?"

"Eleven. I'll be 12 on September 17th."

Cindy was obviously looking forward to becoming a year older; I felt a pang in my heart as I realized how many decades had passed since I looked forward to getting older. Gyan and Cindy climbed into the truck, and Stellan crossed the street with me to follow them in my car.

"You have the cat that ate the canary look," he said to me. "What gives?"

"Can we let this ride until tomorrow?"

Stellan smiled at me. "It must be a dilly. You look wound up pretty tight."

"I feel wound up," I said.

We arrived at Gyan's house, and all three of us spent the afternoon carrying boxes and furniture, unpacking the boxes, moving furniture around, checking the furnace, the water heater, and the refrigerator, and hanging some curtains. I unwound. Toward the end of the afternoon, Gyan and Cindy made a trip to the grocery store in my car. I was worn out and sat down with a sigh in the now reasonably tidied living room. Stellan sat across from me, and didn't appear to be doing much better.

"I think I've had it," I said. "When Gyan and Cindy get back, I'll give you all a lift to your house, and then I'm heading for the barn."

"Me too, but I have to help Gyan get the U-haul back to the rental place. It's been a long week, but it's nice to have Gyan and Cindy here and hopefully somewhat settled. Good thing it's summer vacation, so Cindy won't have to change schools in the middle of a school year."

"How is Cindy taking her mom's move to Italy?"

Stellan sighed, "I'm sure she's hurting, but Gyan is paying her a lot of attention and trying to make this transition as smooth as possible. I suppose she'll really miss her friends. Do you think we could stop by the Hobo Pool tomorrow? I'm sure that would be a highlight for Cindy."

"We'll make a point of it." We sat quietly for a while, and then I suggested, "What if you and I take the truck and trailer back? We could stop by your house to get your car, and then take the truck back. You're cleared to drive it, aren't you?"

"That's a good idea," Stellan said and began to rouse himself. "Maybe Cindy's not too far off thinking you're a mental giant. You do come up with some good ideas every once in a while."

Stellan offered a hand to help me up, and I was glad to accept it.

We were moving slowly, but we returned the truck and trailer, and picked up Stellan's car. By the time we got back to Gyan's house, he and Cindy had returned and were putting away groceries. I started to take my leave, but Stellan stopped me and asked Gyan for his car keys. "If you could drop me by my house, I'll bring Gyan's wheels over here and take mine back home. Everything will be straight then."

"You aren't bad at coming up with good ideas yourself," I told him.

"9:45 at my house tomorrow morning," I called out to Gyan as we left.

I was tired, so I slept well that night. The next morning, I was busy putting the finishing touches on the picnic lunch, loading all the food and picnic paraphernalia into the car, and remembering at the last minute to grab some towels and my swim suit for the Hobo Pool. I called both Cass and Maggie to let them know we would be stopping at the pool, so they should bring swim suits. I was ready.

Cass arrived punctually, and the others dribbled in over the next ten minutes. I made introductions and stowed the extra clothing in the trunk of the Cadillac; we were only late by five minutes of my estimated departure time. We were slightly crowded with six people, but the day was sunny, the temperature balmy, with only a slight breeze. A lovely day. My passengers spent some time getting to know each other, and I was pleased Cindy was included in the conversation and joined in without having to be cajoled.

I turned the conversation to Civalia. I'd been thinking about the barriers to creating a domain experiment being more social, political, and relational than physical and technical. One of the thorniest problems I had encountered was the demographic structure of a small community. I had read of studies showing groups of up to 25 people were cohesive and social. Over that number, the groups tended to divide into factions and become internally competitive.

If we planned for a community of about 25 people, split approximately evenly between males and females, what should the age distribution look like? Will the residents of domains live longer, shorter, or about the same as residents in our existing society? Will the incidence of old age infirmity be more, less, or similar? The information available for making these types of judgments was slim. One data point I thought about was the lives of Helen and Scott Nearing, activists for living the simple life, whose lives might approximate people living in a domain community. Both survived to nearly 100 years old, and were reasonably active throughout their lives.

If a domain-based community was formed with all members approximately the same age, the community would age and die roughly together, posing problems with reproduction because domains would not be available until the residents were well beyond child bearing age. This type of structure would only be viable if many communities of varying ages coexisted.

If the community had 25 members between ages 0 and 99, and they were approximately evenly spaced, all the residents would be about four years apart. Assuming males and females were interleaved, the next older and younger persons of the same sex would average eight years difference. This arrangement would present problems of close companionship. More residents would help, but could potentially introduce the problem of splintering into factions.

If there were clusters of people, mini generational divisions, of say four per cluster, there would be about six clusters with an average 20 years between clusters. This might be a more workable structure than an evenly spaced one, but inbreeding might be a problem unless a network of domain communities could offer a variety of possible partners. I decided to ask Cass about these issues.

"Cass, how many people do you think we should plan for in our first stab at Civalia? I've read research showing groups of about 25 people are cohesive and get along well, while larger groups fragment and generate infighting. But a community of 25 doesn't seem large enough to have the coverage of skills or the breadth of demographics needed to keep the community viable."

"I've read that research," Cass said. "The number 25 comes from research done in the United States, one of the most competitive nations in the world where we glorify individualism and competition. Cooperative societies, emphasizing group activities and cooperation, are able to sustain larger groups harmoniously. Let me give you an example. The Iroquois Indians were a matrilineal society with members of the extended families living in longhouses."

"What's a longhouse?" Maggie asked.

"It was a family living structure 20 to 23 feet wide and averaging about 60 feet long," Cass explained. "There were some in the 300 foot range, and the longest one recorded was around 400 feet. Each longhouse was divided into residential sections about 20 feet long, and each section divided into two family quarters by an approximately 10 foot wide central hallway stretching axially down the longhouse. The central hallway contained hearths for cooking and heating. There would be a wooden bench along the outside wall for sleeping and shelves above it for storage."

"That's only about 100 square feet of dedicated space per family!" Maggie exclaimed. "They couldn't have had nearly as much junk as we tend to have!"

"Undoubtedly that's true. They probably also spent considerably more time outside than we do. Each family area was owned by one of the related women in an extended family. When a woman married, her husband came from another family and moved into his wife's living area. We don't know for certain how large the individual families were, but they probably needed at least an average family size of five, a mother and father with three children, to maintain zero population growth. So even the average longhouse would have a minimum population of around 30 and a 300-foot longhouse could have had a population around 150."

"Wow," Stellan said. "I can't imagine living with 149 other people. I think I'd go crazy."

"You probably would," Cass told him, "having grown up in

this culture, with the idea of your own room, your own bathroom, your own television set, your own everything drilled into you from birth, maybe even before birth. Consequently, you are not as likely to play well and share well with others."

"There'd be a lot of kids to play with," Cindy said.

I joined the conversation. "There'd have to be a lot of sharing, and whenever I've tried sharing some of my tools with other people, I've been sorry. They come back dulled, broken, scarred, rusted, sprung, and bent."

Cass leaned forward so I could hear her clearly from the back seat. "In your statement you're showing you suffer from the unconscious assignment of lesser value to things belonging to someone else. Don't you value your own tools more than anyone else's? Admit it. If you're working with someone and your tools get mixed, don't you generally separate yours first, and then gather your partner's tools? What if all the tools belong to someone else, are you as careful with them as with your own?"

I'm certain I must've looked a little stricken, because Cass went on. "The idea of individual ownership engenders these types of responses, but when people are raised in an environment where there's community property, they have a different outlook. You may have experienced this within your family. Did your family have a family car you took pride in and helped keep in good shape?"

"Yes. Yes, it did. Dad had a pickup I really liked. I washed and waxed it, and even worked on the engine."

Stellan changed the subject, "Are we then to think the community size could conceivably be as high as 150?"

Cass answered, "That depends on how you define 'community.' For communal living, where everyone lives in the same space and shares most everything, there definitely is an upper limit. Cooperative community living, where people share some things and don't share other things, probably has an upper limit, but it would be much higher. And, of course, populations with isolated residences where little or nothing is shared seem to be unlimited, as can be seen by the urban sprawl of Colorado's Front Range or the Los Angeles area."

"I think," I said, "we will have to share a great deal, if we are

164

to get our average entropy production down to much lower levels."

"How do you measure your entropy production?" Maggie asked.

"That's hard to do," I answered, "since there's no such thing as an entropy meter. So what we can do is estimate it from our power consumption. I calculated my direct power consumption for last November and came up with 9.5 kilowatts."

"That doesn't mean much to me," Maggie said. "More to the point, what do you think it would take to get your entropy production to lower levels?"

"Almost all of our power consumption eventually ends up as entropy, i.e. unavailable energy," I said and launched into a long winded explanation. "Power multiplied by time is energy, and the energy divided by . . ."

Stellan interrupted. "Some research John dug up shows we can have a satisfying, secure life with about a tenth of John's November consumption, somewhere around a 1,000 Watts. We just can't survive on 1,000 Watts in our current single family, or individual living arrangements."

"I agree," Cass said. "That is why I promote intentional communities with large sharing components."

"So," I asked Cass, "what would be your recommendations for a workable number of residents in Civalia under the most optimal conditions? I assume communal living requires the least amount of energy expenditures as well as the least amount of embodied energy."

"Where to start," Cass said. "In the 1990s, Robin Dunbar found a correlation between the average social group size of primates and their brain size. Based on the average human brain size and extrapolating from the primate data, he proposed humans can only maintain about 150 stable relationships. Perhaps this is why not many longhouses were over 300 feet long. There is, of course, controversy over Dunbar's number, the main one being whether humans, given training in cooperative living, could learn to live harmoniously in larger social groups."

"How many kids would there be?" Cindy asked.

"I'd guess about eight kids within a couple of years of your age, Cindy," Stellan said.

Cass continued. "From my experience with intentional communities in this country, they tend to struggle between 40 and 75 people, because 40 or more people don't seem to be able to connect with everyone else, but over 75 some functional subgroups tend to form, meeting people's needs. A historical example of a larger community is the Oneida Community. You may have heard of Oneida silverware; the silverware company was started by the community and outlived it. That community had about 300 people at its peak, but they had a complex bureaucracy of 27 standing committees, almost 50 administrative sections, and it was a religious community. Modern Israeli kibbutzim average almost 400 members. Again they are hierarchical and bureaucratic. Neither of these sounds as if they are compatible with your ideas of Civalia."

"No, they don't sound compatible," I said. "You stated there is controversy whether Dunbar's number is valid given training in cooperative living, so do you think it's possible for Civalia to exceed the 40-person limit you stated with careful organization and education about cooperative living?"

Cass sighed, "I don't know for sure. I would like to think it's possible, and some communities have succeeded. Twin Oaks is an example. The ones that succeed generally are fairly structured."

Gyan spoke for the first time in this conversation, "If Cass is right and Civalia will function best with about 40 people, it would make sense to start with a small number. After all, there are only four of us now, and if we plan well, we can build up with both people and infrastructure. Perhaps the growing process can give us an idea of whether or not 50 will work and how best to reach that number. Regardless of whether or not the size of Civalia or similar communities can reach 50 or more, there is a reason to plan Civalia for at least 50. I foresee there will be people interested in at least learning about Civalia and the *Declaration of Life*, if not beginning to live with this paradigm. I think having room for visitors and temporary residents is essential."

"That makes a lot of sense to me," Stellan offered. "If the Civalien Project grows, the first community, Civalia, will undoubtedly be the gateway."

"It will also be the beta test," I added. "There will be a lot to learn, and I only hope we can create something that can be adapted and modified into a workable community."

"You will have your work cut out for you," Cass said. "If, as it appears to me, you are headed toward a conscious anarchy, a consensus society by definition, I suggest you will need an educational program, and in your educational program you will need to train your residents on conflict resolution and egalitarian relationships. A few years ago, I worked on a study of specific systems in community life relating various factors to satisfaction, among other things. We found conflict resolution, egalitarian relationships, and income sharing were the three top things correlated with satisfaction. I don't know how we plan to handle income."

"You said 'we,' Cass. Are you part of this venture also?" Maggie asked.

"Maybe it was a Freudian slip," Cass answered. "I've certainly been thinking about it a lot. I think I probably will."

"That would be great, Cass," I said. "As for how we plan to handle income, I. . . um," I looked desperately over at Stellan.

He shrugged and said, "Well, we don't, uh . . . . I think we were here before."

Gyan saved us again. "Cass, when we first met, I said I'd get together with you and tell you about the financial issues with Civalia. I'm sorry that slipped my mind."

"It's not like you didn't have anything else to do," Cass said. "Moving's tough on everyone."

"Thanks," Gyan said, sounding grateful. "I probably told you then the economics of Civalia are complex, relative to the economic system we are living in now. It will take me a lot longer than we have before we get to Saratoga to tell you about it, and I'd bore everyone else to death. So, I hate to put you off again, but may I suggest you and I arrange a time to get together? I'm also very interested in learning about the agricultural systems in the communities where you've lived. Perhaps you could tell me about those when we meet. Is there a time you're free?"

Cass considered Gyan's request for a moment, and when her silence dragged on a bit, Gyan added, "I'm looking for a position on the campus, and there are some relatively quiet study rooms in the College of Agriculture. We could meet there."

"Okay," she said. "I will have some time on. . ." she consulted her schedule, "tomorrow afternoon. Will that work, say 1:30?"

"Yes," Gyan answered, "room 1046."

Cass then addressed all of us. "One other thing that is really, really important is to carefully select your members. I'll see if I can get us some related references."

This last statement by Cass allowed me to segue into the next tough subject; one I had thought a lot about, but hadn't reached any hard and fast conclusions. "Assuming we have a handle on the number of residents in Civalia and are aiming toward a community with domains, the domains being of significant size, approximately 100 acres, what do you think the basic organization should be? Should we have a village of individual or family residences? A rural landscape of scattered homes on domains? An apartment building with individual apartments?"

I paused as I thought of more options. Stellan chimed in, "A tent city? Tree houses? Mud huts? No living structures, such as the Australian Aborigines?"

Stellan and I often find our minds racing along the same path. I took up the challenge. "We could do cardboard boxes like some of the homeless in the cities, or we could do tipis. Igloos?

Gyan added his two cents worth. "Sod houses? Log cabins? Grass Huts? Caves?"

"How about Yurts?" Maggie asked.

Stellan got a faraway look and then said, "Hey, are you familiar with the underground city of—of Capattalia, no Cappecoken? Hell, I'll look it up." Stellan took out his smart phone and punched in an internet search. "Here it is, Cappadocia in Turkey." He continued to scroll down. "There is another one, Uplistsikhe in Georgia. And here is another one in Naours, France. Nushabad in Iran. Derinkuyu in Turkey. Derinkuyu could have housed 20,000 people and had eleven underground layers. Wow!"

"Are you talking about living in a cave?" Cindy asked. "That'd be icky."

Gyan laughed. "Not exactly," he said. "There would be rooms just like we have now, but they might be earth-sheltered."

"I've heard of Derinkuyu," I said, "but I didn't realize that there were so many others. Maybe that should tell us something. We do have some cliff dwellings in this country." I realized we were getting side tracked and tried to bring the subject back to the type of community to aim for. "Cass, what are your views on how our community should be organized?"

"I've been listening to all of you talk about physical structures, but in my view, the most important factors are human values, relationships, fulfillment, and fellowship. They should dictate the physical structures. In my experience, some of the characteristics and values that are vital for any worthwhile human community are cooperation, tolerance, and helpfulness. Building individual homes on domains of 100 acres would physically, socially, and emotionally isolate most everyone. You seem to have ruled out a hunter/gatherer society by the mere fact of designating domains. To be unified, I think your community should definitely include a significant amount of communal space, if not be totally communal."

"How about individual personal space?" I asked. "Sometimes I like to be able to get away from everyone else, particularly to sleep. I still remember one night when I was in kindergarten, and spent a miserable night with a friend. I lay awake all night on the very edge of a double bed, while my friend snored away, taking his half out of the middle. I've never wanted to do that again."

"Yup," said Gyan, "Cindy, you had a slumber party last month. Remember that? I certainly could have used some private space to get away from all of you giggling girls."

"Dad!" Cindy said with a trace of embarrassment in her voice.

Cass laughed. "Yes, there is need for people to have a place to retreat to, some personal space, but it's small compared to the communal space."

"Can you put any numbers on those space requirements?" Stellan asked.

"All I can tell you is about the sizes of the communities I was in," Cass said. "The most successful, and to me the most satisfying one, had individual residences ranging from about 200 square feet up to homes for a couple of around 1,500 square feet. Most were what might be called tiny houses. Then, there were community structures of various sizes and function. There were multiple kitchen/dining room combinations, where residents ate a couple of communal meals a day.

"How many people would there be in a single dining room?" Gyan asked.

"Again, they varied in size, from about 10 to 20. They were more restaurant-, maybe cafeteria-style, and not all of the residents ate at the same time. Small groups would come through, friends eating with friends. Meals times are important bonding times for the residents. We had a central, multipurpose, community meeting building of 2,000 square feet, but there were other smaller special purpose garages, sheds, and shops; all communal. Generally those were sized to match the usage."

"How many people were in that community?" Stellan asked.

"It varied during the time I was there, but I think there were 72 when I left."

"Getting back to the question of the organization," I said, "it sounds like we are headed toward a significant communal component in Civalia. Is that the consensus?"

"What's a consensus?" Cindy asked.

"That just means everyone agrees to do something, Cindy," Cass said. "It's like when you and all your friends decide to go to a particular movie together. All of you may not eagerly agree on the same movie, but those who don't particularly want to see it go along for the sake of keeping your group together."

"Sometimes it takes us a long time to decide," Cindy said.

Cass laughed. "Yes, it also sometimes takes a long time to come to consensus."

"Couldn't you use majority rule?" Maggie asked, drawing on her legal background.

"Are you always happy with majority decisions?" Cass asked.

"Well, no," Maggie said, "but I usually just suck it up and try to live with the will of the majority."

"Okay," Cass said. "So, if the majority decides to make a law saying you must have your feet bound, do you just live with it?"

"No way!" Maggie said. "I get your point."

Stellan said, "John thinks our *Declaration of Life* is the definition of an anarchy, which would require consensus for all decisions."

"That's right," I said. "But if I don't like what's going on, I'd be free to go live by myself on my domain."

"What's a an-r-key?" Cindy asked.

"That's where everybody decides for themselves what they should do," Gyan told her.

"So if you tell me to take out the garbage, I can just not do it?" Cindy asked.

"Just like I could not fix supper when you tell me you're hungry," Gyan answered. "When we care about other people and love them, we decide to do a lot of things to make life easier for all of us to be together."

Glancing in the rearview mirror I could see Cindy looking a little pensive, and then snuggling into Gyan's side. "I'll empty the garbage," she said in a small voice.

Gyan said, "It sounds like we generally agree Civalia should have some private space, some communal space, and some greenhouse space for food production. Is that right?"

"That pretty much sums up my thoughts," Stellan said, "but I'd also add some space for cottage industry."

"Sounds good to me," I said. "What do you think, Cass?"

Cass answered my question with her own question. "Are you thinking of separate structures for all these different spaces, or are some or all combined into one?"

"I'm for putting everything together, since the volume to surface area ratio will be better for reducing heat losses," I said. "Gyan, what do you think?"

"There're pluses and minuses for both approaches. I'll have to think about it some," he said. After a pause he added, "You've had the advantage of experience with your apartment in a shop arrangement."

"As long as there's someplace to get away once in a while," Stellan said, "I'd go for a combined space."

The turn off to CR-798 came up on the left, and at least for me, the time had gone quickly. The conversation quieted as I turned, and everyone began looking at the surrounding land. They remained quiet, conversing in low murmurs, until we reached the turnoff into Ralph's land. He'd left the gate open for us, and I began driving slowly along the two-track road beside the forest boundary fence.

"That's a weird fence," Cindy said.

"It's called a buck and pole fence," Gyan told her. "Those A-frames are the bucks, and the horizontal poles are, of course, the poles. People usually just call them buck fences for short."

"It's the forest boundary," I added, "and they use this type of fence, because the elk and moose don't knock it down like they do wire fences."

Maggie said, "The wild flowers are pretty." There were murmurs of assent from more than one person.

We approached the barren ridge, and I didn't see the top of Ralph's truck, so I assumed we had arrived first. That was not the case. When we came over the top of the ridge, I saw Ralph sitting on the log he used for watching wildlife at the salt lick. There was a haltered, saddled horse grazing about two thirds of the way down the meadow, and a doe with her fawn bounded across the meadow. I pulled to a stop; the deer also stopped and turned at the edge of the meadow. The horse raised his head, still chewing the grass he had bitten off, and Ralph stood and dusted off the seat of his pants. When my passengers started bursting out of the car, the deer faded away into the trees, the horse went back to grazing, and Ralph started toward us. I got out of the car and headed for Ralph. We met about halfway between the car and the log, and hugged.

"I've missed you," I said.

"An' I've missed ya' too," he said.

"Let me introduce my friends to you."

I made all the introductions, and listened to the small talk that erupted, most of it exclaiming on the beauty of the place and asking about the visible features. Cindy was transfixed by the horse. I began unloading the picnic food and supplies, and Stellan came over, ostensibly to help me, but probably more to quiz me.

"How long have you known Ralph?" he asked.

"A week," I said. "I met him last Thursday."

"And you know him enough to give him a hug, and to picnic on his land? At least I assume this is his land."

"Stellan," I said, "have you ever met someone you feel like you've known all your life? Like you have some . . . some intense connection? Well that's what I experienced, and I think it is mutual."

Stellan considered this. "I've experienced that once, but it was not mutual. I think I came on too strong for the other person."

"Well, I think this is mutual, and Ralph asked to meet all of you, except maybe for Maggie."

"Speaking of Maggie, why is Maggie along?"

"Because I screwed up. It's like this. I made an appointment to see her today, and then I set up this picnic, also for today. Since the appointments conflicted, I asked her if she would like to come along. She surprised me by saying yes." I changed the subject. "Ralph has a lot of the same ideas we have. Except he thought them up when we were just kids, and he doesn't use the same terminology."

"That's probably because he doesn't have an engineering education," Stellan said.

Stellan and I carried the picnic stuff over by the log and began to set out the food. I looked up and saw Cindy on horseback, with Ralph leading his horse on a walk around the meadow. The rest of the group was watching their progress. Cindy was hanging on to the saddle horn for dear life, but her smile was a mile wide.

"I can finish setting up the picnic, Stellan. Why don't you go join the others?"

"I think I'll do that," he said and walked off to intercept the group.

As I watched, Ralph brought Cindy back to the group and helped her down. He turned his horse loose, and it began to graze again. I watched as the group then migrated toward the north edge of the meadow with Ralph in the middle. I couldn't hear what was being said, but their body language indicated they found Ralph captivating. I hoped the feeling was mutual.

Even after everything was ready, I delayed calling them in.

But when I noticed the ants, yellow jackets, and flies had started to congregate for their part of our feast, I couldn't hold out any longer. The worst intruder was a camp robber, which was getting bolder by the minute, flapping his way right up to the food. I gave a loud whistle and waved them in.

The picnic was one of the most enjoyable I have ever had. Stories flowed, camaraderie bound us closely, the sun smiled down on us, and we enjoyed feeding the camp robbers, three of them by then. That afternoon was one of those times that I wished could go on forever.

Eventually, the sun began heading for the hills to the west of us. I looked at my watch and informed my friends we'd better get moving, if we wanted to get to the Hobo Pool. I invited Ralph along, but he declined. I was a little surprised, but not totally, when Stellan also said he would rather pass, and asked Ralph if he could stay and talk with him while the rest of us went swimming. My surprise turned into a tad of jealousy.

Everyone pitched in to load the picnic supplies and the food, but we left a few tidbits for the camp robbers and the insects. After bridling his horse, Ralph rode off through the trees at the bottom of the meadow. We piled into the car and drove back on the county road to Ralph's house, where we left Stellan. I could hear Stellan being scolded by Gerald when he approached the porch. The rest of us headed for the Hobo Pool.

What can you say about the Hobo Pool? It's a free public hot spring with a small inlet pool, very hot, over 120 degrees Fahrenheit, called the Lobster Pot. There is really only one way to get into that feature. I jumped in from the surrounding rocks, and then stood absolutely still. I think this allows a thin film of water next to your body to cool somewhat. When I moved to get out, I was instantly way, way too hot. The larger pool varies in temperature depending on the water currents and distance from the Lobster Pot. There is almost always somewhere comfortable and just right. We enjoyed our soak and the desultory conversations.

I was half floating on my belly by the side of the pool, keeping my head above water by hanging onto the side, when Cass paddled in and joined me.

"I've be wondering how you are planning on powering Civalia. Will you hookup to the power grid?" she asked.

"We haven't discussed that issue in depth yet."

"But I'm sure you have some thoughts on the matter," she said.

"We probably won't connect to the grid. That would make us dependent on some unknown people and forces we'd have no control over."

Cass persisted. "That's a problem every intentional community I've lived in has, and none of them had a completely satisfactory solution. Net metering was about the best, but it was costly. Don't you have other ideas?"

"Of course, I've thought of a lot of different schemes, wind power, PV panels, Stirling engines. In fact, I've been thinking a lot about a liquid piston Stirling engine . . ."

At that moment we were interrupted by Cindy splashing in between us, followed immediately by Gyan. A water splashing session followed, and our conversation was lost. Eventually, we were all sufficiently waterlogged and stewed, so we got out, dried off, and dressed.

The drive back to Ralph's was quieter than the drive to the hot springs. All of us were more relaxed and mellow. Cindy even went to sleep against Gyan. When we drove into Ralph's, he and Stellan were sitting on the porch. All of us got out and thanked Ralph for letting us picnic on his land. Cindy shyly thanked him for letting her ride on Lester. That was when I learned Ralph's horse's name.

"Why do you call him Lester?" I asked.

"Lester's just a good friend uh mine," Ralph said vaguely. "I've knowed him for years. He's reliable an' has helped me a lot, an' old Lester here is one of the most reliable horses I've ever had, an' he helps me a lot, too."

"Can I come back and see Lester?" Cindy was not at all shy about asking for more time with the horse.

"Of course," Ralph said smiling. "Anytime. Lester'd like that too, since I don't get out with 'im as much as I used ta."

We all said our goodbyes, and I noticed a special look that passed between Ralph and Stellan. Again, I felt just a twinge of jealousy, but I killed it by hugging Ralph again before I headed for the car.

"Stellan," I called out, "Would you drive us home?" My mind felt too busy to focus on driving, plus everyone else was likely to be talking about their experiences of meeting Ralph, seeing the land, and swimming in the Hobo Pool; these factors were bound to make me a hazardous driver. "The keys are in the ignition," I told him.

"All right," he agreed, changing his path toward the driver's door of the car.

I turned to Ralph and said in a lowered voice, "I'll be in touch . . . very soon."

"I'll be lookin' forward ta that," he replied.

CHAPTER 9

I was quiet on the ride back to Laramie, not quite certain of my internal, private, emotional state. The others made up for my reticence, except for Stellan. He was also quiet, and I wondered if Ralph had affected him like he had me.

Cass said to me, "You weren't just kidding when you told me what Mickey Mouse said."

I generated a wan smile for her.

"What did Mickey Mouse say?" Cindy asked.

"We will frolic all day in the happiest way, and we won't get back home until dark," Cass told her.

Cindy clapped her hands. "Oh, we did that, didn't we, Dad?"

Gyan put his arm around her, "We sure did. How'd you like the Hobo Pool?"

"Great! Can we go back sometime?"

"You, bet!" I answered for Gyan.

Cindy and Gyan, sitting in the front seat with Stellan, continued to banter about their afternoon, while Cass and Maggie, sitting next to me in the back seat, talked about the landscape, the scenery on the drive, and finally segued into sharing personal information. I might have learned quite a bit about both of them if I had been listening closely, but I did not. They talked softly and the noise from the road and the car masked their conversation. I let the travel motion and the soft sounds of their voices lull me into a light sleep.

I roused from my slumber when I realized Stellan, Cass, and Gyan were discussing possible configurations of a Civalia structure. "Hey," I said, "fill me in on what you've been talking about."

Gyan turned toward me and said, "We were discussing possible layouts for Civalia, and Dad made the point we need to carefully consider heating, ventilating, and air conditioning requirements if we want to reduce our average energy consumption to the one kilowatt range. The volume to surface area ratios of structures, as well as the insulation and air exchange factors, are what determine the necessary HVAC energy flows."

"We also were discussing how food independence is necessary to keep our energy consumption low," Cass said. "We'll undoubtedly need greenhouse space to achieve that goal."

I agreed with both of these statements, so I asked, "What conclusions have you reached?"

"Dad mentioned spheres have the best volume to surface area ratio, but they make awkward structures. In general, the next best shape is cylindrical. So, we're thinking along the lines of an earth sheltered cylindrical structure."

"Cool," I said. "So, would you have a separate circular greenhouse or a circular greenhouse with various rooms around the outside?" I recalled the earth sheltered structure I had seen in my dream. It fit with what my friends were considering.

"We're not thinking of it in exactly that way," Cass said. "The first arrangement you suggested would make the greenhouse a totally separate structure, and limit the attention it would receive. I wouldn't like to go out to it if a blizzard was raging, even if we had an enclosed breezeway. The second plan you just suggested would make the communal space chopped up and awkward. Instead, we think the communal space should be in the center and the greenhouse a ring around that."

Stellan spoke for the first time. "I think we'll need some sort of cottage industry space, which by definition is communal space. I've suggested it should go in the very center. Other communal space, dining areas, meeting rooms, a library, a laundry, a music hall, class rooms, laboratories, and so on, will then be a ring around the cottage industry space. The greenhouse, a colossal conservatory if you will, is then another concentric ring."

"They talked about personal space being a third concentric ring," Maggie added.

In a quiet voice Cindy said, "They didn't say where the playroom was going to be."

Gyan was immediately contrite and put an arm around her. "Of course there could be playrooms in the common area, plus you could have your own personal play room in the private area. A greenhouse would be a lot like playing outside, so I'm sure there could also be some playgrounds there."

I pictured such a structure in my mind, and while there were many pleasing and exciting things about it, the size seemed to grow as I thought about the greenhouse space needed for around 50 people to be food independent, the space needed for cottage industry, the areas needed for people to socialize and pursue other interests, the space needed for utilities and maintenance, and the list went on. The size and complexity of such a structure spelled many dollars. I knew I didn't have the financial resources for such an undertaking, and I didn't know anyone else associated with our project that did. I did not want to borrow the money, so I became the wet blanket.

"That all sounds fantastic, my friends, but I don't think it's affordable. Can we maybe build a collection of some sort of smaller units?"

There was silence as the cold water I'd thrown on their dreams cooled their enthusiasm. Then Gyan spoke one word, "Keyhole!"

The rest of us looked at him blankly.

Gyan continued excitedly, "If we built the cottage industry space, and a wedge of the common area, the greenhouse, and the private area rings, it would have a keyhole shape. It'd be a fraction of the cost of the whole cylinder, and Civalia could be completed in stages as we get resources to expand it."

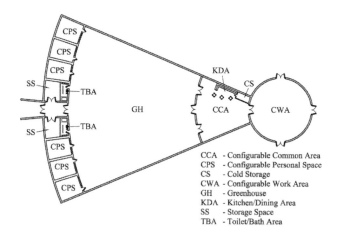

CCA - Configurable Common Area
CPS - Configurable Personal Space
CS - Cold Storage
CWA - Configurable Work Area
GH - Greenhouse
KDA - Kitchen/Dining Area
SS - Storage Space
TBA - Toilet/Bath Area

The excitement built again, and this time I was part of it. Ideas flew, and it seemed like only moments had passed before Stellan pulled into the driveway in front of my garage.

When we got out, I addressed Maggie. "You said you have something on tap for tomorrow, but can I make an appointment for sometime early next week?"

"Why don't you call me Monday morning, and we'll set up a time," she said.

"Okay. Thanks for coming with us today. I hope you had a good time."

"I did indeed. I needed a little time away from my desk."

Maggie got in her car and drove off, and I turned to Gyan and Cindy. "I don't have to ask if you had a good time," I said to Cindy.

She nodded enthusiastically. "I want to ride Lester again." She frowned. "That's a funny name for a horse. I think I'd call him Prince or King or Rusty. He's kind of rusty colored."

"Ralph said he named him after one of his friends. Did you hear that?"

"Oh, yah," she said, "but if he was mine, I'd name him something different."

I looked up at Gyan. "Thank you both for going with us today. I'd like to hear your impressions of the area. Perhaps we could get together again; maybe sometime next week, since you still have a lot of work to get settled in."

"We'll work out something, but right now we need to get home. I'll call you on Monday or Tuesday."

Gyan and Cindy left, but not before giving Stellan, Cass, and me hugs.

"Would the two of you like to come in and talk for a while?" I asked Stellan and Cass.

"I would," Stellan said immediately.

Cass looked at her watch and then said, "I can for a short time."

We went in and sat down in my living room. Stellan began the conversation. "Ralph is truly a unique person. I don't know how you found him, but it is like finding a treasure."

"I didn't find him, he found me," I said. "Last Thursday, when you were gone, I had worked out a game and I was feeling really restless, so I decided to just go over by Saratoga and look around. I drove the Cadillac over there and turned off on county road 798. I'd driven a couple of miles in when I noticed a striking difference between the land on the south side of the road and the north side."

"I noticed that, too." Stellan said.

Cass joined in. "I was in the back seat on the right side of the car, so I mainly saw what's on the north side. It looked well cared for. I only got glimpses of the south side. What was the difference?"

"The land on the south side had been cleared and planted to crested wheat grass sometime in the past," I explained. "Crested wheat grass is a non-native species, and some people are now classifying it as invasive. Ralph's land on the north side is almost all native plants and is not overgrazed, like the south side of the road is. I parked and got out to take a longer, closer look. Ralph drove up and stopped because he noticed my Cadillac. He told me he had owned one and remembered it fondly. We got to talking, and I spent the afternoon with him."

"You must have had quite a talk, because Ralph indicated he had learned a lot from you. Did you discuss our project him?" Stellan asked.

"Yes, I did, but what I found was Ralph was way ahead of us. Decades ago Ralph had figured out most of the principles we are basing our project on. He just didn't have the technical terms we have from our engineering education."

"That explains one thing I was wondering about," Stellan said. "He was questioning me about subjects I was not expecting him to know anything about." Stellan looked thoughtful for a moment and then asked, "Did you play your game with him? When I walked through his house to use the bathroom, I noticed what looked like a handmade game on his table."

"Oh!" I exclaimed as I sat up a little straighter. "I'd completely forgotten about the game. I should have picked it up when I came home Tuesday. I'll have to try to remember it the next time I'm over there."

"You stayed at Ralph's for . . .," Cass counted to herself, "five nights?"

"No, I came home Thursday night, but I went back Saturday morning."

"There seems much more to this story than you have told us," Stellan told me sternly.

I felt like a guilty child caught in a lie.

Stellan continued. "Perhaps you should answer a question I have and then tell us the whole story. Ralph told me to tell you, he is satisfied the conditions are met. What does he mean by that?"

Both Cass and Stellan were looking at me intently, and I felt shocked. I took a deep breath. "Ralph has agreed to sell me, that is us, a 40-acre parcel of land, the meadow where we had our picnic, for building Civalia."

"You're shitting me," Cass said. "You've known him for what? Something like a week, and he has agreed to sell you some land? What's the catch?"

Stellan jumped on me. "Well one catch is 40 acres isn't nearly enough for Civalia."

"Let me explain," I said. "If we're planning on 50 people, 5,000 acres in that region would cost at least somewhere north of five million dollars. I – I mean we – don't have that kind of money to start Civalia, so I thought if we bought on the national forest boundary, we could ostensibly use the forest as our domains until we can acquire more land. The forest land's not likely to be developed, and even if we don't have total control, it can probably function as domains."

Stellan and Cass both look skeptical.

"Besides," I said, "the Lazy HZ ranch was originally about 27,500 acres, but a land developer stole over 13,000 acres by eminent domain. Ralph didn't rule out selling us more land in the future."

"Provided we are good enough neighbors for him," Cass said.

Stellan responded to Cass's comment. "You used the word 'we.' Does that mean something?"

Cass hesitated before answering. "As I told you, I've been thinking a lot about what I've been learning from the three of you, the four of you if you count Cindy, and what you've said makes a lot of sense. I've been about two thirds of a mind to join in with you, but I was hesitating because I wasn't sure you were committed to making Civalia a real community. I guess my slip of the tongue and your working toward the step of acquiring land kind of cements my position. May I join? If you will have me, of course."

I answered Cass, while Stellan dug out his phone and dialed someone. "Cass, I've been thinking you would be a real asset to our project, and I have been trying to think how I would ask you to join. Of course I'm for it."

Stellan turned away from us and spoke into his phone. "Hi, Gyan. We've just had an unexpected inquiry into joining our project." A pause. "As a matter of fact it is. How did you know?" Another pause. "Uh-huh . . . Uh-huh." He turned around and smiled at Cass. "I guess that settles it then. I'll talk to you later. Bye now." Stellan pocketed his phone. "I guess you heard," he said to both Cass and me. "Welcome aboard! By now, you probably have a good idea of what you're getting into with this crazy man here," Stellan indicated me, "and with Gyan, Cindy, and me."

"I do," Cass said, "and from what I know now, this is going to either be one hell of an interesting community, or it is going to run headlong into bureaucratic roadblocks. Either way, I think I can learn a great deal, and I can contribute a great deal."

"You already have," I said. "Contributed a great deal, I mean."

Cass laughed. "I've also learned a lot, and I plan to learn more. I've never heard of a liquid piston Stirling engine. You'll have to clue me in on that, John."

"Let's get back to this land," Stellan said. "So you're proposing to buy 40 acres of Ralph's land, and I'm detecting some weaseling in what you're saying. Let's have the rest of the story."

"Well, actually, Ralph said he wanted to give us 5,000 acres of land, but I didn't want him to."

"Why not?" Stellan asked, his eyebrows rising in surprise.

"Yes, why the hell not?" Cass added.

"The issue is Wainright. That's Ralph's uninvited neighbor, who took half his ranch. Wainright claimed the land was not being used, because Ralph was taking excellent care of it and not overgrazing and despoiling it in the name of development, like all of his neighbors are. Wainright convinced a judge to give it to him for economic development for only $200 per acre. I figured if Ralph gave us 5,000 acres, it might incite Wainright to try to take more at an unfair price or for free."

"I see," said Stellan. He looked at Cass. "The plot thickens." He looked back at me. "So, what kind of a deal did you strike with Ralph?"

"When I thought about using the national forest land as our ostensible domains, I told Ralph about that idea, and he offered to sell us 40 acres for $1,000 per acre."

"That's an extremely low price for that land," Stellan said. "Might that also incite Wainright to go after more?"

"That's what I thought, so I offered Ralph $3,000 per acre."

Cass asked, "So, you are going to buy those 40 acres we looked at for $120,000?"

"No," I said. "Ralph told me he wouldn't take a nickel over $2,000 per acre. I've started gathering the money from my accounts, and I'll be talking with Maggie about the legal aspects early next week, as you heard."

Cass was frowning. "Is it a good idea to go into a location with an obviously grasping neighbor like Wainright? I admit that your land deal is outstanding, but a bad neighbor can ruin everything."

"I have the same concern," Stellan added.

I sighed, "I think Wainright can be taken care of, and I want to help Ralph do that, regardless of whether we locate Civalia there or not."

"So there is even more to the story?" Stellan asked.

"Yes, the only access to the land Wainright ripped off is through Ralphs place. You may have noticed the road that goes by his house is heavily traveled. We looked into it, and there's no easement for the road. Since Wainright's been using it less than a year, Ralph said we could block it off to maintain the private road status. I helped him do it last Monday."

"Can't Wainright build a road somewhere else?" Cass asked.

"He could, but it would have to be either over some more of Ralph's land or over some terrain which would make it very costly.

Access to highway 230 could also cause delays or be denied."

Cass and Stellan looked at each other, and Stellan said, "I'll have to think about this some more, and perhaps look over the situation myself. I'd also like to discuss this more with Ralph. How about you?" he asked Cass.

"Yes, I need some time to digest what John has told us, and I'd also like to personally analyze the situation. Since I have not had time to talk with Ralph alone, going there with you is probably the best idea. Is there a time we can make a trip?"

"Let me see about when I can get away from work, and I will give Ralph a call to see when he is available. Do you have any work-around times?"

"No," Cass said. "I can make any time this next week work. Should we try to get Gyan to go also?"

"I'll check with him," Stellan said.

I felt a pang at being excluded from a trip to see Ralph, but I could understand why they didn't want me around. I also did not want to tell them I was certain Ralph's land was the absolute right place for Civalia; I had seen it there in my dream.

I needed something to keep my mind occupied for the next few days, so I decided to work on designing the liquid piston Stirling engine, an LPE, using solar energy as the heat source. I was having fun and became engrossed in the task. Part way through my investigations, the idea of using carbon dioxide, CO_2, for a working fluid came to mind. Some of the properties of CO_2 are very attractive for use in a LPE; it is available, condensing out of highly compressed, cooled air. If accidently released, it is non-toxic up to concentrations of about five percent. CO_2 is not flammable, actually being used in fire extinguishers; it is much less viscous than water but denser than water at pressures above 300 psi; and it is non-corrosive if it's not mixed with water. I set about trying to design a LPE cycle using CO_2.

This work occupied me through Friday and over the weekend. I made some progress, but I was happy when Monday came and I could call Maggie. Fortunately, she could meet with me that morning at 10:30. I was fifteen minutes early, and Maggie was about five minutes late. It seemed like hours before she arrived, and then I wasn't certain how to start my conversation with her.

"Did you enjoy the picnic last Thursday?" I asked lamely.

"Yes, and the Hobo Pool afterward. It has been years since I've been over there, and every time I am, I resolve to go more often. But I never do."

That conversation was not heading in directions that I wanted, so I tried again. "What did you think of Ralph?"

"He is a very nice older gentleman. Why are you asking? Does he need some legal help?"

"No. . . No. I need some help."

Maggie looked confused. "Is something going wrong that you haven't told me about?"

"No, I just don't know how to explain these issues to you."

"Well," she said, "you're on the clock, so I suggest you give it a try." She leaned back in her chair and began fiddling with a pen, passing it from hand to hand.

"Okay," I said, "Stellan, Gyan, Cindy, and now Cass, and I have been working on developing a community based on . . . on minimizing entropy increases, and . . ."

Maggie stopped fiddling with the pen and sat forward. She interrupted me, "I don't know what you are talking about. What is entr . . . ent. . .?"

"Entropy," I said. "It's a measure of unavailable energy."

"That doesn't help very much. Can you give me an example?"

I thought for a moment, and then pointed to her cup of coffee sitting on a coaster on her desk. "You poured yourself this cup of coffee a short time ago, and there was a given amount of heat energy in the coffee. That heat immediately began leaking out of the coffee, first into the cup and the air, and now into the coaster, your desk, and into you as you drink the coffee. All of the heat energy is still in existence, but it is unavailable to you. The measure of how much of it is unavailable is entropy."

"Would you spell that, please?"

"E-N-T-R-O-P-Y"

Maggie wrote the word "entropy" down on her pad. She arched her eye brow. "And what does entropy have to do with the problem you have come to see me about?"

"Years ago, Stellan and I came to the conclusion that life based on entropy considerations would be very different from those we are generally living. We developed a statement based on these principles; we called it the *Declaration of Life*." I handed Maggie one of my *Declaration of Life* cards.

She took the card in one hand and read it. She then took a two-handed grip on the card and read it again with a frown on her face. She looked over the card at me and asked, "The first part of this is just the Declaration of Independence, but the second part doesn't make any sense to me. Can you explain it?"

"Well, you know you couldn't live very long if you didn't have air, food, and water, don't you?"

"Yes, of course. So what does that have to do with having a right to life?"

"Let's just talk about air first," I said. "What you really need is oxygen, and the oxygen in the air comes from plants using solar energy to convert water, and the carbon dioxide we breathe out, into oxygen and carbohydrates. The carbohydrates are the primary basis of the food we eat, and you know we need the oxygen to stay alive. So if we don't have enough plants to do all this for us, we will not live as long as we could otherwise."

Maggie closed her eyes, and thought about what I had said. She opened her eyes. "I think I understand what you are saying in your Declaration; you have to have enough plants dedicated to you for you to have a right to life. Are there other ways the carbon dioxide could be converted? Submarines can spend months underwater without any of the crew dying."

"Submarines either store oxygen in pressurized tanks, or they generate oxygen from water by electrolysis. They take the carbon dioxide out of the air by chemical reactions in scrubbers. It all takes a lot of energy to do those functions, and that energy doesn't just disappear, but it becomes unavailable like the heat from your coffee cup. The crew's time is limited, because they don't have ways to get all of the entropy, the unavailable energy, out of the submarine. If they are underwater too long, they die well before their natural deaths would occur. Plants also produce entropy when they convert the carbon dioxide and water into oxygen and carbohydrates. That entropy's in the form of heat, and it's exported into outer space as radiant heat."

"That's a lot to take in right now, so suppose I take your word for it. What's the problem you want my help with?"

"This community we're trying to develop requires considerable land area per person, and the legal system of land ownership creates problems for people having what we're calling a domain by right."

"What is the problem? Can't they just buy the land? How much land is this per person?"

I drew a deep breath. "I'll answer your last question first. A world average is about 100 acres, but it varies with the biological activity in a given area."

"So, how much are we talking about in Wyoming?"

"Wyoming is a little below average, so Wyoming averages about 125 acres."

Maggie sat back again and looked thoughtful. "That is quite a chunk of land. My family of five would need about 625 acres then?"

"That's right," I said, "almost a section, a section being 640 acres. Of course one problem we foresee with people buying land is the cost, but probably a bigger problem is the fact it can legally be taken away from them. If they get in arrears in their taxes, the land is sold for delinquent taxes. It can be seized by the police if they even suspect it might have been used somehow in illegal drug activity. If the courts rule the owner is incompetent and a guardian is appointed, the guardian can sell the land to someone else; or it can be seized by eminent domain for some perceived greater good. There are probably other ways I am not aware of that land can be legally taken away. You'd know more about these issues than I do. Then when a person dies, the heirs may want to subdivide or turn the land into a toxic waste site, or do something else we didn't want to happen."

"I see your point," Maggie said. I could see the wheels of her mind were starting to turn. "Do you have any suggestions?" she asked.

"I'm wondering whether we could form some sort of corporation as a land holder to eliminate some of these problems and at least reduce the risk of losing the land; a 501(c)(4) social welfare organization perhaps?"

"Tax law is not my specialty," Maggie said. "I know generally what a 501(c)(3) is, but I haven't heard of a 501(c)(4) social welfare organization. I don't feel comfortable giving you advice on this subject."

"I appreciate you being up front with me about that," I said, "but I really didn't come here today to get your advice about a social welfare organization."

"You're just a fount of mysteries today," Maggie said. "So, what DID you come to talk about?"

"Ralph has offered to sell us 40-acres to build our community; the meadow where we had our picnic last Thursday. I need to know the legal issues with building a community, initially for six to ten people, and eventually housing up to 50 people on that location. We plan to grow our own food in a greenhouse, provide our own water by capturing rainwater and recycling water in the greenhouse, and handle and recycle our own wastes. Are there zoning issues we need to be aware of? I will need a contract with Ralph, but should I buy it personally and then put it into a corporation, or should I form a corporation first and have it buy the land directly?"

Maggie was scribbling notes as I was talking. "Let me do some research on these issues, and get back to you. If nothing else, I can find some people who do know about these topics, so either I can learn something about them or I can put you in touch with them directly. Meanwhile, I would suggest you work out the exact terms of your purchase with Ralph. We'll need those details to write the contract. How soon do you propose closing on this land?"

"I expect to have the money in hand by the end of the week or early next week. I'd like to move quickly, so I'd say sometime next week."

Maggie looked surprised. "Usually real estate deals take considerably more time than that, with inspections, title searches, and such."

"I don't think the title search will take long because the land has been in Ralph's family since it was homesteaded. I'm eager to get things moving, and so is Ralph."

"Okay. I'll have time today and tomorrow. Why don't you get back to me on Wednesday; say 2:20?"

"Got it." I took my leave.

After talking with Maggie, I realized much of what we wanted to do was unorthodox, and I needed to try finding out for myself how we could fit our project into the existing social-legal structure. I began by looking up the Carbon County Zoning Map and the Carbon County Zoning Regulations. I began reading.

These resources led me to the conclusion it was possible to build Civalia within the existing zoning framework, but we would need to carefully dot all our i's and cross all our t's. We needed a site plan, which required a land survey, but that was also needed for the land purchase anyway. To design and develop the viable, self-sustaining Civalia community, we needed data on geophysical, meteorological, materials, and soils; plant and animal surveys; water and mineral rights information; and a whole host of other information on the North Platte River Valley community. The scope of the project was daunting, but also exciting.

Then the reticence of Stellan and Cass came to mind, and my enthusiasm dimmed but did not go out. I called Stellan; his phone rang several times and then went to voice mail. I left him a message asking when they planned to visit Ralph. I then checked with my broker, and found out my funds would probably be in my bank account by Thursday; an unusually swift response from my financial institution.

I then called a friend who worked for an engineering survey firm and inquired into surveying services. He told me they were fairly busy, but he could probably have a crew free in about a week and a half. I made a booking for their services, and then made a trip to the Geological Services office on the University campus to pick up the relevant quad maps, both paper and digital. The Civalien Project was beginning to assume concrete form for me. I hoped it was also becoming more real for Cass, Gyan, Cindy, and Stellan.

That evening Stellan called.

"Hi," he said, "All of us met with Ralph yesterday. Why don't you come over and let's talk about it."

"Aren't you going to give me a hint about what you think?" I asked. Stellan can be a man of few words, and his brusqueness worried me.

"Nope. Just come over and we'll talk."

"Okay," I said, and hung up.

When I arrived at Stellan's, I found the whole group was there; Stellan, Cindy, Cass, and Gyan. Stellan offered us all something to drink, but I declined; too nervous. Stellan opened the proceedings.

"All of us are very impressed with Ralph and the depth of his knowledge of the land and the biome of the region. What he has done with his ranch is extraordinary, given the social pressures to put monetary returns ahead of all other considerations. Our opinion is the Lazy HZ would be a suitable location for Civalia . . ."

My heart leaped . . .

". . . except for the issue of Mr. Wainright."

. . . and plunged back down.

Stellan looked at the others, and they all nodded.

"We would like to hear what you have to say about that issue."

I sat for a moment, trying to calm myself and gather my thoughts. "Wainright is certainly an issue," I said. "Ralph may have told you about our blocking his access, and his reaction."

Stellan nodded.

"Closing the road on that day increased his costs significantly, and further actions along those lines are bound to put more pressure on him. I don't know for certain, but Ralph told me rumors are circulating; he may be getting static from his banker. Did Ralph show you the building Wainright calls his office complex, but is probably really his house?"

Cass answered. "No, Ralph did not show us any of Wainright's buildings. Are they significant?"

"What's significant is that particular building is ostentatious, at least on the outside. I, of course, have not seen the inside. Actually, most everything the man does is showy and over the top. He drives a Hummer with a vanity plate that reads 'TOPDOG,' and when we went into town to have dinner one evening, we saw him in a bar with a group of sycophants. He was holding court, very loudly dominating the conversation, and commanding the center of attention. Even his clothing is flashy. The man wears an actual ten-gallon hat, for God's sake. If he is building the Jim Baker's Retreat on borrowed money, he is vulnerable."

"Is there any way to find out for sure if that's the case?" Gyan asked.

"I think it's pretty clear he is. Ralph told me he checked with the County Clerk's Office in Rawlins, and there is a healthy mortgage on the land, and another one on the office complex, the only completed building. Unless I miss my guess, there either is or soon will be one or more contractors' liens on the new construction caused by our little caper of closing the road. I'll check next week to see if anything has shown up in the legal notices or the Clerk's Office. The concrete supplier can't be happy after what happened with his trucks, and probably the general contractor is also unhappy. Unless he, George Callaway is his name, walked out of the site, he was trapped there for over 24 hours. He probably didn't have much to do, since a concrete pour was scheduled and didn't happen. To add insult to injury, he was trapped with Wainright; not a situation I'd want to be in."

"Things could get ugly," Stellan said.

"Yes, they could, but I think in the long run, Ralph will prevail.

His standing in the community is excellent, and Wainright's is shit. Ralph and I discussed dialing up the pressure. Then even if Wainright takes the issue to court, Ralph has enough legal standing to at least delay things for long enough to severely damage or kill his construction project."

Stellan looked at the others and then looked at me with a grim look. My heart sank.

"Here's the deal," he said. "We think there is merit in building Civalia on the land offered by Ralph. There is much to recommend it. Not least is the fact it's an affordable solution to get started with the Civalien Project. However, the potential for significant friction with Wainright cannot be ignored, and since he has come face to face with you, and he is likely to come after you as well as Ralph, we do not think you should be among the initial residents of Civalia."

Stellan's words cut me, and yet they did not. Had I not seen me walking away from the construction of Civalia in my dream?

Stellan continued. "Obviously, you will still be a part of the Civalien Project, and as we see it, your main job right now is to obtain the land and set up whatever structure is best for preserving and protecting Civalia and the land. We'll adopt Gyan's ramp-up strategy, starting with a small portion of the Civalia residents and infrastructure, a group of six to eight individuals, living in Gyan's keyhole. We'll add more residents as we are able to expand."

Stellan shifted in his chair and faced me more directly. "Cass has the immediate responsibility of identifying and recruiting a couple of other key initial citizens of Civalia; a chemist with a broad knowledge base and a medical person to initiate early and effective population control. Cass will cut her current work to half-time, and I will supplement her income until we have some sort of residence available on the land. I have decided to retire from my consulting work and devote my full time to the design of Civalia. We will have to farm out some of the work, but you and I will do the bulk of the design. Gyan has secured a lecturer position at the University, and he will continue to teach until we have some sort of initial greenhouse structure completed. He will then leave his job and move into Civalia. Cindy will keep us all entertained and prevent us from being too serious. When we have a suitable design, all of us will participate in the construction."

"I guess it's time to break out the gray pants," I said past the lump in my throat. All of them looked at me blankly, and I realized they had no idea what I was talking about. "Stellan," I said, "will you take a walk with me?"

"Sure," he said. We both got up and walked out his front door, his arm around my shoulders.

The evening was cool, but thankfully not windy. We walked along in silence for about half a block, and then I spoke, "Stellan, I know this was very difficult for you, as it was for me, but I knew it was coming."

Stellan stopped and spun me around to face him. "What do you mean?" he asked. "Did someone tell you about our discussions and decision?"

"No," I recounted my dream to him, and we resumed walking. "I had on gray pants in my dream."

"I wondered about your comment on gray pants, but I've also been wondering why you were so positive about Ralph's meadow being the spot for Civalia. Your dream answers both of those questions."

We walked a ways farther in silence. Stellan again spoke. "That was one of the hardest things I've done for a long, long time; telling you we didn't think you should be one of the original residents in Civalia."

"That was difficult for me, also," I confessed, "but I'd probably have bowed out anyway."

"Why is that?" Stellan asked, sounding incredulous.

"If we form an IRS social welfare organization or some other kind of non-profit corporation, the directors cannot benefit directly from the corporation. Some very dedicated directors having the best interests of Civalia in mind will be absolutely necessary to make certain it doesn't get hijacked like the non-profit I told you about. I'm probably the logical person to head up the Board of Directors."

"How many directors do you need?

"The statues call for a minimum of three."

"Do you have others in mind?"

"I thought I'd ask Ralph, and then see if Maggie would be the third. If she accepts, she will also keep us in line legally."

Stellan and I had walked around his block and we were approaching his sidewalk. He stopped and gave a little shiver. "Somehow this whole endeavor seems to be a lot bigger than just the five or six of us involved in it."

"It does seem that way, doesn't it," I said

We began walking up to the door. "When do you think you might actually buy the land?" Stellan asked.

"I'll have the money in hand by the end of the week, and I'm meeting with Maggie Wednesday. I hope to finalize my plans by the end of next week. I've arranged for a survey in about a week and half, and I'd like to get everything wrapped up in about two weeks. But to be safe, call it a month."

Stellan whistled, "That is quick. Is Ralph on board with all that?"

"I'll probably either call him or go visit him tomorrow, or sometime Wednesday, and lay out my plans."

We stopped in front of the door. "I think I'll go on home from here," I said. "You can tell the rest of them about my dream if you want."

"I think I'll keep that to myself," he said.

We embraced and I walked back down his sidewalk.

CHAPTER 10

The next morning I began the day working on my LPE project. I called Ralph after I figured he was back from his morning chores. He was, and I told him about my thoughts on buying the land with a non-profit social welfare organization to avoid some of the difficulties associated with private ownership. He allowed that made sense, so I asked him if he would be one of the three directors of such a corporation. Ralph agrereed. The third thing I asked him was if he could come to Laramie the next day, Wednesday, to outline exactly where the land boundaries would be, and to meet with Maggie and me. Ralph said he could, and we agreed to meet at 1:30. I next called Maggie and set a meeting time for 3:00.

I went back to the LPE project and worked on it the rest of the day. I definitely needed to keep my mind busy and off thoughts of Civalia. Some of the mathematical models of the LPE had begun to look very interesting. Furthermore, it appeared to be a project with a very small entropy footprint. If the engine block was constructed of something like reinforced concrete, the working fluid was CO_2, the heat input came from solar radiation, and the output turbine was constructed of a ceramic material, the engine would have few parts producing large amounts of entropy in their manufacture. The generator, the high-pressure tubing, the wiring, and the controls would all be highly entropic, but if the engine had a long service life, possible because of very few moving mechanical parts, the overall entropy footprint ought to be small.

I decided to build a prototype LPE and began rounding up materials. Some I had or knew where they could by obtained. A main piece, the solar collector, I had; a seven-foot diameter, aluminum, parabolic dish; a microwave antenna in its previous incarnation.

Polishing the aluminum would turn it into a dandy high temperature solar collector. I also had a couple of small variable displacement, high-pressure pumps, and the required tubing and fittings could be obtained from distributors in Denver. I also had much of the required electrical components. The turbine was another matter.

When I began doing calculations on the turbine, I received a pleasant surprise. Because liquid CO_2 is less viscous than water and is denser at the pressures envisioned for the LPE, the turbine could be smaller than a comparable water turbine. For the prototype, the best way to produce a turbine might be to have it 3D printed. However, the time and expense for that option made it impractical. Instead, I decided to use a standard hydraulic gear motor as an energy conversion mechanism. Such a motor might not last very long, since it would be poorly lubricated by the working fluid, but should last long enough to prove the concept. I might even be able to replace the metallic gears with some self-lubricating ones. Since the liquid CO_2 would be moving back and forth in the LPE chamber, I needed a fluid rectifier to run the generator in a single direction. This was easily accomplished with standard check valves. An accumulator smoothed the fluid flow.

I managed to occupy my time until Ralph arrived at my door. He was slightly early, but that was okay because it gave him time to tour my shop, exclaim on my antique car collection, and have some iced tea before we sat down with my set of quad maps. Ralph outlined the area he was thinking of for the forty acres, and having seen the area, I could not imagine having a better layout.

"Are you sure this is what you want to sell?" I asked Ralph. "The area you've outlined includes some of the best features in the whole area."

"Sure is," he said. "Wouldn't be much sense in doin' it if they weren't."

I got out my engineering scales and drawing equipment, and we roughly laid out where Civalia would be located.

"If it's okay with you, I'll arrange for some surveyors to stake this, probably next week," I said.

"The sooner the better," he answered.

"And after the contract is signed, I'd like to send in a geo-technical crew to get a picture of the subsurface. Would that be alright?"

"Ya do it right, John. We wouldn't want no buildin' on Civalia ta collapse, not if it's gonna last. I assume ya ain't gonna put up any shacks that'll collapse in a week. What're you plannin' on buildin'?"

"We have yet to design the building, or buildings, for Civalia, but if I have my way, they will be very substantial and last for hundreds of years."

We wrapped up our planning session and headed off for Maggie's Office. I brought the quad map with the proposed land purchase drawn on it. Maggie greeted us, and after the initial "How was your drive over?" and other pleasantries, she got down to business.

"First, I discussed your tax issues with one of my colleagues, and his take on it is no organization form fits it exactly, because what you're trying to do is way outside the mainstream of normal commerce. So your social welfare organization, a type of catchall category, is about as close as you can get. His suggestion is you incorporate as a non-profit, apply for C4 status, and be prepared for a long, drawn-out, debate with the IRS. We can help you pre-pare your IRS application to maximize the probability of a favor-able ruling. This leads us to the non-profit corporation. Have you given any thought to that?"

"Yes," I said. "As I understand the corporate structure, we will need a board of directors with a minimum number of three; a president, vice president, and secretary/treasurer."

"You're correct," Maggie answered. "I think those people are more critical than usual for officers of an ordinary non-profit, since your goal is to protect land in a multi-generational frame. I think I heard you throwing around the number 500 years last Thursday."

"You heard correctly," I said.

"I would suggest you do not make a membership organization, since if you do manage to grow, the logistics rapidly become unmanageable, and you cannot know the mindset of the future members. I would also suggest you make a self-perpetuating board, and you build in some pretty stiff requirements for board members, perhaps even a probationary period. Do you have some prospective board members in mind?"

"Well, yes," I said. "Ralph is one."

Maggie looked sharply at Ralph. "I expected you to be a member of the community; Civalia did you call it?"

Ralph grinned at Maggie. "Oh, I'm expectin' I'll have a lot uh contact with Civalia. So far, they're all people I like really well, but I'm gettin' along in years, an' I'll probably be just as happy in my own home. I'll just ride Lester up there once in a while so Cindy can go for a ride."

"You know, don't you, that you cannot receive any compensation for being on the board of directors?" Maggie asked.

"Yes, ma'am. John, done told me that, but I figger I'll get lots uh compensation, just not in dollars an' cents. I'll get ta see the land I've work hard ta protect for most uh my life pass on ta those who'll do the same. A man can't ask for more'n that, can he?"

"I guess not," Maggie said. She looked back at me. "Any others?" she asked.

"Me," I said.

Now Maggie looked really surprised. "You? How can you be on the board of directors? You're a founding member of Civalia. If you're living there and receiving substantial benefits from the social welfare organization, you can't be on the board."

"I won't be living there," I said. "I have other things to do, such as seeing that the land can be domains for the citizens of Civalia; plus Ralph and I have a crusade to wage against his interloping neighbor."

"That's right," Ralph said. "We're goin' after that skunk."

"Nothing illegal, I hope." Maggie said, regaining some of her composure.

"Of course not," I told her. "We plan to use the legal system to try to stop what he has done through the legal system. We just plan to be a little more competent than he has been. Obtaining Ralph's land without legal access was a powerful mistake on his part."

Ralph and I told Maggie the story of how we had blocked the private road into Wainright's project, and how we planned to continue the crusade.

I then asked her about my involvement. "If I . . . No, I mean, when I purchase 40 acres from Ralph," Ralph gave me an approving glance, "how will that effect Ralph's standing with Wainright, and what will that do to my standing? Wainright knows I exist, because I was helping Ralph, and he confronted me directly."

Maggie sat back and studied the ceiling for a few moments. Then she sat forward and looked at me. "I don't see your actions changing anything for Ralph, but it might open you up to actions from Mr. Wainright."

"Would you represent me, if Wainright does come after me?" I asked.

"That might be fun," she said. "I'd certainly consider it."

"Just like a lawyer," Ralph said, "a definite maybe."

We all laughed. "Getting back to our prior subject," I said, "would you consider being the third person on our board of directors?"

Maggie again looked surprised. "I'll consider it," she said, and then looked embarrassed. "A lawyerly answer," she added, looking at Ralph.

Ralph grinned at her, and then said, "Let's get ta the meat uh this here meetin,' if'nya'll pardon an old rancher his awful pun. We need a contract for this here land sale."

Maggie appeared glad to change the subject. She opened a drawer in her desk and pulled out three copies of a standard real estate sales contract, handed one to each of us and kept one for herself. The three of us read in silence for a while, and then began a spirited debate of various clauses. In general, Ralph and I were for simplifying the language and the terms, and Maggie argued for more lawyerly language. In the end, we arrived at a contract both Ralph and I considered understandable, concise, and what Ralph said his father called a woman's skirt contract; long enough to cover the subject, and short enough to be interesting. We couldn't complete the contract at that time because we didn't have the legal description. I told Maggie, I should have that by the end of the following week, so we made an appointment for the Wednesday two weeks away to complete the contract.

"I'll get on setting up the non-profit corporation," I told her, "and I'll try to get it done by early next week."

"That would be good, if you wish the buyer to be the corporation," she told me.

We all shook hands, and Ralph and I left. Outside, Ralph said, "She's a nice lady."

"That she is," I said, "but I think we need to start looking for a third member for the board of directors. Usually, when a lawyer says they will 'consider it,' the answer is negative. Do you have any ideas?"

Ralph thought about it for a while and then said, "Maybe. I'll have ta check."

We continued home. Ralph left for the Lazy HZ a short time later, but not before I extracted a promise from him to come and spend some time with me, maybe taking in an antique car show coming up a few weeks later.

The next two weeks were excruciatingly slow for me, but I did get a lot accomplished on my LPE project. I also developed the articles of incorporation for Civalien, Inc., and delivered those, plus the filing fee, to the Wyoming Secretary of State. I also met with Maggie and we began drafting the application to the IRS for social welfare organization status for my new corporation. We tried building some of the language about domains into the application, emphasizing the energy side of things and avoiding the use of the word entropy since we had no way of knowing what the level of understanding would be for the reviewers of the application. Most people have some understanding of energy, but few, in my experience, have an understanding of entropy. The days dragged on.

The survey came in on time, and the legal description was completed. The plot of land that Ralph directed the surveyors to stake was actually 41.256 acres, and I spent a little time arguing with Ralph about the extra 1.256 acres. He wanted to include the extra acreage in the original $80,000 price and I wanted to add $2,513.65, the cost for those extra 1.256 acres plus just one penny shy of the nickel per acre he refused to accept. Eventually, I partially won. Ralph agreed to accept the $2,512 for the extra land, but he balked at accepting the extra four cents per acre. We shook hands on the deal.

"In the long run, we may not be done with these negotiations," I told Ralph, "because your land is worth more than we're paying you."

"We'll see about that," Ralph answered.

These negotiations had taken place after I dropped off a copy of the survey for Maggie to finish the contract and write the deed, and I'd driven over to the Lazy HZ to show Ralph the results of the survey. We were sitting on Ralph's front porch, under the watchful eyes of Gerald. He must have been getting used to me, because he did not scold me nearly as long as he used to. Ralph said, "If ya've got the time, there's someone I'd like ya' ta meet."

"Sure. Are they coming over?"

"Nope. We'll have ta go there."

Ralph and I took his truck, because he told me the roads weren't very good. That was an understatement. We drove back to highway 230, then toward Riverside before turning off to the left onto a two-track road. It got worse. There were gullies to cross, rocks sticking up, and pot holes that seemed a foot deep. The Cadillac would not have had a chance. About three miles in, we came on a rustic cabin with a few out buildings, one of them being an outhouse with the classic crescent moon cut into the door. There were some corrals around what I assumed was a barn. An elderly woman, her gray hair done up in a bun on the back of her head, stood in the doorway of a medium size cabin. She wore a long white dress that looked like it was probably in style in the early 1900s. A medium-sized crockery bowl rested in the crook of one arm, and she held a large wooden spoon in her other hand. A cat was rubbing against her ankles, which were encased in high top, lace up boots.

"'Bout time you comed to see me," she shouted as we climbed out of the truck.

"Maybe we'd come more often if'n ya'd fix yer road a little," Ralph shot back.

The woman snorted, "Keeps the riffraff out 'ceptin' you. This here the young man, the one ya tol' me about?"

"Yup. Geraldine, this here's John Tantivy." Ralph held out a brown paper sack, which had been resting on the seat of the truck. "I brought ya some uh those tarts ya like so well."

I almost burst out laughing when I realized the source for the name of Ralph's squirrel. I must not have hid my mirth very well, or I had a shit-eating grin on my face, because Geraldine looked at me a little fiercely and said, "So, I kin see you put two an' two together, and figgered out that Ralph here named that crazy squirrel after me. Cept'n he didn't figger out Geraldine didn't have no tits until I told him. So Geraldine became Gerald."

Both Ralph and Geraldine burst out laughing, and I joined in. "I'm pleased to meet you," I said, having to wipe tears of laughter from my eyes. What an introduction.

"You all better come in and have some tarts while I finish up these cinnamon rolls," Geraldine said as she turned and went back inside, leaving the door open for us. The cat followed her in.

"Geraldine's 're some uh the best cinnamon rolls ya'll ever have," Ralph told me. "I bribe 'er with tarts ta keep her makin' me some once in a while."

The easy banter continued between these two, and I came to appreciate the deep bond that must exist between them. Ralph began to explain their connection.

"Geraldine was a neighbor uh mine until Wainright split us up. I used ta ride Lester over here once in a while ta visit, but I can't do that no more. So Geraldine looks after the land on this side uh that there ravine. She runs a few sheep an' some goats, but she's as interested in the land as me. Her grandma homesteaded this place 'bout the same time Grandad did mine."

"Granny was a real corker," Geraldine said, waving her wooden spoon. "One of 'er hired hands shot 'er in the neck one time, an' dumped 'er in the crick, stole her strong box, and rode away with it in 'er wagon. Her dog drug 'er out an' she went after the guy when she'd recovered. Took 'er eight months to find 'im, and two weeks to drag 'im back."

Ralph added to Geraldine's story. "She means it when she says her grandma dragged 'im back. Brought 'im back at the end of a rope, and when he tripped or couldn't walk no more, she'd sometimes drag 'im behind her horse. Guy was a little worse for wear when she got 'im back here. The judge felt a little sorry for 'im, an' figger'd he'd been punished enough. Set 'im free, but he wasn't much more'n a beggar; couldn't walk much or use his arms or hands right."

I was fascinated. These two people had so much history behind them, and apparently so much love of the land. "How did you come to understand the land so well?" I asked Geraldine.

"Oh, I've lived here ever since I was a girl, an' Granny told me things, Ma told me things, an' I noticed things. Old Ralph here helped too. He explained a lot of things to me. I've never had no formal education, did learn a little readin' an' writin' from Ma."

"Maybe you're lucky," I said. "If you'd have gone to school, they probably would have tried their best to teach you it was not only your right, but your duty, to plunder and destroy this land. You'd have been taught to 'maximize your return.' That means make the most money from it possible, even if that leaves it in ruins."

"Maybe you're right 'bout that, if'n Wainright's any example," she said.

Geraldine uncovered a large crockery bowl that was filled with dough. She dumped it, punched it down, rolled the dough out, covered it with the cinnamon sugar mixture she had finished mixing in the medium sized bowl she had been carrying. She then rolled the dough into a long cylinder.

"Why'nt you cut these," she said to Ralph, "while I fire up the stove."

Ralph picked up a knife from the counter and went to work on the cylinder while Geraldine added some wood to the fire box on the stove and adjusted the dampers. I'd noticed that the stove was warm already, but soon it was roaring. I looked around Geraldine's home while the two of them worked on the cinnamon rolls, Geraldine placing the rolls in the pan as Ralph cut them.

There were a number of framed landscape photographs on her walls and several more wildlife photos. They were very good. When Geraldine and Ralph finished getting the cinnamon rolls in the pan, she covered it with a tea towel and slid it into the warming oven.

"Let's go out on the porch," she said. "It'll be cooler."

We went out, and I sat on the steps while Ralph and Geraldine sat in the two chairs on the porch.

"Ralph told me you might like me to be a director or some such thing for a company yer formin'" she said to me. "I ain't never been such a thing, an' I don't know much about it. What'd I have to do?"

"We'd have to meet occasionally, at least once a year," I said, "and we'd have to guard against anyone doing something they shouldn't to the land."

"Ralph tol' me that much. I want ya to tell me more."

The three of us spent the rest of the afternoon discussing Civalia, what we hoped to accomplish, and the underlying ideas. Geraldine got up once to put the cinnamon rolls in the oven to bake, then again a couple of times to turn them or move them to an upper shelf, and after the tantalizing smell of freshly baked cinnamon rolls had just about killed all of our conversation, she took them out of the oven. They were delicious, and I had to agree with Ralph's assessment. They were also the best cinnamon rolls I'd ever eaten.

The evening was coming on when Ralph stretched, patted his stomach, and began to make noises about leaving. After two, or maybe it was three, cinnamon rolls, I was feeling ready for some really leisure activity or maybe even a nap. Geraldine went into her house and returned with the paper bag, now containing some of her cinnamon rolls, which she handed to Ralph.

206

"Give this young whippersnapper some of these before he goes home," she told Ralph, and she turned to me and said, "Come back sometime, an' I'll be one a yer directors."

I told her I would be back, and I thanked her profusely. Then Ralph and I bumped back down her road to the highway. We were mostly quiet on the way back, but I did remark to Ralph, "Geraldine is a remarkable woman."

"More than you know," Ralph said. "'Er mother died when she was in 'er early twenties, an' she has run that place ever since. Did ya notice that there stone fireplace?"

"Yes, it's beautiful."

"Well, Geraldine decided one day she'd like a fireplace, so she built herself one. Gathered all them rocks 'erself an' laid 'em all. I think she did get a book from the library on fireplaces, but no one else helped 'er any. It works good, too."

Ralph insisted I spend the night, and I was not too inclined to object. He fed me well, and I slept soundly. Ralph was out, probably doing some chores, when I got up and moving, so I left him a note thanking him for his hospitality and the cinnamon roll I took as my breakfast. Before I had driven very far, I had eaten the cinnamon roll and wished I had taken two.

When I got home, the incorporation papers from the Secretary of State's office were finally in my mail box. They had been much slower coming than I expected, but everything seemed to be coming together. I made a trip to my bank, opened an account for Civalien, Inc., and then transferred monies for the land with an added 20% for other expenses into the account.

When I got back home, I called Maggie to verify she had everything ready. She did, and I made an appointment for the next day, again at 3:00. I told her we had found a third person for the Civalien, Inc. Board of Directors, and Maggie told me she was glad, because she didn't really think she could do it, and besides it would be a conflict of interest if I continued to use her for the corporation's legal needs.

I then called Ralph, arranged for him to come to Laramie, and since we needed to have the inaugural meeting of Civalien Inc., asked him to invite Geraldine. He agreed to ask her and said he'd let me know if she couldn't make it. If she couldn't, I told him I'd make a run over there in the morning. I suggested they both bring overnight supplies because our business might run late.

I called Stellan and asked him if he could round up the rest of the Civalia team for dinner Wednesday evening starting at 5:30, so we might all share our latest news. Stellan called me back later and told me Cass and he could make it at 5:30, but Cindy was playing softball and had a late afternoon game. She and Gyan would not be able to come until shortly after 6:00.

I'd made all the arrangement I could, but I still felt wired. More work on the prototype LPE was the therapy I prescribed for myself, and polishing the solar collector seemed the right kind of mindless activity. I spent several hours working on the dish. It was a weird experience, since being above the dish, even though I was not in the exact focal point, the sound reflections gave all sorts of strange effects. I took to humming and singing to myself to hear the sound distortions and variations in loudness. Sometimes I'm easily entertained. These activities did help me take my mind off the upcoming Civalia events.

Ralph called back that evening. Yes, they both could make it to Laramie, and no, they could not stay overnight. There were animals to care for, but they could stay for dinner. I had to be satisfied with that.

Sleep was slow in coming, and when it finally did, it was restless. I was groggy in the morning, but a hot and then cold shower helped. I tried working on the LPE engine. However, after successively ruining two tubing fittings, I gave up and just paced the floor. Ralph and Geraldine drove up at exactly 10:42. I knew that, because I'd been watching the clock as well as pacing. I opened the door before they could ring the bell and welcomed them in.

"I've been tellin' Geraldine 'bout yer cars," Ralph said. "We better have a look at those before we get down ta business."

"Sure," I said and led them into the shop.

"They're beautiful!" Geraldine exclaimed when I removed the car covers.

"Those are the most common words out of everyone's mouth the first time they see these cars," I told her.

"Well," Ralph said, "I remember seein' some uh 'em back when I was a kid, an' I don't remember any uh 'em lookin' this good."

"Me neither," Geraldine added.

We poked around the cars and the rest of the shop for a while and finally went back into the apartment. I got us some glasses of water, and we all sat down at the table. I called the meeting to order.

"As the incorporator of Civalien, Inc., I call this meeting to order and hereby appoint you Ralph Hertell and you Geraldine . . ." I realized I did not know Geraldine's last name. I'm sure my face turned beet red. "I'm sorry," I said, "but I've never been told your last name."

Geraldine and Ralph laughed. Ralph said, "I guess I plumb forgot to tell ya. I'll try again. John, this here's Geraldine Olsen. Her folks hailed from Norway back in the 1800s. We growed up next door to each other, an' she was like the little sister I never had."

"An' he was my ornery older brother," Geraldine said. "Still is."

"Okay," I said, "so I'm appointing both of you to be temporary directors until we can adopt bylaws and select directors according to the bylaws. I've got the Articles of Incorporation here." I passed them copies of that document. "These Articles of Incorporation I filed are just boilerplate and a formality, and these preliminary bylaws," I picked up a second stack of papers, "are also boilerplate. But we need to develop bylaws which really reflect how we plan to run this company." I handed out the boilerplate bylaws.

Ralph and Geraldine quickly read through these two documents, and when I saw that they were finished, I said, "I've made some changes to the bylaws, which I think address the needs of the Civalien project. So I need you to read these." I handed them each a third document. "We need to discuss these, make any changes necessary, and then vote to adopt them."

The two of them took their time reading this set of bylaws. Then Geraldine startled me by being the first to speak up, "You've written into the purpose for these 'ere bylaws lots of stuff 'bout energy, entropy, and such. Now don't you go gettin' me wrong, but this here stuff don't belong here. These here bylaws are public, and the public reading this here'll not understand it and think we've gone around the bend. Put this here stuff in a policies an' procedures manual."

Ralph nodded. "Makes sense ta me."

I was dumbfounded and speechless, realizing I had badly underestimated Geraldine. Ralph was grinning at me, obviously enjoying my discomfiture. "Ah-h-h. Good point," I said.

We argued briefly about the best wording for the purpose, and when we were done, I had to admit it was better than what I had come to the meeting with.

Ralph hit me next. "This smacks uh three dictators, you, me, and Geraldine, sittin' here decidin' what's best for a whole lot uh other folks. Now I know we can't have meetin's with hordes' uh folks all tryin' ta have their say, but maybe we ought ta have some sort'a advisory panels from each Civalia, if'n we get more'n one. That'd at least give them folks some sort uh suggestion box."

"Hear, hear," Geraldine said.

This went on for a lot longer than I had ever thought it might, but in the end the bylaws we approved transcended what I'd written by the proverbial extra mile.

"The next agenda item," I said, "is to elect officers, a president, vice-president, and a secretary/treasurer."

"I nominate John fer secretary/treasurer," Ralph said.

"I second it," Geraldine immediately added.

For the second time in the meeting, I was dumbfounded and speechless, realizing I had been assuming I would be the president of Civalien, Inc. "Discussion?" I managed to croak.

Ralph provided the explanation. "Well, this here company's goin' ta need lots uh money ta build these here Civalias, an' me 'n Geraldine are sort uh home bodies. So we figger'd you're the one ta go raise the cash, an' we'll stick around here, an' help 'em get things up an' runnin.'"

I had to admit Ralph had a point, but my ego was still bruised. I managed to ask, "Anymore discussion?" There wasn't any, so I called for the vote; two for and me abstaining.

"Look," Ralph said, "I know this is hard on ya. This here's yer baby, an' ya want ta be there when it grows up. But ya can't do ever'thing for 'em. Sometimes, ya just have ta step back, and let 'em get bucked off. Ya can help 'em get back on, but ya can't get bucked off for 'em."

I rallied and asked for nominations for vice-president.

"I nominate Ralph," Geraldine promptly said. I could tell these two had talked among themselves and decided how things were going to be before they arrived. They probably had a good reason, so I capitulated and seconded the nomination.

"Discussion?" I asked.

Geraldine gave the explanation that time. "Ralph is goin' to be sellin' this here company some land. It wouldn't look good for the head honcho to be benefitin' from his position."

"Any more discussion?" I asked. There was none, so I called for the vote for the position of vice-president. It was unanimous this time.

"I nominate Geraldine for President," I said before either of them could start the nomination.

"I second it," Ralph said.

"Discussion?" I asked. There was none, and the vote was unanimous. I turned the meeting over to Geraldine.

"How 'bout a treasurer's report, since you got the bank account?" she asked me.

I read off the balance in the bank account, followed by my motion, "I move Civalien, Inc. buy 41.256 acres of land from Ralph Hertell for the sum of $82,513.65."

"Why the 65 cents?" Geraldine asked.

I glanced at Ralph and then told Geraldine, "Ralph said he wouldn't take a nickel more than $2,000 per acre for the land, so I'm just making certain he gets the most possible for his land, $2,000.04 per acre."

Geraldine looked at Ralph, who was sporting a sort of re-signed smile. She looked back at me and said, "Well, you've put in your two cents worth, so I'll put in my two cents worth, makin' it four. I second the motion,"

It was my turn to grin at Ralph.

"At least ya didn't make it five cents," he said. "That might uh sunk the deal." He smiled at me.

Geraldine called for the question and the motion was passed with two ayes and Ralph's abstention.

We closed the meeting, I hurriedly wrote up the minutes of the meeting, and we left for Maggie's office.

Our meeting with Maggie was business-like. I introduced Geraldine to Maggie, produced the incorporation papers for Civalien, Inc., and then produced the minutes from our first meeting. Maggie read all of the documents thoroughly, and then produced the paperwork for the sale of the land. We all read the contract carefully, and then Ralph signed as the land owner, and Geraldine signed for Civalien, Inc. Maggie had their signatures notarized by her office staff.

I then wrote out a Civalien, Inc. check, payable to Ralph, for the sum of $82,513.65, signed the check as treasurer, and had Geraldine countersign. I handed the check to Maggie, and she handed Ralph a warrantee deed to sign, transferring the land from him to Civalien, Inc. Her secretary notarized Ralph's signature, and Maggie looked over all of the documents again to make certain they were in order. Finally, she handed the check to Ralph and the deed to Geraldine.

"Congratulations," Maggie said.

Pandemonium broke out. We hugged, laughed, shook hands with Maggie, tipped over her waste basket, and I wiped the tears from my eyes. Civalia had a home.

PART III

THE DEVELOPMENT OF CIVALIA

CHAPTER 11

I had made reservations for our celebratory dinner in the back room of a local Mexican Restaurant, Poncho's Inn. Geraldine, Ralph and I were the first ones there, arriving a little early, but we were not even seated and settled when Stellan and Cass walked in.

"Hi," Stellan greeted us and looked questioningly at Geraldine.

I addressed Geraldine. "I'd like you to meet Cassandra Martine and Stellan King." I turned to Stellan and Cass. "May I present Geraldine Olsen. Geraldine's a rancher, a neighbor of Ralph's. I'm going to postpone telling you about Geraldine's connection to Civalia until all of us are here."

Ralph and Geraldine smiled, but both Stellan and Cass looked puzzled. I began getting people seated with an eye to distributing our Civalien, Inc. board members among the Civalia crew. A waiter arrived to take drink orders, and conversation began to pickup. A short time later, Gyan and Cindy hurried in and I introduced them to Geraldine.

The conversations around the table increased in volume as the others began to warm to Geraldine, whose temperament seemed remarkably similar to Ralph's. I was mostly quiet, merely enjoying the growing camaraderie among our group. The waiter took our orders and soon began setting portions of our meals in front of us. The food was savory, the volume and intensity of conversation continued to increase, and I felt like a grandfather basking in the animation of his extended family.

Toward the end of the meal, when about half of us had finished our deserts, I arose from my seat and tapped my knife on my glass. The resulting thunks were disappointing, and I realized my "glass" was made of plastic. I utilized Geraldine's beer bottle to produce some louder glass sounding tings, although they were lower frequency than those produced by traditional water glasses. However, they did the job, and our group quieted down and looked expectantly at me.

"Friends," I said, "the Civalien Project is moving forward, and we have formed a corporation to be the land holder for Civalia. To tell you about the actions and plans of Civalien, Inc., please welcome the President, Geraldine Olsen."

There was a shocked silence followed by a sudden increase of murmurs from some of our group as I sat down and Geraldine stood up.

"I'm lookin' forward to gettin' to know ya all better, as we're workin' to make Civalia happen," Geraldine told us. "Civalien, Inc. has been set up as a social welfare organization, an' us three, me an' Ralph an' John, are the Board of Directors, an' our mission is to help ya all build Civalia an' to protect the land."

Geraldine took a sip of beer and continued, "To help ya best, we've decided to have a Civalia Advisory Panel, that's you all's job, to tell us what's needed an' how best to help ya. As of today we've also purchased some land from Ralph for you all to build on. So get to work."

Geraldine sat down, and silence reigned for a second or two before several people tried to speak all at once. Cass stood up and quieted the others. "Geraldine, Ralph, and John, we are honored to have you here, and we are grateful for your assistance in the effort of changing Civalia from a dream into a reality. We have also been at work, although you have just given us the incentive to work even harder. All of us have been contributing in our areas of expertise. I've been working in the area of what some would call human resources, a phrase I detest. I would rather consider myself a human community facilitator or perhaps a human amalgamation trainer; a person who works to combine unique individuals into a synergistic whole; with an acronym of H-A-T. Does that make me a 'hat'?"

She got a laugh from the whole group for her question, and then she continued, "Finding the individuals to create Civalia and helping to forge them into a cooperative community is awe inspiring work for me. I am thankful to have the opportunity to be a part of this effort."

Cass looked around at the other Civalia citizens, then back at Geraldine. "I think we understand why you have the formal organization to own and protect the land."

"And probably to provide a way to finance Civalia," I added.

Cass smiled at me, and then looked back toward Geraldine. "That too," she said, "but Civalia cannot be governed by such a formal organization as a corporation. We will be organized, but it will be a mutual benefit, consensus arrangement based on the *Declaration of life* with the long range goal of minimizing our entropy footprint. Knowledgeable individuals will provide leadership in their areas of expertise when needed, and we'll all provide labor when and where it's needed."

Cass sat down, and Geraldine stood up and applauded Cass. "Couldn't a said it better myself, an' we're here to clear the path for ya as best we can. You'll just have to let us know what ya need."

Geraldine sat down and I stood up. "Cass, I can understand you feel a little skeptical about having a corporation as a landlord, but with the existing legal structure we're all living under, this was the best way we could find to protect your domains from outside predators and, yes, even inside predators. We don't plan to micromanage the use of the lands, but we don't want people like Harold Wainright able to encroach."

Ralph spoke, so I sat down "I brought some copies uh the Civalien, Inc., bylaws, so's ya can read about what we've got in mind. Ya'll see we're goin' ta have a policies manual ta keep some uh yer ideas out uh the public eye." Ralph handed out copies of the bylaws. "Cass," he said, "it'll probably be up ta ya ta figger out how ta get some sort uh advisory board going. Why'nt you come over an' talk ta me an' Geraldine 'bout this here advisory board an' policies manual someday real soon?"

"I'd love to," Cass said. "I'll get your contact information from John and make arrangements with you."

"As host for this celebration," I said, standing up again, "I propose a toast to the launch of Civalia."

"Here's to Civalia!" the group chorused, raising their glasses and bottles high. We drank deeply and our dinner dissolved into excited talking and trading of information, particularly between Stellan and Geraldine.

Stellan turned to me and changed the subject. "I've noticed you've been sort of out of the loop of our planning lately, John, and now I can see why. The fact is you three," Stellan indicated Ralph, Geraldine, and me by a wave of his hand, "have established a major milestone in the creation of Civalia. That gives us added motivation to do our parts, the community structure by Cass, the biological infrastructure by Gyan, and the physical structure by me. We'll need all the help we can get to accomplish these goals, but I am confident we will."

The next day, bright and early, Stellan came over. "Let's go for a walk," he said to me.

I slipped on my jacket and we headed down the street. "I don't quite know how to say this to you, John, but the feelings I've experienced since we started this project, are . . . are a little over the top. It's like I'm on a train with all the rest of you in the Civalien Project, rushing off to some destination; I'm not quite sure where. I can walk around in the car, visit with all of you, but by the time I've made the circuit of the train car, we are in some new country. And yet there is a thrill to it all, and I don't want to not be on the train."

Stellan and I walked along in silence for about a quarter of a block. I scuffed my feet some, and then said, "I think I know how you feel. This whole thing of forming Civalien, Inc. and buying the land has an unreal quality about it. Meeting Ralph, meeting Geraldine, forming the corporation, and starting Civalia; that's a lot to take in."

"You expected to be President, didn't you?" Stellan asked.

"Yes," I said.

"What happened?"

I told Stellan about our first meeting the day before and how

Ralph and Geraldine had obviously talked things through together and then ramrodded me as Secretary/Treasurer and Ralph as VP.

"I'll bet that was a shock."

"It was," I said.

"What do you think about it? Is this some sort of insurrection we need to do something about?" Stellan asked.

"After Ralph and Geraldine told me their reasoning, and I've had time to think about it some, I've come to accept it as the best way to proceed. They thought I might be too much in Wainright's gun sights as president, Ralph couldn't be president because the sale of his land might look like a conflict of interest, and they thought I should be the one to work at raising the money to complete Civalia. I think their reasoning is sound, but I was still shocked. My first thought was I had missed the train altogether and was left standing at the station."

"I can see why you might feel that way," Stellan mused. We walked on for another half block, each of us lost in our own thoughts.

"If it gives you any consolation," I said, "I think Ralph and Geraldine are feeling somewhat the same about being on the train; maybe more so than we do, since we've had a lot longer to think about these issues than they have."

"Geraldine seems like a very strong woman," Stellan observed.

"Did anyone tell you the story of her Grandmother?"

"No. I assume it's interesting."

I told Stellan about Geraldine's grandmother homesteading the land where Geraldine was living. I related the story of her grandmother's hired hand shooting her in the neck, dumping her in the creek, and taking off with her wagon, horses, and other worldly goods. Then I told him how she was rescued by her dog dragging her out of the creek, and after her recovery, her months' long trek to find the guy and drag him back, sometimes literally, to face justice for his acts.

"Ralph later added a detail to that story when we were back at his place. He told me his grandfather was the one who supplied Geraldine's grandmother with a pair of horses to go after the guy."

"Wow!" Stellan said. "If Geraldine is anything like her grandmother, she must be one tough woman."

"As far as I can tell, she is. She also has a sense of humor."

I told Stellan about Ralph's squirrel being named after Geraldine, and the mix up with genders. Stellan laughed heartily. I joined his laughter, and that seemed to dispel the tension we had both been feeling during the first part of our walk. We headed back, telling each other our thoughts about Civalia.

"One reason I came over to your house so early," Stellan said, "was to see about getting together with you to work on the design for Civalia. Do you have time this morning?"

"If I didn't have time, I'd make it," I answered.

"Good," he said. "Gyan and Cindy will be joining us later, and will bring Cass."

Over the next couple of weeks, some combination of our team met almost daily to hammer out a concise set of design specifications for Civalia. In the process of developing these specifications, we discovered several unique ways of achieving our goals.

The first specification, a structural design life of 500 years, was the most contentious and took the most time. Such a long design life is not possible using common contemporary materials. One morning found Stellan and I sitting at my table where we argued over a suitable design life and the materials to achieve the lowest per-capita, per-year embodied energy for Civalia. Our search for long-lasting materials began when Stellan observed the 500-year design life I was advocating is more than twice as long as the United States has been in existence. That sobering thought brought to mind ancient structures, such as the Parthenon, now more than 2,000 years old; Stellan mentioned the Great Pyramid, approaching 3,600 years old. His comment sparked a memory, something I had read years ago, and I struggled to remember what it was. Then it came to me.

"Just a minute," I told him, and went out into my garage where I had stashed some boxes of books. I hadn't looked in those boxes for a number of years, but after 10 minutes of digging, I found the particular book I had in mind.

Design Specifications

- 500 years—structural design life
- 50 residents
- 3,000 sqft—per-capita Greenhouse area
- 1,000 sqft—per- capita common space area
- 1,000 sqft—per-capita private space area
- 750 sqft—per-capita work area
- 45% maximum relative humidity
- 25 gallons—maximum per-capita daily water consumption
- 15,000 gallons minimum water storage capacity
- 4—minimum number of water storage tanks; 2 hot and 2 cold
- 6 psi—maximum water pressure
- 300 cfm—minimum air ventilation rate
- 100 lbs—per-capita maximum annual solid waste generation
- 1,200 Watts—maximum per-capita average power consumption; both direct and embodied
- $10 million—maximum total cost
- 2,700 Calories—minimum average per-capita daily food production
- Minimum factor of safety 1.25
- 8.0—minimum average residential Satisfaction with Life Index value

When I got back, Stellan was at the counter refilling his coffee cup. He looked pointedly at his watch and said, "I'd hate to have to wait a few minutes for you instead of just a minute." Stellan had not been idle while I was gone, because he said, "Do you realize the Civalia structure we are considering will cover around 43% of the land area under the Great Pyramid?"

I was shocked, and Stellan must have picked up on my expression, because he smiled wryly. "This is no small project, is it?"

"No," I said, "but your wait for me will be worth it." I held up the book I had retrieved. "This book has something really interesting to say about the Great Pyramid." I handed him *The Book of Stone*, by Joseph Davidovits, Dr. rer. nat., Ingenieur E.N.S.C.R.

Stellan paged through the book, "Give me a synopsis."

"Davidovits studied the stones from the Great Pyramid and thinks there is evidence they are artificial. He thinks they were made from silt deposited by the Nile River mixed with a hydrated phosphate of copper and aluminum, sodium carbonate, and an aggregate composed of small shells. This mixture was cast in place, where it polymerized into the stone blocks of the pyramid. He thought this accounted for the astonishingly excellent fit of the stones, which don't have marks from stone working tools. He called the resulting stone geopolymer, and he has worked out some formulas to make it. If his work is valid, and we can build Civalia with similar material, we could design for a 500-year design life, or maybe even longer, judging from the age of the Great Pyramid."

Stellan set the book down and picked up his tablet computer. He was engrossed in his web search for a few minutes and then handed his computer to me so I could see what he had found. "Look at this, John. Geopolymers aren't a major industry yet, but they appear to be making some inroads. I wonder if this has any connection with Roman concrete."

On Stellan's computer screen I saw there were a variety of people and companies working on geopolymers, and I saw something else very interesting. Fly ash can be a basis for them. I also saw Dr. Davidovits was still around, president of the Geopolymer Institute. "Interesting," I said and gave the computer back to Stellan. "This all brings to mind another piece of information I learned many years ago. Some people have advocated using sulfur in place of concrete. Molten sulfur can be poured into forms with reinforcing, just like Portland cement. A great feature of using sulfur is it can be re-melted and modified or repaired or reused."

"Hold that thought," Stellan told me. "I just did a search on Roman concrete, and some of that concrete work is still around today with little or no wear after 2,000 years. There are a number of articles that point to research on the composition of this material and how to make it. So, Roman concrete might also be a possibility for long design life material. Let me look up your sulfur concrete." Stellan worked his keyboard again. "There are a few references, but not very many. Probably the greatest disadvantage of sulfur is that it burns."

"What is the autoignition temperature?" I asked.

"Let's see." Stellan searched for the 'ignition temperature of sulfur'. "232 degrees Celsius."

"That's just slightly less than paper." I said, imagining a structure nearly half the footprint of the Great Pyramid on fire. "I think we can rule out sulfur concrete. The fire hazard would be unacceptable, but it might make a good material for sealing cracks and making weight distribution pads for columns. I've seen it used for that purpose on concrete test samples. So where are we now?"

"Geopolymers and Roman concrete put a design life of 500 years within the realm of possibility. The fact geopolymers may be made from industrial waste, such as fly ash, can drive the cost down. That's intriguing. I'll look into it more."

During this time, Stellan developed a technology that would have an immense impact on the viability of Civalia. This technology involved growing artificial shell material, basically calcite. His process had a biologic basis, and was driven by solar energy. He was not able to develop it sufficiently for basic construction purposes, but it was far enough along to supply smaller, incidental items. Where it really excelled was in developing optical coatings for various energy collection and distribution systems, and for entropy export systems.

Since greenhouses produce a lot of water vapor, I dreamed up a solar powered dehumidifier. Besides reducing mold and mildew issues, dehumidifying the greenhouse had a side benefit of producing sufficient potable water to more than meet per capita water needs in Civalia. The extra water could be ponds, waterfalls, small streams, or fountains.

Gyan suggested using bamboo grown in the greenhouse for water distribution pipes, since we were planning on a low-pressure water system. Although bamboo pipes would not have a 500-year design life, replacements can be grown rapidly, and bamboo is useful for many other purposes.

To control heat transfer through the greenhouse glazing, both

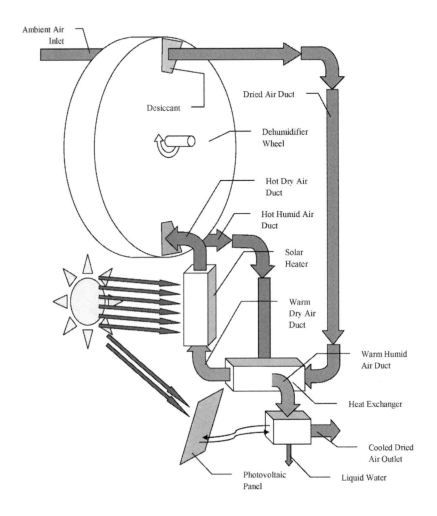

Ambient Air Inlet

Desiccant

Dried Air Duct

Dehumidifier Wheel

Hot Dry Air Duct

Hot Humid Air Duct

Solar Heater

Warm Dry Air Duct

Warm Humid Air Duct

Heat Exchanger

Cooled Dried Air Outlet

Photovoltaic Panel

Liquid Water

excess heat gain and heat loss, I dredged up an innovation I had experimented with in the distant past, wet foam, essentially soap suds. When air is bubbled through a suitable fluid mixture contained between two layers of glazing, foam is generated. When the air is shut off, the foam decays over time, so the insulating properties can be adjusted to suit the environmental conditions.

Cass developed a Civalia-specific Satisfaction with Life Index, based on *Maslow's Hierarchy of Needs* and our perceived happiness, contentment, and satisfaction. We all considered this an outstanding measuring tool for how well Civalia works. All of us could hardly wait to try it out when living in Civalia, because when we applied it to our pre-Civalia lives, our scores were not stellar.

Stellan and I worked together to accelerate development of my solar powered LPE using liquid carbon dioxide as the working fluid. The story of how my LPE project became an integral part of Civalia began when Stellan dropped by one morning in the second week of our planning.

"One reason I came over to your house so early," Stellan said, "was to see about getting what data I could from you on your wet foam insulation. That's probably going to be a key item to keep the supplemental energy requirement low."

"I'll have to dig it out for you, since I haven't worked on that project for several years."

We went into my shop, and I began looking through the filing cabinets, which held information on my various projects over the years. Stellan wandered over and began examining my LPE project.

"What's this?" he asked

"That's my liquid piston engine," I answered, still pawing through file folders. "I haven't had time to tell you about it."

"Does it work?" he asked.

"Close," I said, as I extracted the 'Wet Foam Experiment' file and shut the file drawer.

Stellan was closely examining the LPE, and his eyes followed the hoses snaking out through a window and out of sight.

"Where do those go?" he asked.

"I've got a parabolic dish on the roof to heat the working fluid."

"Which is? The working fluid, I mean."

"Carbon dioxide," I answered and then explained my reasoning for using CO_2.

Stellan and I fell into the type of technical give and take that had brought us together originally. Before we knew it, we were aligning the parabolic collector and attempting to fire up the LPE. The file on the wet foam experiment was forgotten.

When we finally broke for a very late lunch, the LPE was running. It was eerily quiet, just a swishing noise from the U-tube and some mechanical sounds from the gear motor. Over some hastily assembled sandwiches and canned soup, Stellan and I discussed how the LPE could be improved and used in Civalia.

We talked about using the energy available through the separation of salt and fresh water as a secondary backup system for converting solar energy into electrical power. However, development of robust, ion-exchange membranes was the hang-up for the salt water technology. Additional research was still needed to deal with fouling and short life span of these components. Such a system, however, has the interesting, unique feature of gaining higher potential over time as water evaporates from the stored brine, thereby increasing the salt concentration. Solar stills, used to produce the concentrated brine and fresh water, are another attractive feature, because they are one of the most economical of all solar collectors. We decided to keep this technology in mind, but not pursue it for Civalia.

There were many other innovative design details I am not able to describe in detail, since I was not present at the meetings when they were conceived. I was not in attendance at these meetings for two reasons. First, I was working on getting the permits and background information needed to construct Civalia; and second, I was spending more time with Ralph. Both of these factors came up after we had the LPE running, and Stellan said, "I'd like to show this to the rest of the crew. Are you going to be around the next couple of days?"

"I thought I'd go back over to Ralph's and see what is happening with Wainright, then make a trip to Rawlins to start getting whatever permits we'll need," I told him. "But I can give you a key," I added.

"How about access to your files on the LPE project?" Stellan asked.

While we were still thinking about it, I gave him access to my computer and the files I had generated while I was designing the LPE. We progressed to a discussion of what needed to be done and the scheduling required.

Stellan told me, "You may remember we talked about using a keyhole model for the construction for Civalia, but I've been thinking a pie model may work better."

I must have looked confused, because he hastened to explain.

"The central common area dedicated to workshops is cylindrical, but our very first construction could be a wedge-shaped chunk of that cylinder, a piece of pie. We can then use the slice of pie to set up our mold and form construction equipment, and perhaps some of our geopolymer mixing and molding facility. As we extend that first wedge out through the common area, we could put in temporary quarters, and some or all of us could move in. Living on-site could accelerate the construction of the greenhouse and the private quarters."

The first actual residents in Civalia was a thrilling thought, but I was also thinking of the problems associated with making a strong joint between two blocks poured after one had already cured. This is a definite problem with ordinary concrete. I asked, "Wouldn't problems arise from joining the pieces of pie together as the first wedge is connected to its neighbors?"

"I've been in contact with the Cold Climate Housing Research Center, the CCHRC, in Fairbanks, Alaska, and learned one of the beauties of geopolymer is its stickiness. Unlike Portland cement, a new pour will adhere to an old one. I've been thinking if we make dovetail joints on ends of each outer wall section of the rings, new extensions to the wall will be almost as good as a single pour. We'll try experimenting with this technique soon."

"What about the side walls?" I asked. "Won't that split the finished cylinder into a bunch of wedges?"

"I think we'll try making those walls temporary and movable. They'll probably have to be segmented and hollow, but we'll plan on moving them each time we make a new wedge. To start with, I'm thinking the roof is going to be a double layer tent roof like the Denver airport. I thought we'd try using your wet foam between the two roof layers to control the insulating factor. That reminds me, where is that information on your wet foam project?"

Stellan and I went back into the shop to look for the folder. It took a little while, but Stellan finally located it on the top of the bolt cabinet slightly above eye level. I'd obviously stashed it there but had no memory of doing so. We laughed together over the "lost tools and parts" phenomenon we had both experienced many times in our "shopping," as we called our time spent in our shops.

"What do you think your building schedule is going to be?" I asked.

"Well, our core building's a very simple structure and is fairly independent of the remainder of Civalia. The main connection with future construction is going to be the outer cylinder wall. It will serve as the inner wall, and the support for the roof of the communal ring. We've decided to make the floors of both of these sections similar to the ancient Roman hypocausts. That way, we can install all of our utilities later, and change them in the future if we develop better ones or our requirements change. To answer your question, we'll be ready to start building about a month after we get some geologic data."

Stellan looked at me enquiringly. "Did I understand you were going to get rolling on the geological data?"

I sighed. "Yes, I was, but I've lost a little focus on that task. I'll move it to the top of my list."

"It's not like you haven't been doing anything," Stellan told me with a sardonic smile. "And this development of yours," Stellan gestured toward the LPE, which was still quietly swishing away, "more than makes up for any tardiness on the geological data. This is going to be a key contribution, and will have a very small entropy footprint." Stellan gazed at the apparatus with a contemplative expression.

"The entropy footprint can't be too small," I said. "We'll still need some metals for the valves, the turbine, the pumps, and the spray nozzles, not to mention the high-pressure tubing."

"Maybe it'll be better than you think," Stellan said. "There're some things I haven't told you yet. First, last week Cass located a chemist interested in working with me on the artificial stone."

"What's his name?" I asked.

"Not him—her," Stellan replied. "Her name is Manjinder Kumari, and she has a son named Anand.

"Tell me about her," I said.

Stellan spoke up again with an enthusiastic note in his voice. "Cass found Manjinder at the University, where she is an assistant professor of chemistry. She has looked at my experiment on growing artificial shell, and has already helped me speed up the process. She recognized my setup was similar to a 3D printer, so she suggested we generate the protein for the shells separately, and then seed the initial substrate in a specific pattern, grow the calcium carbonate for a time, and then reseed the protein for the next layer. We tried it earlier this week, and although we have a lot of work left to make the process as precise as existing 3D printers, we did create a crude 3D lotus flower."

Stellan pulled a plastic bag out of his shirt pocket and handed it to me. Inside was a small, lotus-flower shaped piece of artificial shell. It was somewhat crude, but still thrilling.

"Stellan, that is fantastic! Are you telling me we might be able to print a turbine for the LPE out of shell?"

"Maybe," Stellan said. "In the mean time, we'll stick with more conventional manufacturing processes. Rome was not built in a day and neither will Civalia be. The full development of Civalien technology will take decades, and neither you nor I will be alive to see it all."

"You're so right, Stellan, but I want to give it the best start we can. I'm sure you do too."

"Yes," he said, with a mischievous smile, "and there's more."

"What more could there be?" I asked.

"After you suggested calcite could be made clear, and Gyan suggested light pipes for distributing light to the common and private areas of Civalia, Manjinder and I've been working on printing some light pipes with light distribution panels using the same technology as LED screens."

"What!" I said. "That's really cool. When can I see what you're doing?"

"Yes, it's cool," Stellan said, "almost no heat buildup like there is with light bulbs. We don't have anything to show you yet, but you'll be the first to see it when we do."

―――∞∞∞―――

After Stellan had left, taking the information I had given him, I began calling to find someone to do geotechnical investigations. Local geologists were all busy for the rest of the summer, so I started investigating regional firms. I struck pay dirt with a firm in Fort Collins; I got the principle of the firm on my first try, an unusual occurrence.

"Yes," she said, "We might be able to help you. What do you need done?" She sounded eager.

When I explained what I was looking for, there was a long silence on the line.

"Hello?" I asked.

"Are you with Callaway Construction Company?" she asked in a belligerent tone.

"No—No," I answered. "Not at all. Were you doing work for CCC?" I asked.

"Yes, we were," she answered, very formally.

"This may take some face-to-face explanation," I said. "May I visit you at your office?"

"You may," she said, "but I'm not sure it will do you much good. I don't want anything to do with something connected to Mr. Wainright's project."

"I understand completely," I said. "I can be at your office by 4:15 today, if that will work for you."

"I suppose," she said, sounding reluctant.

"By the way, my name is John Tantivy, and yours is?"

"Diane Matthews."

I hung up, threw together some of the paperwork for Civalien, Inc. and Civalia, and headed south in my Cadillac. The time was tight and I must admit I exceeded the speed limit a little in a few places as I raced the clock. I didn't quite make it. It was 4:18 when I found the offices of Matthews Geotechnical Consultants and entered the office.

"I thought you might not be coming," Diane said.

She stood up behind her desk and extended her hand. This was probably a rote action of a seasoned business woman, because she did not appear very happy to see me. I decided to get right down to business.

"Are you aware of how Harold Wainright acquired the land for his project?" I asked.

"He did brag about what a great deal he got, paying something like $200 per acre for it. Why do you ask?"

"You knowing exactly how he obtained the land will make my explanation of our needs a lot simpler and shorter," I said. "Mr. Wainright had the land declared underutilized or abandoned and employed eminent domain for purposes of economic development. He was able to acquire it for a song from the Lazy HZ Ranch, owned by Ralph Hertell, because the district courts set the land value at $200 per acre."

I paused while Diane thought about this. She looked troubled and frowned.

"Did you and your people get caught in the road closure about a week ago?" I asked.

"Yes, we did," she answered, "and work has been suspended since."

"I'm afraid Ralph and I are to blame for that. Wainright planned to eventually cut a road out to the highway, and he somehow neglected to get an easement on the road through the remains of the Lazy HZ. We closed it off to preserve Ralph's right to maintain it as a private road."

"So that's what happened," she said. "CCC hasn't been very forthcoming about anything. All they told me was our work was shut down until further notice. They've put me in a bind, and they haven't responded to my billing them for what work I've done. I've been scrambling to find more work. Probably Wainright hasn't paid CCC either." Diane leaned forward some and looked more interested. "So what are you here about?"

"Several decades ago, a friend and I began to look at the world and society in a different way based on our understanding of entropy. Are you familiar with that term?"

"I've heard it before in some science classes, but I can't say I know what it means," Diane confessed.

"It's not a 15-minute lecture topic, and I'm still finding my understanding of it deepening," I told her. "Suffice it to say, Ralph had come to understand the principles and concepts of entropy decades before we did, and he did so without any formal education on the subject. Consequently, he began treating his land very gently, recognizing the contribution of plants and soil to the well-being of all animal life, including us. As you drove into Wainright's site, did you notice how verdant the land you were working on was compared to some of his neighbor's land to the south?"

"It did look appreciably better," Diane admitted.

"That's what got it tagged as underutilized, and taken away, stolen, really, for $200 per acre." I let this sink in for a moment. "Anyway, we see eye-to-eye with Ralph, so he has sold a group of us about 40 acres to build an intentional community based on entropy principles. We need geotechnical data on this site for designing our new home."

I slid the quad map with our 40-acre Civalia homesite outlined next to the National Forest boundary. "We do have rights to this site and we do have access," I said, as I also laid a copy of the deed on her desk, showing a deeded access route to the county road.

Diane looked more interested as she studied these documents. "I always felt like there was something a little off with Wainright," she said. "Could he still cause trouble?"

"We're certain we haven't heard the last of him, but we're confident he can't interfere directly with this project. We don't border him, and our access is to the south."

Indecision showed on Diane's face, "I don't know. This work looks legitimate, but it's awfully close to Wainright's, and I've still got trucks and equipment up there."

"You don't have to make a decision right this minute," I told her. "May I suggest you come up to the site, look it over, meet Ralph, and maybe some more of our group, before you make a decision?"

"Okay," she said, looking slightly relieved, "I don't have anything else to do, so I suppose I could drive up tomorrow. Will that be okay?"

"Let me check with Ralph," I said and pulled out my cell phone.

I called Ralph, explained where I was, what the situation was, and asked whether we could meet there tomorrow. Ralph readily agreed, and Diane and I concluded our business. I left, reasonably certain we would be able to get the geotechnical data we needed through her firm.

The next morning, I drove to the Lazy HZ and was greeted first by Gerald, and very shortly after by Ralph, when he came out of his house. I was very glad to see him. Almost two weeks had passed since we were last together, and it seemed like forever. We sat on his porch, and Gerald was soon at Ralph's feet, begging for peanuts. Each time I had been there, Gerald would come closer to me. This time Ralph handed me a peanut, and I placed it on the porch floor about two inches from my foot. Gerald jerked back and forth for a while, finally screwing up his courage enough to grab the peanut and scamper away.

"What's the latest news about Wainright?" I asked.

"I ain't heard boo," Ralph said. "It's been kind uh quiet. He's driven out a few times, but I ain't seen no construction activity. Sources in town tell me he's been spendin' a lot uh time at 'is lawyers. They're also sayin' he's become real frugal."

I laughed. "I'll bet he has. He owes the lady who's coming up today some money. I'm going to go to Rawlins later today to start figuring out what kind of paperwork we need for Civalia, and I thought I'd drop by the court house to get any information I can on what mortgages Wainright has on the land and his house. Do you want to go along?"

"Well that sounds right intrestin'. Don't mind if I do. When's your lady friend due?"

"She said she would be here about ten, so she should be here most any time. Gyan is also coming over. He's interested in learning what the soil and subsoil look like."

We sat in companionable silence for a while, and then Ralph said, "Maybe it's time we closed that there road permanent like."

"Perhaps it is. I've been thinking that myself. The question is: do we do it when Wainright's at home or when he's away?"

"Now, that's an intrestin' question," Ralph responded. "Do we want him having trouble gettin' in or gettin' out?"

We both sat and contemplated that thought for a while, but before we could try to answer the question, a pickup truck came up the county road and turned into Ralph's drive. Diane got out and came up to the porch. I offered her my chair, while Gerald began scolding from the nearby tree. I sat down on the step.

"We're waiting for one of the members of our group," I told Diane after introducing her to Ralph. "He's on his way from Laramie and should be here soon."

"I've been by here before," Diane told Ralph. "I was doing geotechnical exploration for Wainright."

"So I heard," Ralph responded smiling, "but we won't hold it against ya."

"I'm surprised," she said. "What he did to you wasn't very nice."

"Naw, but it's getting me some really nice, new neighbors here." Ralph looked over at me, and Diane obviously caught the meaning of what he was saying.

We engaged in small talk for a few minutes before Gyan and Cindy drove up. After the usual introductions and Cindy's inquiries about Lester, we drove in Diane's and Ralph's trucks up to the land. I rode with Diane. When we got there, I sat on Ralph's log and let Diane wander around the meadow with Ralph, Cindy, and Gyan.

When we were back at Ralph's home, before we got out of her pickup, I asked Diane, "What do you think? Is this a job you would like to do?"

"I'd like to think about it over the weekend," she said, "and it would take me that long to work up a proposal, if I do decide to bid on it."

"Fair enough, but I do have a proposal for you right now." I was thinking of my conversation with Ralph about closing the road. "You said you have a truck and some equipment on Wainright's site?"

"Yes?" Diane arched an eyebrow, obviously wondering why I was asking about her equipment.

234

"How about if you move your things onto our land where it can be out of sight and available if you do decide to work for us. If you don't work for us, it will be readily available to move elsewhere. You never know what might happen to the road into Wainright's."

Diane looked at me sharply. "Are you trying to tell me you're going to close the road again?"

"You never know," I replied.

Diane looked back at the road, "Sounds like a good idea."

"Gyan can help you," I said, volunteering him without his knowledge. "I'd help, but Wainright's met me in very unfavorable circumstances, so I'm on his shit list, and he won't let Ralph on what used to be Ralph's own land."

"Nice guy," Diane said sarcastically. "Actually, it will be a relief to get my equipment out of there."

When we got out, I explained my offer to Gyan, Cindy, and Ralph. Ralph looked amused, Cindy looked ecstatic, since she'd have some time to spend with Lester, and Gyan, well, Gyan looked determined as he and Diane drove off toward Wainright's construction site. I hoped they could get out without a confrontation.

Ralph suggested we take the Cadillac, a car well known to Wainright by now, up to the land. Gyan's car was not known and would be okay. It would explain Cindy being around, and I could make myself scarce if Wainright happened to come by. We carried out Ralph's suggestions, and then went through the stables to the lower pasture. Ralph gave a sharp whistle, and before long, Lester came ambling up the hill.

The three of us went into the stable after Ralph fed Lester a handful of grain, and Lester dutifully followed. Ralph saddled and bridled him, then led him outside. I boosted Cindy up into the saddle, and Ralph led Lester along the road for a while, before returning back to the stable door.

"Open that there gate ta the corral," Ralph told me, pointing with his chin to indicate which gate he was talking about.

I opened the gate and Ralph led Lester through. As I closed the gate, he passed the reins to Cindy, gave her a few instructions, and patted Lester on the shoulder. Lester set off at a slow walk around the corral, and Ralph came back over by the gate. We watched one happy girl moving slowly around the circle.

Lester stopped suddenly, turned his head toward the road leading to Wainright's, and pricked up his ears.

"Looks like we may be gettin' company," Ralph said. "Open the gate, an' go into the stable an' stay out uh sight. Might not be necessary, but better safe than sorry."

I did as Ralph instructed, and the last thing I saw was Ralph leading Lester out of the corral, across the road, and up by the house. I could now hear engine noise, and I found a crack in the stable wall I could look through without being seen. My cell phone rang. Gyan was calling, and he told me he was leading in the drill rig truck. Wainright was following them, so he planned to turn toward the highway to avoid letting Wainright know the truck would be on the land. He assumed Diane would understand and follow him.

The truck rumbled by, followed by Diane in her pickup, the bed now loaded with miscellaneous equipment. Wainright's Hummer with his TOPDOG vanity plate was right on Diane's tail. I moved to the wall facing the county road and found a new crack to spy through. All three vehicles in the convoy turned left onto the county road. I then lost sight of what was going on.

Ralph later told me Wainright had passed the two trucks in a burst of speed and disappeared down the road. When he was out of sight, Gyan had stopped and conferred with Diane. The two of them had then driven on. I called Gyan, who told me Wainright had been very unpleasant and suspicious, and had not wanted Diane to remove her equipment. Diane thought he was following them to make sure they were headed back to Fort Collins. I explained the situation to Ralph.

"We'd better do a thing or two here," Ralph told me. "I stood Lester an' Cindy so's Wainright couldn't see them plates on Gyan's car when he went by, but I think we'd better get it out uh here. He's left his keys in it, so whyn't you drive Cindy up ta the land, an' I'll come and get ya. Cindy'll have ta stay in the house out uh sight when we get back."

We set to work carrying out Ralph's new suggestions. When we were done, I called Gyan again. He and Diane had reached Highway 230 with no sign of Wainright, so they had decided to drive as far as Three Forks so see if he was there. If he wasn't, it would be safe to assume he had turned toward Saratoga, and they would head back. If he was there, well, that was another story. They planned to head toward Laramie and see if he continued to follow.

Ralph, Cindy and I waited in Ralph's house, playing my entropy game to pass the time. Another half hour later, Gyan checked in. He reported Wainright had been sitting at Three Forks, but he had not followed them farther when they turned toward Laramie. They thought he had started back north, and they'd stopped at a turnout a few miles east of the junction. I suggested they wait there for a while to see if he came back to Jim Baker's Retreat. We gave him forty minutes, but he made it in thirty-one. He accelerated past Ralph's house, his tires spinning and raising a huge dust cloud.

"We're goin' ta close the road," Ralph said grimly.

I called Gyan, and the convoy of two started back.

It was mid-afternoon before Diane's truck and equipment and our cars were safely out of sight on the land, and we were all once again gathered in Ralph's house. Lunch hour was long gone, but Ralph made us some toasted cheese sandwiches on some of his homemade bread.

"I'm sure glad you helped me get my truck and equipment out of there," Diane told us. "That guy is a mad man. I'll never do any more work for him or any of his contractors."

"You'll probably never get paid for the work you've already done," I told her.

"You sort uh missed getting' ta Rawlins," Ralph told me.

We were all beginning to wind down, and the time to disband

had arrived. Ralph drove Cindy and Gyan up to the Civalia site, and the two of them headed for Laramie. I went to Ralph's shop and began organizing the barricade materials. Diane went with me and looked over what we had built.

"You're really going to do it, close the road, aren't you." Diane's comment was a statement, not a question.

I answered anyway. "Yes, we are."

"Tonight?" she asked.

"We're not sure yet," I told her. "We haven't decided whether we should close it with Wainright at home or away."

"At home," she said firmly. "That way you have some idea of where he is and what he might be up to. It will also limit his access to outside help. Let me make a call, and I'll help you."

Diane stepped outside and made a call while I continued to get the barricade materials ready.

When Ralph came back, the three of us loaded the first barricade into his pickup. When dusk was shading into the dark of night, we headed down the road towards Wainright's. Ralph drove without lights. We setup the barricade by the last vestiges of sunset, then by starlight.

When we were done, Diane looked at the barricade critically and said, "This won't hold him. He'll drive right around the end." She looked back up the road. "You had some more barricade materials in the shop didn't you?"

"Yup," Ralph said. "When we first closed this here road, we barricaded this end and the end by the county road too. Course, then we had Elaine ta keep 'em from drivin' 'round."

"Elaine is a lieutenant with the County Sheriff," I explained.

"Well, Elaine's not around, so how about we do something else." Diane started walking back up the road, looking from side to side. Ralph and I followed.

After we had gone a few hundred yards, passing through a slight bend where the road curved around a grove of trees, Diane stopped and waited for us to catch up. "Here," she said. "These trees on the left are close enough to prevent anyone driving around a barricade, and those rocks over there on the other side can be moved to block access between the road and those trees farther out."

"I'll get the pickup," I said and hurried back down the road.

I had noted Ralph had left his keys in the truck, and I had also noted Ralph was tiring. I drove slowly back up the road, again with the lights off, and picked up Diane and Ralph where they were resting on one of the rocks. I drove us back to Ralph's shop, and we loaded the rest of the barricade materials in the pickup.

"Ralph, do you have a chain somewhere?" I asked.

"Over there," Ralph said, pointing to a cabinet in the far corner.

I found a suitably stout chain, and some clevises and hooks, and loaded them into the truck. Then I took Ralph aside.

"Ralph, you look very tired."

"I'm a bit tuckered," he said.

"You stay here and get to bed," I commanded. "Diane and I will finish putting up the barricade."

Ralph left without a protest, and I knew that meant he was exhausted. I watched him go into his home, and my heart ached for him. I hoped we were doing what was best for him.

I turned to Diane. "I didn't ask if you are willing to work into the night to set up this barricade. It's been a long day for you also."

She had been standing by the passenger door of the pickup during my exchange with Ralph, and her reply was terse, "Let's go." She opened the door and climbed in. On the way down to the new barricade site, she elaborated. "In my business, I have had to work with a lot of men like Wainright, but he's one of the worst one's I've ever met. He wouldn't even talk to me when we went after MY truck and MY equipment. He addressed all of his misogynistic comments to Gyan. Maybe tomorrow I'll feel different, but right now I'd be happy if we could seal him in so he'd never get out of his place again."

We set up the second barricade at the spot Diane had selected and used Ralph's pickup to rearrange some of the rocks to form the west side barrier. It was near midnight when we finished, and a crescent moon had risen, shedding some light on our work. Again, Diane looked over our handiwork and said, "It's too flimsy. Wainright can drive right through that barricade with that Hummer of his."

"Maybe Ralph and I can reinforce it in the morning," I said.

"It's awfully late and you still have a long drive home."

Diane was silent as she stared at the barricade. "We need some posts behind this," she said. She turned to me. "Does Ralph have some posts lying around?"

"I did see a post pile in back of the stable, but I'm not sure we could dig even one posthole in this road . . . even if we work all night," I added. "This road is hard."

"We'll use my drill rig."

"But the noise might alert Wainright your truck's still in the vicinity," I objected.

"When I start working on your site, he'll hear it anyway." Diane moved toward the pickup. "Let's go get my rig."

We retrieved Diane's truck and, on the way back to the barricade, I stopped and picked up half a dozen posts. I also located a tamping bar in Ralph's shop. When I got to the barricade, Diane had moved it aside, positioned her truck, and was raising the mast. She paused and handed me a hard hat and some safety glasses. I got one of the posts from the pickup and went back for the tamping bar.

"I think we can drill these post holes without running the engine at full throttle," she yelled at me over the sound of the drill rig engine. I really couldn't tell the difference whether it was full throttle or not. It seemed loud enough to wake everyone within ten miles.

Diane worked the controls so the drill descended and bit into the road. I was amazed at how quickly a posthole was drilled. "Piece of cake," she said to me as she throttled back the engine.

I set the post into the hole and then realized I had forgotten to bring a shovel. "I forgot the damn shovel," I told Diane. "I'll go get one."

"No problem," she said and produced one from a toolbox on the drill rig.

I set to work shoveling dirt back into the hole and tamping it around the post. Meanwhile, Diane repositioned the truck and had another hole drilled before I was finished. Five hours and five more posts later we repositioned the barricade and stepped back to look at our work. There was no way anyone was going to get through without breaking something, moving some rocks, or cutting down some trees.

"There is one last thing we need to do," I said.

"What's that?" Diane asked, sounding none too interested. We were both exhausted.

"There's a finger of Jim Baker's Retreat land, that's what Wainright calls his place, which sticks out to the south. Wainright included that finger of land in the eminent domain theft to get a spring that's a little ways down the hill. We need to cut him off from going out that way."

"This guy sounds more odious whenever I hear something more about him, but I don't think I have it in me to build any more barricades."

"This one's easy," I told her. "We just have to redirect some water. Do you want to go along?"

"Why not?" she said.

"If you want to take your drill rig back to the Civalia site, I'll pick you up there, or you can drive your pickup back to Ralph's ."

"I'll bring my pickup back."

We loaded the tools and chains back into Ralph's pickup and Diane's truck. She secured the drill rig mast and headed out. I drove Ralph's pickup back to his house and put away the tamping bar, the chains, the clevises, and the hooks. I was dragging. It had been years since I had pulled an all-nighter; I was definitely not used to it. Nevertheless, I walked around to stay awake and waited for Diane.

In due time she drove into the yard, parked, and got into Ralph's pickup. I drove to the gate near the stock tank where I'd first gone with Ralph. I got out to open the gate, and Diane slid over and drove through after I had it opened. I got in on the passenger side and directed her down to the tank.

"Somewhere down here there's a shutoff valve for the tank from the spring. I've never seen it myself, but Ralph shut it off when we first barricaded the road. The spring overflowed and made the finger of land with the spring impassable. Why don't you angle the pickup to illuminate the hillside over there?" I indicated the direction I thought the line ran. We got out and began searching.

"This way," Diane said, pointing off to the right of where I thought the line was.

"How do you know?" I asked.

"It's been disturbed."

I couldn't see any difference between the direction I was headed and where Diane was pointing, but I followed her lead. She was right. About fifty feet up the hill there was a covered box set into the ground. We removed the lid and found an open pipe headed vertically down, but we couldn't see what was down in the pipe.

"There must be a shutoff valve in there," I said. "We probably need a long handle of some sort to turn it. Maybe Ralph carries it in his truck. I'll go look."

I went back to the truck, but had no luck finding anything that looked like it might be a handle. When I turned to go back to the valve box, I saw Diane had found the valve handle clipped to the underside of the lid and was already extracting it.

"Ralph is a very organized person," I told her. "I should have known the handle would be readily available."

"Yah," she said, "I don't think I've ever seen a rancher's pick-up so clean."

Diane got the valve closed, the handle replaced, and we slid the cover back on. Our drive back was quiet, and the sky was markedly brightening in the east.

Ralph met us when we drove up to his house and ushered us inside to a hot breakfast. That was very welcome. When Diane made some noises about heading for home, he firmly sent her to the guest room to get some sleep and took me out to the bunk house. We had to rearrange a few things before I could collapse on the bed. I remembered little else.

CHAPTER 12

I had no idea how long I'd been sleeping when I was awakened by the sound of an approaching siren. I staggered to the window of the bunkhouse in time to see a rural fire truck go past Ralph's house toward Wainright's place. By the time I got into enough clothes and got my shoes on, I had heard a couple more vehicles racing past. I went out to see what was going on. Diane was already outside shading her eyes and looking toward Wainright's. I joined her.

"Do you know what's going on?" I asked.

"No," she said, "but there is smoke not too far away."

A mixture of black oily-looking smoke and light gray smoke was billowing above the trees. I estimated the distance put it just about where we had been working last night.

"Do you suppose we did something or left something there that caught fire?" I asked.

"I sure hope not," Diane answered. "I can't think of anything it might be."

As we watched, the color of the smoke changed with some white smoke and vapors mixing in with the older colors. I looked around and noticed Ralph's pickup was gone.

"I hope that's not Ralph," I said. I was getting worried. "Shall we walk down the road a ways, and see if we can tell what's on fire?"

"A ways," Diane answered. "I was caught in a brush fire once, and I don't like getting too close to this kind of fire."

We walked down the road far enough to see the fire truck was parked on the near side of the barricade, which was burned and scorched. The top board was burned in two and hanging in a V-shape, but the barricade fire appeared to be extinguished. Behind the fire truck was a military surplus tanker, and in back of those two vehicles was a Sheriff's pickup with the light bar flashing. There were still flames shooting up beyond the barricade from what must be the source of the black oily smoke. I didn't see Ralph's pickup, and my heart sank.

Diane nudged me and pointed off to the left. The nose of Ralph's pickup could be seen past a screen of bush only about a quarter of the way toward the action on the road. I had missed it because I was focused on the road, and his pickup was closer than I'd expected. Best of all, Ralph was leaning against the front of the truck and watching the action. We walked over to him.

"What happened?" I asked.

Ralph was a little startled, having not heard us approach, but he quickly recovered. "I don't rightly know fer sure, but that there's Wainright's Hummer that's burnin',"

I was dumbfounded.

"Was he in it?" Diane asked?

"I don't think so," Ralph answered. "When I got here the barricade was burnin' an' the front end uh the Hummer was burnin'. I didn't see no sign uh Wainright. Course ya can't see in ta it with them there tinted windows. I called it in, an' it took the fire department fifteen or twenty minutes ta get here. By then the whole thing was burnin'. The tires popped off 'fore the fire truck got here, an' the fuel tank went too. Is that what waked ya?"

"I'm not sure," Diane answered. "Something woke me up a little before the fire truck came by."

"The fire truck is what woke me up," I said.

The flames had died down and the smoke was diminishing. We saw some firemen spread out with backpack spray units and examine some of the surrounding foliage.

"There was some brush an' trees on fire over there ta the east when I first got here," Ralph said. "They sprayed that an' the barricade before workin' on the Hummer."

Now that Ralph had pointed it out, I could see where some of the trees and brush were blackened. "It a good thing it's not drier and the wind wasn't blowing," I said.

"Yah, sure is," Ralph said. "This could uh really took off if'n there was a stout wind."

The volume of smoke had just about vanished. The sheriff's department officer came back toward his pickup and I recognized Melvin. He saw all of us and walked over.

"Melvin, was anyone in the Hummer?" I asked.

"It doesn't look like it," Melvin said. "But we'll need to close off this site until we can complete our investigation." He pulled a notebook and a pen out of his shirt pocket and got prepared to write. "When did you put up this barricade?"

"John an' Diane put this here up last night," Ralph answered. "I told 'em ta do it. Wainright was getting' ta be a pest; didn't want this lady ta get her own equipment off uh his place, an' he wouldn't pay her. You've any idea what happened here?"

Melvin finished writing some notes and then hesitated before he said, "This is just my guess, you understand. There won't be anything official until after we've completed our investigation. There's a gas can beside the road, and one is missing off the back of the Hummer, so I think Wainright splashed some gasoline on the barricade and tried to burn it down. Either the Hummer was too close to the fire, or some of the gasoline ran back down hill and the fire followed."

"There's another barricade a ways down the road," I volunteered. "Wainright would have had to get past that one too. Have you looked at it?"

Melvin wrote some more in his notebook. "I wasn't aware of a second barricade. Perhaps we should take a look at it. Lead the way, but please give this site a wide birth."

We tromped through the brush and trees to the west side of the road, staying off it at Melvin's insistence, until we approached the lower barricade. It stood as we had left it last night, but there were definitely some tracks going around the west side. To my inexperienced eye, they looked like whoever had made those tracks was in a hurry and was spinning their wheels.

Melvin wrote some more in his notebook, and then shepherded us back to Ralph's pickup. "We may need statements from all of you. I'll need your contact information. Ralph's I know, but I'll need yours," Melvin looked at me, "John is it?"

I gave him my contact information, and Diane handed him a card.

"Is there a way to get to Wainright's place?" Melvin asked Ralph.

"I could lend you my horse," Ralph told him with a mischievous grin. "Otherwise you'll have ta walk or ride one uh them there trail bikes."

"I'll call for one of those," Melvin said, "and some backup."

Ralph drove us back to his home. We were all hungry again; it was about 2:30 in the afternoon. Diane and I helped Ralph make some lunch.

While we were eating, I commented, "You were absolutely right about Wainright, Diane. He didn't let that first barricade even slow him down, and if Melvin's right, he wasn't going to let the second one stop him either."

"It slowed him down,"

"Stopped him, actually," I said.

"Ain't that that truth," Ralph's expression became more serious, "but I hope he weren't burned. I don't wish that on nobody."

"We owe you for your help," I said to Diane. "We wouldn't have stopped him without it. When, I guess I should say if, you prepare a proposal for doing our geotechnical work, please add in something for your time and effort here."

"Well, you helped me, too. Maybe we should just call it a wash."

I shook my head. "It's hardly that."

"Have ya given Wainright the data ya generated for his place?" Ralph asked.

"Technically, I was working for CCC, but the money was coming from Wainright. And no, I haven't delivered any data yet."

"Well, that settles it then," Ralph said. "We'll just buy that there data from ya. We may just need it sometime, or it might help out with the Civalia site."

"That's a great idea," I added.

Diane looked pensive for a moment and then brightened. "Okay, I'll work up a report and get it to you—ah—next Wednesday?"

"Fine—fine," Ralph said.

"And I'll have a proposal for doing the work on the Civalia site then, too. I really should head back home now, but I'd like to unload some of the equipment I have in my pickup. Will it be okay to leave it by the drill rig?"

"That'll be fine," I said, "and I'll go help you unload. I need to pick up my car, too."

When Ralph and I got back from the Civalia site, Ralph suggested we check what was happening at the burn site. We found the fire engine and tanker were gone, but now there were three Sheriff's vehicles and a couple of trail bikes. Melvin came forward and motioned us to park a ways away. We got out and he came over.

"How's yer investigatin' goin', Melvin?" Ralph asked.

"It's interesting," Melvin said. "We biked into Wainright's place and didn't find anyone at home. We scouted around, and it looks like he had a dirt bike that someone, we assume it was Wainright, rode southeast, away from the construction site. We didn't follow that track, because we want to get some pictures and tire track casts."

"That's a lot uh investigatin' fer a trespass case, ain't it?" Ralph queried.

"Well, it's a bit more than that." Melvin said. "There is arson and destruction of private property."

"Wainright's the one goin' ta suffer the most," Ralph said. "Them Hummers ain't cheap. You suppose Wainright made fer the Highway?"

"Probably," Melvin said, "he either rode his bike to town or had someone meet him. We haven't been able to locate him yet."

"Is it okay if we go out to the side and take a look at the Hummer from a distance?" I asked.

"I guess that's okay," Melvin said hesitantly, "but stay back at least 50 feet."

Ralph and I headed out near the tree line on the west side of the road and walked around till we could get a good look at what was left of the Hummer. It was a burned out hulk. The tires were burned away except for the tangle of steel belts, the alloy rims

247

were melted, the windows were gone, and the rear of the vehicle was exploded out where the fuel tank had been. The ground was littered with ash and miscellaneous items burned beyond recognition.

"Not a pretty sight," I said. "I'll bet he was really angry and was careless with the gasoline."

The posts Diane and I had installed looked like they had been the particular object of the arson attack. They were severely burned near the ground line. A couple of them had burned enough to have broken off and fallen over.

"That's a mess that'll take some doin' ta clean up," Ralph said.

"Amen to that," I added. I wondered where Wainright had gone.

Ralph and I went back to his home and speculated about what would come of this incident. Eventually, I made arrangements to pick Ralph up on Monday for a trip to Rawlins, bid him goodbye, and drove home. I was very tired and did not do much the rest of the day. I also took advantage of Sunday being the day of rest. I was feeling better by late Sunday, so I called the Civalia crew and asked them to come over for dinner. All of them could make it on short notice except Manjinder. I figured I wouldn't have to tell the story of what happened on the road to Wainright's so many times if most of them were together at once.

The crew's reaction to what had happened at the barricade was shock followed with wild speculation. In the end, we just had a lot of questions; the main one from Cindy was whether Lester was okay. Stellan and Gyan were both pleased to hear that Diane was going to give us a proposal for the geotechnical investigations by Wednesday. Stellan brought out some plans for the initial building on the Civalia site, but everyone was probably a little disappointed to see just an empty pie shaped building.

"Don't worry," Stellan assured us, "we'll fill it up. John, I've been meaning to ask you if we could convert your shop into a form building facility in the weeks before we start actual construction."

"Of course," I said. "I'll rearrange the antique cars, and the modern ones will just get parked outside. I was going to tell you I had planned on going to Rawlins on Friday to start the permitting process. I guess you understand why I didn't get there, but I'll make the trip tomorrow."

"We'd like to use your truck and trailers, also," Stellan added.

"No problem," I said.

Stellan continued. "I've been in contact with the Denver airport roof manufacturer and will be getting information, and hopefully some quotes, within the next two weeks."

"You've been quiet, Cass," I said. "How are your efforts going in finding some more residents?"

"It's heavy going," she said. "Getting people to understand the theoretical basis of Civalia is tough. Manjinder was fairly easy, because she had a basic understanding of entropy to begin with. I'm having a lot more difficulty finding others, particularly a medical person."

"Would the game I put together help?" I asked. "It's over at Ralph's right now, and every time I'm there, it seems like something dramatic happens, so I keep forgetting to pick it up. I've been thinking I should make another one."

"Perhaps you should. I've not played your game, so I can't tell you whether it would help or not. Why don't you get that one from Ralph, or make a new one, and then let me know. We can get together and see how it goes."

"You can probably help me improve it." I looked at Stellan and asked, "What are you going to use for the basic ingredient for the geopolymer?"

"We're working with the CCHRC and the fly ash from the Laramie River Station in Wheatland to optimize a formula for the Civalia geopolymer. We plan on getting bulk trona from the mines in Green River. We'll need aggregate, but we'll find a local source for that. Two other things we need to think about are a labor force to help us pour that first 'pie' of Civalia, and how we're going to mix the 300 to 500 cubic yards of geopolymer."

"I have a thought on a temporary labor force," Cass said. "Why don't I visit one or two of the intentional communities I've lived in before and see if I can recruit some people for temporary labor. If we can provide room and board and some reasonable compensation, I think some of those people would be intrigued by the concepts of Civalia, the geopolymer, and the chance to spend a little time in the mountains; a mini working vacation if you will. Having the Saratoga hot springs close by won't hurt either."

I tackled the mixing problem. "We are going to be building on Civalia for quite some time into the future, so I suggest we find a reasonably priced continuous concrete mixer, or we design and build our own. We don't know what will happen in the future, but if other Civalias are built, such a machine could be very useful. If we combine it with a concrete pump, it could be a stationary unit."

"I'll look into that," Gyan volunteered.

"Manjinder sends her regrets she can't be here," Stellan told us. "She has a paper due Tuesday and is working late to get it done. She is making progress on the 3D printing, and she asked me to show you this."

Stellan pulled the second 3D printed lotus flower from his shirt pocket and passed it around. This one was noticeably more precise than the first one. There were several "oohs" and "ahs" as it made the rounds.

"I want one," Cindy said.

Stellan smiled. "You can have this one. There'll be others. Several are growing as we speak."

We wrapped up our business and sat down to a convivial dinner. "This is what community is all about;" Cass said, "cooperation, security, intellectual challenge, sharing, a feeling of belonging." We all agreed.

On Monday morning I headed out for Ralph's. We took another look at the mess on the road before heading for Rawlins. The area still looked and smelled just as dismal as it had on Saturday, but now it was surrounded by crime scene tape. Ralph told me there had been quite a bit of activity the rest of Saturday and most of Sunday; not so much yet that Monday.

When we arrived in Rawlins, I headed for the planning office and Ralph tagged along. We sat down with one of the staff, and

Ralph, having greeted him as an old friend, introduced him as Alan Hanson.

"Alan's folks ran sheep over by Wamsutter," Ralph told me. "Alan here was a kind uh wild kid, but he sure could rodeo."

Alan grinned. "Those were the good old days. What can I do for you today and," he paused, asking what he really wanted to know, "what happened over by your place?"

Rumors of Saturday morning's events must have been rife in the office, so the news of our presence spread like wildfire. Shortly, the whole office was there, including the director. Most of them were acquainted with Ralph, and they were eager to hear what had happened from someone close to the source.

"Well, we don't rightly know," he told them. "But I've not been happy with all that there construction traffic over my north meadow road; you know the land what Wainright took from me; so I closed 'er off. John Tantivy here helped me set up them barricades."

"We heard about that," the Director said. "Wainright came in here last week and was really pissed. He wanted us to do something about it, but in his original proposal to us, he showed the access going out to Highway 230. We told him we'd look into it, but the County Attorney told us there was no legal easement on your meadow road. When we told him that over the phone, he was pretty abusive."

"He was pretty crude with Sally, over at the Sun, an' Elaine, an' John, too." Ralph told them.

"We heard about that, too, through the Sheriff's office. But what happened on Saturday?"

"Well, Friday, a young lady from Fort Collins wanted ta get some uh her equipment off uh Wainright's place, an' he didn't much want it gone. So, I gave her permission ta use the road, an' we helped her get her stuff out. Wainright wasn't in a very good mood, so I decided ta shut 'er down again. The young lady an' John helped me do it. Saturday morning I seen some smoke risin' up over the trees an' went down the road ta where we'd put up a barricade. It was burnin', an' so was a vehicle on the other side uh the barricade. Some trees was beginnin' ta burn too. I called 911."

"We heard the vehicle was Wainright's Hummer," one of the planners said. "Was he in it?"

"It was probably a Hummer all right, but I didn't get close enough ta see for sure whether anyone was in it. Then the fire truck an' Melvin showed up. They told me ta stay back. Me and John went down ta look at 'er this mornin', an' ever'thing is burned clean. It sort uh has the shape uh a Hummer, but it don't look a lot like one now. The gas tank blowed up, an' so'd a gas can on the back, so the back end's kind uh mangled. It don't look like anyone was in there, but ya can't tell for sure."

Another one of the planners said, "I talked with Wayne, he's a fireman, and he said no one was in the Hummer."

I was amused, and not too surprised, to watch Ralph work the planning staff, getting more information from them than he was giving. This conversation went on for another fifteen minutes or so, and we learned Wainright had been in Rawlins several times during the last week, visiting not just the planning office, but also a couple of lawyers, contractors, and the concrete company. We had expected the latter, since the Walden concrete supplier was not likely to do further business with him.

When we finally got down to business, the director sat in on our meeting. I told them our corporation, a social welfare organization, had purchased 40 plus acres from Ralph, and our goal was to build an experimental single household dwelling on the land with sufficient greenhouse facilities to feed the entire household. Our plan was to maintain the land around the dwelling in as pristine condition as possible, continuing the care for the land that Ralph had initiated.

On the drive to Rawlins I had discussed with Ralph the best ways to approach the planning commission for our rather unorthodox project. Consequently, I purposely did not tell them the full scope of what we were planning at that time. I did mention our household would be composed of some related and some unrelated persons, with common, shared food preparation and eating facilities. I also mentioned we had some ideas for cottage industry, but the main venture would not be dependent upon it since the corporation would insure adequate funding was available for construction and operation of the household.

What we had to offer to the community was research into some interesting subjects, including perennial, indeterminate, edible plants; geopolymer construction; wet foam insulation; artificial shell materials; and renewable energy systems. I emphasized some of this research was ongoing, and we intended to incorporate as much of it as we could into the dwelling. I showed them the first artificial shell lotus flower Manjinder had printed and showed them pictures of my prototype LPE. By the time I was finished, the planners at least looked interested. I asked what documentation we needed to supply them to obtain a permit for our project.

The director produced a copy of the zoning regulations and a five-page document outlining the submittal requirements for their review. We had a little back and forth over some of the wording in the zoning regulations, but in the end they agreed our project fell under the Rural, Agricultural, and Mining (RAM) land use category, our dwelling did appear to be a single family household, and the fact we were building on more than 35 acres relieved us of needing to file a subdivision plat. It was a good start.

Ralph and I left the planning office and headed for the Sheriff's Office to see if we could gather any more information.

"What do you think happened to Wainright?" I asked Ralph as we walked along.

"I think he booked," Ralph said. "Skedaddled."

"So do I, and if he did, I'll bet he didn't go empty handed," I said. "Is there any way we could find out about that?"

Ralph walked in silence for a time and then said, "Maybe. I know a guy at the bank might tell us somethin'. Let's go there first."

We changed directions and soon approached the Rawlins National Bank.

"This here's a local bank and has a branch in Saratoga. Started out in 1899, an' it's the bank I use. Wainright might've used it too."

We went in and approached the receptionist.

"Is Lester in?" Ralph asked.

My imagination went wild. I started to say, "Is your . . .."
Ralph silenced me with a look.

"Yes, he is, Ralph. I'll let him know you're here," the receptionist picked up her phone.

Ralph herded me over to some seats, and we set down. "Lester
England's an old friend uh mine; been in the bankin' business for
a long time," he told me, speaking emphatically.

I got the message. It was not too long before Lester came out
and took us into his office. Ralph introduced me, and then he and
Lester engaged in ritual small talk for a while before Lester asked,
"What can I do for you today, Ralph?"

"Well," Ralph said, "since Harold Wainright's my neighbor,
an' he's caused some damage ta my property with a fire on Saturday, I was wonderin' if ya might know if he was still around so's
I can get in touch with 'im. He does his bankin' with ya?"

"He did," Lester answered, "But he closed out his accounts
last week. He claimed he was dissatisfied with our service. It hurt.
He wasn't an inconsequential customer."

"Ain't that the truth," said Ralph. "He was spendin' millions
on that there place."

"Yes," Lester said, "the flow was quite large, and he claimed it
was going to go up into the tens of millions. I can't tell you where
he is now. I assume he's at his place next to you." Lester fidgeted
for a moment and then asked, "I heard about the fire on your place
and there was a vehicle involved. Was it Wainright's?"

"Near's we can tell, it was," Ralph told him. "It was plum
gutted by fire, an' the fuel tank an' a gas can on the back blowed
up, an' Wainright ain't around."

Lester paled. Ralph asked him, "Ya got an interest in that there
Hummer?"

Lester hesitated again, finally saying, "We have the loan on it."

"Really?" Ralph asked with just a hint of surprise in voice.
"How much did he owe?"

Lester was quiet for time. "I really shouldn't be telling you
this, but he owed $95,000 on it." He looked somewhat sheepish.

"It was a luxury model and very low mileage; less than 5,000."

"Sheriff Johnson know 'bout this?" Ralph asked.

"Not yet, but I think he will," Lester said.

"Ya might want ta look at his credit report, too," Ralph told him.

"Do you know something I don't?" Lester asked.

"Nah, but I've got my suspicions," Ralph replied. "If'n I find out anything, I'll let ya know. Course, ya'll do the same for me, won't ya?" Ralph asked.

"Sure," Lester said.

We left, and Ralph was quiet for while as we walked down the street. "Sure would like ta take a peek at that there credit report," he said. "I'll have ta see if'n Lester'll pony it up after a while."

"I'm beginning to think burning the Hummer might have been intentional," I said. "If he took off and drove the Hummer, eventually bounty hunters would be after him when the note went out for collection."

"Intrestin'," Ralph said.

"And if Wainright rode a dirt bike out to the highway, he probably had someone pick him up, because the dirt bike also could be traced."

Ralph looked at me sideways. "Ya do have a devious mind, John, but I think ya could be right. How'd ya think we could find out?"

"If what I'm thinking is true, he'd ditch the bike, because eventually it might turn up somewhere and lead the cops to him. I think we should look for the dirt bike."

"Where do ya think it might be?"

"It wouldn't be far. I suppose he could have dumped it in the river, but I don't think so. It might make an oil slick, or some fisherman might see it. Are there some side roads that might lead to a hiding place?"

"Nearest one's Geraldine's road. Geraldine'd probably have heard him, if'n he went there. Think we ought ta go look around 'fore we visit the Sherriff's Office?"

"It'd be nice to have something for them to work on," I responded.

We reversed our course and went back to the Cadillac, and shortly headed back to Ralph's. After we had passed Saratoga and then Riverside, we began looking for possible places Wainright could have ditched the dirt bike. Some of the roads were passable by the Cadillac, but many were not.

"Let's go get my truck," Ralph said. I readily agreed, so we drove to Ralph's home and transferred vehicles. Ralph headed out toward the barricade. "I'd like ta take another look at that there Hummer," he told me. "There's uh pair uh binoculars in the glove box. Whyn't ya get those."

We parked back a ways and walked around the crime scene tape to get a good look at the Hummer. Ralph looked at it through the binoculars for a time and then handed them to me. I looked for a time and mainly saw an awful lot of scorched metal. I did locate where the gas can had been lying in the borrow pit, the outline marked on the soil with surveying paint and a number. I assumed they had taken the gas can to look for further evidence.

"See anything missin'?" Ralph asked.

"No," I said.

"Look on the rear,"

"There's a lot missing on the back," I said. "It's mangled."

"Look at that there license plate holder,"

I did, and although it was distorted to some extent, it was not damaged enough to account for the missing license plate. "The license plate's gone," I said stupidly.

"Yup," Ralph said. "The front one's still there. Ya reckon he wanted a souvenir?"

Scanning the ground behind the Hummer to make sure it had not been blown clear, I didn't spot anything. I then examined the license plate holder carefully to see if I could tell whether it had been removed after the fire. I could see no marks indicating it had been, and the screws were definitely missing.

"Interesting," I said. "So Wainright drives around the lower barricade, runs into this one he can't get around, pulls a can of gas off the back of the Hummer, douses this barricade, and sets it on fire. From what we learned from Lester, he'd probably already decided to skip the country. So then he either intentionally or accidentally set the Hummer on fire. The missing rear license plate would indicate intentionally, but we can't be sure."

I was thinking some more about what might have motivated Wainright. "You know, Ralph, you or your place might have been the real target of Wainright's arson. Maybe he got stopped short, and thought perhaps the forest would catch and take you out." I shivered, thinking about what might have happened.

"Well, if'n that's the case, he didn't succeed. Let's go see if'n we can find a dirt bike."

We drove back to the county road and headed for the highway.

"He would uh had ta hoof it back ta his place ta pick up his dirt bike," Ralph said, "that'd take him some time, an' not knowin' when the fire might be discovered an' fire trucks comin', I'll bet he didn't go north. So let's go up by Geraldine's road, an' start workin' our way south."

"That sounds reasonable"

Ralph drove to Geraldine's turnoff, turned around there, and started back southeast. Before we got back to the county road, there were a couple of side roads on the river side, which we explored. Neither proved to be promising. We continued on southeast toward the Colorado border, and the roads became farther apart, and even less promising.

I told Ralph my opinion. "Unless he had someone meet him a long way off the road, none of these roads show much potential. I also can't envision him going this far on the highway. The risk of being seen and remembered would be too high."

"Maybe we're wrong, an' it didn't happen the way we're thinkin'." Ralph said.

He turned around and started back. As we approached the county road turnoff, Ralph said, "Let's go have another look at where he might uh come over the hogback."

"Sure," I said, somewhat dispiritedly, thinking Ralph may have been right and we were not analyzing Wainright's actions correctly.

I was looking out the passenger window toward the river, feeling discouraged we hadn't found any likely hiding places. When we approached what would be the boundary between Ralph's land and the Jim Baker's Retreat land, Ralph slowed and I shifted my attention to the left side of the highway. Both of us scrutinized the terrain and looked for anywhere Wainright might have hidden a dirt bike. Nothing jumped out at us.

Ralph then accelerated, and I turned back to looking out the passenger window, seeing nothing but a sharp drop off to the willows along the river.

"We'll turn around at Geraldine's road an' go back," Ralph said.

We were passing by the mouth of the ravine over the land still owned by Ralph when a thought struck me. "Stop," I ordered Ralph.

"Did ya see somethin'?" he asked, as he guided the truck to a stop on the edge of the highway.

"No, but I want to take a look at something."

I scrambled out of the truck and slid down the embankment to where the creek bed ran under the highway in a pair of four- or five-foot diameter culverts. I was at the lower end of the culverts, and a small stream of water was running out of the closest one. The other one was dry. I leaned out from the bank to look inside the first one, and I could see through to the other end. It was empty. I had to climb back up the embankment part way and go over the top of the first culvert to get to the second one. I walked out on the top of that culvert and lay down to look over the upper lip. That culvert did contain a dirt bike. It was lying on its side near the upstream end.

Eureka! I slipped and slid as I battled my way toward the top of the embankment. Ralph was standing beside his truck when I emerged on the roadway.

"It's there," I shouted and ran back, dusting off my clothes before I climbed into the truck.

Ralph got in on his side and grinned at me. "I reckon it's time ta visit the Sheriff," he said, and we took off for Rawlins again.

It was getting to be late afternoon when we arrived back in Rawlins. This time we parked by the Sheriff's office, and we were lucky to find Elaine was in. Ralph did not beat around the bush this time. He began telling Elaine directly what we had discovered. He mentioned the missing rear license plate. Elaine looked startled at that bit of news.

"Could it have been blown off by either the gas tank or gas can explosion?" she asked.

"We don't think so," Ralph said. "Mind ya we didn't get real close; stayed well outside yer tape, but we scanned the whole area with binoculars an' didn't see nothin'. John here looked at the mounting plate carefully an' it didn't look tore up bad enough ta have been ripped off, an' he couldn't see where it'd been taken off after the fire."

In short order she moved us to the conference room and called the Sheriff in to listen to Ralph's story. He started in again from the beginning, told them we surmised Wainright was in the process of stiffing a number of vendors; we knew of two, the concrete company in Walden and the geotechnical exploration company in Fort Collins. There were undoubtedly others. He told them we were pretty sure he was defrauding the Rawlins National Bank by stopping payments on the Hummer loan and destroying the vehicle, and we were guessing he had probably defrauded the Amalgamated Bank of Omaha.

Ralph suggested the Sheriff's Office should check into Wainright's finances to see if our deductions were correct and, if so, the extent of Wainright's financial thievery. He told them the reason for his interest was his concern for what might happen to the land in light of these goings on, and whether things might not turn out worse than having Wainright for a neighbor.

He also told them we were thinking Wainright intentionally torched not only the barricade we had set up, but also the Hummer, and possibly Wainright really intended to torch something besides the barricade. The implications of this were not lost on Elaine, and she called Ralph on this point.

"I assume you think he might have been targeting you," she said. "Do you have any solid evidence to support this allegation?"

"Naw, I don't have solid evidence, but ever'thing's pointing ta him making plans ta cut and run, an' we think he took the rear plate off uh the Hummer as a souvenir, 'cause he planned ta burn the Hummer somewhere, an' he was headed toward my place. He just couldn't get there, because John an' Diane put in a barricade what he couldn't get 'round. But he had a schedule ta keep, so he just set fire ta it right there an' hoped fer the best. Then he done hot footed it home, rode his dirt bike down ta the highway, abandoned it in the culvert under the highway, an' caught a ride out uh the country with someone."

Elaine had stopped taking notes and stared at Ralph as he finished talking. The Sheriff also sat up straighter and was staring at Ralph, who remained composed and appeared impervious to their stares. Elaine found her voice.

"You've seen this dirt bike?"

"I ain't seen it myself, but John here has," Ralph said calmly.

"Melvin followed the tracks of the dirt bike, and they angled up onto the highway heading south toward Colorado," Elaine said. "We thought he headed south. Are you sure you saw Wainright's dirt bike?"

"Well, we can't say fer sure whose it is, but there's a dirt bike in the upstream end uh the culvert." Ralph sat back and smiled at Elaine. "It'd be a real coincidence if'n it belongs ta anyone else."

Sheriff Johnson spoke up. "We'll check that out ASAP. Give us the details."

Ralph told him exactly where to find the culvert, and the Sheriff got up and left the room. While he was gone, Ralph asked Elaine, "When ya find out what Wainright's done with the land, can ya let me know?"

"I think so," she said. "The Sheriff'll probably make a public statement about this as soon as we have an idea of what really happened. He'll be asking the public for information and leads on Wainright's location. I'll try to get him to let you know before he goes public. Sounds to me like there might be a small army of people out there who would like to see him caught."

The Sheriff returned and told us two deputies were on their way to check out the culvert, he had cancelled the wrecker that

260

was scheduled to retrieve the remains of the Hummer the next day, and he had scheduled the forensics team to return and see what they could find out about the license plate, or the lack thereof, as the case may be. He thanked us for our information, and we headed back for the Lazy HZ. Before leaving Rawlins, we stopped for a bite to eat at a local restaurant that Ralph liked. The food was excellent, as I expected it would be.

The evening was late when we got back, and I needed to get to Laramie to start working on the planning office application. However, I needed more to spend time with Ralph. We sat on the porch and talked as the light faded and discussed what had happened with Wainright and how he had figuratively, and now literally, burned so many bridges with the folks in this neck of the woods. We agreed he would be in danger of being tarred and feathered and rode out of the county on a rail if he showed his face again.

"Do you think the Sheriff's Office will really try to find him and prosecute him?" I asked. "I'm betting he made off with a pile of money. He doesn't seem like the kind to just take off if it wasn't worthwhile."

"I don't think so," Ralph said. "Sure, there're some things he might do jail time for, but not much, if any. They might fine 'im, but no one got physically hurt, an' the bank'll probably get some money out uh the insurance company. If'n he stiffed the bank in Omaha, well, they're a long ways away. I think it'll just die down after a few days. Probably sell a few papers though."

We sat, watched the stars appear, and listened to the night insects calling. Ralph stirred.

"If'n you an' Diane hadn't put in that there second barricade with posts, we might not be sittin' here tonight," he said.

"I've thought that, too," I said. "I think Wainright was out to get you, or do some serious damage to your place here." I paused. "Or both," I added.

"I think so too," he said. "I 'preciate what ya done."

"It was Diane's idea. I think she might have known him a

little better, having worked around him for a time. I just met him that once. I was tired and ready to quit after we put up the second barricade, but she insisted we put in those posts."

"I'll have ta thank 'er, too."

We sat for a while longer in companionable silence.

"John, I've been thinkin' an' this here's what I'm goin' ta do. I ain't spent the money Wainright paid me for the land, so I'm going ta donate it ta Civalien, Inc., an' ya're goin' ta use it ta get back as much uh that land as ya can fer Civalia or maybe fer more uh 'em if'n other people get interested."

I was surprised into silence, and then I voiced the first thought that came into my mind. "Ralph, that's a lot of money. We can't accept that much."

"Why the hell not?" he asked. "Ya ain't a rich man are ya?"

"No," I said

"Well, if'n I remember right, ya gave a right big chunk ta buy that upper meadow, an' I think ya been fundin' the construction. Am I wrong?" he demanded.

"No," I said in a low voice.

"Well, then ya just let an old man do with 'is money as he pleases."

I was taken aback by Ralph's vehemence, so I apologized as best I could. "Ralph, I care a lot about you, and I wouldn't want to do anything that might hurt you, now or in the future. What if you need the money later on?"

"Pretty lame, John. I could say the same 'bout ya," Ralph said smiling. "Ya really believe in this here Civalia, an' so do I. Ya wouldn't want anyone ta deprive ya uh the opportunity ta make it happen would ya?"

"No," I said even more softly. "You're right. We're in this together."

I looked into his eyes when I said this, and the warmth flowing from them was intoxicating. We began talking about the logistics of trying to reclaim some of the land, and I told Ralph it would be nice to know how much Wainright had borrowed and how much he might have made off with. Ralph said he'd follow up with the Bank, although, even if he was able to pry the information from the bank, it might not be accurate. Wainright might have been using more than one bank.

We agreed a trip to Omaha was likely to be in the cards, and Ralph told me I would have to go there on my own. Travel was hard on him, and he had his animals to care for. I told him I would plan on going as soon as the information we needed was in hand. We called it a day; it had been a long and eventful Monday for both of us.

CHAPTER 13

The next day I did go back to Laramie and checked in with Stellan. He was making good progress on the construction plans for Civalia. He also told me Cass had a lead on a medical person, Gyan had started some experimental plantings, and Manjinder and he had made more progress on the artificial shell project. He estimated construction could begin late July or early August, if the geotechnical information was available and I could get the permit from the planning office in time.

On another subject, Stellan told me he had a preliminary quote on the fabric roof for the first pie shaped wedge of the workshop area. The quote made me wince, but I assured Stellan we would be able to cover the expense.

In the afternoon, I began putting together the materials for the planning office submittal, and also materials I thought might be needed for a trip to Omaha. I looked up the Amalgamated Bank of Omaha on the internet and began to familiarize myself with the bank to the extent I could.

Wednesday came and I got a call from Diane.

"I have the proposal for the geotechnical work on your Civalia land prepared, and I've got an invoice for the work on the Jim Baker's Retreat site," she told me. "To whom should these be addressed, and where should I send them?"

"We have a social welfare organization that is incorporated as Civalien, Inc., and Geraldine Olsen is the President. Address your proposal and invoice to her." I spelled Civalien for her. I added, "We will hold a board meeting to approve them. If you would like, you can attend the meeting and present your proposal in person, but if you don't want to make the trip, send them to me, and

I'll make sure we get this done promptly."

Without hesitation, Diane said, "I'd like to attend the board meeting."

"Good," I said. "I'll set up a time and get back to you. Ralph wants to tell you something, so he will be pleased to see you."

I called Ralph, and he said he would arrange a time with Geraldine and get back to me. I continued working on my planning proposal and on the Omaha trip materials. The rest of the day became a blur, but by the end of it, arrangements had been made for a board meeting the next day at the Lazy HZ Ranch. Diane would meet us there, and I had given Stellan a heads up about the high probability of him needing to meet with Diane on Thursday or Friday to communicate his design work requirements to her. The phone rang and rang again. I needed time to myself, so I went for a walk and stopped at the library.

Since much of my activities involved financial concerns, I looked into information on that subject and found a Bank of England quarterly report on the creation of money. It was eye opening, and it brought back memories of my earlier investigations into money and the capitalistic system. I had the vague sense, originating from I don't know when or where, that commercial banks received deposits from customers, paying them a certain interest rate for the use of their money, and then lending that money to someone else at a higher interest rate. Was I ever wrong!

When commercial banks make loans, they create money with the stroke of a pen, or I should say by keystrokes in this digital day and age. Their main obligation is they maintain their reserve requirement, which is about ten percent. When a bank makes a loan, the loan amount is credited to the borrower's account in the bank and becomes a checkable deposit. The amount of money which can be loaned is the inverse of the reserve requirement. In short, only about ten percent of any loan is actually backed by bank depositors. The sleight of hand comes in when the bank demands collateral for the loan, a mortgage on the property if the loan is for real estate. Now the bank does have an actual asset for the money they created. They can then loan out even more money on the basis of this new asset.

I walked home with my mind whirling, and sleep was long in coming that night.

Wednesday dawned and I was fuzzy headed, but a long shower and a good breakfast before I left for the Lazy HZ cleared my mind. As the miles rolled by, I thought about all that had happened. If construction was to start on Civalia, I still had much to accomplish in the next few weeks. I wondered if Stellan was experiencing the same sort of pressure.

When I arrived at the Lazy HZ, both Diane's pickup and a second pickup, probably Geraldine's, were parked by Ralph's house, but no one was on the porch. Even Gerald was absent as I went to the door. The inside door was open, and through the screen door I could see the three of them sitting around Ralph's table. I knocked lightly and let myself in.

"Come on in," Ralph said, looking up. "We're just playin' yer game."

I smiled. "You're getting a lot of mileage out of my game." I greeted Geraldine and Diane.

"This game is interesting," Diane said. "When we met, you mentioned the background on your project was not a 15-minute lecture, but this game makes the entropy principles behind your project fairly clear in a short time."

"Thanks," I said. "So, are you ready to sign up?" I asked jokingly.

"I'll have to think about that," she said with unexpected seriousness.

"She'll indubitably decide not to, with all of us old folks around fer company," Geraldine said.

We all laughed and Ralph moved the entropy game board to a side cabinet as we settled around the table.

"This here meetin'll come to order," Geraldine said. "Do we need minutes from the last meetin'?"

"I think we can dispense with those, since this is not a regularly scheduled meeting." I said.

"Fine." Geraldine looked at Diane. "I un'erstand you've got a bill for what work you did on . . ." She paused, seeming not to know what to call Wainright's land. "It don't hardly seem right to call it Wainright's, seein' as how he's skipped the country."

"Why don't we call it Ralph's land?" I asked.

"Just what it is," Geraldine said, and Ralph got a pleased look.

"Anyhow, you got a bill for your work on Ralph's land?" Geraldine asked Diane.

"Yes," she said as she pulled an invoice out of her brief case and laid it on the table in front of Geraldine. Ralph and I moved sideways to be able to read the invoice.

"$13,652. This here says ya worked eleven days," Ralph said. "That ain't enough 'cause I knowed ya were here at least fourteen, an' that's not countin' that day ya helped put up the barricade."

"And you aren't charging enough for your drill rig," I said. "It's worth at least a thousand a day."

Ralph got a scratch pad off of the counter and began calculating. "I think it's closer ta $26,000," he said. "Is this what you'd 'a charged Wainright?" he asked, tapping the invoice.

"No," Diane said in small voice. "But you folks are so nice and if it wasn't for you, I'd be taking a loss on the whole amount, and maybe incurring a loss on some of my equipment too."

"What would you've charged that there skunk?" Geraldine asked her.

Diane borrowed Ralph's scratch pad, pulled out her diary, and began paging through it and writing down numbers on the pad. "Be honest now," Geraldine added.

"It looks like the bill would have come to $27,312," she said.

"So, If'n we paid ya' $26,000 we'd be gettin' a hell uh a bargain, wouldn't we," Ralph said to her with a grin.

I could see Diane was beginning to tear up when she answered in a choked voice, "Yes, and so would I."

Geraldine took a pen from Ralph and scratched out the original invoice total and wrote in $26,000. I took the pen from her and initialed her change. "I move we pay this here invoice," Ralph said, and I seconded the motion. "All in favor?" Geraldine asked, and we voted unanimously to pay Diane's invoice.

While I wrote out a Civalien, Inc. check to Matthews Geo-technical Services, Diane pulled a fairly thick report along with a flash drive from her briefcase and laid them on the table. "Here's the report on . . ." She hesitated, and then reached for the pen, scratched out Jim Baker's Retreat on the cover of the report and wrote in, "Ralph's Land."

"Now, let's see your proposal for geotechnical site investigations for Civalia," I said.

Diane pulled a second document out of her brief case and laid it in front of me. I scooted it over so we could all look at it. This was basically a time and materials proposal, so I checked to make certain the schedule of charges and the total estimated time looked reasonable. I looked at the schedule, and it was one which would work with our plans for starting construction later in the summer.

"I move we accept this proposal from Matthews Geotechnical Services for the Civalia site investigations." I said.

The Civalien, Inc. board of directors also unanimously accepted Diane's proposal. I opened the checkbook again and wrote out a down payment check for Diane's services. Ralph and Geraldine signed both checks, and we adjourned the meeting. Ralph then got out his own checkbook and wrote her a check for $2,000.

"This heres's for your help with the barricade," he said as he handed her the check.

"I can't accept that," she said. "You've already done too much." She was still a little teary.

"Well," Ralph said, "you don't know what you done for me."

Ralph proceeded to tell Diane about what we had discovered and the likelihood Wainright was on his way to do some serious damage to Ralph, or his home, or both. Ralph then began to set out some lunch fixings, but not before he had taken me aside and told me he had heard from Elaine, and she had some information for us. He asked if I'd be willing to go to Rawlins to find out what she had. He called Elaine, and I grabbed a quick sandwich, excused myself, and set out for Rawlins. The Cadillac was certainly getting a workout.

I sat down with Elaine in her office and she told me several people in the region had voluntarily given her information of Wainright's financial machinations, so she could pass this information on to Ralph and me. She gave me a quick rundown on what she had learned. He had moved over twenty million dollars through the Rawlins National Bank, but she could only account for between three and four million from local vendors.

She asked me, "What do you plan to do with this information?"

"I'm going to approach Wainright's lender, the Amalgamated Bank of Omaha, and see if I can recover any of Ralph's land. Do you have any information on the timing of Wainright's transactions, especially his deposits?"

Elaine mulled this over for a moment and then said, "I think I can get that information. When do you plan to approach the Omaha Bank?"

"If you get the information, I think I'll be ready early next week, maybe Monday or Tuesday."

"How are you going to approach them?" she asked.

"I'm going to drive out there. I've found personal contact generally gets the best results, and I want to get Ralph the best results I can."

Elaine looked thoughtful, and then looked directly at me. "I may want to go with you. Is that okay?"

Elaine's request was unexpected, and I was a little taken back. "May I ask why?"

"I think there may be more going on with Wainright than we have a lead on here. Call it an investigator's hunch, and an investigative trip to prove or disprove that hunch."

"Okay, sure. Let me know if you get any more information, and we'll make plans." I gave Elaine my contact information.

I drove back via the Lazy HZ and stopped to talk with Ralph. Geraldine was still there. I told them what I had learned from Elaine, and we speculated about what Wainright had been up to.

"If I make a trip to Omaha, I'd like to have some pictures of the burned barricade, the Hummer, and some of the Jim Baker's

Retreat improvements, if you can call them that. Do you suppose I'd get into trouble for trespassing on the land?"

"There's another way to do 'er," Geraldine said; "telephoto lenses."

"Geraldine's a cracker jack photographer," Ralph said.

I thought back to the framed pictures I had seen on her walls. "Are those your framed pictures I saw at your house?" I asked Geraldine. She nodded yes. "Will you take some pictures for me then?"

"I'd be happy to," she said, "but if'n ya're goin' on Monday or Tuesday, I wouldn't get 'em back by then."

"Geraldine uses real film," Ralph said. "It's gettin' hard ta find, but she still likes it."

I considered options. "Geraldine, if we were to buy you a digital camera, would you use it to get those pictures for me?"

"It might take some gettin' used to it," she said, a little doubtfully.

"Let's give it a try," I said, and ushered the two of them out to the Cadillac.

This time I headed for Fort Collins through Walden, and after having an enjoyable dinner at an Italian restaurant, we spent the evening shopping for a camera with telephoto lenses. Geraldine was at first hesitant, but as she became more familiar with the "new fangled" cameras, she became more enthusiastic. By 9:00 PM she had identified her camera of choice, and we added a couple of telephoto lenses, some spare batteries, a bag, and some flash drives. I added a tablet computer and a color printer, so she could view and print her photos.

"You shouldn't get me all that stuff," she objected.

"Oh, we'll get our use out of it," I said. "We'll make you the official historian of the Civalien Project."

Geraldine continued to grumble, but she looked pleased. We headed back to the Lazy HZ. It was quite late when we got back, so both Geraldine and I stayed over at Ralph's. I took the bunk house again.

<hr>

I spent the remainder of the week working with Stellan on plans for the first stage of Civalia, and on the application for the planning office. Diane came to visit Stellan, and the two of them went over the plans for the site investigation. Diane told us she'd start the site work on Monday. Stellan brought me up to speed on the progress to perfect the geopolymer formula and obtain the ingredients. He told me Gyan had a lead on some volumetric cement equipment, and definitive word on this equipment should be available in the following week. I visited my financial advisor and made arrangements for an additional transfer into the Civalien, Inc., bank account. The costs for Civalia were beginning to mount.

The time was strange, seeming to both crawl and leap. My departure for Omaha seemed far in the future, yet I would end a day wondering where all the time had gone. Keeping track of everything needing to be done was difficult, but slowly, or at least it seemed that way, progress was being made.

I received pictures of Jim Baker's Retreat from Geraldine, finished the planning office application except for the site and construction plans, and some other technical materials I needed from Stellan, and gathered materials for the trip. Elaine called, telling me she had obtained a detailed statement of Wainright's account. She would not be able to show it to me, but she would be able to tell me some generalities. We made arrangements to head east on Monday morning. I called and made room reservations for us in Omaha for two nights, since I doubted we would want to head back on Tuesday. I also called the Omaha bank and made an appointment for Tuesday morning. I then serviced and fueled the Cadillac and packed for the trip.

Monday morning finally came and Elaine arrived at my door along with the rising sun's rays. We transferred her things to the Cadillac and headed east on I-80. I drove the first leg to North Platte, where we stopped for some food and fuel. Elaine drove the rest of the way. I was glad she was driving, because we came into Omaha during the afternoon rush hour. We found our way to the hotel, ate dinner in the hotel restaurant, and turned in for the night.

Elaine and I talked a lot while we were driving. I had inquired about her life and her connections with Ralph. I learned she was a longtime resident of Carbon County, having moved to Rawlins when she was in grade school, and lived there since. She had married her high school sweetheart and they had two children, a dog, and two parakeets. Her husband was the local State Farm Insurance agent. Since Ralph used State Farm Insurance, she had first learned of Ralph through her husband. Then when Wainright had taken Ralph's land, she had become much more aware and acquainted with him through the legal system.

Elaine asked me about Civalia, and I told her about our thinking, our plans, and how they meshed with Ralph's thinking and his care of his land. She confessed she didn't really understand what I was saying about entropy, so I suggested she talk with Ralph about it if she thought she would really like to understand it. I told her how Ralph had figured out the intricacies of entropy on his own and was able to explain it much better than I could with my formal education approach. She said she would think about doing that.

What we didn't talk about was Wainright's finances. I tried talking about them, but she put me off and explained she needed to keep secret some things showing up in her investigation of the circumstances involving Wainright's disappearance. She did tell me she thought there might be some information coming out in our meeting with the bank that could help me, if not immediately, then down the road. She also told me frankly the budget of the Carbon County Sheriff's office would not support a trip for her to Omaha, and going with me was a way for her to personally get to talk to the bank representatives. I accepted her explanation, and we avoided the subject for the rest of the drive.

Tuesday morning, we set out early to find the bank. After locating it, we found a nearby restaurant for breakfast. At 8:30 AM we were in the bank for our appointed meeting, where we were met by a Mr. Al Gifford, a loan officer of the bank, and taken to his office.

"What can I do for you?" he asked when we were settled.

I looked at Elaine. She glanced at me, and then took out her Sheriff's Office ID.

"Mr. Gifford, John introduced me as Elaine Thompson, but that should be Lieutenant Thompson, with the Carbon County, Wyoming Sheriff's Department. One of your bank's customers has some holdings in Carbon County, and some things he has done have come to our attention. I believe he has a substantial loan with your bank."

Elaine handed Mr. Gifford her ID. He looked it over carefully and then asked, "Who might the customer be?"

"Mr. Howard Wainright, and he's calling his project Jim Baker's Retreat."

"Just a minute," Mr. Gifford swiveled to his computer. He adjusted the monitor to make certain we couldn't see it and then tapped some keys, frowned, tapped some more keys, and then said, "Yes, he has a loan from us that is currently in good standing." Mr. Gifford emphasized the words "good standing."

"Records from our end show he has currently borrowed $23,228,678 from you in construction loans. Is that correct?"

I tucked that information away in my mind for future use, but I also felt devastated. The monies from Ralph would hardly make a dent in that loan. I'd be lucky to get back a tenth of what Wainright took.

Mr. Gifford looked very uncomfortable. "I really can't say. Our client's records are confidential, and . . ." He paused. "Do you have a search warrant?" he asked.

"Will I need one?" Elaine responded. "We are just trying to help you out here, Mr. Gifford. Mr. Wainright has disappeared, and we think he might have taken some of your money with him."

Now Gifford looked patently upset. "I need to get some other people involved in this."

Gifford ushered us out of his office and led us upstairs to a conference room. He seated us and then went out the door. "I'll be right back," he said.

He was back shortly, and there were three other men and a woman with him. He made hasty introductions, most of their names forgotten by me before they were out of his mouth, but Elaine had taken out her notebook and quickly wrote down names. I did catch their titles. We had a bank VP of something, I didn't get what, the CFO, an internal auditor, and the woman, who was an administrative assistant to the VP. The administrative assistant had setup a laptop computer and had it operational by the time the introductions were completed.

Elaine repeated her request for the total loan amount. The VP cleared his throat and said, "You are correct within a couple of percent."

"Mr. Wainright had a substantial deposit arrive at a Rawlins National Bank a couple of weeks ago. I assume this was an installment on his construction loan. Is that correct?"

The VP also looked uncomfortable, but he said, "Yes, we made such a transfer to his account. He made the required progress report, and we transferred the funds for ongoing construction expenses."

"May I see the progress report?" Elaine asked.

"Now see here," The VP said. "This is highly irregular, and we can't let just anyone see these confidential records."

"Then let me ask you another question," Elaine said. "Did Mr. Wainright submit an invoice from Mathews Geotechnical Services out of Fort Collins, Colorado?"

"Yes," the VP answered.

"And is that invoice in the amount of slightly more than $27,000?" Elaine asked.

There was stunned silence on the Amalgamated Bank of Omaha side of the table, and then a wild whispered conference broke out among the four bank representatives as they leaned toward each other. They stopped, settle back in their own chairs, and the VP said, "It looks like we might indeed have a problem here. Do you have a copy of this invoice you are referencing?"

"Yes, I do," Elaine said without making any move to produce it. "May I suggest that you produce your progress report from Mr. Wainright, and I will produce my copy of the invoice from Mathews Geotechnical Services so we can compare them?"

Another conference ensued and the administrative assistant

left the room. The bank representatives all sat in silence, staring at most anything but us, while they waited for her to return. When she did, she was carrying a large, rather thick manila envelope, which she laid in front of the VP. He pulled a sheaf of papers from it and began to page through them. As he did so, I caught sight of a picture, and my breath caught in my throat.

Elaine opened her brief case, removed several stapled sheets of paper, and laid them face down on the conference table.

The VP removed a similar, much thicker pile of stapled sheets and also laid them face down.

"So, what is the invoiced amount on your copy of the Mathews Geotechnical Services invoice dated June 23rd of this year?" Elaine asked.

The VP was looking positively sick. "$593,325," he said.

I discretely bumped Elaine's foot and cleared my throat. "Did Mr. Wainright supply you with pictures of the progress of his project?" I asked.

All the bank representatives turned their attention to me, and the VP said in a weak voice, "Yes."

"I don't suppose it looked like this picture taken three days ago did it?" I said casually, as I laid one of the photos, which Geraldine had taken, out on the table and slid it toward the center of the table facing the bank representatives.

The VP's face lost all color. His hands trembling, he pulled a sheet from the sheaf of papers and laid it beside my picture. It was not the same angle, but there were enough features to identify it as the same geographical location with Wainright's house behind the main construction. The similarity ended there. The construction project on the Bank's picture showed advanced construction with parts of a building approaching exterior finish. There were also many vehicles, and lots of equipment around the building. Several luxury vehicles were parked around Wainright's house. My picture showed some foundation slabs, a few raw concrete walls, pipe stubs sticking out of the slabs. There were no vehicles of any description around Wainright's house and no equipment around the slabs.

"My picture was taken three days ago," I said, "as you can

see by the time stamp on the picture. Or if this is not sufficient to convince you, you are welcome to send you own representative to verify this stage of construction. Your picture is Photoshopped," I said confidently, indicating Wainright's picture.

The bank representatives excused themselves to confer, and Elaine and I took the time for our own conference.

"Did you know Wainright was running this kind of fraud?" I asked Elaine.

"I had a strong suspicion. The numbers I was finding were not adding up. How did you know about the pictures?"

"I glimpsed one when the VP was paging through Wainright's progress report," I told her.

"It's a good thing you had those pictures with you," she said.

"Where are you going to take it from here?" I asked her.

"I don't think I can take it much farther. I'm willing to bet Wainright is out of the country, and we certainly can't follow his trail there."

"Could it be made a Federal case?"

"If it is, the bank will have to initiate it," she said.

"Could the Rawlins National turn it into a Federal case?"

"The only loss they'll have is going to be the Hummer loan, and insurance will probably take care of it. This bank is the only one that is going to really suffer. We'll have to see what they've got in mind."

I examined the picture from Wainright. The Photoshopping was very good, but with very careful studying, a couple of discrepancies were visible. The most telling one, in my mind, was a shadow out of place on one of the cars around Wainright's house.

The bank representatives came back, reinforced by the bank president. A frank discussion took place and the bank allowed us to see the entire progress report. Elaine had more information on a couple more venders whose invoices had been inflated, and she showed those to the bank representatives. I was shocked at the extent of Wainright's brazen changing of the invoiced amounts. The total reported on the progress report, $8,743,586; more than ten times what I thought Wainright had actually spent; probably twenty times, if the invoice Diane had presented was any guide.

This progress report contained a supposed independent inspector's report. Elaine told the bankers Wainright had obviously had outside assistance, speculating he and the inspector might have been co-conspirators. She reasoned the inspector might have been the person who picked him up when he rode his dirt bike out to the highway.

I showed the bank representatives the discrepancies I'd found in the Photoshopped picture, and told them I'd seen the site from a distance once, and though construction was ongoing at the time, there was not anywhere near that many vehicles or that much construction equipment present. I was conservative in my critique of the pictures and didn't point out all I knew or suspected, because they were already convinced.

The administrative assistant was sent for earlier progress reports on the Jim Baker's Retreat loan, and the same sort of doctoring was evident in them all. Wainright's fraud had been going on since the beginning.

The bank president was grim faced. "We'll foreclose on that property immediately, and sell it. Its over 13,000 acres, so we should be able to more than recoup our money, but if not, there is always the five million dollar building we could sell."

Elaine nudged my foot, so I began my spiel. "There is a problem with that," I began. "The piece of property you are talking about is virtually land locked, and that's the reason Wainright absconded with your money at this time. Had he not been blocked from accessing the construction site, he would undoubtedly have continued to steal a lot more money from you."

I proceeded to tell them the story of Wainright's acquisition of the land from Ralph by eminent domain, and about his failure to obtain an easement through Ralph's property. I told them how the land was bordered by the national forest, Ralph's land, and the river, with the highway right-of-way passing through the eastern side. I emphasized how the land in question was sandwiched between two parcels of Ralph's land, since Wainright had taken a chunk out of the middle. I showed them pictures of the road and the barricade we had erected, and pictures of Wainright's burned out Hummer. I showed them pictures of the hogback and explained why making an access road through there would be very expensive, and why it would take a long time to get permission to connect to the highway, if such permission would be granted at all. I laid it on thick.

Elaine added to my narrative by telling them while the Sheriff's office was not yet absolutely certain, they were pretty sure Wainright had torched his own vehicle, and had intended to inflict harm on Ralph. Although she had never seen the inside of Wainright's house, she also speculated it was not much more than a shell, as evidenced by the progress on the rest of the project.

While Elaine was talking, I had been thinking desperately about how I could get a reasonable chunk of Ralph's land back from the meager monies he'd been paid for it. I thought back on what I'd been reading about banks creating money and then getting paid interest on what they'd created. I then came to a decision. I'd try offering them a settlement based on the reasoning they really only had a tenth of the amount they had loaned at risk to their depositors, they were entitled to about 20 percent annual profit on that money, and they were entitled to a certain amount of overhead. I'd see if I could get back at least some of the land using that formula. What did I have to lose?

When Elaine finished talking, I leaned over and whispered to her that I really needed to see the data she had from the Rawlins National Bank. This time she did not hesitate to surreptitiously pass the sheet under the table to me. I hastily ran the calculations to determine the time average of the loans to Wainright and multiplied that number by 1.5. I came up with $2,439,011, and I rounded that to $2,440,000. I could use the remainder of the$275,000 Ralph had been paid to bargain with them. This, of course, was all predicated on whether or not the bankers would even talk to me about such low numbers.

After Elaine had finished what she had to say, the bankers had again been conversing with each other in whispers and low murmurs while I was making my calculations.

I cleared my throat to get their attention and said, "Gentlemen, in light of the fraudulent progress reports you have before you, I'm certain you can get title to this land, maybe through a some-

279

what lengthy foreclosure proceeding, but more likely through a summary judgment within a very short time. Is this not so?"

"Certainly," the bank president said, "and we will do just that. Seek a summary judgment, I mean."

"Yes," I said. "I represent the prior owner of this land, Ralph Hertell, and I am authorized to offer you $2, 440,000 to purchase back this property."

There was shocked silence for a moment and then a babble of voices. One shout stood out, "No Way!"

Sensing failure, I stood up and Elaine followed suit. She surprised me by saying, "Well, we will probably be seeing a lot more of you gentlemen in court in Wyoming when Ralph sues you for failure to perform your fiduciary duties."

As we walked down the stairs and headed for the outside door, I asked Elaine, "Could Ralph really sue them?"

"He probably could. If he got them in front of a jury, and all this mess came out, the jury might be sympathetic to Ralph and give him something for what he's suffered. On the other hand, juries are fickle. A lot of it would depend on the lawyers."

"I know a pretty good one," I said. "I'll follow up on that angle."

"Why did you offer such a low amount?" Elaine asked.

I told her my budget was limited to the monies Ralph had received for the land, and I'd come up with a formula giving them a 20 percent annual profit plus 30 percent annual overhead on 10 percent of the amount they had loaned to Wainright. This formula was within my budget and gave me a little negotiating room. As I was about to explain why I'd only used 10 percent of the loan amount to calculate what I'd pay to the bank, we went out the door and started walking across the parking lot to the Cadillac. I was fishing in my pocket for the car keys when Mr. Gifford came running after us, panting from the exertion.

"Wait," he gasped.

We stopped and he stood trying to catch his breath. When he could speak again, he said, "Come back up, and let's talk about this some more."

We followed him back inside, up the stairs, and back into the conference room. The VP was missing.

The president indicated the bank was willing to make some concessions, given the nature of these transactions, and he tried to bargain with me by offering to settle for a mere $10,000,000.

"Look," I said, "I don't think you realize how difficult it will be for you to sell this land if you do foreclose on it."

I pulled out the ownership map of the area again and placed it on the table in front of the bank president. I used my pen to indicate boundaries and again went over the land locked situation.

"This parcel of land is bounded on the north and south by land belonging to Mr. Hertell. He's the one from whom Wainright obtained this land by eminent domain. I can guarantee you, Mr. Hertell will not grant you access from either the north or the south side of that land. On the west you have the national forest. I'm sure you know getting access through National Forest on that side would be a bureaucratic nightmare, if you could ever get it at all. On the east side is State Highway 230, and getting access through that side would be another bureaucratic nightmare. The connection to the highway is either on a fill or in a cut for most of the way across the eastern end, making it difficult and expensive. Plus, as I told you before, you have this hogback running down toward the highway and ending in this ravine. The ravine, as you can see, is on Mr. Hertell's property. Making a road through the hogback would be difficult and very expensive. Wainright could have taken this option, but he didn't."

"That's right," Elaine said, "and the local residents are not happy with what Wainright's done, particularly to Mr. Hertell. I predict, after what has happened now, there will be a lot of local opposition to any more construction work. That goes for any effort to sell the land to some outsider too."

"To even show it, you would need for your prospective buyers to walk in, ride in on a trail bike, or come in by helicopter, and I don't know if there is a good place for a helicopter to land," I said.

"And a jury would love to hear about how you helped rob Ralph by paying Wainright," Elaine added.

I thought about discretely kicking her to keep her quiet, but I refrained. She was probably actually helping my cause, but I was embarrassed by her words. However, what she said was effective;

it just wasn't how I would have said it. The president conferred with his CFO and auditor via passing some notes.

The president then turned to us and said, "Will you settle with us for $3,000,000?"

"$2,500,000 is the max," I said.

There was a long silence. "Okay," he said, "but there has to be a legal agreement that you won't bring any legal action against the bank, and you can't publicly discuss the settlement. Will you agree to that?"

Threat of legal action did seem to be the key to making this deal work, and I was grateful to Elaine for applying that pressure. I now felt really glad she had come with me.

"Yes," I said. "We have a corporation that will be handling this transaction for Ralph, who is the vice president of the corporation. You can work out a purchase agreement, which includes your non-disclosure agreement, with our lawyer. We'll sign it, and then our lawyer will send it to you for your signatures. When you obtain the deed for the land, we will set up a closing. Elaine and I will return to Wyoming tomorrow, and Thursday I will begin moving money to our lawyer's trust account. Everything should be in place on our end by sometime next week."

I traded contact information for Maggie, myself, and Civalien, Inc. with the bank representatives, and Elaine and I left for a victory dinner and a good night's sleep before the long drive home. I was elated, but at the same time felt a sense of guilt. I had just extracted, maybe you could say robbed, more than twenty million dollars from a bank.

CHAPTER 14

Elaine was quiet on the drive back from Omaha.

"Is something bothering you?" I asked.

"A little," she answered. "I'm really happy you were able to convince the bankers to return Ralph's land for even slightly less than he was paid for it, but I've been thinking about all those people who've deposited their money in the bank and lost it to Wainright. I don't think we'll ever be able to find him, and even if we did, we probably wouldn't be able to recover their money. But I can't believe the bank accepted your offer of only two and half million."

"It's not exactly like that," I told her. "The bank had considerably less than two and half million of depositors' money at risk as a reserve requirement. The rest of their loan to Wainright was created money."

"What do you mean by that?" she asked. "I thought banks loaned depositors' money and charged interest to make a profit."

"That's what they'd like you to think, but what really happens is the bank only has to have a certain reserve in long term deposits, about ten percent, and then they create the entire loan amount by adding it to the borrower's account in their bank. The money comes out of thin air. It is created by pushing some keys on a computer."

"You're shitting me," Elaine said.

"I wish I was, but I'm not."

I drove in silence for a while, then Elaine asked, "So why don't they just go wild and loan out billions or trillions of dollars?"

"Some have done that and I'm sure some continue to, even today. What happens is they get overextended, get too greedy, and then when someone comes in and wants to withdraw their savings, the bank doesn't have enough available cash to pay them. Other depositors get wind of this shortfall and come to the bank demanding their money. It's called a run on the bank, and the bank has to close its doors."

Elaine was quiet while she digested this information.

"Excessive borrowing also fuels inflation," I added, "so the cost of everything ratchets ups. In this country, and most countries in the world, banking laws have established legal limits on how much money they can create. These rules are crafted to try to keep everything growing at a slow rate, about two percent. Even with these rules, a few banks still manage to get in trouble and close, about half a dozen to a dozen a year in the United States."

"Well, I know a few bankers," Elaine said, "and they are very respectable people. I like them."

"Yes," I said, "so do I. You've probably heard the saying, 'When someone gets something for nothing, somebody, somewhere, sometime, gets nothing for something.' Well, I think it's more true to say somebody gets a whole pile of entropy, or as Ralph would say, 'shit'. If you ask bankers, they believe they are very instrumental in making the world a better place by making the economy grow, but they're not making the world a better place. In fact, continual growth will eventually destroy the Earth by entropy build-up, as surely as continued growth of a cancer will destroy a person. What we've thought to be life-giving really brings death."

Elaine mulled over what I had said, finally stating, "I don't understand all you have been telling me, particularly about entropy, but I have personal experience with death from cancer; my mother. And yes, I can understand how things can't grow forever. Rawlins has grown some, and water and sewer problems have reared their ugly heads. We've seen new problems arise in the Sheriff's Office from growth of the community."

She brooded some more. "You've relieved my mind somewhat about the bank's depositors, but I'd still like to get Wainright somehow," she said.

"If he's out of the country, that might be hard to do," I replied.

"Maybe, but if he was on his way to burn down Ralph's house and perhaps kill him, I don't think he'll give up easily."

That was a sobering thought to me. "Do you really think he was trying to do something?"

"I think it fits his profile, and the evidence of his burned Hummer points that way. I wouldn't be surprised if he didn't try to get even with Ralph sometime in the future."

"How could he do that?"

"He could put out a contract on him, but I think he might want to be more personally involved, seeing Ralph suffer for ruining his fraud scheme."

"You're scaring me," I said.

"I'd hope so," she said. "You and your Civalien project might also be targets if you begin using and building on the land Wainright regarded as his. Just being friends with Ralph might put you on his shit list."

"What would you suggest we do?"

"Let me think about that for a while," Elaine answered.

I drove for about 15 miles before Elaine broke the silence.

"From what you told the bank people, Ralph has given you, or the corporation you've formed, the money Wainright paid for the land, and the corporation will then buy the land from the bank. Is that right?"

"Essentially," I said. "The money hasn't been transferred yet, but that's what Ralph said he wanted to do."

"You and your project will probably be safer if Ralph personally buys back the land, keeping you and your friends out of the picture. I think Ralph will also be safer.

"How so?" I asked.

"I think he's already a target," Elaine said. "I'd bet on it. Guy's like Wainright don't like to be defeated in any way, and Ralph, with your help, cut his fraud scheme short. I'm thinking if Ralph buys the land back, it will become the focus of Wainright's resentment and give us a much better chance of detecting his plot and stopping him. I think it might be the best way to protect Ralph from him, since we'd have some idea of the direction from and how he might be attacking. In other words, it narrows the possibilities some."

We were both quiet for a while as I thought about what Elaine had said. "How do you think Wainright might come after Ralph?" I asked.

"He probably won't come after him personally, because I'd guess he's out of the country. The bank records show transfers into out-of-state banks and eventually into off-shore banks. I also can't see him putting a contract on Ralph, because that'll cost him and won't make him any money in the long run. I'd guess it might come in the guise of his agent attempting to somehow obtain or sabotage the land, or it might be some type of legal action."

"His house," I said. "There's a separate deed and mortgage on the building and a few acres of land. If he has control of that, he would have a foot in the door to go after Ralph, both legally and physically."

"You may be right," Elaine said. "I'll have to look into that."

"If it's okay with you, I'll work on that angle too."

"Be my guest," she said. "I don't have the resources to work on this full time. In fact, it will probably be a low priority. How'd Wainright get the house and a few acres separated from the main deed on the land? Wasn't it included in the original eminent domain purchase and money borrowed from the bank in Omaha?"

"I don't know," I said, "and I forgot to bring it up with the bankers. I'll have to look into that angle too."

We talked more, but we just didn't have enough information to make any firm judgments about the best course of action.

We arrived back in Laramie late in the evening, and I asked Elaine if she would like to stay over rather than drive home in the dark. She decline, climbed into her car, and headed home. I opened the front garage door to put away the Cadillac, but another one of my antique cars was already in there. I closed the garage door, locked the Cadillac, pulled the mail out of the mailbox, and went into my apartment. The curtained window in the door to the shop was glowing, and fairly loud construction sounds could be heard.

I opened the shop door to a very welcome sight. Stellan, Cass, Gyan, Cindy, a woman and a boy I assumed were Manjinder and

Anand, and two other people I didn't know were busy among stacked pallets, large containers of various descriptions, and equipment of various kinds, including a cement mixer. Stellan saw me, dropped what he was doing, and hurried over.

"It's good to see you back," he shouted over the noise. "Let's go inside where we can hear." He turned me around and ushered me back through the door.

"What's' going on?" I asked excitedly, at the same time Stellan was asking, "How did it go?"

"Why don't you go first?" Stellan asked. "What I have to report will take a lot longer."

"Okay," I said, and proceeded to tell Stellan about what had happened in Omaha. "So, they've agreed to sell all of it back to us for two and a half million," I finished.

"You're kidding!" Stellan said. "What did you do? Hold a gun to their heads? Where's your mask?"

I explained what I'd done and my reasoning behind it.

"It'll take me a while to digest all that," Stellan said.

"Right," I said, "so tell me about what's going on in the shop."

"Wait here a second," Stellan said, and he slipped back into the shop. He was back almost immediately with a roll of drawings, one of which he pulled from the roll and spread out on the table. "As you know, we're starting on the inner cottage industry area, the workshop area, with a wedge shaped piece. The only permanent parts of this first wedge are the hypocaust floor, the outer cylindrical wall, and the center column to support the roof." Stellan pointed out these various parts on the drawing. "We're going to build temporary wing walls from the center column to the outer wall."

"How do you plan to build the wing walls?" I asked.

Stellan grinned. "Cindy came up with a great idea for those," he said, and he pulled another sheet from the roll and spread it out.

"That looks like one of my childhood toys, American Wooden Bricks, or the more modern LEGO® blocks," I said.

"Exactly," Stellan said. "Right now, out in your shop, we're putting the finishing touches on a series of experiments with geopolymer materials to design the molds for full size blocks.

They'll have slightly tapered pegs and sockets to make them fit snuggly together. We're designing in some tongue-and-groove structures along the edges to help seal them from the weather, but we'll probably have to put something over the outside to block the wind and keep moisture out. We hope to start pouring blocks next week, but that's dependent on getting enough material to make the first mold."

"Perhaps you should leave a groove for chinking," I said. "What are you going to make the molds out of?"

"They'll have a backing of geopolymer, but there will be a flexible polyurethane liner that'll help release the cast block from the mold. Your idea of a chinking groove is a good one. I'll talk with the others and we'll consider adding that feature."

I examined the drawing carefully and mentally made some estimated calculations. "With these dimensions, two feet by one foot by four inches high, these would weigh about 100 pounds. How many of them do you think we need?"

"Probably about 1,800, but we're planning to make about 2,000. Having some extras won't hurt. However, they'll only weigh about sixty pounds, because we're going to build in some empty space in the same way a LEGO® block is not solid on the bottom."

"Oh, I see that in your drawing," I said, and I modified my estimated weight calculations. "So, the total weight of all the blocks will be somewhere in the 60 ton range. That's less than a rail car of material, so it should be workable. And if you're making them here, it would only take twenty trips with my truck and trailer. It's definitely possible, but the time frame doesn't look like it will work. With the blocks taking seven days to set enough to handle, you'll have to make hundreds of molds to get the job done."

"I think we will make it, unless we get a horrible blizzard in September. Geopolymers can be handled in two or three days. We're planning to ramp up to about 100 molds within a month and transport the molds to the Civalia site as soon as we're confident they will produce blocks to specification. Meanwhile, we have a lot of other work to get ready for actual construction."

"That's an understatement, if I ever heard one," I said. "What else is going on?"

"Well, I had Diane concentrate on the most likely location for the Civalia complex, and she has completed enough of the geotechnical data to allow us to break ground. Gyan located some continuous cement equipment, and we'll be going after it soon. Which reminds me; can we use your truck and trailer for that, and I need to get with you to see about funding some of these efforts."

"Right," I said, but a quick mental inventory of the financial status of Civalien, Inc., told me I'd have to put in some more money before much of anything could happen. I put that task on my mental to-do list. "Can you get me a cost estimate of what you are going to need in the next couple of months? A timeline with it would be nice, but don't waste a lot of effort on it. We've got to make blocks while the sun shines."

"I'll get it to you ASAP," Stellan said. "Let's go out, and I'll introduce you to the others."

Stellan rolled up the drawings, and we went out to the shop. He halted some of the noisiest work and introduced me to Manjinder and Anand, and to the two people I knew nothing about. They were two of Manjinder's graduate students, Denise Boechard and Larry Pindergast. I didn't visit with them long, since I didn't want to interfere with the work. I signaled to Stellan to start up the work again and went back inside, taking Stellan's roll of drawings with me.

I looked through the drawing set and began to earmark supplemental materials I'd need for the building permit application, mainly the building plans. I was deep into this work when the noise from the shop quieted down, and the slamming of the back door a few times indicated the crew was leaving. Stellan came in through the shop door, turning off the light as he came into my apartment. We sat and talked for a while, and I briefed him on the drawings and ancillary materials I'd need for the building permit.

"We'd better get the permit underway," I said, "or it will be a major roadblock for the project."

"I'll get right on it," Stellan replied. "Our crew is great, so I don't think I need to be here all the time. I think I can get it to you tomorrow, probably later in the afternoon."

"Wonderful," I said. "I'll plan on heading for Rawlins with the permit application this Friday."

We'd both had a long day, so we decided to end it.

Thursday dawned, and I began the day by visiting with my
financial advisor and transferring more funding to Civalien, Inc.
I called Ralph, and after lunch I headed out to visit with him. I
did not go directly to his ranch, but instead drove to Rawlins to
research the deed and mortgage on Wainright's house.

The deed looked ordinary enough, a tract of land 375 feet
square with all the improvements thereon. The house was centered
in the square and the square was oriented with the house structure. The deed was in Wainright's project name, and the mortgage was held by an investment company named Embuscadoes
Investments, Inc., in Key West, Florida. These two documents
were accompanied by a release from the Amalgamated Bank of
Omaha for the house and the few acres it sat on. All three documents had been recorded three days after our first barricading of
Ralph's road. My con alarm went off. I tried contacting Elaine,
but she was not available, so I made four copies each of the deed,
the mortgage, and the release. I then went to the Carbon County
Library to use their computers for some internet searches.

A search for the mortgage company yielded zero results. I
found the web site for the Florida Secretary of State, and tried
looking up the company in their corporation database. I couldn't
find it, but there was one with a name only off by a single letter,
Ambuscadoes Investments, Inc. It had been incorporated the day
before the mortgage was filed—with a fictitious name registra-
tion. It was all rather confusing to me, so I recorded the contact
information for the registered agent, and tried calling Elaine. She
was still not available, so I left a message for her. I then called the
planning office and made an appointment for the next day, Friday,
at 1:30, and finally headed for Ralph's.

Just driving up to Ralph's home was soothing to me. It seemed
like all the cares and problems churning around in my mind faded

in importance. Ralph was waiting in his rocking chair, and Gerald was sitting up on his hind legs next to the chair checking me out. When I climbed out of the car, he headed for his tree, scolding as he climbed.

Ralph stood and we embraced. "It seems like it is always too long between when I see you," I said.

"Sure does, don't it," Ralph said, as I sat down in the other rocking chair. "Tell me 'bout yer trip ta Omaha." By then Gerald had stopped scolding and was headed back down the tree.

I described our meeting with the bank loan officer and how Elaine had opened the door to a more serious meeting. When I told Ralph I'd learned Wainright had borrowed over twenty million dollars from them, he was surprised to say the least.

"No shit! How'd he do that?"

"Fraud," I said. "He submitted inflated invoices from his contractors, faked progress reports, and bogus inspections."

"So how'd you make out? A couple 'a mill don't go far for land that's costin' more'n twenty mill." Ralph looked somewhat crestfallen.

"Well," I said, "we got them to release the whole mortgage for two and a half million."

Ralph stopped rocking and leaned forward. "Ya pullin' my leg? What'd ya do; pull a gun on 'em?"

"No, I'm not pulling your leg, but there are problems."

Ralph settled back in his chair. "Figgers," he said. "Sounds a little too good ta be true."

"Oh, it's true alright. We should be able to complete the transaction within the next couple of weeks, but I don't think we're done with Wainright."

"That figgers too," he said. "Tell me what that skunk's up ta now."

Ralph listened quietly while I told him about the deed, the dicey mortgage on the house and a few acres around it, and the release from the Amalgamated Bank. I told him about my dead end searching for the mortgage holding company in Key West, Florida, and the weirdness of the incorporation of a company with an almost identical, fictitious, name. I tried to explain to Ralph the concept of a fictitious corporate name in Florida, but I wasn't too clear on it myself and probably made a hash of it.

"Elaine thought it would be best if you purchased the land back directly, instead of having Civalien, Inc., buy it," I told him.

"Why's that?" Ralph asked.

"If Wainright's out to get revenge, she thinks it may focus Wainright on you and make it easier to detect what he's doing and stop him."

"So," Ralph said, "he'd be less likely ta go after ya an' Civalia. Ain't that right?"

I was again amazed at how perceptive Ralph was. "Yes, that's what Elaine thought. I've left a message for Elaine to call me, so I can tell her about this weird transfer of Wainright's house."

We both sat rocking for a time, thinking about the ramifications of what I'd found. Ralph was occasionally, absentmindedly, feeding Gerald peanuts.

I was the one to speak first. "It seems to me, we should try to close the deal with the Amalgamated Bank as soon as we can. If we wait too long, this whole thing could blow up into a legal nightmare and take years to settle. Even now, it may take a little longer than I originally thought, because I don't think the Amalgamated Bank knows about the transfer of this little chunk. We'll have to look into the legality of it, and it may hold up the bank getting a clean title to the land. Hopefully, it won't be a major problem, because Wainright's not likely to appear to defend his fraudulent invoices. Maybe the house can be included in a summary judgment."

Ralph leaned forward, and we both stopped rocking. "I agree with ya. I was thinkin' some uh the same things a few minutes ago, but got ta thinkin' 'bout some other things needin' done, just didn't tell ya 'bout it," Ralph said.

"Oh," I said, "what else are you thinking we need to do?"

"Wainright must be figgerin' on usin' that there house fer somethin' no good, so soon as we can, we ought ta fence it with somethin' not too easy ta get over and install some uh them there trail cameras where they're kind uh hidden." Ralph sat back and resumed rocking.

"That's a good idea," I said. "When I talk with Maggie tomorrow, I'll see if we can get something in the purchase agreement about letting us put in a fence and some security. I'll also ask her what she thinks about how we should bring up the issue of this transfer with the bank."

The evening was creeping up, and although I didn't really want to leave Ralph, I forced myself to head for home. I had much to do the next day, Friday, to prepare for an equally busy weekend.

I stumbled out of bed early the next morning and began writing up a narrative to give to Maggie about the bank meeting and my findings about the additional mortgage. Stellan and his crew were at work around 7:00, and Stellan brought me the materials for the building permit application. I thanked him and continued writing. He looked at me questioningly, but as I didn't have time to get into everything I was working on, I told him I'd catch up with him on the weekend. As early as possible, I called Maggie and asked if I could drop by for a few minutes. Fortunately, she said she could spare me about 15 minutes. I rushed out the door.

"Hi, Maggie," I said as I plopped down in her client chair. "I went to Omaha with Elaine Thompson, she's a lieutenant with the Carbon County Sheriff's Office, and met with the Amalgamated Bank of Omaha representatives. They were loaning Harold Wainright money to buy and develop Ralph's land. I've written a short narrative about what happened, and it includes some more information I found yesterday. I'd like you to read this over. . .," I laid my papers on her desk in front of her, "and then work out a purchase agreement with the bank for the land Wainright took from Ralph."

"Whoa," Maggie said. "How long is your narrative?"

"It's about five pages."

"Why don't I read this quickly, and then ask you any questions I have. Then we can go from there. Okay?"

"Sure," I said. I settled back and while Maggie was reading, I got out my checkbook and wrote out a check for ten thousand dollars, figuring we'd need some earnest money.

Maggie finished reading and laid the sheets of paper down. "I'm impressed. You must have really scared the bank to have them settle for only two and half million, but this glitch with the real estate transfer may cause trouble."

"That's what I'm afraid of," I said. "What do you think is the best way to handle it?"

"I don't know. Let me research and think about it. I'll start writing a purchase agreement, and get back to you next week. If I have questions, I'll call. Will that do?"

"It'll have to," I said. "Of course, I'd have liked to have it yesterday."

Maggie laughed. "Your fifteen minutes are up, Buster."

I hurried home, called Ralph to see if he would like to go to the planning office in Rawlins with me. He said he would, so I gathered the building permit application and all the other materials I thought I might need and headed out.

We barely made it by 1:30, I had to push the speed limit a little to make it, but we did. We were shown into a conference room, and Ralph helped me arrange the materials on the table.

Alan came in and greeted us. "I'm going to be the lead planner for your project," he said.

"So you'll be our case officer." Ralph declared. Both Alan and I laughed, and we got down to business.

Ralph and I laid down the checklist they had given me and then laid out the various documents in the same order. We began going through them with Alan, and when we got to the plan set, he was visibly impressed. Stellan's OCD paid off. The main architectural sketch, a rendering of the completed keyhole design we were starting with, was surrounded with magnified detail drawings showing the various features of Civalia. Alan began paging through the drawings and asking questions.

"I don't see drawings showing the electrical service, lighting, power distribution, etc.," he said, "Where are those?"

"First," I answered, "this is an off-grid structure. We aren't going to be hooked to the grid. Second, most of our space will be dynamically configurable, and we have this hypocaust floor system where we can run utilities as necessary for a particular use." I showed Alan the floor drawings. "As for lighting, we are developing natural lighting options and will only have a minimal amount of portable electric lighting."

I pulled out a model of the light pipe solar lighting scheme Stellan had given me a couple of days before. When I put the light pipe portion of the model into a shaft of sunlight shining on his desk, the panel glowed brightly. Alan was intrigued.

"Why don't you keep this?" I said, handing the solar lighting model to Alan. "The light distribution on this model is not as even as we would like. We're still refining these and need to scale them up, but they do work."

"Thanks," Alan said, putting the light pipe into the shaft of sunlight and turning the model this way and that to see how it worked.

"They're tellin' me they don't need lots uh 'lectric lights, 'cause they're plannin' on goin' ta bed with them chickens," Ralph said. "Sounds like a great idea ta me."

"Me too," Alan said, putting the solar light model down. "Sometimes, it just seems like there's no end to the work, not enough hours in the day. And this building permit application is looking like a lot of work. This isn't your usual construction project, is it? Parts of it look like a cathedral." He indicated some of the details of the common area with curved outer walls, fluted columns, flying buttresses, and arched ceilings. "And having this much greenhouse is unusual. I've seen large atriums and courtyards, but this greenhouse is the biggest part of your structure."

"Right," I said, "we're planning on eventually producing all our own food and water and recycling all of our own wastes. Perhaps we can make your review of our permit application a little easier for you by showing you the site and our construction preparations in person."

"Sure," Ralph said, "one of them there guided tours. Get ya out of the office for a while, and have a nice day in the sun. Bring the family along."

Alan brightened and then frowned. "I'll have to talk it over with my boss. He'll have to okay it."

"Let me talk ta 'im," Ralph said. "I've known ol' Bill fer years."

Ralph got up and went down the hall to Bill's office. I asked Alan about his family, and soon had him talking about his wife and kids, what they were all doing that summer, their hobbies, and their aspirations for the future. After a while, Ralph and a person I assumed must be Bill came back down the hall.

"Alan," Bill said, "Ralph's been telling me some really interesting things about this project you're reviewing, and I think it would be a good idea for you to go see for yourself what they have in mind. Why don't you plan on going over to the site sometime next week?"

"That'd be great," I said, "We'll plan on having some other members of our group there to tell you about our plans."

"That's right," Ralph said, "an' if'n it's a nice day, bring yer family. We'll probably end up at the hot springs before the day's over, an' I'll see to a picnic lunch. Bill, ya can come too, if'n ya want to. "

"Well, I probably won't be able to, since I've got some reports to get done for the county commissioners meeting next week," Bill looked clearly torn between duty and wanting to have a vacation day.

"How about next Thursday?" I asked. "I think we can get everything together by then. About ten o'clock?"

Alan consulted his calendar and addressed Bill, "I have the Piedmont permit application that is due before the commissioners meeting on Friday, but I think I can get it to you before Thursday. Will that work?"

"As long as you get it done, it's okay," Bill answered. "What's this?" Bill asked, picking up the light pipe model from Alan's desk.

"That's a model of how these gentlemen plan to light their structure," Alan said. "Here, let me show you how it works."

Alan took the light pipe model from Bill and stuck the end into a sun beam. The panel glowed. Bill took the model back from Alan, and began experimenting with it like Alan had done earlier.

"Ver-r-r-y interesting," Bill said. "Well, I've got to get back to work," and he headed back down the hall, taking the light pipe model with him. Alan looked crestfallen.

"Don't worry," I told him. "We'll make you another one. It should be done by next Thursday."

Alan brightened and added the trip to Ralph's ranch onto his calendar. Then the talk dissolved into some rehashing of the events surrounding Wainright's disappearance. There was not much new material, at least any I was willing to divulge, so it wasn't long before Ralph and I left the planning office and headed for the Sheriff's Office.

We were in luck. Elaine was in, and I told her about my findings on the documentation of the transfer of Wainright's house.

"Good work," Elaine said. "I knew there was a transfer of the house and a small acreage, but I didn't know it was so dodgy. Have you thought this might gum up the works with your purchase of the land from the bank? Does the bank know about these documents?"

"Yes, I've thought those documents may jeopardize our purchase agreement," I said, "and no, I don't know if the bank knows about them. Before I do anything, I thought I'd ask your opinion on how to approach this matter."

Elaine was quiet and looked thoughtful for a while, but Ralph interjected, "John told me how ya thought I should personally buy back the land, so as Wainright would come after me, an' not them. This here might be a lever ta get that there change done. If'n the bank don't know about it, it could be somethin' ta make 'em more eager ta get clear of this whole mess. If'n they knowed 'bout it, an' they didn't tell ya, John, that's a strike again' em. Either way it might make 'em readier ta deal."

"Ralph," I protested, "That'd make you a target, and I . . . we don't want you to be a target of anyone."

"Elaine's right," Ralph said gently, "Wainright's likely ta come after someone whether we want 'im ta or not. So we might as well have 'im focus on me. It'll make it easier ta catch 'im."

The three of us argued for a time, but eventually I lost, two to one. We worked out a rough plan of action going forward.

I was to have Maggie call the Bank and introduce the issue of the transferred house. She would try to find out whether the bank was aware of it or not. From there she would try to renegotiate the deal and to have Ralph purchase it back personally, and whether they knew about it or not, we would take on the issue of dealing with the house transfer in order to save time. Through Maggie, I would also try to get an agreement with the bank to immediately take steps to isolate the house and the associated acreage, ostensibly to prevent any incursion by Wainright, but actually to try to trap him or his agents.

Elaine was to look into this dicey real estate transfer, which was recorded in the Carbon County Courthouse, and investigate paths, legal of course, for getting it invalidated. Some of her work would depend on whether or not the bank had knowledge of these documents.

It was late in the day when Ralph and I took our leave. Our conversation on the drive back to Ralph's focused on how to isolate Wainright's house. Our final plan was to put up an eight-foot-high security fence with barbed wire arms on the posts sloping outward, all carefully placed to avoid the disputed property. A locked gate would complete the perimeter. We planned some obvious surveillance equipment, and some not so obvious.

I spent the night at Ralph's and headed for Laramie early in the morning, but not before having another of Ralph's memorable breakfasts. I appreciated a good night's sleep and the relaxed time I had with Ralph. I knew the next week would probably be very busy.

When I arrived back at my shop, even though it was Saturday, it was bustling. All of the lights were on, music was playing, and what seemed like a dozen people, though it was really only the same nine I had seen previously, were engaged in production activities. One group was operating the cement mixer and pouring the geopolymer into molds. Another group was moving the filled molds to some racks that were being pushed through a heated tunnel. A third group was taking the molds from the other end of the tunnel, extracting the cured blocks from the molds and rolling the blocks out the back door on a cart.

I slipped back into my apartment and changed into work clothes. When I joined the work team, Stellan welcomed me back and sent me to work with the de-molding team, since that was the heaviest work, and I could give them a little respite. I joined Manjinder's grad students, Denise and Larry, and they showed me how to remove the molds.

I watched as they opened a flap on one end, released six latches around the top of the mold, and then lifted it off. This revealed the bottom of the block with eight cylindrical holes and a chinking groove around the perimeter of the bottom edge of the block. They then turned the bottom of the mold over, with the block still inside, and removed eight bolts along the long sides of the mold. After that, they were able to work the mold off the block. The top side of the block had the eight cylindrical protrusions that would fit into the holes of a block placed above it. The next operation was new to me; I watched them put a puller arrangement on the side of the block and pull a piece of mold material out.

"What's that?" I asked.

"Those are the handholds," Denise answered, and demonstrated how they work by slipping her gloved fingers into a slot in the block left by the mold piece. "It's slightly curved upward, so you can get a good grip."

I started to try it, but Denise said, "It's a little warm, so you better put on some gloves." I got a pair, and by the time I got back they had finished extracting the mold pieces for the remaining three handholds. I helped Larry transfer the block to a cart, and the handholds worked well. We headed out the back door, and Denise began reinstalling the handhold molds back into the bottom part of the mold.

"What was the flap on the end of the mold for?" I asked Larry.

"You might have noticed, we're standing the molds on end and filling them through those end flaps," Larry said. "That's the only way we can completely fill this complicated geometry."

"Oh, right," I said.

When we were outside, Larry picked up an angle grinder with what I assumed to be a masonry disk, and dressed the region of the block where the flap had been, the sprue from the molding process. We then pushed the cart over to a series of planks placed on cinder blocks to create a series of shelves like a bookcase and transferred the block to a shelf. About a dozen blocks already rested on the planks.

"How many of these can you make in a day?" I asked.

"When everything works right, we can turn out a block about every ten minutes," Larry said as we headed back inside.

Denise had already started on the next mold, and I began helping where it looked like I wouldn't be in the way. Larry suggested I be responsible for taking them outside for a while, and then he'd spell me. An hour later I had taken five more blocks out, and while they were somewhat heavy, I'd worked out a way to partially slide them onto the shelf so I wouldn't have to lift the entire weight. When I went in after the sixth block, everyone was taking a break. Stellan, who had been working with the mixing crew, greeted me and asked about my visit with the planning office.

"They were impressed with your plans," I said, "but they were somewhat overwhelmed by all the unfamiliar features."

"I take that as an understatement," Stellan said. "So, what's the prognosis?"

"I invited Alan Hanson, the planner who's reviewing our application, to visit us at the site next Thursday. I figured we could all be there and give him a great dog-and-pony-show, which I'm certain will help him come to a positive conclusion."

"So," Larry said, "if you can't dazzle him with brilliance, you'll baffle him with bullshit."

Some of us laughed. Manjinder added some explanation. "Larry's been working on a research proposal that is running into some bureaucratic hurdles."

"I couldn't help adding that," Larry said. "That's what's been happening, and what I've been doing with my research proposal."

"Perhaps," I said, "if things go well with getting a building permit, we can come up with a graduate research project for you on something for Civalia."

"Seriously?" Larry asked.

"Seriously," I said. "There's a lot we don't know about what we're planning to do. We could use some research. How about you too, Denise?"

"I think I'm already working on your project," Denise said, "since I'm on Stellan's artificial shell project."

I turned to Stellan, "So can we find something for Larry to do?"

"No problem," Stellan said. "I've got several problems he can choose from. Now, time is wasting and we need to get back to work."

By the end of the day, I was exhausted, but there were another 27 blocks on the shelves. I had also learned a great deal. Running the blocks through the oven cut the curing time from the range of 48 to 72 hours down to 24 to 36 hours, and cut the mold removal time down to ½ hour. The blocks on the shelves were considered "green," and they could stand gentle handling, but not impact loading. I found this out when I dropped one. The crew granted me the butter fingers award of the day.

Stellan and Cass stayed for a while after the others had left, the lot of them agreeing an early bed time sounded wonderful. When the three of us were settled around my table with some hot chocolate and cookies, I gave them a full picture of our visit to the planning office. I also brought them up to date on the issues with the documentation on the transfer of Wainright's house.

Cass was troubled. "This could escalate into something really ugly."

"True," I said. "Ralph and I have made plans to isolate the house with deer, and hopefully human, fencing to keep four and two legged critters away. But we also think it gives us a way to detect any incursions."

"How are you going to do that?" she asked.

"I'd rather not give you all the details," I said. "Some of it will be overt and some will be clandestine. The fewer who know all the details, the better it will work."

"Fair enough," Stellan said. "We'll depend on you to keep us safe while we focus on building Civalia."

"I feel left out of that to some degree," I said, "and I wish I could spend more time working with you. I'm sorry I broke that one block."

"That's not the first block broken," Stellan said. "We destroyed several before we got our assembly line operational. It's part of the learning curve."

I was mollified by his words. "This project is awe-inspiring to me," I said. "I seems like I'm learning new things and doing new things all the time. New vistas are opening up for me nearly every day. What you've accomplished here," I indicated the door to the shop, "is . . . is simply amazing." I began to get a little teary.

"You need some sleep," Stellan said a little gruffly, and his eyes were also a little shiny.

Cass didn't say anything, just reached out and took one of each of our hands in hers. Stellan and I completed the circle, and we sat that way for a time, and then it was time to go. As Stellan and Cass got ready to leave, I asked, "Can you come back tomorrow to plan for Alan's visit on Thursday?" Both agreed. After they had left, I headed for bed knowing Sunday was going to be another busy day.

CHAPTER 15

Sunday was busy, and Monday was worse. I barged into Maggie's office as soon as she opened her doors. After some explanation for my unannounced visit, and her perusal of my copies of the mortgage and release documents, we began strategizing on how to proceed. I showed Maggie the Florida web site which listed the corporation I thought might be the one holding the mortgage. She was almost as puzzled as me about fictitious corporate names.

"This is going to require some research," she told me.

Maggie decided we should contact the Amalgamated Bank to find out if they were aware of this mortgage, and if they had executed the release. She dialed the bank. After several transfers between bank employees, Maggie finally reached the person we had been given as the contact person for our transaction with the bank, Tyler Kelly. She put him on speaker phone.

"Good morning, Tyler. This is Maggie Porter, and I have John Tantivy here with me on speaker phone. We are calling in reference to the purchase agreement between your bank and Civalien, Inc. I've been given your name as the bank contact for this transaction. Is that correct?"

"Yes," Tyler said. "I'll be handling that matter. What can I do for you today?"

"Well," Maggie said, "we are unsure how to deal with the release from your bank and the separate deed and mortgage for about three acres and Wainright's house. How do we handle that?"

"Say what?" Tyler seemed genuinely puzzled.

"Why, I have here in my hand copies of a deed for a small tract and Wainright's house, a release from your bank to Jim Baker's Retreat, Inc., and a mortgage from Jim Baker's Retreat, Inc. to the Embuscadoes Investment Co., all three documents filed in the Carbon County Clerk's office."

"You say you have copies of these documents?" Tyler asked. He was beginning to sound agitated. "Who signed the release?"

"Yes, I do, and John has seen the originals. He made the copies. I can't exactly read the signature, since it's just a scribble. It might start with an A or an O. Maybe it's a D. I can't tell for sure."

After a short pause, Tyler asked, "Why don't you fax me a copy of the release, and I'll see if I can figure out who signed it?"

Maggie winked at me. "Can't you look at your copy of the release? I'm sure it will be clearer than a faxed copy."

Tyler was silent for a time, but we could hear the rustling of papers. "Uh," he finally said, "I can't seem to locate that document right now. Perhaps I can search for it and call you back after I've located it."

"That won't be necessary," Maggie said. "We'll fax you a copy of the signature. John, why don't you talk with Tyler for a moment while I send this fax?"

"Hi Tyler," I said.

"Uh, hi to you," Tyler said warily.

"When I was at your bank about a week ago," I continued, "the subject of this separate ownership of Wainright's house didn't come up. That little glitch appears to affect our agreement, so we might have to make some adjustments. I'm sure you can understand a chunk of land of three acres in the middle of 13,000 plus acres can be a difficulty. We're concerned the owner, apparently Mr. Wainright, might trespass over the rest of the land to get access to this small piece. As you're aware, he has caused damage to some of his neighbors' property, and we want to prevent any more of that if at all possible. I'm sure you do too, since you're the current mortgage holder for the rest of this parcel."

"Of course," Tyler reluctantly answered.

"Prior to the closing on the main parcel of land, we'd like a preliminary agreement to allow us to enter and fence off the parcel with Wainright's house."

"I think we could do that," Tyler said hesitantly. "When do you want to have that agreement?"

"This afternoon would be great," I said. "I'll have Maggie send you a draft within the next hour."

"I don't know about that," Tyler said. "That's awfully quick. We'll need time. . ."

I interrupted him, "Here's Maggie back. I'll give you back to her," I said. I grinned at Maggie as I handed her the phone. She gave me a thumbs-up.

"The fax call has finished, so you should have a faxed copy of the signature on the release by now."

"Just a minute," Tyler said. "I'll have to go get it." It was almost five minutes before he returned. "Uh, I showed this faxed signature to my boss, and he wants to speak with you."

"Hi," a new voice said, "I'm Phillip Weston, an internal auditor for the bank. John, I think we met when you were here about a week ago."

"Of course," I said, remembering him more from the sound of his voice and his title than from his name. "Good to hear from you again, but I'm sorry we have to bring up these problems."

"Quite all right," Phillip said. He paused for a moment and then said, "We have no record of the release you describe, and we do not believe the signature you faxed was written by anyone working for the bank. Could you fax us the entire release document, so we can evaluate it?"

"Are you saying you think this release may be a forgery?" Maggie asked.

"Yes," Phillip answered.

"In that case, I'd better not send it to you," Maggie said. "The release is likely evidence of a crime, and we should immediately stop having anything to do with it."

"We'd better turn this over to the Carbon County Sheriff's Office," I said. "You remember Lieutenant Thompson don't you? I'm sure she will be eager to have you verify whether the release is fraudulent or not."

Phillip sighed, "Yes, I do remember Lieutenant Thompson. When do you think you might get this to her?"

"I'll call her right away," I said, "and she can take it from there. I expect you will be hearing from her, if not today, then probably tomorrow."

"This changes the situation somewhat," Maggie said, "can we talk about how all this affects the purchase agreement we're supposed to be negotiating?"

"Yes," Phillip again sighed, "but I'll have to round up some other people to negotiate that. How about if I call you back at, say, two o'clock?"

"Is that your time or my time?" Maggie asked.

"Let's make it my time."

"Okay, we'll talk to you then. Bye now." Maggie punched the phone off.

The first thing I did was to call Elaine. Fortunately she was in, and I told her what I knew about the release and mortgage on Wainright's house and the 3.23 acres of land.

"That's most interesting," she said. "It sure sounds like Wainright was establishing some kind of a way to get back here, maybe to maintain a toehold, but probably to take his revenge. I'll see what I can do to get those documents as evidence. I'll get a search warrant, if I have to."

After my call, Maggie and I talked some more. Then I told her I had lots to do and couldn't get back to her office after lunch. I did, however, tell her exactly how I would like the access agreement and the purchase agreement spelled out and the reasons why. In particular, I told her the access agreement was the highest priority, so we could fence the house as soon as possible. I then headed home and began searching for and rounding up surveillance equipment and fencing supplies. This task took me to Cheyenne and Fort Collins with my truck and trailer.

Later in the day, before Maggie was likely to leave her office, I called for a progress report. The news was good. The bank was willing to let us install fencing around Wainright's house, and Maggie expected to get a signed agreement faxed to her in the morning. The paper copy would follow by mail. She also said she had some other news, but I asked if it could wait until I had time to visit with her. I wanted to stop by Diane's while I was in Fort Collins.

I caught Diane in the office, working on a report for Stellan, and she agreed to meet us with her drill truck to help us build fence the next afternoon. I told her I'd call her in the morning to tell her either we were leaving Laramie or the access agreement was held up. I also told her to be prepared to stay, because the work would undoubtedly go into Wednesday.

She smiled at me and said, "In my line of work, I'm always prepared for one or more overnight stays."

A mad dash to Laramie had me back before the assembly line in my shop disbanded for the day, and I interrupted production to recruit some help for fence building. Gyan, Cindy, and Denise agreed to go with me. I called Ralph to let him know our plans, and then late into the evening I was loading tools, equipment, camping gear, and food.

Tuesday morning dawned and I crawled out of bed, took a shower to wake up, and waited impatiently for a call from Maggie. The production crew assembled in my shop, and to keep my mind off the call I was expecting, I helped them. There were some new faces, and Stellan told me Cass had found some laborers, not anyone interested in Civalia, just some guys who wanted some day work.

At eight thirty, the call came. The access agreement was in place, and I could pick up a copy at any time. I was out of the shop in a flash, telling my crew we would leave as soon as I got back. I'm thankful Laramie is a small town with light traffic, because the round trip only took me fifteen minutes. I called both Diane and then Ralph to let him know we were on our way. Gyan became the designated driver, and I thankfully sank back into my shotgun seat.

We'd only been on the road for about fifteen minutes when I thought of something I should have done. I pulled out my phone and called Alan at the planning office. "Hi Alan," I said. "I need to ask you about a situation that's arisen, and consequently some fencing we need to do."

"Is this on the site where you plan to build Civalia?" he asked.

"No, it's not. Do you remember our talking about Harold Wainright's land, and how it appears he's left the country?"

"Sure, what's up with that?"

"A bank in Omaha holds the mortgage on Wainright's land, but there is a small parcel, a little over three acres, around Wainright's house, which is mortgaged to a shell company in Florida. The bank in Omaha is working to foreclose on Wainright's land, and neither they nor we want anyone trespassing to get to that house. We have written permission from the bank to build a fence around that house parcel, so I need to know if we need a permit."

"That's a lot to take in," Alan said. "I don't understand why you would be building the fence. Shouldn't the bank be doing that? And if Wainright put a house on three acres, he certainly should have gone through the planning office. I'll check, but I don't believe we have any records on that. He could be liable for a fine for not permitting such a small acreage, and probably he needed to file a subdivision application."

I decided to tell Alan that Ralph would likely be getting the land back. I also decided to ask him to keep that information to himself, although I was quite certain it would quickly become common knowledge.

"Well, Alan, please don't spread this around, but it looks like Ralph may get his land back; at least most of it. So he has a vested interest in protecting the land against trespassers."

"Really!" Alan said. "That would be great. Let me see. That parcel is bigger than 35 acres, isn't it?"

"Yup," I said, "over 13,000 acres."

"Well, we wouldn't have anything to say about a fence on a tract that large. Now if it's on the three acre parcel, we certainly would become involved."

"We're going to make sure it's all on the big tract," I assured him.

"If the fence blocks someone else's right-of-way, we'd also have something to say."

"There's nothing in the documents I've seen giving anyone a right-of-way to the house," I told him. "So can we proceed to build a fence?" I asked.

"You can as far as our office is concerned," Alan said.

I thanked him, and rested easier as we traveled down the highway.

"What was that all about?" Gyan asked.

"Alan is the planner who's reviewing our building permit application," I told him. "I didn't want to surprise him with anything he might think is questionable about our actions while he's working on our permit. In fact, I'm going to be bending over backwards to dot all of our i's and cross all of our t's. Our project could get controversial, and we don't want to give anyone a legal wedge to stop us."

Diane and Ralph were waiting when we arrived at the Lazy HZ, so we didn't waste time at Ralph's house, but continued on. A few days earlier, the Sheriff's Office had hauled away Wainright's burned Hummer, and Ralph had cleared the wreck of the barricade enough for us to drive through to Wainright's construction site. Diane followed in her drill rig. I hadn't personally seen Wainright's construction project up close before. From this perspective, it looked even less finished than it had in Geraldine's pictures.

When we pulled up by this unfinished construction, I got out, unloaded some equipment, and then setup the most important item, the camp latrine. A couple members of our party were grateful. The survey equipment I had rented the day before was next. With Denise's help, I began laying out a fence line about twelve and a half feet outside the legal boundary of Wainright's house parcel. When we had moved sufficiently far up the first side of the parcel, the south side, Diane moved her drill rig into place and began drilling post holes, starting with the second hole.

When Cindy asked Diane why she was not starting with the first post hole, Diane said, "I'm starting with the second so I can drive my truck straight out when I'm drilling the holes for the last side. That first post hole will be the last one I drill."

Gyan and Cindy started putting posts into the drilled holes and backfilling the holes. We had decided not to cement the posts, because eventually we'd probably remove the fence. Backfilling the holes was the hardest work on the project. So, when Denise and I finished laying out the fence, long before Diane had finished drilling post holes for the south side, we joined the post-planting crew. Denise teamed with Cindy, and I began working with Gyan. We worked steadily until noon, took a short break for lunch, and then worked steadily till about 3:30.

We took a break when Ralph arrived with some refreshments. All of us were flagging by then, and the break, and his food and drink, were most welcome.

"What ya' have in mind fer dinner?" he asked me.

"I've brought some food." I said, indicating a couple of coolers on the back of my truck.

Ralph moseyed over and took a look in the coolers.

"How 'bout I add just a little ta yer dinner?" Ralph asked. "Cindy, why'n ya come help an ol' man fix a little grub for all ya hard workers?"

Ralph had obviously seen how tired Cindy was, and I was grateful for him giving her an excuse to stop working. After Ralph and Cindy left, the rest of us soldiered on. By six, we had all graduated from flagging to dragging. Diane had turned the corner and was well on her way down the west side. Her organization and work efficiency were amazing to watch, which I found myself doing more and more often, when I leaned on my tamping bar or shovel for a moment of rest. When Ralph's truck drove out of the trees near where our first barricade had been built, we all stopped working long before he parked.

Ralph built a fire in a fire pit Calloway Construction had left at the site, and I think we all enjoyed the heat, rest, and the wonderful smells as Ralph cooked us some dinner. I know I did. Cindy seemed to be revived and helped Ralph. I used the respite to call Stellan and check on preparation for Alan's tour of our site on Thursday. He told me preparations were going well, but he'd need my truck and trailer to haul some blocks and other items to the Civalia site on Thursday. I told him I'd get it back Wednesday night, but it might be late. I also told Stellan about our progress on the fence.

"It's going to take us longer than I thought. I estimate Diane had only drilled about a third of the post holes and the rest of us had only installed about a fourth of the posts. None of the chain link fencing has been installed. We certainly won't get finished by tomorrow night."

"Would more help make a difference?" Stellan asked.

"Not a lot, unless you're talking about a half dozen more skilled laborers and a lot more tools. I think we'll just have to slog through to the end, which looks like will be sometime this weekend."

"This does bring up the issue of building Civalia," Stellan said. "Our group doesn't have nearly enough hands to get the first section of our cottage industry area built before the snow flies."

"I think I remember Cass saying she was going to check on whether she could get some help from one or more of the communities she's lived in. Do you know if she's looked into that?"

"I doubt it," Stellan said. "We've been working long hours to get where we are with manufacturing the blocks. By the way, Larry thinks we should call them Megos, short for Monster Lego® blocks."

I laughed. "Sounds good to me. Perhaps you should check with Cass, and if she hasn't contacted any of her old communities, see if she can begin working on that. After we get this fence finished and I get the building permit well under way, I can pick up some of the slack. I've missed working on all the construction projects you've been doing."

"We've missed you, too, having you poke your nose into all the nooks and crannies of what we've been doing," Stellan said.

I laughed again. "Ralph has some food ready now," I told him, "so I'll see you tomorrow night."

I put away my phone and dug into Ralph's chow. After the meal was over, all of us unloaded the camping gear and set up camp. No one seemed interested in staying up late, and I crawled into my sleeping bag before dark.

I awoke to the smell of frying bacon. When I was able to move some, accompanied by a few groans for my many sore muscles and joints, I poked my head out of my tent and saw Ralph busy at the fire pit. I realized I was ravenous. After I dressed, not without difficulty, I joined him.

"Yer lookin' a little worse fer wear, John," Ralph said. "an' yer also lookin' hungry."

"I feel like I've been rode hard, as you would say," I replied, "and I am hungry."

"Well, ya' better get them others up, so's they'll have a chance ta get some chow 'fore ya eat it all."

I began waking the others. From the sounds I heard as they woke up, they weren't feeling much better than I was.

Ralph's breakfast put new life into us, and while Ralph took care of the breakfast mess, we began the day's work on the fence. All of us worked a little slower than we had the day before, and we took more breaks. Even so, by the end of the day, Diane had completed drilling all of the post holes, and we at least had posts setting in all of them. Backfilling was another matter. Only about half of the holes were backfilled, but we'd started installing the rails too.

Nevertheless, I needed to get back to Laramie. Gyan, Cindy, Diane, and Denise decided to camp overnight and work some more in the morning. I recruited them to help me unload the rest of the fencing supplies, and I then headed for Laramie with the truck and trailer.

Stellan woke me early, and by 6:00 we were loading the finished Megos and boxes of equipment and supplies he had waiting. Moving was painful, but I did the best I could. We planned to get away by eight o'clock, but we were beginning to run late. And then I remembered I needed to get fuel.

Ralph phoned. "How's it goin'?" he asked.

"We're running late," I said, "so I can't talk long."

"G-o-o-d," Ralph said.

"What do you mean, 'good?'" I asked, feeling out of sorts.

"Well, I was just callin' ta suggest ya have a flat tire, or somethin' that'll delay ya for 'bout an hour or so."

I was bewildered and argued with Ralph. "But we can't be late meeting with Alan. This is important, and we don't want to give him the wrong impression."

Ralph chuckled, "Oh, I don't think Alan'll mind ya' bein' a little late. Just take yer time, an' we'll see ya' 'bout eleven. Okay?"

"Okay," I said hesitantly.

I'd come to trust Ralph, and he probably had a good reason for wanting us to be late, but it was against my nature. I couldn't help feeling anxious. Still, it was a relief having a little extra time to get ready. Stellan was also happy for a reprieve. We finished loading, remembering a couple of items we would have surely forgotten if we hadn't had the extra time. Then after a trip to the filling station, we picked up Cass, Larry, Manjinder, and Anand, and headed for the Lazy HZ and the Civalia site.

When we pulled up at Ralph's home, a car with county plates was nestled among Ralph's, Diane's, and Geraldine's pickups, but nobody was in sight. All of us got out and went up to Ralph's door. Through the screen door, I could see several people sitting around Ralph's table. I rapped once to announce our presence and entered. Ralph was there along with Geraldine, Gyan, Diane, Alan, and a woman, who I assumed was Alan's wife. They were playing my N-Trō-P game. I didn't see Denise or Cindy.

"I'm sorry we're late," I said.

Ralph grinned broadly and said, "I told 'em ya got away from here real late last night an' had ta load up a bunch uh stuff this mornin' 'fore ya came." He then proceeded to make introductions.

"An' Alan and Kathy's girl, Wendy," Ralph finished, "is out with Denise, Cindy, an' Lester. Denise's a fine horsewoman, an' she's givin' them girls some lessons. We was just playin' yer game."

I understood then why Denise and Cindy were missing. I also noticed Alan kept glancing down at the N-Trō-P board, but Kathy seemed to be happy to have the play interrupted.

I addressed Alan, "What'd you think of our game?" I asked.

"It's very interesting. I think . . . I think it kind of ties together some things I didn't know needed tying together. Ralph was telling me about how it did the same for him. It's given me lots to think about."

"We've got a few more things for you to think about on my

truck and trailer," I said. "Why don't Stellan and I take this stuff up to the Civalia site, and all of you can wander up when you get ready."

"An' I'll bring lunch," Ralph said.

On the way to the meadow, I said, "Stellan, Ralph is a wily guy. It will probably help our cause a lot if Alan understands even a little about the physics of entropy. I understand now why he wanted us to be late, and I think he's right, Alan won't mind a bit."

"Yah, the more I'm around him, the more impressed I am with his knowledge and understanding."

"You're not the only one," I said.

When we got to the meadow, we unloaded everything but the Megos. Stellan started opening boxes and totes, and then began to assemble the LPE prototype. Since I was familiar with the LPE, I relieved him of that duty. When he began unloading and stacking some of the Megos into a wall, I abandoned the LPE to help him. I was curious about how they worked. With the two of us using the handholds, one on each side of a block, stacking them in an alternating brick pattern was easy and quick. I was surprised at how snuggly they fit together.

"Do they come apart as easily as they go together?" I asked.

"Lift up on this one," Stellan said, and we applied upward pressure on the block we had just set. It took a fair amount of upward force to break it free, but it was not unreasonably difficult.

"You've done a great design job on these," I told Stellan.

"Only after several trials," he said.

When the wall section was about seven feet high, Stellan removed a Mego from a box, and we placed that particular one on the top of the wall. It looked somewhat different from the others.

"What's with this one?" I asked.

"It's got a light pipe embedded in it," Stellan answered as he was digging in a box for something else.

He lifted out a clear, rectangular panel about two feet long and one wide. "Can you give me a hand with this? Here hold it." Stellan handed me the panel and retrieved a stool. Standing on the stool, he took the panel from me and attached it so it was cantilevered out from the top Mego on the shady side of the wall.

"So that's a larger version of the model light panel," I said. "Did you make that or did you take it from an LED screen?"

"Manjinder made it," he said. "She's amazing. I couldn't have done all this without her."

"I haven't had time to get to know her, but I'd sure like to," I said.

Stellan jumped down and rummaged around in the same box, this time coming out with what looked something like a piece of gutter, only it was deeper than a standard gutter, and much more rounded and wider at the top. We went to the other side of the wall, and Stellan, again standing on the stool, attached this gutter along the edge of the top Mego. When we went back around the wall, the panel was glowing brightly, considerably lighting the shadow of the wall.

"That's a trough collector on the other side," Stellan said. "It's made of artificial shell."

"Impressive," I said. "I'd better get back on the LPE."

While I finished assembling the LPE, Stellan mounted the parabolic collector on a tripod. I connected the LPE hoses to the collector, and Stellan aimed the collector at the sun. In short order, the signature swishing sounds could be heard.

"I brought an inverter and Ralph loaned me his induction cook top," Stellan said. "He plans to do a little cooking for lunch. I sure hope this setup works."

"So do I. What else have you got?"

"Well, I put together a series of isometric drawings showing the various stages of construction."

"That'll be a good show and tell," I said.

"And Manjinder made another light pipe/panel model for Alan. It's better than the first one. She also made a couple of bracelets for Alan's wife and daughter."

Stellan showed me these trinkets. Manjinder had indeed significantly improved the artificial shell process. These pieces were outstanding.

"How'd you make the solar collector?" I asked, indicating the trough at the top of the wall.

"That's done with optical layering," he said. "We're learning to introduce certain substances into the calcite and control the thickness to make optical layers. Those layers can control radiant energy, reflecting it, refracting it, or passing it through. We still need to improve the precision of our processes and learn more, of course. Wait till you see this."

Stellan began pulling some insulated tubes about a foot in diameter out of a box and assembling them into a long tube attached to another well-insulated box. I kept quiet and watched Stellan work. When he was done, he arranged the assembly so the tube was pointed at the sky in a northern direction.

"Let me guess," I said. "You've made a refrigerator."

Stellan grinned. "I can't put much over on you, can I?" He hooked up a meter to some thermocouple wires leading out of the box, and we watched as the temperature reading began to slowly drift down. "This phenomenon exists in deserts; sometimes a bowl of water will freeze at night, even in the summer," Stellan said. "But the same as in the desert, this will only work on clear days when there're very few particulates in the atmosphere. It's a good thing today is sunny, clear, and the wind isn't blowing."

"How'd you get the weather to cooperate?" I asked. "And what's in the tube?"

"Manjinder and I made some clear calcite plates with layers to reflect shortwave and transmit long-wave radiation. There are a couple of layers of these plates with a vacuum between them in the tube."

"So you're sending long-wave radiation into outer space," I said. "Stellan," I said, my voice husky with emotion, "this may be the most significant thing you've done so far. You are transporting entropy off the earth into outer space. This can significantly help reduce our entropy footprint."

"Yes," Stellan said, and we both stood silently watching the temperature in the box slowly decrease.

We both turned as the sound of approaching vehicles reached us. Ralph's pickup came over the ridge, followed by Alan's car. The bulk of the crew was riding in the bed of the pickup. Kathy was Alan's only passenger. The vehicles stopped, disgorging their passengers, and the crowd surged forward, bringing with it picnic baskets and paraphernalia, cameras, laughter, and smiles.

Somehow, I felt a million miles away. I drifted over to my trailer and sat down. I felt like I had done my part to bring this group of people together, and now it was up to the other Civalien Project members to convince Alan that Civalia has merit and substance. I watched as Stellan, Manjinder, Gyan, and Larry talked with Alan, while Ralph and Geraldine went about cooking and preparing the picnic lunch. Denise, who had ridden Lester up to the meadow, was giving rides to the kids while Kathy looked on. Diane came over and sat down beside me.

"You look tired," she said.

"I suppose I do." My normal reaction to such a statement would have been to crack a joke, but I just didn't feel like it.

"Are you feeling a sense of let down?" she asked.

Surprised by her question, after a moment of reflection, I had to admit I did. "Yes, I guess I am."

"I've felt the same thing when I've passed along a project to someone else after I've put body and soul into it." Diane reached down, picked a blade of grass, and twiddled it in her fingers. "However, I don't think your job is done here yet." She stuck the blade of grass between her teeth and gazed in the direction of the group surrounding Alan. "You hold the purse strings for this operation, so you're the only one who can assure Alan this project will go to completion and won't become just another failed pile of junk. He's probably seen a lot of those. There's one right down the road." She turned back to look at me. "Wainright's mess is likely to make the planning office a little skittish."

I met her eyes and stood up. "Thanks," I said and offered my hand to help her up.

We moseyed back down to the festivities, and Diane peeled off to help Geraldine and Ralph. I continued on and was just in time to join Stellan's presentation of his isometric construction sequence. The first plate showed the center cylinder for what, after much argument, we had decided to call the common work area, composed of a hypocaust floor system, the outer division wall segment, the far side temporary Mego wall, the dual layer fabric

roof, and a cut-away of the near side temporary Mego wall. Together these features formed the first wedge of Civalia, an eighth
of the common work area for the complete Civalia cylinder. We
had decided to call this space a "work" area to avoid the economic
connotation of the words associated with industrial or shop activities.

Stellan discussed the technical issues of the construction,
pointing out the advantages and efficacy of using geopolymer
materials, answering clearly and succinctly the various questions
Alan asked. He even had small samples of the geopolymer feed
materials, which he mixed and poured into a small mold, a per-
sonalized paper weight for Alan.

At that point, I intruded and discussed the overall cost for
what was shown on Stellan's first drawing, indicating it would
be entirely financed by me without any borrowed money. Stellan
added that we hoped to get this phase of the project completed by
winter. He turned to the next drawing.

On this drawing, the common work space wedge was extended
to include a common living area. This common space was formed
by extending the hypocaust floor, building a second outer division
wall, putting up temporary Mego walls on either side, and roofing that portion with an earth-sheltered arched ceiling. Also on
the second drawing, additional wedges were added to both sides
of the original common work space wedge. The drawing showed
additional hypocaust floor, extensions of the outer division wall,
and the temporary Mego walls moved outward. Again, Stellan
expertly presented the features.

I followed with a discussion of the cost estimate. Stellan started to turn to the next sheet, but Alan asked, "Is this your work for
next year?"

"No, we plan to do more next year," Stellan answered. "Besides
this common space, we also plan to put in the greenhouse and the
private quarter sections." He turned to the next drawing, which
showed the greenhouse section. "We'll also be completing the
common work space. By the end of next year we hope to have
what Gyan calls the keyhole stage of Civalia done." Stellan turned
to the next drawing which showed the isometric view of the completed second stage of construction.

"Wow! That's ambitious," Alan said. Stellan had turned to the last plate, which also showed a plan view of Civalia at that stage. Alan said, "And the plan view does look like an old fashioned keyhole."

"This is as much of the construction of Civalia we are trying to permit at this time," I told Alan. "We'll have six to eight residents at that stage, who will be working to get it fully operational, but we won't be permitting anymore of the final structure until we get this first section working correctly. The major task at that time will be getting the greenhouse established. I'm certain we'll have learned a lot and have some great innovations to include in any further expansion."

Stellan laughed and Alan laughed with him. "That's an understatement," Stellan said to Alan. "The amount I've learned so far is enough to make my head spin sometimes. And from my previous experience, putting plans into action drives the learning curve way up."

I continued, "We don't know how long it will take us to iron out all the wrinkles, but we don't plan to build further until we have high confidence all systems are go, and we have more people interested in becoming residents. I'll also be financing the project throughout this stage," I added. "We don't intend to borrow to make this project happen."

"Well planned. Impressive," Alan murmured.

"How about I go help Ralph and Geraldine with the picnic?" I said to Alan, "and you and Stellan can look over the details of these next sections of Civalia."

I departed and made my way over to the picnic area.

"This here induction cook top ain't heatin' real well," Ralph told me.

I went to check on the LPE and immediately saw a problem. The sun had moved, of course, and the light from the parabolic reflector was not falling fully on the heat exchanger. I adjusted the reflector and the swishing sounds from the LPE began to pickup.

"That's better," Ralph said.

"Can I help?" I asked.

"We'll be ready in 'bout ten minutes. Why'nt ya an' Diane go round up the critters?" Ralph waved his spoon toward the group down toward the lower part of the meadow. They were clustered around Lester.

I had a lot more appreciation for sheep dogs, and Ralph's characterization of the people as critters, by the time Diane and I had the kids, adults, and Lester back up by the picnic area. We feasted on Ralph's cooking and Geraldine's baking.

After lunch Cass, Ralph, and Geraldine organized a tour of the Civalia site with Alan and his family. I made a move to tag along, but Cass waved me back. I relaxed and watched Larry, Denise, and Diane examining the LPE and Manjinder and Stellan's refrigerator. Diane continued on to examine the Mego wall and its lighting fixture with Denise as her guide. I finally roused myself and asked Stellan if he'd organize a trip to the hot springs for Alan and his family, and any of the other adults that wanted to go. Meanwhile, I'd see if I could talk Larry, Denise, and Diane into working on the fence some more. I was successful in my quest, and Stellan drove us over to the fence project. We took up the fencing tools and started working.

CHAPTER 16

Late in the afternoon, Stellan returned and drove us to Ralph's house. Alan and his family had returned to Rawlins directly from the hot springs, and the others had returned to Ralph's, where they had finished unloading any equipment and the Megos still on the truck and trailer. We sorted out who was going back to Laramie and who was staying to work on the fence. Both Manjinder and Gyan had class obligations, so they were going back, taking Cindy and Anand. Cass decided to return also.

At first Stellan was going to stay and help us with the fence the next day, but when I explained we needed some more equipment and supplies to unroll and stretch the chain link fencing, he agreed to make a round trip to Laramie.

Ralph and Geraldine fed us picnic leftovers, and we all rehashed the day. Stellan had some interesting things to say.

"Alan is very positive about this project," Stellan said. "While we were at the hot springs, he quizzed me a lot more about it and about you in particular, John."

"Really? What did he want to know about me?"

"Oh, basically how deep your pockets are. You'll have to admit, a project like this, using conventional building techniques, materials, and contractors, would run in the tens of millions."

"So what did you tell him?" I asked.

"I didn't tell him anything directly. I thought telling him we're pretty confident we can get through these first two years for around one million would just raise a con alert with him, so I just invited him over to Laramie to take a look at your shop facilities."

I was bewildered. "What do you think visiting my shop will do?" I asked.

"John, I think you realize most men walking into your shop

are struck by a bad case of shop envy. What you don't realize is most of them are also thinking you must have a lot of money, because a shop like yours is so far out of their reach. Then when they see your antique cars, the die is cast. They automatically compare you with a certain well known TV host and a certain very popular author. I'll arrange it so you don't have to be there when he visits. You might find it embarrassing."

"Yah, I guess I shouldn't be there, because I'd probably blow it."

"You probably would," Stellan said. "There's something else I should tell you. I put a couple of flaws in those drawings I gave him."

"What'd you do that for?" I asked indignantly.

"If you were preparing a set of plates for Alan, I'll bet with your OCD you'd slave over them till everything was perfect, right?"

"Of course."

"Well, most people, Alan for instance, feel like they're not doing their job unless they find something to improve, to leave their mark on it."

"Stellan's exactly right," Diane said, "but you can't be too blatant or too trivial about it."

"It's a dog markin' his territory," Ralph added. The others laughed except for Cindy and Anand. They were falling asleep.

"Sometimes," I said, "I think I'm out of my league with all of you."

Our gathering began to break up. Stellan was taking those returning to Laramie in my truck, pulling the empty trailer. He would return in the morning with some more equipment and supplies to help with the fencing. After we all said goodnight to Ralph and Geraldine, Diane drove Larry, Denise, and me to the fencing site, where we all crashed for the night in our tents and sleeping bags.

We finished stringing the last wires, installing the gates, and clicking the gate lock closed on Saturday afternoon. We were just in time, as an afternoon rainstorm swept across from the northwest. We waited in the truck till it had passed and then broke camp. Stellan drove us home and I dozed most of the way. We must have all been tired, because it was a very quiet trip.

Sunday was recovery day. I did practically nothing, so by Monday I was prepared to check on the progress of the purchase agreement with the bank by phoning Maggie

"We finished installing the fence around Wainright's house," I told her. "We still need to install surveillance equipment, but that work shouldn't take as long. However, I'd like to get it done before we close on the land with the bank. When do we need to have funds in place to close? What have you heard? Is our land deal still on? What's going to happen with Wainright's questionable filings?

"Take it easy," Maggie answered. "I'll update you on what's happened, and if you have questions after that, we'll deal with them one at a time." I could hear her rustling some papers. "First off, I'm 90% certain they knew nothing of this questionable deed, mortgage, and release on Wainright's house and the small piece of land around it. They've been in contact with Elaine, as I have, and the consensus is the release is forged. Eventually, the deed and mortgage can probably be declared null and void."

"I was thinking that too," I said. "Is this going to slow down the land sale?"

"Quite the opposite," Maggie said. "The bank is more eager than ever to put as much distance between them and this mess as possible. They don't want any publicity about this situation, which paints them as complicit. So here are some questions for you. Why do you think Wainright set up this little fraud, and are you, or whoever gets title to the land, willing to take on the risk? Wainright might have something planned, as well as the hassle involved in clearing the title. By the way, I was going to tell you the other day when you called from Fort Collins, to show you how much the bank wants out, they lowered the purchase price by $100,000."

"Wow!" I said. "I guess they really do want out." I remembered Maggie telling me she had some more news for me, and I was chagrinned I had not gotten back to her.

"There's some conditions on that sale," Maggie continued. "It's provided you'll take on the responsibility of dealing with the mess surrounding Wainright's house, and you can close by this next Friday, or as soon as they can get a clear title. Oh, and they agreed to selling it directly back to Ralph. In fact, although they didn't say it in so many words, I think they thought selling to Ralph might offer them some positive kudos if word of this whole affair did leak out."

"I don't know what Wainright's game is," I said, "but I've been thinking about it this last week. I'm guessing it could be one of three things. One, he is just poking a stick in the eyes of all of us who brought his scheme to an end. This would include all the banks involved plus Ralph and, probably, Diane and me at a minimum. But there may be others we don't know about yet. Second, he could be setting up something to make the place, and maybe a lot of land around it, unusable for anyone else. Something like what he did with the Hummer. Or third, he might have set it up as a trigger device, to tell him when something is happening with the land, so he can put some other, as yet unknown plot into motion."

"None of those sound very inviting," Maggie said. "So, are you willing to take these on?"

"I am, but I'll have to talk to Ralph about it," I said, "and I'll do that as soon as I can, and get back to you." I paused and thought about another issue. "I should also ask, are you willing to take this on? It might turn into a nasty fight."

"Isn't that what lawyers are supposed to be searching for?" Maggie asked. "It's sure to run up some pretty impressive fees."

"I take that as a yes," I said. "An extra $100,000 will at least help defray some of the expenses we will encounter, including yours."

"My guess is your expenses may go over $100,000," Maggie observed. "I base this on the fact the Amalgamated Bank is offering a discount, which probably means they think they'll be saving money in the long run."

"If Ralph is willing to move on this," I said, "I'll see about getting the monies to you as soon as I can. Hopefully, we can get it done before Friday."

"Keep me posted," Maggie said.

I called Ralph as soon as I had hung up from Maggie, but he was not in. I left him a message. This week was beginning to shape up to be as busy as last week. I called Cass. She was in, and I asked her if I might drop by and talk about construction labor with her. She said I could, so I hustled over to her home.

"It's obvious to me we need a fair amount of additional construction help if we're going to get the first part of our work space done by winter time," I said.

"Yes, I think that's obvious," she said.

"I seem to recall you talked about approaching some of the communities you lived in previously to see if you could hire some of them."

"Yes, and I've been following up with that source of labor. I've got reservations to fly to Missouri on Wednesday." Cass hesitated. "I realize you've been extremely busy these last couple of weeks, but having another copy of your game would be a great help. As you probably noticed, it made a big difference with Alan last Thursday. I'm sure it can make a difference with my former colleagues too."

I was flummoxed. I had come to Cass's home to cajole her into moving on finding additional construction labor, and here she was taking me to task for not fulfilling my word. "My apologies," I said lamely. "It slipped my mind."

"I'm sure it did," Cass said.

"Would you have time to help me put one together?" I asked. "Today would work best for me, if you have time. Tomorrow may get really hairy, and the day after that, you'll be headed out."

"I'll make time," she said. "Let's get started."

We returned to my home and began constructing another game board. Cass suggested we make the board much larger, since many of people in the communities she'd be visiting would probably be interested in playing. She also suggested the larger board would let us use larger sized energy/entropy tokens and we could make them by modifying poker chips with permanent markers. These were great ideas, and I headed out to a local discount store to find the poker chips and markers. Cass started making the various environmental areas for the board by scanning some landscape pictures I'd gathered when I made the previous game. Before leaving, I hunted up some extra dodecahedron dice I had purchased in my effort to make the first game.

When I got back, Cass said, "Ralph called. He said to call him back."

I dumped my purchases on the table, picked up the phone and called Ralph.

"Hi, Ralph," I said. "There's some more news about Wainright's house and the purchase agreement with the bank."

I told Ralph about my discussion with Maggie, about her dealings with the Amalgamated Bank, and about the bank's response. We discussed the possible dangers and whether Ralph was willing to expose himself to that possibility.

"Ya ever seen a cornered badger?" Ralph asked.

"No, can't say as I have," I answered.

"Well, they don't turn tail an' run. They hiss an' spit an' 're ready ta take on whatever's out there, even if'n it's ten times bigger. That's how I feel 'bout takin' on Wainright. He's worked at takin' away an' destroyin' what's important ta me, an' that includes ya' too, if'n we quit now. He's got my dander up, so let's go after 'im."

"Alright," I said. "I'm with you. Now we get to the unpleasant part, money. We'll need to put together the money to buy the land from the bank by Friday, if possible."

"What's unpleasant 'bout money?" Ralph asked. "It's just a tool for gettin' things done. I'll just close out them there CDs I put that there money into when I was paid fer the land."

"Won't you lose a lot of interest if you cash them in early?"

"Maybe, but getting the land back's more important. I'll start doin' it right away. Ya tell me where that there money's gotta go, an' we'll get it there by Friday."

When I finished talking to Ralph, Cass, who'd of course been listening, commented, "You and Ralph are taking a lot of risk going after Wainright. Is there another way, such as ignoring him and just leaving his house alone?"

"I've thought about taking that route, Cass, but I think Wainright's at least sociopathic, if not psychopathic. If we ignore him, I don't think he will ignore us. Also, I'm starting to worry he has done something to damage the land, or Ralph, or us. Somehow his house seems to be involved."

"Well, be careful," she admonished me.

I excused myself from working on the game for a short time longer while I called Maggie, giving her the word to go full speed ahead on wrapping up the land purchase. After taking care of that chore, I settled into working on the game.

By noon we had most of the game hardware done, so I took Cass to lunch. When we returned, she excused herself and headed for home after I promised to package the game, including instruction sheets, and deliver it to her no later than six o'clock.

It took me a couple more hours to print the instructions and another hour to package the game. After delivering it to Cass, I turned my attention to surveillance of Wainright's house. Using a quad map of the area, I began to plan how to deploy the equipment I'd purchased. It was a daunting task. How to watch over more than 20 square miles of land? I realized I was not up to the task and probably didn't have the right equipment.

Stellan and his crew were hard at work in my shop, and it was getting later in the afternoon, so I snagged Stellan for a consultation. I showed him the map and laid out my concerns about keeping tabs on what Wainright might do. Stellan studied the map for a while, then sat back and gazed at the ceiling for a while.

Finally he spoke. "Your reasoning Wainright planted the bogus documents in the Carbon County Courthouse makes sense. The question then becomes, why? He had to know if a land sale of the main parcel ever occurred, they'd be discovered. The title search would turn them up. The most benign interpretation is he was just leaving a little bump in the road to annoy the next buyer."

"I've thought of that," I said, "but it doesn't seem consistent with the rest of Wainright's actions to date."

"I'll grant you that," Stellan said. "So, that leaves at least three more possibilities. One, it gives him a heads up when a transaction is taking place, and legal beagles begin looking into the mortgage holder. Two, it triggers a nasty legal battle, or maybe even a physical battle, if someone sets foot on the property."

That caught my attention. "I sort of like that explanation. It would fit with Ralph's closing the road. An eye for an eye. What's your third possibility?"

"He might have had some scheme in mind requiring more time than he had available, so it might be a delay tactic."

"Your possibilities don't seem to be mutually exclusive. All three could be part of his plans."

"True," Stellan said. "So, what to do?"

"Well, we've fenced it off to help prevent anyone from accessing the lot or house without our permission."

"That's also true," Stellan said, "but it won't prevent anyone from going over, under, or through the fence."

"Going under is very unlikely," I said. "So can we detect over or through?"

Stellan and I brainstormed for a while and finally decided to instrument the fence with some strain gauges and accelerometers to detect anyone going over or through the fence. To power the system, we settled on solar lights with sufficient solar panels to charge batteries large enough to power the lights and the security system, said system being comprised of instrumentation, recording, and alarm subsystems. We decided at least one of the lights would be non-functional. The non-functional light would create a dark section of fence to act as a decoy for someone coming in at night with the intention of gaining access.

When we finally kicked back, Stellan stood up with a sigh. "I'm beat," he said. "You have to take it from here." He went back into the shop, and a short time later the sounds of work diminished and shortly the shop lights went out.

I worked late, refining the plans and generating a parts list. The next day I went shopping, having to go as far as Denver to find some of the items I needed, and began assembling them when I got home. Thursday I couldn't stand not knowing what was happening with the land transfer, so I called Maggie. Ralph had gotten the monies into Maggie's trust account, but there were hang-ups with the Amalgamated Bank getting their Quit Claim Deed validated and recorded. I was thankful, because I was running behind. We definitely needed to have our system in place before the deed for the land was actually transferred. Friday I continued work on assembling the lighting/surveillance system. On Saturday, Stellan joined me. Together we made a bench system work. Sunday found Stellan and I on the road to the Lazy HZ to install it.

Ralph was happy to see us, and Gerald scolded us longer than usual, since Stellan was there.

"Let me help ya," Ralph said.

"We never turn down help," Stellan said.

"An' I'll call Geraldine, an' see if'n she'll come over too," Ralph added.

Ralph was as good as his word, and an hour later, the four of us were installing strain gauges and accelerometer units out of sight in the fence rails, highly visible lights on posts, a solar powered battery unit inside the fence line, and buried instrument wiring across the road to the incomplete slab. We'd decided the slab was a place where we could install the recording and transmitting equipment without arousing suspicion. Stellan and I had made a geopolymer box that resembled a pile of dumped concrete. The transmitter antenna looked like a rusted rebar sticking out of the pile.

The day was fading when we finished and were sitting on the concrete steps of Wainright's unfinished lodge.

"Ralph and Geraldine," I said, "we can't thank you enough for helping us put all this surveillance equipment in place. But we do have another request of you." Both of them looked my way. "Would you be willing to monitor this system? If someone comes, it might be in the middle of the night, and there could be some false alarms. We've tried to set it so even an eagle landing on the fence won't trip the alarm, but if a deer or elk bumps it, the alarm might go off." I looked from one to the other of them.

"Well, I certainly don't mind none," Ralph said. "Course we'll let you know if 'n somethin' happens, an' it might be the middle uh the night." His eyes were twinkling.

"Same fer me," Geraldine said.

I looked at Geraldine. "There's something more I'd like to ask you to do."

I reached into the box in which we had transported the instrument package, pulled out another, smaller box, and set it down by Geraldine.

"When I was at your place, it appeared like there's a location up by your barn, where you can see the northwest corner of Wainright's house. If the alarm system does trip, could you check it out? And if it looks like someone is messing around, get some video footage? There're a regular video camera with a telephoto lens and an infrared night vision scope with a built-in video camera in this box. There're also some extra battery packs, some extra USB memory sticks, and a parabolic microphone. I have a couple of tripods in the truck"

Geraldine's smile lit her face. "Why sure. I've always wanted to make one them there movin' pictures."

"There's plenty of data storage," I said, "so feel free to experiment with the equipment."

"I shoulda had these the other day, when you an' them kids was buildin' the fence. I could of watched ya from the comfort of my porch 'stead of standin' out by the barn."

"I'm glad our work didn't go unnoticed," I answered. Geraldine smiled a mischievous smile.

"You an' that young girl—Denise is it?—work right well together," she said and laughed.

As it was beginning to get dark, the lights on the fence snapped on, except for one near the northwest corner.

"Ya got a light out," Ralph said. "Ya want to fix it now, or wait till tomorra?"

"That's intentional," Stellan said. "If someone comes in the night, they'll probably avoid the lighted parts of the fence. We expect they'll head for that northwest corner, and there's where Geraldine will have the best view of them."

"Ya think of ever'thing, don't ya," Ralph said, shaking his head.

"Let's test this system," Stellan said. He showed Geraldine and Ralph how to turn on their monitors, and then he walked over to the fence, carrying a ten pound weight with a long hook we had brought with us. He reached up and, none too gently, hung the weight on the fence. Nothing happened. But when he began to pull heavily on the weight, the alarms went off. Stellan tried it in various places with satisfactory results. Prolonged shaking also tripped the alarm, as did opening the gate. We high-fived each other when he returned.

We locked the gates, packed up, and got ready to leave. Before driving away, I told Ralph I would be back, probably in the next day or two, to check on the progress of the building permit. As we drove away, in my rear view mirror I saw Ralph with his arm around Geraldine's shoulders. I'd always thought they should be a couple, and maybe they were.

When I checked in with Maggie on Monday, there was nothing new to report, so I prepared to head for Rawlins via the Lazy HZ. Stellan and I had discussed the logistics of moving the Megos being built in my shop to the Civalia site. Loading pallets of them on the truck and trailer could be done at my shop with my fork lift truck. Unloading them at the site was another matter. We had decided to enter into a long term lease of a skid-steer loader from a friend of mine to solve that problem. With the various attachments for the loader, we could handle materials, move soil, and drill holes. I planned on taking the skid steer, along with a couple of pallets of Megos, to the Civalia site on my way to Rawlins. Loading those items took a good part of the morning. The shop was again bustling with activity and noise, and I was happy to get away by 11:00.

Traveling to the Civalia site, unloading the skid steer, dropping the trailer, picking up Ralph, and traveling to Rawlins put us at the planning office an hour before closing. Ralph and I greeted Alan and enquired about his family.

"They're fine," he said, "and they really enjoyed their time on Ralph's ranch and the hot springs in Saratoga. Say, John, those antique cars of yours are beautiful. And thanks, Ralph, for allowing Wendy to ride your horse. She can't stop talking about that."

Ralph smiled broadly, "She's welcome, an' old Lester likes the girls. They're lighter than an old fart like me. I'll just mosey on down an' visit with Bill while ya' two tend to business."

I was surprised Alan had seen my antique cars. I'd known Stellan had invited him for a visit, but I didn't know it had happened.

"Beautiful is the most common description of those cars I hear when people see them for the first time," I told Alan. "I think in those days a lot more artistic effort went into the design of cars."

As soon as etiquette permitted, I asked about progress on our building permit.

"It's moving right along," Alan told me. "I have found a couple of things that will need to be changed. Here, let me show you."

Inwardly I smiled and congratulated Stellan for his prescience. In fact, Alan had found not two but three things. Two of them were the errors introduced by Stellan, but the third was a genuine problem neither Stellan nor I had foreseen or caught. I was impressed.

". . . and so," Alan was saying, "here's what I think you'll need to do to correct these items."

He handed me some stapled pages with hand written notes on the three defects in our permit application. I was further impressed by his thoroughness.

"We'll attend to these directly, and get them back to you. Can we e-mail you the corrections?" I asked.

"Certainly," Alan said. "That way we both have clear records of what was sent and when."

"Do you have any idea when your review will be completed?" I asked.

"I'm essentially done with my part of it, but I estimate the review process will take about another week. It'll have to make the rounds of the planning office, so everyone has a chance to voice their opinions. Bill's already aware of it and is on board, so I don't expect any problems in this office. Because your total cost is below a million dollars, it doesn't have to be Okayed by the County Commissioners. I'm still amazed you can build such a substantial structure for so little money, but after seeing your geopolymer process and your Mego assembly line in operation, I'm sure you can do it."

I didn't know there was a million dollar threshold in the review process, but I was glad we had not triggered it. Getting some plans as unconventional as ours through a political review might have been difficult.

"Stellan's work in this area is really amazing, isn't it?" I queried, not expecting an answer, but I did get one.

"Totally," Alan answered, "and there is so much more." He slid open one of his desk drawers and pulled out the model light pipe and distribution panel we had given him. "Take this, for instance. From what Stellan explained to me, there is really nothing new here, but it is using known technology combined in a new way to cut way down on energy consumption."

Alan put the model back in the drawer and slid it shut. "I don't want my connection to your project to end with approval of your building permit. I'd like to drop in once in a while to see what kind of progress you're making. Would that be okay with you?"

It was my turn to say, "Totally." I continued, "We'd be happy to have you check it out." I glanced at my watch. "We're about to keep you overtime," I said, "so I'd better roundup Ralph and let you get home."

After Ralph and I had caught a bite to eat and were headed back to the Lazy HZ, I told Ralph about my talk with Alan. I mentioned he thought our building permit might be issued in about a week.

"Bet 'cha it don't take no week," Ralph said.

"Oh? Why not?"

"I was tellin' Bill how ya'll 're real careful uh the land, an' ain't gonna make a mess like Wainright did. I told 'em 'bout Stellan makin' raised board thingies for Diane to back in on and then drive straight out on, and put her drillin' cuttin's on so's not to mash all them flowers. An' how ya backed in to unload yer displays an' Mego things on the road, 'stead uh making a big circle in the meadow. An' how ya an' Stellan set up them there displays on bare spots. Bill's office needs a little somethin' goin' right for 'em after all the heat they been takin' for givin' Wainright a permit."

That Ralph noticed our care with the land surprised me, because doing so was second nature to both Stellan and me. I had not taken any particular notice of our actions. But I shouldn't have been surprised, because Ralph was always keenly aware of how people treated their environment.

"All right," I said. "I'll take your bet, because the wheels of bureaucracy always seem to grind slowly, but I'll be very happy if I lose."

I spent the night at Ralph's, finished unloading the pallets of Megos in the morning, and called Maggie to see if anything was happening with the land deal.

"There's some movement," she told me.

"What does that mean?" I asked.

"They asked for verification the monies are available, and I had my bank verify the funds are in place. I have to admit, this is the largest balance I've ever had in my trust account."

"When this transaction happens, will Ralph need to be present?"

"I don't think so," Maggie said. "Ralph signed the purchase agreement the other day, and now the Bank has to sign over the deed. I expect it will happen by the end of the week."

"Only about a week late. Not bad," I said. Maggie laughed.

After bidding Ralph goodbye, I headed back for Laramie with the trailer. The rest of Tuesday seemed to creep by, but Wednesday was much more interesting. Stellan was showing me a collection of Megos that had not turned out quite right when we decided to test a couple. We rigged up a hydraulic test machine, broke two of them in the presence of our assembly line crew. Everyone cheered when the first one passed the design loading, and we held our breath as the load climbed higher and higher. The block finally broke in two at a safety factor over two. The second block performed as well. I took everyone to lunch to celebrate.

Thursday an omne trium perfectum, *The Rule of Three* to translate from the Latin, happened. Cass returned from her trip to her former cooperatives with firm commitments from seven people to supply labor for construction of the first part of Civalia; Maggie called to tell me the land transaction was complete and Ralph was now again the owner of his land; and I lost my bet with Ralph. Alan called to tell me the building permit was approved, and I could pick it up at my convenience.

Friday. Well, Friday no work got done. Everyone, including Maggie and Diane, traveled directly to the Lazy HZ. That is, everyone except me, and I went to Rawlins, picked up the building permit, and picked up Geraldine on my way to the Lazy HZ from Rawlins. We all spent the rest of the day eating, drinking, and celebrating these milestones.

CHAPTER 17

W e dived into construction of the first segment of Civalia. I was able to put about half time into construction activities, the rest of my time being occupied with trying to sort out the legal status of Wainright's house and parcel. It fell on Maggie to try to contact the mortgage holder, while Elaine pursued the possibly forged release. I helped where I could.

I scrounged a sample of Wainright's writing from an unpaid bar tab in a Saratoga bar, and found a handwriting expert to compare his signature with the scribble on the Release. The results were indeterminate. The sample size of the scribble was too small to yield good results. The next tactic was to try locating the notary on the release. This took a little doing, since the notary was supposedly in Omaha. The notary's writing was just as illegible as the signatory's, and the stamp was smeared almost to the state of being illegible. The one thing I thought I could make out was the year the notary's commission expired, which happened to be prior to when the document was supposedly executed. I took my findings to Elaine.

Elaine explained, "The Bank sent me a list of those with authority to sign such a release and included samples of their signatures. From examining those, I don't think there is any question the document is forged. The problem becomes one of finding incontrovertible proof and a motive."

"Neither of those is proving to be easy," I said. "I found a sample of Wainright's signature, and I did have a handwriting expert look at it. There wasn't enough to make a definitive judgment, but he didn't think it matched. It certainly doesn't look the same to me, but that is not to say Wainright didn't attempt to disguise his signature. As for motive, or at least a partial motive,

I think Maggie's efforts to find the mortgage holder might add weight to the hypothesis this is all an alarm to let Wainright know something is happening. She has not been able to contact the Mortgage holder. The phone number listed has been disconnected, and the address does not turn up with a Google Earth search. The Florida Secretary of State's Office has also not been helpful. There is a post office box listed, but she found it's one of those private mail drops. They wouldn't give her any information on the box holder. We haven't tried writing to them at the box yet."

"So, you're saying if something is sent to that P.O. Box, Wainright knows the mortgage is being investigated. This sounds more suspect all the time."

"That's what we think. I have one other possible bit of evidence," I said.

Elaine appeared not to have heard my last comment, since she was drumming her fingers on her desk, deep in thought. "You did tell me you were going to set up surveillance on the house, didn't you? Has that been done?"

"Yes, we finished last week. So far nothing has tripped our surveillance system."

"Have you been testing it?"

"Yes."

"So, the options appear to be narrowing down to doing nothing but waiting for Wainright to do something, or sending an inquiry to the P.O. Box, and maybe triggering a response. The house appears to figure into his plans somehow," Elaine mused.

"Stellan and I think so," I said, "and I have something else that leads to that conclusion."

"What's that?" Elaine asked.

"The company name listed on the mortgage is Embuscadoes Investment, Inc. It's a Florida corporation"

"It sounds sort of Spanish," Elaine said. "So?"

"There's no Florida corporation by that name, but there is a corporation named Ambuscadoes Investment, Inc. The P.O. Box listed on the mortgage is in a private mail drop location in the same area as the Ambuscadoes Investment, Inc. address, which doesn't show up on Google Earth."

"Where does all this lead?" Elaine asked.

"The kicker is," I said, "Ambuscadoes can be defined as ambushes. Ambuscades comes from embuscadoes, via middle French, which comes from the Latin prefix in- and the Latin root bosco, translated as forest."

"Wow!" Elaine said. "Either that is a hell of a coincidence, or Wainright is a more slippery, arrogant, and egotistical character than I've been giving him credit for."

Elaine drummed her fingers on the desk even harder for a time before speaking again.

"Here's what I think," Elaine said. "Doing nothing is likely to provoke an unplanned response, which could be something completely unexpected, making it harder to detect and stop. If something is sent to this P.O. Box, it will mesh with Wainright's plans, and he may get a little careless, congratulating himself on how smart he is and how dumb we are. So, I think our chances of intercepting and defeating his plans are better with the second option."

"So, should I have Maggie send a letter to the box?"

"I think you should go full bore on this and file a lawsuit to get the release, deed, and mortgage declared null and void. Send the filing via register mail to the named mortgage holder at the P.O. Box and see what happens. If they do respond, you will at least have turned over a rock to see what kind of troll is living under it. If there's no response, and that's what I'll bet on, it'll give us more information to go on, and you'll get a summary judgment."

"And it will clear the title to the land," I added. I thought about this course of action for a moment. "I see your point. Something else it might do is force his hand sooner than he plans, assuming, of course, Wainright is behind this."

"Is there really a question about that?" Elaine asked.

The next day I showed up at Maggie's office when her office hours began.

"You're getting to be a regular visitor," she said. "What kind of problems are you bringing me today?"

I launched into an explanation of Elaine's suggestion we file a lawsuit to have the deed and mortgage documents declared null and void.

"Sounds reasonable," Maggie said. "So, you want me to file a civil suit in District Court in Rawlins naming this Embuscadoes Investment, Inc., as the defendant, and send a registered letter to the P.O. Box, which you think is this Ambuscadoes Investment, Inc."

"That's about the size of it," I said.

"And you're prepared for the fireworks from this action?" she asked.

"As ready as I'll ever be."

"Okay, I'll get on it and probably have the paperwork ready in a couple of days. Ralph will be the plaintiff, since he is the current landowner. He is on board with this, isn't he?"

"I don't really know," I said, suffering from a sudden stab of guilt. "I haven't talked with him about it, but I guess I'd better do that."

"I guess you should," Elaine echoed.

"Why don't you start on the paper work, and I'll check with Ralph. I'm pretty sure he'll go along with this action."

When I got home, I called Ralph. When I explained what I had found, my conversation with Elaine, and what I intended to have Maggie do, his comment was, "John, I ain't never had a friend what thought as much like I do as you. I just would uh done it sooner. I'll jingle up Geraldine, an' tell her ta be on 'er toes."

The die was cast, so I went back to helping with the construction project. A few days later, Ralph dropped in at my shop shortly after lunch, looking over our assembly line and telling me he'd been by Maggie's office to sign the complaint. When he asked, I supplied him with some coveralls, and he joined our assembly line. Stellan gave him one of the easier jobs, but still Ralph impressed our younger workers with his stamina for his age, and also for his wealth of stories and lore of this region in days long gone. The afternoon passed swiftly.

We quit work early, so all of us, our Civalia crew and our outside laborers, could enjoy a meal with Ralph before he had to head for home. We had a rowdy pizza picnic in the park not far from the shop. As the evening wound down and Ralph departed, Stellan and I set on a park bench and talked.

"Where's Gyan? I noticed he hasn't been here the last couple of days. Is his work keeping him tied up?" I asked.

"No, as a matter of fact he has gone to Texas to pick up a volumetric continuous flow mixer. You might have noticed that the batch mixer is a bottleneck in our Mego manufacturing process."

"I did notice that. But you have some of the crew working on molds. Does that mean you'll be ramping up Mego production with the new mixer?"

"Partly," Stellan answered, "but some of those molds are for the hypocaust floor slabs. We need to get moving on those, since we'll need to get the floor in before we finish both of the Mego block walls."

"Will those need reinforcing?" I asked.

"Yes, they will, along with the center column and the outer permanent wall."

"What do you plan to use?"

"We don't have a lot of good options for that purpose, given the 500 year design life. Ordinary rebar won't last that long. Stainless steel rebar might."

"That would be costly," I said.

"Wouldn't it, though."

Stellan and I sat in silence for a while, both thinking about reinforcement.

I broke the silence. "The geopolymer material has better properties than concrete, and GFR could maybe make it better."

"I'm not familiar with the term GFR. What's that?" Stellan asked.

"Glass fiber reinforcing," I said.

"Is glass the only type of fibers used?" Stellan asked.

"No, a wide variety from steel to plastics, but probably glass is used the most."

"I'll look into it." Stellan was quiet again for a time, and then he said, "Manjinder and I have been experimenting with making reinforcing bars with the artificial shell process, and it likely will work. But we haven't figured out a way to solve the scale up problems yet."

"That sounds like it would be ideal," I said enthusiastically, "so what about using something known for now, like stainless steel rebar or glass fibers, and then introducing your shell material later? After all, the amount of floor scheduled for this first section of construction is relatively small."

"That does sound like a workable solution," Stellan said, then changed the subject. "I think you should stop helping with the Mego manufacturing. . ."

"What?" I interrupted. "I know I've been somewhat in and out, with the land deal and everything, but I want to help build Civalia."

"You didn't let me finish," Stellan said patiently. "Something else needs done, and you, my friend, are the one to do it. Assuming we do get the Civalia work space done by late fall, I'd like to move our manufacturing facilities over there. We don't have room here for the feed stocks we will need, and we have to transport our finished blocks to the Civalia site; it's costing us a lot of time, money, and entropy to manufacture here. However, we will most assuredly not have any of the energy control systems in place to make the work space habitable for the winter. It won't be earth-sheltered, there won't be the solar gain potential from the greenhouse, and the thermal mass will be very limited."

"So, what do you want me to do?"

"I think the only reasonable alternative for this winter will be to heat with wood. It is a very ancient means of heating and we do have a local source that's not totally against the principles of Civalia. I've been up into the national forest and there's a huge supply of downed timber from the pine beetle infestation."

"So, you want me to become a woodsman?" I said.

"Yes and no. Remember how we said the National Forest would be our virtual domains?"

"Yes," I said.

"Well, if the forest is our domains, we can't just go out and collect firewood. We need a permit. Furthermore, if you go take a look, I'm sure you'll agree all the downed wood is a fire hazard right next door to Civalia. So, I think you should go negotiate a deal with the forest service where we take care of a chunk of our next-door forest, and the forest service lets us use some of the stuff we clear out."

"I see what you're getting at," I said. "This is another task, like getting Ralph's land back from Wainright, but negotiating with a federal agency can't be easy. Are you sure you don't want to take on the Forest Service and let me work on Mego production?"

Stellan laughed. "Not in a thousand years. You seem to be able to get impossible things done, so this will just be one more to add to your list. After you get permission, you become the woodsman, and bring home the firewood."

Thus began my quest for an agreement with the Forest Service for Civalia residents to take an active role in grooming the forest next door. In thinking about the problem, I decided a workable strategy was to make an analogy with the various civic groups adopting sections of highway to periodically pick up the trash. I also decided Ralph, and maybe Geraldine, would be helpful in making these negotiations.

I began making preparations, the first being to recruit Ralph and Geraldine. I then spent the better part of a week documenting the state of the forest adjacent to Civalia with pictures, researching Forest Service policies, and investigating the proper channels to thread through the bureaucratic maze. When I couldn't think of anything else I could do to get prepared, I gathered my troops and we descended on the U.S. Forest Service Brush Creek/Hayden Ranger District headquarters in Saratoga.

Taking Geraldine and Ralph along with me was one of the best moves I could have taken. They introduced me to Jeremy, the range specialist for the District.

"We heard you got back that land Wainright took from you," Jeremy said to Ralph.

"Yup, an' John here's the one that done it fer me."

Jeremy turned to me. "Yes, and I've heard some rumors you and your friends are going to build some kind of. . . of. . . .." Jeremy apparently didn't know what to call Civalia.

"Call it a cooperative living structure," I said. "We've named it Civalia. You've probably heard rumors of everything from a hippie commune to a communist gulag."

"Well, yes," Jeremy said, having the decency to blush from embarrassment.

"What we're really trying to do is make a living-arrangement for a group of people to live rich, fulfilling lives without worrying about where they are going to lay their heads the next night or where their next meal comes from."

"They may find it difficult to find jobs in the valley here," Jeremy said. "The valley is not exactly a hotbed of economic development."

I smiled. "Our goal is to have a community where no one has to have a job. Oh, there will be work to do alright, but it will not be the mandatory obligation for survival that is the case of jobs in our existing society."

"That sounds utopian," Jeremy said. "Wouldn't everyone just lay back and do nothing?"

"Mark Twain addressed a similar issue in one of his short stories, *Captain Stormfield's Visit to Heaven*. Captain Stormfield arrived in heaven and was issued a harp so he could go sit on the edge of a cloud and sing. It wasn't long before he tired of singing, got up, threw his harp on a huge pile of discarded harps, and set off to find something more interesting to do. We are finding people get enormously creative when they have the time and resources to do so."

"You should see some the things these here people are doin'," Geraldine said. "I've taken a few pitchers."

Geraldine hauled out a stack of pictures she had taken on the day of our last picnic, and began handing them to Jeremy with brief explanations. She showed him our Mego blocks, radiant refrigerator, light panels, and Ralph's cooking being run by the solar powered LPE.

Jeremy got a slightly longing look before he roused himself and said, "I've got a lot more questions, and I'd like to hear more about your project, but I suspect you have some business you'd like to take care of with the Forest Service."

"You're right about that," I said. "There're a couple of things. We're going to complete a small portion of our structure by winter, and some of our people will be living there until spring, making more Megos and other building parts. We'd like to get a firewood permit to supply heat. Can you tell me exactly what I need to do to obtain the permit?"

"Certainly," Jeremy said, sliding open one of his desk drawers. "Here is a brochure giving the procedure and regulations covering the gathering of firewood. Whoever's at the front desk can help you out. What else can I do for you?"

"The second thing is a little more complicated," I said. "Civalia will be not far from the forest boundary. When I hiked through the area to the west of our building site, I noticed a lot of standing dead trees, even more downed trees, and a heavy accumulation of brush and duff."

"It's getting' thick an' heavy these last few years," Ralph added.

"Sure is," Geraldine added. "Gettin' to be a real fire hazard."

"I've got pictures of some of the area," I said, and handed my collection of pictures to Jeremy.

Jeremy sighed as he paged through a few of the pictures. "We're well aware of the conditions throughout the forest, but we just don't have the manpower to do much about it. Ralph, I've seen some of your land across the fence from the forest, and it looks like you've done a better job than we have. There's much less fuel on your place. If we could get the forest to look like that, we'd be much happier."

Ralph smoothed his mustache and said, "Geraldine an' me 'ave been tryin' ta keep the dead stuff from getting too out uh hand."

"But havin' so much just across the fence is worryin'," Geraldine added.

"That's true for us too," I said, "but we want to suggest a possible way for us to reduce the risk." I hurried on before Jeremy could think or say anything else, probably negative. "You know how various civic organizations adopt sections of highway to clean up the trash periodically?"

"Yes," Jeremy said with a little note of caution in his voice.

"What if our group adopted," I wiggle my forefingers on both hands in the air to indicate quotation marks around the word adopted, "a section of forest just to the west of Ralph and Geraldine's land and the Civalia site? We could work at reducing the fuel load, as well as doing whatever else you folks in the Forest Service consider beneficial to maintaining a healthy forest."

Jeremy looked confused and then had the look of a light dawning. "So you would want to have the rights to sell the harvested wood?"

"No," I said. "We would prefer the Forest Service deal with any salvageable wood products from our cleanup efforts; in any way you choose," I added.

Jeremy again looked confused. "But aren't you getting a firewood permit?"

"Yes," I said, "but we don't expect to need wood heating for more than a couple of years at most. We also expect our grooming efforts will take years, probably decades. It might never end, just like trash along the highways doesn't end."

Jeremy shook his head. "That sounds too good to be true. What's the catch?"

"Well, we would like to have a little input into whatever might be planned for the area we are grooming. For instance, we'd probably express our opposition to a mining or drilling operation starting up in the area or a motorized trail blazed across it."

"You and me too," Jeremy said. He began to look more interested and curious. "Most of the people coming in here want something from us. They're what I call takers. They want resources, camping areas, trees to transplant, wedding party areas, mushrooms; you name it. You appear to want to give us something."

"We want to give the land something," I said.

Again, he shook his head. "What kind of area are you talking about?"

"To begin with, we figure we could handle about a square mile," I said. "As Civalia grows, we'd like to add to it. When Civalia is completed, we'd probably be able to take care of about eight square miles, four miles along the boundary and a couple of miles in."

Jeremy again shook his head. "That sounds like a lot of work."

"It certainly will be to catch up," I said, "but not so much to maintain the forest once we do."

Jeremy straightened up and rested his forearms on his desk. "This isn't something I can do on my own. It'll probably have to go to the Forest Supervisor, maybe higher. Will you be willing to present you case directly to the higher ups, if necessary?

"Of course," Geraldine, Ralph, and I all chorused together.

"But I have a question and a request of you," I said.

"What's that?" Jeremy said, evidencing some wariness again with a slight frown.

"The question is whether you will be willing to champion our cause, knowing it might be rough sledding to get it accomplished. There's always a lot of bureaucratic inertia."

Jeremy sat back and sighed.

"You'll just be helpin' us do a project a mite akin to yer Horse Creek Draw project," Geraldine said.

Jeremy brightened a little. "That was some project, wasn't it?" He sat up a little straighter and said, "Okay. I'll take it on. What's one more crusade in this avalanche of paper?" He indicated the untidy stacks of paper covering most of his desk.

Geraldine and Ralph had helped me select Jeremy as the best person to approach with my request for turning some of the National Forest next to Civalia into quasi domains for the residents. They had told me about his championing the preservation of a Native American site in a remote area, named Horse Creek Draw, when the Forest Service had targeted it for a prescribed burn. He had organized some girl and boy scout troops, some church groups, and other just plain concerned citizens, to work like banshees for a couple of weeks to clear a significant amount of the ladder fuel in the area. That effort had almost cost him his job, but it had prevented the archeological site from being destroyed.

"My request," I said, "is for you to visit our site to see for yourself what we're trying to do." I handed him my contact information.

"I'd like that," Jeremy said seriously as the three of us stood to leave. He stood and followed us to the door of his office.

"It was nice to meet you, Jeremy," I said, "and I look forward to seeing you again. I'll be in touch as our plans develop, and I expect I'll be hearing from you as you try to thread our request through your bureaucracy. Hopefully, we won't be too much of a pest to you."

"It was nice to meet you too," Jeremy said, and he stood in his doorway, fingering my card, as he watched us walk down the hall toward the front desk. I bought a firewood permit and collected the requisite instructions and rules.

Back at the Lazy HZ, I thanked Ralph and Geraldine for their help and went on up the road to where Civalia was beginning to emerge. Diane was at work drilling holes for pilings, Stellan had engaged her to complete the foundation piling work, not just for this first section, but also for the remainder of the wedges required for the full work space cylinder. He also had her putting in the pilings for next year's commons section, including extended buffer areas on both sides.

Two of the laborers Cass had brought in appeared to be cleaning out the bottom of some of the holes just beyond Diane's rig. Beyond them were a few sono tubes and stainless-steel rebar cages lying on the ground. Diane waved to me and I walked over by her drill rig. She raised the drill auger, releasing a cascade of soil around the hole, and throttled down the engine.

"How's it going?" I asked.

"Good. We're on schedule."

"It doesn't exactly look it," I said. "Besides these few holes I can see that you've drilled, there doesn't seem to be much else going on."

"Looks are deceiving," Diane said. "Let's take a walk."

We walked farther out into the field, past where the laborers were working, and past the sono tubes and rebar cages. As we got farther out, I could see there were numerous disturbed areas, each with what looked like a concrete piling with rebar sticking up out of the top in the center of it.

"We're trying to minimize the disturbance, so we started at the north end and are working south. That way we minimize travel over this area. Most modern construction plans for a project of this size sequentially drill all the holes, then install the sono tubes and rebar, then pour the concrete, and then backfill the holes. We're working a small area at a time, so we minimize the time the vegetation is covered; you might have seen I have a canvas on top of a grid to catch the soil I'm pulling up with the drill. We can't help creating some disturbance around one of these pilings, but we are able to keep it to a small area."

I was astounded at how little disturbance was visible from where I stood. Yes, there was damage and disturbance near my feet, but when I looked further out in the meadow, not much was visible. Looking closely, I could see some silver rebar poking up among the flowers and waving grass, but they did not stand out. I could see where the grids had been placed around the piling I was standing by, but even that disturbance was beginning to be erased by the growth of the undamaged plants in the area.

"Doesn't taking this much care slow you down?" I asked.

"That depends on how you look at it," Diane answered. "When Stellan first told me how he wanted me to do this work, that's exactly what I thought, but when he explained his thinking, I changed my mind."

"What did he tell you?"

"He pointed out Thoreau's reasoning for not taking the train to go to adjacent towns. Thoreau said if he added the time it took him to earn the money for a train ticket, it would take him more total time than just walking, so he walked. In this case, if we take into account the time necessary to quote, 'reclaim' the land, it takes less overall time to minimize disturbance. I think he's right, because I've seen areas where I've been working where land restored years earlier was not really back to its original condition."

"Now that you mention it," I said, "I've seen evidence Stellan's right. When you stop to think about it, there're some scars on the land still visible after centuries. Oregon Trail ruts are still visible near Guernsey. If the time, expense, and effort it takes to reclaim the land are added, it's more effective to minimize the disturbance, and I must say you are doing an excellent job."

"Thank you," Diane said. "Using this geopolymer material helps make the job go faster, too, since the curing time is so much shorter than for concrete."

"What's the next step?" I asked.

"This area we're standing in right now will be a temporary work space wall. Stellan's going to dig some trenches from piling to piling along the line of the wall, and then they'll pour some beams from piling to piling. The beams will support the temporary wall and will eventually be part of the hypocaust floor supports when the wall gets moved. I think for now he's shooting for enclosing the work space as soon as possible."

"I'm eager to see all of that happen, and I'll likely get to, since I've been assigned to be a woodsman and bring in the firewood for this winter."

"That's what I heard. When are you starting?"

"I plan on gathering my equipment and heading over here tomorrow. I'll be staying in Ralph's bunk house."

"I'll probably see a lot more of you then," Diane said, "but I'd better get back to work."

I scouted the site to locate a place where I could pile wood without being in the way, and where it would do minimal damage to the plants. I checked the area where a couple of travel trailers were located for Diane and the laborers, but decided it would be too far from the permanent structure when the trailers were removed. I called Stellan to get some guidance on the wood pile location. He directed me to just outside the western temporary wall where some extra pilings had been installed. I was to start piling the wood at the far edge of that area, and in a few days, they would install some flooring and a portion of the temporary wall in that region. I could then build some ricks next to the wall, and the construction crew would help me transfer the cut wood to the ricks. I found the area of extra pilings and then examined the buck fence and sketched a plan for a stile to get over the fence and a slide to pass firewood under. I then headed home.

The next day I gathered my equipment, debating for quite a while about using my gasoline engine powered chain saw. I finally decided against it. I loaded my electric chain saw, and figured I'd use the LPE generator/inverter, which was still at the Civalia site. The time I could use the saw would be limited by that setup, but it would be a lot more consistent with our project goals. I also loaded a selection of hand saws and other hand tools. In a moment of inspiration, I added the Bruck to the load.

A trip to the lumber yard for materials for the stile and slide completed my preparations, so I set off with my truck and a trailer load of Megos. When Stellan had learned I was headed for the Civalia site to begin cutting firewood, he had hastily put his crew to work loading the trailer, so my trip could be multipurpose. He had also arranged for Cass to go with me and bring the truck and trailer back to Laramie.

Cass and I had interesting conversations on our trip to the site. She was enthusiastic about the progress being made on the structure of Civalia, and she was also pleased with the deep relationships developing among all those committed to being part of Civalia. As I listened to what she had to say, I felt a sense of sadness, because I was not a direct part of that growing—family, group, clutch, kin, clan, coterie, gang, team, band? I realized I could not find a particular word to accurately portray the group of people making up Civalia.

I mentioned this to Cass, and she said, "I know what you mean. I've experienced the same thing when I've been trying to tell other people about the advantages of cooperative living versus competitive living. Our language is just not geared to express those ideas well. You've probably had a similar experience when you've tried to tell other people about entropy."

"You're right about that. Even most of the scientists and engineers I've worked with can't seem to make the connection with the social and environmental problems we face and entropy buildup. Their solutions to the problems generally produce a lot more entropy."

"That's somewhat understandable, isn't it?" Cass challenged me. "Even we are producing more entropy as we are building Civalia."

"True," I said, "but we're trying to minimize our entropy production in the process, balance our production with entropy export into outer space to the best of our ability, and in the long run, if Civalia has a 500-year design life, keep the average entropy production per person per year consistent at about 1,000 to 1,200 Watts energy consumption. Even now we're low compared to the entropy production from the 400 to 800 25-year design-life homes it would take to house a similar number of people for 500 years."

"Entropy is a complicated subject," Cass said.

"That it is, and not having common language to describe it makes it worse."

I asked about Cass' efforts to find other individuals interested in joining Civalia, specifically those with skills needed in the community. She told me some people had expressed an interest, but she hadn't much time to follow up those leads. Construction efforts were the main focus, not only for her, but for all the others committed to Civalia.

"Except for me," I said. "It seems like I haven't been able to spend much time on construction."

"We don't think that's true," Cass told me. "You've been clearing the way, providing the resources, and dealing with problems that could slow us down. I've always thought that's exactly what the managers should be doing in companies I've worked for. Instead, most of them are throwing up roadblocks, taking away resources, and creating problems."

I laughed. "That's been my experience too. I hope I haven't been doing any of those things."

Cass asked me about the issues with Wainright's house, and I brought her up to date on what was going on with the house and the paperwork associated with it. I asked her about the workers she had recruited to help us with the construction; she called them "Dancers," since most of them came from the Dancing Rabbit Ecovillage. She told me how they were intrigued by the construction techniques we were employing, and how, at the very least, they would be taking some of those back to their respective communities. They had also occasionally been playing my entropy game in the evenings. Some were beginning to ask some questions, indicating they either might be interested in joining Civalia, or in taking some of the Civalien philosophy and technology back to their communities.

We arrived at the Civalia site, unloaded the Megos and my woodcutting gear, and Cass headed back to Laramie with the truck and trailer. Using the Bruck, I began moving my equipment up to the forest fence. That attracted the attention of the Dancers, and a group of them came over to inspect the Bruck, as well as to help me transfer my gear over the fence. It was near lunchtime, and the Dancers took the time to ride the Bruck up and down the road. We ate together, and after lunch they helped me haul the Bruck over the fence, along with the LPE equipment. I set out to begin gathering firewood.

Over the next couple of days, I cut downed beetle-kill into short lengths, hauled them to the fence, and fed them through it. At lunch time, and late in the afternoon, I cut the logs into stove lengths, and using a wheelbarrow I had brought along, transferred the wood to the designated location. When I had about a half dozen wheelbarrow loads of stove length wood, I took the time to split the larger logs and stacked everything in temporary piles. I was able to harvest about a third of a cord that first afternoon. At dinnertime, I walked down to Ralph's for a nourishing dinner, and then became a log myself in his bunkhouse.

On the third night Ralph woke me up about 1:30 AM. I was a little slow waking up, but when I understood our alarm system at Wainright's house had been tripped, and Geraldine, using the night vision scope I had given her, was watching someone examining the fence around the house, I was wide awake.

I hurriedly dressed and threw on my coat. Ralph and I then walked down the road and climbed the hill where I had first seen Wainright's work. We found some shelter in a grove of trees from which we could view Wainright's compound without being seen. I scanned the area with a pair of binoculars. There was enough starlight that I could make out the fence, but I couldn't see much else. I scooted back down the slope and texted Geraldine. After a short delay, she called me back.

She told us the intruder was gone, but when she'd first seen him, at least she assumed it was a man, he'd been at the fence where we'd faked a malfunctioning light. From there he'd gone around the fence, staying a distance away to avoid being in any cones of light. He'd then approached the gate to examine the lock, and that's when she'd gotten somewhat of a look at him and snapped a picture.

I was for hot-footing it back to the house and driving over to Geraldine's to see the picture of our intruder, but Ralph had a cooler head.

"That there skunk might be still around, an' if'n we start rushin' around, it'll let 'im know we're on ta 'im," Ralph told me.

I had to admit he was right, so we slunk back to his home and didn't turn on any lights. Ralph called Geraldine for more details, putting her on speaker phone. She didn't know what direction he had come from, but she had watched him head uphill toward the forest boundary when he left. He seemed like a large man, but that was difficult to judge given the distance and the fact she was observing him in the infrared spectrum. She could tell he had on a backpack, and it looked like he was carrying some sort of a grip which he rather frequently passed from hand to hand.

"The bag must have been heavy," I said."

"I reckon so," she said. "He put 'er on the ground once in a while, too."

"Was the pack heavy too?" I asked.

"Might uh been," she said. "He was bent over some. That there bag was cold, so it didn't show up very good. Same with his pack."

When we had all the information we could glean, Ralph hung up the phone, and we sat in the dark and talked about what we should do. Before long, we heard a vehicle go down the county road.

"That's likely him," I said, "and it sounds like a Diesel engine. That means a truck of some sort."

"I reckon it does," Ralph replied as he looked out a window.

"Can't see nothin' but lights though."

"Do you think he saw what we're building on the Civalia site?"

"Don't rightly know, but it don't show from the county road. If'n he knows, would probably be from hearin' rumors."

"I wonder where he was parked," I said.

Ralph ran his fingers through his hair. "There's lots a' little side tracks an' spaces between trees. The Forest Service been tryin' to make it harder to get off the beaten path, but this here section's low priority and ain't seen much work yet."

As the hours in the dark passed, we were still not turning on lights, we discussed what actions to take. We finally agreed to go to Rawlins at first light to discuss this development with Elaine. Another thought, which we agreed to follow up on, was finding a tracker to locate the parking place of the intruder. We hoped Elaine would be able to help us find such an individual. We ate breakfast, did the chores, and left in time to get to the Sheriff's Office by 8:00. Before leaving, we left a message for her, letting her know we were on our way.

Elaine listened intently to our story of the intruder, asked a few questions, most of which we could not answer, and then told us, "Unfortunately, this is not something warranting an in-depth investigation. So far, you have a case of trespass. Yes, I agree with you it is probably sinister, and bodes no good. We can increase our patrols of the area, but until we have more information, there is little I can do."

"Can you help us get more information?" I asked.

"What do you have in mind?"

"Ralph and I have thought we should try to find out where the intruder might have been parked. It's likely, if, more likely when, he comes back, he'll park in the same place. We were wondering if you might know of a tracker we could engage?"

"I don't know of anyone local, but there is a trackers organization in the state." Elaine rummaged in her desk drawer, and finally found a card. "The Wyoming State Trackers; here's the card for one of their main people."

She handed the card to Ralph, who was closest to her right hand, and Ralph passed it on to me. The main number was in

Lusk. "If you'll excuse me a moment, I'll give them a call." I got up and stepped into the hall, dialed the number, and was surprised when it was answered by the Sheriff's Office of Niobrara County. I explained our situation, and the dispatcher took my number and said he would pass my request on to the trackers. I thanked him, ended the call, and went back into Elaine's office.

I told the others the results of my call. Ralph and I took our leave, but not before we brainstormed with Elaine for a short time about other measures we might take. We couldn't come up with anything that didn't require visiting Wainright's house, but we were loath to do so, since we might destroy some of the signs left by our intruder. Waiting seemed like the best option, although it was the most difficult.

Ralph suggested we drop in on Alan at the planning office. We did, and chewed the fat with Alan for a half hour or so. Ralph invited him to visit again to see the progress on Civalia and the care the construction crew was taking to minimize the disturbance. Alan told us he would if he could work it out. We went to a restaurant and killed some more time with something to drink and a sweet roll. Finally, an hour and half later, my phone rang.

I explained our problem to the man on the other end of the line, emphasizing speed was of the essence. He said that a good tracker could certainly help, and he himself could help, but he couldn't get to the site for a couple of days. I asked if there was anyone in our vicinity who could get there, preferably today. He hemmed and hawed for a moment and then told me there was an excellent tracker near Riverton, but he also couldn't meet us swiftly because he didn't have transportation.

"Riverton you say," I said loudly while glancing at Ralph. "What if we pick him up? I think we can make it in a couple of hours." Ralph nodded.

The man said he'd call and see if the tracker was available and get back to me as soon as he could. Again, we waited. The time seemed to crawl, but at the same time zip, since we were operating with a deadline. About twenty minutes later, my phone rang again. The Wyoming State Trackers representative gave me the name and phone number of a tracker living near Riverton, and told me that person would be willing to help us if we provided transportation. I thanked him and immediately dialed the number he gave me.

"Hello?" a young but dignified voice said.

"My name is John Tantivy," I said. "Is this Darren Mayer?" I asked.

"Sometimes," he said, now sounding slightly frosty.

"Did I get your name wrong?" I was embarrassed.

"In a way," he said. "I was named that at birth, but I have since taken a Native name. I suppose you got my birth name from Kevin at the Wyoming State Trackers hotline."

"Yes," I said. "Tell me your true name, and I will use it."

"I am now Kajika Eagle Feather," he said with authority.

"Do I then call you Kajika?" I asked.

"Yes," he replied.

"Native names have meaning," I said. "Will you tell me the meaning of your name?"

"Yes," he said, his voice thawing somewhat. "'Kajika' means 'walks without sound,' and I earned 'Eagle Feather' for saving a lost child with my tracking skills."

"Then you are the man we need. We don't know for certain, but you may be able to save several lives for us with your tracking skills. Did Kevin tell you about our problem?"

"He said you have an uninvited guest who may wish you harm, and you wish to intercept him."

"That's essentially correct," I said. "I understand you don't have reliable transportation, so if it's okay with you, we'll drive to Riverton and pick you up. Our problem may take a few days. Can you stay that long?"

"When will you be there? It will take me a while to get to Riverton," he said. "I can stay for a few days."

"If you're not in Riverton, where exactly are you?"

"I'm in Ethete."

"That is even closer for us. Why don't we meet you there?" I asked. "We'll be driving a dark blue, 4×4, pickup with Carbon

County plates. How will we recognize you?"

"Call when you get into Ethete," he said, and hung up.

Ralph and I headed out. About two hours later, we pulled into Ethete. There wasn't much there, so I pulled into the parking lot of the Little Wind River Casino and called Kajika. A short time later, a slender young man, looking to be in his mid- to late-twenties and dressed in modern outdoor clothing came walking down the road with a sizable pack on his back. Ralph and I got out of his truck and introduced ourselves to Kajika.

"Aren't you a little worried about setting off with two unknown people?" I asked.

"I looked you up on the internet, and saw articles about you and a man named Wainright in the Saratoga Sun. I also called the Carbon County Sheriff's Office, and talked to a Lieutenant Thompson about you two. She vouched for you."

"Yer thorough," Ralph said, "an' that's what we need."

"You can put your pack in the back and ride between us or shotgun, whichever you want," I said.

Kajika slung his pack into the bed of the truck, and chose to ride shotgun. I climbed into the middle, and Ralph headed back towards Rawlins.

On the drive back to the Lazy HZ, Kajika was at first reserved, but as we talked about various subjects and told him about the situation with the land and Wainright's house, he began to get more comfortable with us, and more talkative. We learned that he had been substitute teaching at the Wyoming Indian High School and was currently unemployed. He'd been thinking of going to work in one of the casinos, but was not too keen on the long hours, the ambience, and the smoking associated with those establishments.

"We'll pay ya for your tracking," Ralph said.

Kajika protested weakly.

"No objectin'," Ralph said. "It's worth somethin' for ya ta help us outsmart that skunk, Wainright."

"And," I said, "if you're not working elsewhere, after the tracking is done, we've got some construction work going and could use some help."

Kajika asked about what we were building, and with Ralph's help, I described the building of Civalia. I shied away from discussing the whole Civalien Project, because I didn't know enough about Kajika's world view or his knowledge of entropy. Ralph seemed to sense my reticence to delve too deeply into the explanation of domains and minimizing entropy production, so he also kept the conversation on a more superficial level.

We stopped in Rawlins and picked up a late lunch. Kajika had a ravenous appetite, and I wondered if he'd been on a forced diet. I traded off driving with Ralph, so he sat next to Kajika and worked his magic on him for the rest of the trip. Soon they were trading yarns about the old days, Kajika's tales coming from what he'd heard from the elders of his tribe; comparing notes on riding and working the range, Kajika having done so as a young man; discussing issues of the reservation, of which Ralph demonstrated a surprising knowledge; and talking about Kajika's hopes and dreams for his future. I was again in awe of Ralph's ability to rapidly draw people out and have them feeling like they'd known him their whole life.

We arrived back at the Lazy HZ in the late afternoon and drove directly to Wainright's house. Ralph and I watched as Kajika dug out and donned a pair of moccasins from his pack. He explained that he would be leaving less of a trail with those, and thus be less likely to obliterate the trail of interest. He shouldered his pack and then moved up slowly toward the gate into Wainright's house, examining the ground closely as he went.

"There were a lot of people here walking around this fence," he said.

"That's right. We just finished building it two or three weeks ago. There was some rain the night we finished, but we installed our security sensors later, and I don't think there's been any rain since."

Kajika looked up and his gaze swept the whole area looking toward the west. "You said he left moving west."

"That's right," Ralph said.

"So," Kajika said, "It'll probably save time if I make a north to south sweep west of the fence. Why don't the two of you go a couple of hundred yards to the south? You'll know I have found some tracks if I begin to move west. You can then follow parallel to me."

Kajika moved around the fence, giving it a wide berth, while Ralph and I walked out a couple of hundred yards to the south. I was intrigued with the smoothness and grace of Kajika's movements. He glided, compared to our lurching. We watched as he examined the area to the west of the fence, stooping occasionally to examine something on the ground. It wasn't long before he set out west, and we followed on a parallel path.

Eventually Kajika reached the forest boundary fence, and after examining the fence rails carefully, he climbed over the fence. Ralph and I followed suit, but not nearly as gracefully as Kajika. We then moved up through the trees, sometimes losing sight of Kajika. He was also living up to his name; we couldn't hear him move through the timber. The same could not be said for the two of us. We crashed and crackled, and swore, as we made our way deeper into the woods.

At last we came out on a two-track road. Kajika was waiting for us. He stopped us from stepping out on the road and told us he had found the parking place. He'd taken some pictures of the tire tracks, and discovered the vehicle had both entered and exited from the south. He suggested we back off a ways, and move parallel as he tracked the tire tracks as far as he reasonably could. Ralph and I complied with all our attendant crashing, crackling, and swearing. About a half mile later, the two-track road joined a maintained road, and Kajika let us out onto the road.

"You two would be easy to track," he said with a broad grin.

"No kidding," I said, "and it's beginning to get dark." Ralph was noticeably tiring.

We headed back on the road, and I realized we were somewhere above where I'd been cutting firewood.

"Wait here a few minutes," I told the two of them, and I plunged off into the trees again. Sure enough, I came across where

I'd been cutting and found my stash of equipment. I freed the Bruck and headed into the trees. There was one place where I'd come close to the road, and with a little bit of effort I was able to clear a path. I headed back north to pick up Ralph and Kajika.

Ralph was more than happy to climb onto the bed of the Bruck and sit down. Kajika was fascinated with it and wanted to pedal. I didn't argue. We took another half hour to get back to Ralph's. By then it was completely dark. Ralph and I fixed a little supper, and after eating quietly, we all turned in. Kajika slept in the bunkhouse with me, and I hoped I didn't snore or keep him awake by other means, but if I did, he was too polite to tell me.

CHAPTER 18

O ur intruder did not come back in the night. I was thankful, but I was still not totally rested the next morning when I awakened. Kajika was still sleeping, so I dressed and eased my way out as quietly as I could. Ralph, of course, was already up sitting on his porch. He looked a little tired also. We commiserated a few minutes and then went to do his morning chores.

Kajika was up and about when we returned. I left Ralph to talk with him while I cooked breakfast. I don't think my cooking equaled Ralph's, but it was passable. Again, Kajika ate a prodigious amount. Maybe I was just slowing down and eating less with age. After breakfast, I left the two of them and hiked down to Wainright's house and retrieved Ralph's pickup. It struck me that we'd made an error in leaving the truck next to the house. If the intruder had come back in the night, the truck might have given away the fact we knew something was going on. I resolved to be more careful.

When I got back, Ralph was playing N-Trō-P with Kajika. I excused myself and rode the Bruck up to the Civalia site. The crew was busy, this time digging trenches and installing forms for support beams. Diane came over and asked if they could use the Bruck with the dump trailer. I helped get it attached before climbing over the fence and beginning to cut more firewood.

The day wore on. As I worked, I considered what we should do about the intruder and his truck; at least I assumed it was a truck. If Geraldine could signal us when he was at the house, we could go take a look at the truck, getting a license plate number and seeing if there was any clue in the truck as to what he was doing. I made a mental list of what we might need to take on such an expedition.

When I made my next run to the fence to deliver an arm load of fire logs, I called Stellan and dictated my list, asking him to send it with the next load of Megos. I brought him up to speed on what was happening with Wainright's house, and he said the Megos and my list of equipment would be on their way in a couple of hours. I also asked if he could arrange to have someone drive my Cadillac over, since not having transportation was becoming an issue. He readily agreed.

Ralph and Kajika brought lunch to the Civalia site. Kajika was fascinated by the Megos, and began asking a million questions about what we were doing, and how it was all going to work. When we finished eating, Ralph headed back with the remains, but Kajika stayed and began helping the Dancers. I went back to cutting firewood.

About 2:30, I heard my truck arriving, so I went back to the Civalia site to help unload and get the items I'd had Stellan send. I was surprised to see not only my Cadillac and my truck and trailer, but also another truck driven by Stellan. This second truck was the volumetric mixing unit Gyan had brought back to Laramie from Texas. This was good news, since it meant significant permanent construction was about to begin on the Civalia site. I was excited and began to pepper Stellan with questions.

"Whoa," he said. "We're going to start pouring the center post and the support beams for the temporary Mego walls within the next couple of days, depending on when we can get the materials here. Some storage bins are supposed to show up tomorrow morning, and the materials shortly after."

I looked around at the pallets of Megos. "Do you have enough Megos to build the temporary walls?"

"Not yet. But we probably will by the time we need them. Some of the last ones will be just-in-time blocks." Stellan looked out over the site. "Who's the fellow working with the Dancers? I don't think I've seen him before."

"That's Kajika Eagle Feather, and he's the tracker I told you about on the phone. I think he's getting interested in our project."

"I trust he's a good hand," Stellan said.

"So far, he has been. He easily located where the intruder had parked, and the stuff I asked you to bring is to help us check the truck if he does come back."

"Do you have any doubt?"

"Not really. Where are the items I asked you to bring?"

"They're in the trunk of your Caddy. For the time being, I'm trying to keep quiet about this issue with Wainright's house with the troops, since we don't really know what kind of ears Wainright might have. I figured the fewer prying eyes and questions, the better."

"Good idea," I said.

I helped unload the Megos, then Stellan and I planned where to place the material storage bins. In what seemed to me much too short a time, Stellan and his crew left for Laramie. I gave up for the day, told Kajika I'd be at Ralph's home, and drove the Cadillac down there. Ralph was on the porch feeding peanuts to Gerald when I arrived. I got the items I'd had Stellan bring out of the trunk of the car and walked toward the house. As I walked up, Ralph suggested I park the car out of sight down the road toward Wainright's house.

"That way yer nocturnal visitor won't know yer around," he said.

"Of course," I said, dropping my things on the porch, turning around, and walking back to the car.

When I'd hiked back to Ralph's porch, Gerald had apparently been satiated and was gone. I plopped down in a chair next to Ralph.

"It's early to bed for me tonight," I told him.

"Me and you both," Ralph said. "I'm plum tuckered out."

"What'd you think of Kajika?" I asked.

"Well, he was a little standoffish at first. I've seen that before when colored folks 'ave worked fer me. I 'spose they've been put down all their lives an' have their guard up all the time."

"You seem to have established rapport with him."

"Yup, he just sees me as an old codger what's lived the life he started out doin'; ridin' the range an' chasing them doggies. But he's a might unnerved by ya. Yer game struck a spark with 'im, 'cause his heritage's prob'ly closer ta what yer game's about than ours is. Then he seen yer project up there, an' it really got ta him when Diane explained yer buildin' that there Civalia in a circle. He said his folks an' ancestors been building in circles, an' their tepees were circles."

"I noticed the circular feature when we were in Ethete," I said.

"Yup, so Kajika don't know 'xactly how ta take in these here ideas uh yers. They're kind uh like his culture, but they're taking it deeper, an' that's scary ta 'im. It ain't familiar, but it seems right."

"I think I can understand what he's feeling," I said. "I think I went through a similar range of feelings when I first began to understand the implications of entropy production. What do you think I should do to make things easier for Kajika?"

"Oh, I don't think ya' need ta do anything special. He just needs some time ta' adjust. Don't push 'im too hard. He'll come ta ya when he's ready."

We sat in companionable silence for a while, and then by mutual agreement, we roused ourselves to begin supper preparation. Ralph had been preparing dinner for the entire construction crew, so we practiced large quantity cooking. I think Ralph was glad to have my help, and I know he was even happier to have all of us clean up and do the dishes. He went to bed immediately after he finished eating. After the construction crew left, Kajika and I also turned in.

Geraldine called me at 11:48. I'd called her earlier in the evening and instructed her to call me instead of Ralph, since he was so tired. I roused Kajika. We dressed, slipped into our coats and headed out with the bag of things I had ordered.

When we were outside, Kajika put his hand on my arm to stop me and said softly, "I brought the Bruck down here last night in case we got a call. It will be quiet and a lot faster than walking, especially with that bag you're carrying. It's over this way." He indicated a grove of trees to the west of Ralph's house.

"Just a minute," I said equally softly, and slipped back into the bunkhouse. I gathered a couple of towels and headed out again. "The articulated hinge on the Bruck rattles on rough ground. We can dampen the sound with these towels," I said, showing Kajika the towels. "Your foresight in bringing the Bruck was brilliant."

"Let's go," Kajika said with a gruff edge to his voice.

We moved to the Bruck. I noted Kajika had traded the dump trailer for the flatbed trailer, and gave him another mental mark for thoughtfulness. Kajika climbed onto the driver's seat, so I placed my bag on the flatbed, wrapped one of the towels around the articulation hinge, tied it in place with the other towel, and climbed on beside my bag. Kajika took off.

There was a waxing crescent moon, but it was dark among the trees. I dug into my bag and pulled out a flashlight I'd had Stellan modify with red taillight lens repair tape. Aiming it on the road in front of the Bruck helped. Kajika's speed increased and the ride was smoother. He gave me the "OK" hand signal. I called Geraldine to get an update on the intruder and to tell her we were on our way.

"He had a ladder, an' put it on the fence," she told me, "an' then he climbed up an' throwed something on the fence. He must uh had some kind uh folding ladder cause first thing ya' know he'd put a ladder inside the fence. Then he went over an' went inside. He's still in there."

"Call me immediately if he comes out," I instructed her.

It seemed like hours before we turned off the main road and followed the two-track road to where Kajika had found the tire tracks. Before we reached the exact location, Kajika stopped the Bruck and motioned me to turn off the light. He then motioned for me to stay put, took the flashlight, and cautiously approached the pickup, which was nosed into the trees off the road. He made a circuit of the vehicle at a radius of about 25 feet. I marveled that he could move through the trees with scarcely a sound. I would have sounded like a herd of buffalo. He then made a close circuit of the vehicle, using the flashlight sparingly, and ended up near the tailgate of the truck. He motioned me to approach.

I carried my bag up to the back of the truck, set it down, and removed a tripod. I attached my camera and focused it on the license plate of the pickup. With a slow shutter speed setting and Kajika shining the flashlight on the plate, I was able to get a readable picture. I then whispered to Kajika that I'd like to look through the side windows into the cab. He led me forward and I peered into the cab using the flashlight. I saw little of interest, but I set up the camera and took some pictures at various angles. The other side got the same treatment.

The windows on the camper shell were tinted, so the flashlight was not effective. I again resorted to my bag of tricks, pulling out a blanket and my high intensity LED shop light. Kajika helped me arrange the blanket over my head and camera at the back of the truck like the old daguerreotype photographers. I then placed the LED shop light against the back window and turned it on at its lowest power. I took a few pictures, and spent some time examining what was in the bed of the truck. There seemed to be a collection of various digging tools, dirt, a spare tire, and some trash of various types. These items appeared to have ridden in the truck bed for thousands of miles.

Of more interest were some items which seemed to be much more recent. Two empty cardboard boxes with some packing scattered around, and two more cardboard boxes, appearing to be clones of the empty boxes. These two boxes had not been opened. All of these boxes were in pristine condition compared to the other detritus in the truck bed. I was able to make out a company name on one of the boxes, TalcTech Industries, Inc. There was one other container that looked fresh. It was a square plastic pail with a label, but someone had taken a black marker and scribbled over the printing on the label. A little of the printing could be seen, but I could not make out much that made any sense. There was also some fresh trash, one item being a plastic bag from a Rawlins hardware store, and another item being plastic packaging which had held wire nuts.

I had Kajika take a look, but he didn't see anything I hadn't seen, and he was unable to decipher anything on the plastic pail.

"We could try opening the window on the camper shell," Kajika said.

"I'd like to," I said, "but for a number of reasons, we need to keep this entirely legal. I'd sure like to know what's in that pail," I muttered.

I thought about that problem for a few moments, and then remembered a time when I'd been doing some black touchup painting on one of my antique cars. I'd tried using my LED shop light to see whether I'd gotten the chip completely covered. When I'd shined the light on the touchup with the light on its highest setting, I was surprised to see the light penetrated through the black paint, and I was seeing the underlying primer and metal. I tried that trick with limited success, since now some letters could be made out.

A fairly large letter looked like a capital "P" or an "8" or a capital "B", followed by a smaller letter that looked like an "e," but could be a "c" or an "o." Below these letters was what looked like a word with a smear for the first letter, but definitely something about half the height of the fairly large letter above it. The smear was followed by two low letters, also indistinguishable. Three more letters followed, which I was about 75% confident were "der." Near the bottom of the label I could read "Net Wt. 20 kg" with high confidence. There were two smeary blobs, side by side, on the left-hand side of the label.

I had Kajika examine the label, and he independently verified my observations, except he thought he could see two lighter-colored diamonds in the blobs on the left-hand side of the label. I took several pictures of the label with various setting on the camera, hoping something would show up when we could examine the pictures.

We discussed whether there was anything else to be learned at the truck. When we decided there was not, we discussed our next move.

"I'd sure like to know if he makes another trip to the truck to get any of this stuff," I said.

"Can't you tell that from your sensors on the fence?" Kajika asked.

"Of course," I said. "I should have thought of that, but I'm sure glad you did. Thank you. Shall we retreat?"

"I'm for that."

"There's two more things I need to do," I told Kajika, as I dug around in my bag.

I finally found a small black taped item in my bag, and placed it under the back side of one of the front tires.

"What's that?" Kajika asked.

"It's a mechanical watch I've modified so when the truck runs over it, the hands will be stuck to a pad over the watch face. If it works right and we can find it tomorrow, it will tell us exactly when the truck leaves."

"Ingenious," Kajika said. "I'll have to remember that. It could come in useful."

For the second item on my list, I dug yesterday's Laramie Boomerang paper from my bag and handed it to Kajika. He instantly knew what that was for and stood holding the front page of the paper out near the back of the truck. I took some more pictures of the back of the truck, making certain I clearly got the paper along with the license plate.

As I packed my equipment back in my bag, Kajika carefully eradicated our tracks to the extent he could. I called Geraldine while he was doing this, and told her we were leaving the truck. She told me the intruder was still inside the building, and she hadn't seen or heard anything. I told her to go to bed and to turn off the audible alarm, since the alarm system would record whether he made another trip to the truck and also when he left. She thanked me for small favors.

We headed back and were again in bed by 2:30. Kajika fell asleep, but I was awake for quite a while puzzling over what might be in the plastic pail.

When I finally awoke in the morning, the sun was shining brightly, Kajika and Ralph were gone, and my eyes felt gritty. I got up, showered at Ralph's house, and found some leftover pancakes for breakfast. Something was niggling at the back of my mind, so I took a walk toward the spring to the east of Ralph's home. It was something I'd read, but I just couldn't dredge it up. I came out of a tree line and saw Ralph and Kajika in the distance working on a fence.

Kajika had on a light blue long sleeve shirt with the sleeves rolled up, and as he strained to pull up on the handle of the fence stretcher, an image popped into my mind. I had it! The cover of a book I was trying to remember, *Muscle & Blood*, by Rachel Scott. The cover showed the musculature of a man's arm with his elbow at a right angle. The man had on a light blue shirt with the sleeve rolled above his bicep. During the night my sub-conscious mind had been working on the puzzle of the label on the plastic pail, and somehow a connection with the contents of that book had formed. And then the message of the label flooded into my mind.

I raced back to the house and called Stellan. Fortunately, I caught him before he left for the Civalia site. I held on while he looked for that book in my library. When he had located it and was back on the line, I commanded him, "Bring it with you, and hurry."

"What's this about?"

"It's too involved to tell you now, so just come as soon as you can. When do you think you could be here?"

"I can probably get away from here in fifteen or twenty minutes, so around one and a half to two hours. What's the rus . . ."

I interrupted. "Make it sooner. I've got to go now." For probably the first time ever, I hung up on Stellan.

I called Elaine and asked if she could meet me in Saratoga ASAP. Barring some emergency, she told me she could be there in an hour and half or so. We arranged to meet on the street outside the Hotel Wolf. She was also curious about the "emergency," but I put her off also, since I had more arrangements to make. I called Geraldine and asked her to immediately come over to Ralph's, and then I drove the Cadillac to where I'd seen Ralph and Kajika. I got out and approached where they were still working on the fence.

"Mornin' sleepyhead," Ralph said. "Yer missin' the best part uh the day." Then he must have seen my angst, because he sobered and asked, "What's happened?"

I felt rattled. "I think I know what our intruder is up to, and I'm going to meet Elaine in Saratoga at 10:15, and Geraldine is on her way over here, and we've got to do something about it immediately, and . . ."

"Slow down," Ralph said. "Why'n we go up ta' the house and talk this over? Kajika an' me'll meet ya' there soon's we pick up our tools."

Kajika and Ralph gathered their tools and started for Ralph's pickup. I reversed course and drove back to Ralph's home. The two of them pulled up shortly, and Geraldine came not long after. I'd gotten a little more control over myself, Ralph's imperturbable calm helping considerably. I set up my computer on Ralph's table, and the others gathered around as I downloaded the pictures I had taken early that morning. I displayed one of the pictures I had taken of the label on the pail and began my explanation.

"A number of years ago, I read a book that is still in my library, titled *Muscle & Blood*. The author, Rachel Scott, documented industrial slaughter of workers in the United States. One of the industries she targeted was the beryllium industry."

"What is beryllium?" Kajika asked.

"It's a metallic element, a very light element, with an atomic number of four. The chemical symbol for beryllium is **Be**." I pointed to an area of the label picture that looked as if it could be a "B" followed by what certainly did look like an "e."

"So, what's wrong with this here beryllium?" Ralph asked.

Workers in the beryllium industries were getting sick and dying similar to miners with black lung. As I remember it, beryllium dust was the culprit, and it didn't take much to cause problems.

I did a web search for the OSHA permissible exposure limit for beryllium. The results were shocking; the IDLH was only four milligrams per cubic meter and the TWA was only two micrograms per cubic meter in the workplace.

"What's this here IDLH?" Geraldine asked.

"That stands for 'immediately dangerous to life and health.'" I told her.

"And TWA?" Kajika asked.

"That means 'time weighted average,'" I told him.

"I think the word below the **Be** is probably 'Powder," I said.

"This here looks serious," Ralph said. He looked grave.

I did some rapid mental calculations. "If this is beryllium powder and there's 20 kilograms of it, as you can see by this weight on the label," I pointed to the bottom of the label where the net weight was reasonably visible, "that pail contains more than seven thousand doses of powder capable of making this room we're sitting in IDLH."

"Let me look up something else," I said. I searched for the beryllium safety information. When I found it, we all stared at the screen. Kajika was the first to speak.

"Those two red diamonds I saw. Those could be them. What do they mean?"

"Well, the skull and cross bones are obvious," I said, "that indicates death, but I'm not sure about the other. I'll look it up."

I found a picture showing the symbols. "I was wrong about the skull and cross bones. It means 'Toxic," I said.

"Not really so much diff'rent frum death," Geraldine commented.

"The other one indicates a health hazard," I told the group.

Ralph cleared his throat. "We know that there beryllium powder's sure as hell dangerous stuff, but we don't know fer sure, if'n it's goin' ta end up in Wainright's house."

While Ralph had been speaking, I'd done another search on the company name on one of the boxes. The results were chilling. I showed the others.

I summed the evidence, "At least two of the boxes in the back of the truck were from a company that makes powder metering devices. One of those boxes had been opened and was empty; the other one was still unopened. We don't know what was in the other two boxes, one opened and empty and the other sealed. There was some trash indicating some electrical wiring supplies had been in the truck. I think we can assume the intruder is installing some powder metering equipment in the house, and the powder is sitting in the truck. What are we going to do about it?"

There was silence for few moments, then two or three of us tried to speak all at once. Geraldine prevailed.

"This here meetin' of the Civalien Corporation's Board of Directors is called to order," she said sternly.

We all quieted down.

She continued, "John here has showed us a threat to this here Company an' its projects, an' we'll have ta' figger out what to do.

Ralph, you got any suggestions?"

Ralph thought for a moment before saying, "We could get Elaine ta go after this intruder skunk, but Elaine told me an' John we've only got 'im on trespass so far. He ain't hurt us yet, an' ownership uh that there house's hazy."

"That doesn't do anything about Wainright, either," I added. "If he's behind this, he'll only just try some other nasty trick if we stop this one."

"You could burn down the house," Kajika offered.

"Indeed," I said. "That would stop our intruder, at least for the time being. It would buy us time, but it also doesn't do anything about Wainright." I looked at my watch. "I've got to head for Saratoga to meet Elaine. Stellan should be here within the next half hour with the book I told you about. Could you three wait around here for Stellan and then bring the book and my computer to Saratoga?"

"We'll do 'er," Ralph said. "Where'll we find ya all?"

"I'm going to meet Elaine at the Hotel Wolf, but we'll probably go somewhere else to talk. Why don't you give me a call when you get into Saratoga?"

"Kajika," I said as an afterthought, "could you go find the watch I left with the truck last night?"

Kajika nodded, and slipped out the door.

I left and drove to Saratoga. Elaine was waiting when I arrived, and I climbed into her police pickup.

Without preamble she ordered me, "So, tell me what's going on."

I told her about Kajika finding where the truck was parked, and how we had looked it over early that very morning. I gave her the plate number of the pickup, and she called it in. I continued with a description of what we saw in the back of the pickup.

"Did you at any time enter the pickup?" she asked.

"No, we didn't. We touched the outside, shading our eyes to look through the windows, and occasionally brushing against it, but both Kajika and I wore gloves." I paused. "I did feel the hood with the back of my bare hand to see if it had been driven recently."

"Good. Continue."

I then told her about my tentative identification of the plastic pail as 20 kilograms of beryllium powder.

"So," she asked, "what does that have to do with the price of rice in China?"

"Just that it's extremely toxic."

"How much do you have to eat to kill you?" she asked.

"It's breathing it that'll get you, and it's not much. Do you cook?" I asked.

Elaine looked a little startled at my question, but she answered, "As little as I can get by with."

"But you've used measuring spoons."

"Sure."

"And you have some idea of how big an eighth of a teaspoon is, don't you?"

"Well, yah."

"If the beryllium powder was flour, it would take about a hundredth of that eighth of a spoonful of flour in a cubic meter of air to be, as OSHA put it, immediately dangerous to life and health. Because beryllium powder is denser than flour, it would actually take even less volume."

Elaine looked suitably shocked. "So, you think whoever is doing this. . ."

Just then her radio activated, and I listened to her saying "yes," "uh huh," and other meaningless fillers. When the conversation ended, she turned to me and said, "You've probably guessed, or had a suspicion, the pickup belongs to CCC."

"The thought crossed my mind," I confessed.

About this time Ralph's pickup pulled up behind my Cadillac, and Geraldine walked up to the passenger side window of Elaine's police pickup. I rolled down the window and Elaine greeted Geraldine.

"This is getting to be a regular party," Elaine said. "Let me see if I can find us a secure place to carry on this discussion." She made a short call on her radio, and then directed Geraldine and Ralph to follow her. I told her I'd also follow in my Cadillac and slipped out of her truck. She led us to the Saratoga police station, and we assembled in a private conference room.

After inquiring into Kajika's relationship to this affair, Elaine took on the demeanor of a police detective, as she quizzed each of us about what we knew. I showed her the pictures we had taken and the web sites we had found describing beryllium powder. Ralph produced the *Muscle & Blood* book. Kajika produced the mechanical watch I'd placed under the front tire of the pickup. It was, as I'd expected, a little worse for wear.

"I'll want all of the material you have for evidence," she said. When I looked mournfully at my book, she added, "You'll get it back, but I need it right now. Speaking of now, I have to decide what I'll do about this situation. From a legal standpoint there isn't much of a case, but you've convinced me there is serious danger to all of you."

Geraldine spoke. "We've thought it over an' here's how we're a thinkin' it should be handled. The real scoundrel here's Wainright, an' he ain't available. Ol' George over at Callaway's in it up to his eyeballs, but he ain't the king pin. So, we ought ta let 'im finish his work."

There was a collective gasp from Elaine and me. Elaine started to speak, but Geraldine held up her hand to stop her.

"But we, us an' you, gotta swap out that there beryllium for somethin' harmless. Then Wainright'll think he done killed us, slowly with a fair 'mount a sufferin,' an' Ol' George'll think he done his part. That'll keep 'em both off our backs, an' maybe, just maybe, we'll find Wainright, an' get 'im out uh our hair."

Elaine looked uncertain, but as Geraldine was talking, I saw the logic of her argument. I was again impressed with the savvy and grit of this frontier woman.

"That sounds like a first-class solution," I told Geraldine. "Did you come up with that?

"Some," she said. "Them two," she indicated Ralph and Kajika, "helped a bunch."

Ralph smiled and pointed at Geraldine behind her back. Kajika just looked awed. Elaine looked like her mind was revved up and a trail of emotions drifted across her face as she considered all the ramification of Geraldine's proposal.

She finally said, "Okay, suppose we try that tactic. How do we make it work?"

"The toughest part is swapping the beryllium powder," I said. "We'd have to come up with a substitute, and then somehow get it in that plastic pail."

"Isn't that just about everything?" Elaine asked.

"I suppose so, but we'd have to do it without arousing any suspicion."

Kajika ask the question, "Did this man, George did you call him, make a second trip to his truck last night?"

I looked at Geraldine. "How many alarms did you have last night?"

"Just the two, him comin' an' him goin'."

"Then he'll probably be back tonight to put in the second metering unit," Kajika said.

"He might fill the first unit with powder and then install the second one, or the second unit might just be a spare," Elaine offered.

"Probly ain't no spare," Ralph offered, "'cause he got no way ta get in there when that there fake deed's taken care of."

"Okay," Elaine said, "we have a brief window tonight to maybe get the powder changed."

"May I ask," I said to Elaine, "whether there is any way you can delay Callaway for at least a day? It's going to take a little time to counterfeit the powder and prepare to swap it. That pail looks like it's sealed, so we'll have to change the powder without breaking the seal. We'll also need hazmat gear, and equipment to transfer the powder."

"Let me think," Elaine said, and she stared up at the corner of the room as we looked on. She then looked back at us and said, "Yes, I think I can. The County has been considering building a new parking garage and the Sheriff's Office will be using it. We can arrange a meeting with George to discuss some issues, and ask him for some feedback. That will keep him busy for a while."

"What if George isn't actually the person doing the work at Wainright's house?" I asked.

"That's a consideration," Elaine said, "but the pickup you saw there is a new model, and I assume it didn't have a CCC logo on the side, since you didn't appear to have seen anything. The probability is pretty high it's George's personal truck."

I had to agree with Elaine's logic.

Elaine continued. "As a backup, I can have a patrol in the vicinity near the witching hour, and I'm sure they can find something to warrant a traffic stop. That will probably be enough to discourage an employee, particularly if the officer begins to ask questions about searching the vehicle. If it's Callaway we'll just let him go with a mild warning."

I brought up the next issue. "We'll have to break into George's pickup camper, and we'll in effect be stealing some pretty valuable material. That pail may have cost about $150,000."

Ralph whistled, and Kajika looked shocked.

"I see your problems." Elaine said. "What I'll do is explain the situation to a judge and see if I can get a search warrant. If I specify that we're looking for a toxic material, we can seize it. That'll take care of those problems. I'll have to be present, and I probably should have another officer with me. Will Melvin be OK?"

"Sure," I answered.

"Is there anything else?" Elaine asked.

"The camper shell may be locked," Kajika said.

"Normally we just break in with a search warrant," Elaine said, "but that obviously won't work in this case. I'll see if I can find a locksmith to go along."

"Sounds like we're gettin' quite a party," Ralph said. "Will that there judge want to see some quick justice? See someone in front uh his bench right away?"

"I'll explain we're trying to rope in the king pin, so we're going to let the small fry go for a while, but we'll keep an eye on them. I don't think we'll have any problems with the judge."

Our meeting broke up, and I left for Laramie with an urgency to find and procure counterfeit beryllium powder. On the way home, I made a mental list of relatively harmless powders which might work. The problem was to find something close to the same bulk density, nearly the same color, having no distinctive odor, non-clumping, significantly safer than powdered beryllium, readily available, and possible to prepare by mid-afternoon of the next day.

I thought of common powders readily available in the kitchen, bathroom, shop, and office. Then I considered some industrial and construction powders.

When I got home, I began evaluating these various powders. In short order, I became convinced no single one met all the requirements. The closest was Portland cement, but it was about 20% lighter, and it not only clumps, but it hardens over time when exposed to atmospheric moisture. It also can cause respiratory damage in high concentrations. I then began exploring combinations of two or more powders. The results were almost as dismal. I basically needed a powder denser than beryllium to mate with the lesser density material, but the options for denser powders were strictly limited. After calculating mixtures of various substances, I settle on one candidate, black iron oxide and powdered sugar with a 1.74 to 1 volume ratio.

To verify this formula, I rummaged in my cupboard for some powdered sugar, and made a small quantity of black iron oxide substitute with my angle grinder by grinding some iron scrap and then sweeping up the grinding dust. I got more than one curious glance from the crew making Megos and floor slabs, but I didn't clue them in on what I was doing. When Stellan stopped by and asked what the hell I was doing, I told him I'd clue him in at a later time and I rushed back into the house to complete my experiment. The powder mixture seemed okay to me, even having a slightly metallic odor. My guess was the intruder, probably George Callaway, had never encountered Beryllium before, so an exact match was probably not necessary.

The afternoon was wearing on, so I tackled procuring the grinding dust first. Making it all myself was an option, but some quick calculations showed I needed somewhat less than two gallons. I didn't have sufficient time for the task. The next option was to visit some of my welding and metal working friends. I have to say they were dumbfounded at my request for grinding dust, even though most of them were somewhat used to me having oddball projects. This effort yielded about one and a half gallons, although it would need to be screened to take out larger chunks. I ended the day by visiting my local grocery store, where I purchased six pounds of powdered sugar; more than I needed for the counterfeit mixture.

I was up and about early the next morning, and went into the shop to start grinding iron. As I set up to begin, dreading the day's work, I wondered if I could use a 10-inch cutoff saw and cut a piece of iron repeatedly. I didn't have a cutoff saw, so I called one of my friends whom I had visited yesterday, and asked to use his. By shortly after 8:00 I was making grinding dust. While working at that task, my gaze fell on his older 12-inch grinder with shields around the grinding wheels. With his permission, I took the cover off the end of one of the shields and was rewarded with a significant amount of grinding dust trapped in the housing. The other side yielded more. With these sources, I had enough grinding dust.

My next task was to figure out how to safely take the Beryllium powder out of the pail, and replace it with the counterfeit powder. Since opening the pail was not an option, I decided we'd have to cut a hole in the bottom and then repair the bottom of the pail. I gathered tools, hazmat gear, plastic material, plastic epoxy, and a new 5-gallon pail with a lid to hold the liberated Beryllium powder. As a last-minute addition, I disassembled my abrasive blasting glove box and stuffed it in the trunk of the Cadillac. I had to take out the spare tire, and even then, it barely fit.

By mid-afternoon, I was on my way back to the Lazy HZ. I'd called Geraldine, and she reported no one had tripped the fence alarms last night. I tried calling Elaine, but she was not available, so I left a message. Ralph told me everything seemed to be proceeding as planned, or at least he hadn't heard otherwise. Kajika was helping with the Civalia construction. I worried about a flat tire all the way, but I made it before dinner and relaxed on the porch with Ralph and Gerald. It felt good to just let my mind drift for a time.

Elaine called to tell us she and Melvin were in Saratoga, and had motel rooms for the night. Her ploy with George the night before had worked, and the fact the intruder had not returned indicated the intruder was indeed George. She had obtained a search warrant from the judge, and went further, also getting wiretaps on his phone and computer connections. She was sorry she hadn't returned my call earlier, but she'd been busy.

"So have I," I said. "I've got some counterfeit Beryllium powder and what we need to change it; I hope," I added.

"We're counting on you. Call us at this number, if and when George makes his appearance tonight, and we'll hot foot it out to Ralph's," she told me.

"Right," I said. "We'll go out before you get here and set up. I'll send Kajika back to get you with the Bruck. We're using it to get there quietly, since vehicle sounds may carry as far as Wainright's house."

I went back to sitting on the porch for a while.

"How is construction going?" I asked.

"'Pears ta be movin' right along," Ralph said. "Them Mego things go up real fast. They'll be quittin' soon. You might wanna mosey up there and take a look."

Ralph drove me up to the site in his truck, and I was surprised to see Mego walls taking shape. When we walked over to them, I was even more surprised to see some excavation for what I assumed would be the footings and posts for the hypocaust floor support system. The crew was wrapping up for the day, and they invited Ralph and me to eat with them.

"How did you get the wall footings done so fast?" I asked

Gyan and Cindy were there, and Gyan answered. "Manjinder made us some mirrors, and we were able to heat the footers with solar energy yesterday. They cured really fast."

"It's awesome," Cindy said. "I was going to put my initials in it, you know, like you see on the sidewalks around town, and they got too hard before I could do it."

"There'll be another chance," I said, laughing.

We didn't stay long, since the crew was tired and planned to turn in early. Kajika rode back with us, and we all sat on the porch for a while, watching the night come on, listening to the insects' calls, and hearing the noises of nocturnal birds and animals.

After loading all of my paraphernalia on the Bruck, the three of us turned in early. I had a terrible time going to sleep, tossing and turning and going over the swapping of the powders in my mind. I couldn't seem to turn it off. When I finally did go to sleep, it seemed like I'd only been out a couple of minutes before the phone rang. It was Geraldine.

"Show time," I said to Kajika as he rubbed his eyes and began to get out of bed.

I called Elaine while Kajika was dressing. I dressed, and then we went out and started up the hill with the Bruck. I was pedaling this first leg of our journey, since Kajika needed to make a round-trip to transport Elaine and Melvin. My perception of the trip was different when I was doing the work than when I was a passenger. The rocks and tree roots appeared much larger, and the noises of the Bruck sounded much louder. When we crested the hill and started down the side road toward our target location, I was grateful for the reduced strain, but I was still sweating by the time we approached the location where the truck had parked. At first, I thought it was not there. However, as we rolled closer, I saw the truck was just a little farther off the road.

We quickly unloaded the Bruck on the side of the road opposite the truck, and Kajika started back. I selected a location a short way down the road, thinking the intruder would probably back onto the road when he left. So, if we could not get all of our paraphernalia out of the area before he left, his headlights would not sweep over them. I setup the tent and put the equipment and supplies I'd gathered to transfer the beryllium powder in the tent. Then I waited.

Eventually, after what seemed like hours, I heard the faint sounds of the Bruck returning. Kajika pulled up with three passengers. Elaine took charge, motioning Kajika to join me while she, Melvin, and the third person, whom I assumed was a locksmith, approached the back of the truck. Elaine used a small pen light to verify the truck was the correct truck for her search warrant, and then shined the light through the rear window of the camper shell. She murmured to Melvin and the locksmith, and then walked over to where Kajika and I were standing.

"It looks just as you described it," she said in a low voice. "We'll open it up and take a closer look. Did you bring a scale?"

I nodded yes, as I watched the locksmith first test the handle and then extract some tools from a kit he was carrying. Melvin was writing in a notebook, recording the times and actions taken.

I touched Elaine's arm to get her attention, and then told her, "I've also got some plates to place next to the pail to mark exactly where it is located, and an adhesive dot to put on the pail to mark the side facing backwards."

I gave Elaine these objects, and she returned to the back of the truck with them. The odd thought crossed my mind that if we didn't have a search warrant, what we were doing would be called a "crime," but since we did and we were doing something legally, I could think of no antonym to describe our act, nothing exactly the opposite of "crime." I immediately felt chagrin at having trivial thoughts while engaged in such a momentous action.

Fortunately for me, my thoughts were redirected to the problems at hand when the locksmith opened the camper shell hatch and stepped back. Elaine and Melvin looked into the back of the truck, and then eased the tailgate of the truck open. Elaine began dictating a list of the contents of the truck bed, and Melvin recorded the list. Then Elaine leaned in, attaching the adhesive dot to the side of the pail and placing the plates I had given her. Then Melvin traded places with her and picked up the pail. He grunted as he took the weight.

While the two of them had been at their tasks, I'd set up and leveled the scale on the bed of the Bruck. Melvin carried the pail over, set it on the scale, and recorded the weight. Then it was my turn.

I carried the pail into the tent, where I turned it upside down. Using a gasket cutter, I cut a disk out of the bottom of the plastic pail and taped an extra heavy plastic bag like a hat over the pail. I put this assembly into my makeshift glove box and turned the pail back over to empty the beryllium powder into the bag. The most difficult part was getting the last of the powder out of the bottom of the pail. I tilted, tapped, and shook for some time until I was reasonably certain I'd emptied the pail.

At that point, Elaine had me sample the powder, and also the counterfeit powder I'd made. We weighed the pail, the disk, and the plastic bag of powder, to verify the weight of the powder, and then, with the pail upside down on the scale, I prepared to refill it with counterfeit powder.

Just then my phone vibrated. It was Geraldine. The intruder had gone back over the fence and was headed our way. From the data we had gathered in his last visit, we had about ten minutes before he would be back at the truck. Panic struck.

"How were you going to seal the pail?" Elaine hissed.

"I was going to epoxy the disk back in," I said. "But there's no time for that now."

"Well, get it together, pronto," she commanded.

I started to pour the counterfeit powder, but thought better of it. Instead I picked up some rocks from the road, and began dusting them off and putting them in the pail. When the pail was reasonably full of rocks, I checked the weight. It was only about two thirds the weight of the beryllium powder, but it would have to do. I dug out a roll of clear packaging tape I had brought along to help hold the disk in place while the epoxy set, and put just tape over the hole. I prayed it would hold as I turned the pail upright. Kajika whisked the scale away as soon as I had lifted the pail, and the others had been moving everything else over to the tent where they threw my camouflage sheet over it. Kajika jumped onto the Bruck and headed up the road to find a place to conceal it.

I gingerly felt the bottom of the pail as I carried it toward the truck. The tape appeared to be holding, although I could feel the bulges of the rocks above the hole. I carefully placed the pail to match the plates, and then removed the adhesive dot and picked up the plates. I then froze as I realized I had not noted which side of the pail the bail had been on.

"Melvin," I whispered, "where was the bail?"

He thought for a moment, and Elaine whispered urgently,

"We've only got two more minutes!"

Melvin pantomimed picking up the bucket to aid his memory and whispered, "It was to your right."

I placed the bail and backed up. Elaine and Melvin eased the tailgate of the truck closed, leaning against it to get it latched without a lot of noise. I helped them. Elaine eased the camper shell hatch closed, and the locksmith stepped forward and re-locked it.

We all faded back into the trees on the west side of the road, Kajika orchestrating our moves to minimize our noise and visibility. We were none too soon, because we could now hear someone approaching us from the east. He did not appear to be taking precautions to be quiet, and as he approached, I could hear muttering and cursing as he crashed through the brush. Finally, the person came out of the woods, opened the back of the truck, and turned on an overhead light in the camper shell.

I'd seen this man before. He was one of the men around Wainright's table the night Ralph and I had dinner in Saratoga. I'd only caught glimpses of George Callaway as he drove past Ralph's home before we'd shut down Wainright's construction project, but this man looked familiar from that standpoint too. I mouthed the question, "George?" at Elaine. She nodded yes.

George rooted around in a tool box for a while and then closed the back of the truck, making far more noise than we had, and headed back east. We waited until Geraldine messaged us George had again crossed the fence before we became active again.

"You're lucky," Elaine said. "What if he'd come back for the pail?"

"It was a calculated risk," I said. "He'd not been gone nearly as long as the other night, and I was guessing he hadn't had time to install the second apparatus he had in the back of the truck. I also figured he might think someone had stolen the Beryllium powder, since it is really quite expensive."

"Right," she said, "I think you told me that pail cost something like $150,000. Still, you are lucky."

We set to work again, much easier this time, since George had neglected to lock his camper shell. George must have bumped the pail while he was looking for his errant tool, because we could see it was sitting at a slightly different angle. I repeated our previous procedures and then dumped the rocks, poured in my counterfeit powder, and glued the disk into the bottom of the pail, all without further incident. We then replaced the pail and argued for a time about whether we should leave the camper shell unlocked or lock it again. We finally decided leaving it unlocked would arouse the least amount of suspicion. We all headed back to Ralph's home, ready to head for the trees to hide if Geraldine told us George was on his way out. No call came.

CHAPTER 19

The excitement of Wainright's predations, what Ralph and Geraldine called *The Great Brain Robbery*, him trying to kill us off slowly, faded away, and I fell back into my role of being an assistant, i.e. not having a domain of my own, but helping, to the best of my ability, those who did. I returned to cutting firewood. Kajika elected to stay on and help with Civalia construction.

Elaine called a few days later, telling us the powder was indeed beryllium, and George did not appear to have noticed any switch, since an e-mail from him to an address associated with a foreign location could be interpreted as mission accomplished. She also told me she and Melvin had decided to intercept George's garbage, an act, which done correctly, did not require a search warrant. She had recovered the boxes we'd seen in the back of George's pickup, along with some installation instructions. If I was interested, I could take a look. I was interested, and arranged to meet with her in a few days.

I called Maggie to find out what was happening with the deed to Wainright's house. She told me the wheels of justice turn slowly. The court date was still three weeks away. No, there had been no response from Embuscadoes Investment, Inc., but the registered letter had not been returned. All we could do was wait, so I continued to cut firewood, and the Civalia workspace continued to rise from the meadow.

When I met with Elaine, she showed me the boxes they had retrieved from Callaway's trash. These gave me some insight into what might be installed in Wainright's house, namely some sort of powder metering device with a supply hopper. One box appeared to be a repurposed box with no return address on it. I was very curious about what it might have contained, but there was no way of knowing.

"It might not even be from George's trash," Elaine explained, "because we had to have at least one other trash pickup mixed in with George's to legally take it without a search warrant."

I continued to cut firewood. The wood pile finally contained ten cords, the maximum allowed by our permit. I thankfully ended that task and began serious negotiations with the Forest Service for Civalia adopting a section of forest as volunteer keepers. When time permitted, I helped with construction, mainly by transporting Megos from Laramie to Civalia. The days and weeks passed.

Finally, the day came for the hearing on our lawsuit to have the deed and mortgage on Wainright's house declared null and void. Maggie and Ralph, with me as an observer, went to Rawlins and appeared in District Court. Maggie presented all of our evidence to the judge and asked for a summary judgment. The judge looked over the material Maggie had presented, including the failure by the court to locate and serve the supposed owner of the deed and the mortgage recorded in the Carbon County Court House; the fact said owner, a Florida corporation, did not exist; an affidavit from the Amalgamated Bank stating they had not issued such a mortgage release for the original owner, Howard Wainright, DBA Jim Baker's Retreat; and an affidavit from the Carbon County Office of Planning & Development stating no applications for subdividing the land had been received by them and no permit to do so issued.

The judge perused the documents Maggie handed her for a short time, and then stated, "This appears to be a straightforward case of fraud."

"Yes, Your Honor. We think it is." Maggie said.

"Don't you want to take this to trial and seek damages from the perpetrator?" the judge asked. "You'd be almost assured of prevailing."

"If we thought we could find him, we certainly would. However, to the best of our knowledge, he appears to be out of the country and the time and expense to maybe find him and attempt to extradite him would be prohibitively expensive."

The judge considered Maggie's words. "If he does show up, you could still bring suit against him, but then your main demand would be punitive damages, so your case would be much weaker."

"We'd prefer to just put this behind us, and move on to rectifying the damage that's been done," Maggie said.

"Okay," the judge said, "I hereby find in favor of the plaintiff, and order these recorded documents to be declared null and void. The property will revert to the owner of record, in this case Mr. Ralph Hertell." The judge went on to precisely enumerate the documents to be voided.

When it was all over, the three of us, happy to have this ordeal in the past, took the judge's verdict to the Court House and initiated the process of having the recorded documents removed. Getting all the paper work done would take a couple of days. Maggie then headed back to Laramie, Ralph and I went back to the Lazy HZ. On the way back we reminisced about all that had gone on with Wainright and the land, and talked about the future.

"What do you think you're going to do with Wainright's house?" I asked.

"Well," Ralph said, "I been thinkin' 'bout that. First thing we gotta do is check 'er out an' find out what they did ta 'er."

"Of course," I said. "That goes without saying. But then what?"

"I thought about just tearin' 'er down, but that seems a waste."

"Yes, and if you include the concrete slab, a lot of expensive work," I added.

"What're ya thinkin'?" Ralph asked.

"We could use a place for our laborers to stay. A staging area, if you will. We could rent it from you, and . . ."

"Ya'll do nothin' uh the sort," Ralph said sternly. "After all ya've done fer me, I'd be some sort a Scrooge ta charge ya', an' I'll throw in the rest uh the money ya' saved me on the land, 'cause knowin' Wainright, you'll have ta fix 'er up some."

"I'm sure you're right about that. That's very generous of you, Ralph. I'm grateful, and I'm sure the others will be, too."

"It's just a fair trade," Ralph said. "Ya'd do the same, if'n ya was in my shoes. When're ya goin' ta check 'er out?"

"I thought I'd talk to Stellan about it, and we'd try to look it over in the next two or three days."

"Good. I'd like ta see what ol' Wainright's done there. Let me know when you're goin' ta be there. I'd like ta see 'er too."

Ralph and I chatted about many other subjects on the way back to the Lazy HZ, and the trip went swiftly. After dropping Ralph off, I headed for Laramie, arriving home in the late afternoon. I called Stellan and made arrangements to meet in the morning.

"I'll be at your shop anyway," he told me. "Just let me know when you want to talk."

The next morning, I was up early, but Stellan was already at work in the shop. I opened the door and asked him if he would like to come in and have some breakfast with me while we talked.

"In a minute," Stellan said. "I've got to get the oven for the Megos heated before everyone gets here for work."

I watch for a moment and then started cooking breakfast. Shortly, Stellan came in and joined the breakfast preparation.

"What's up?" he asked. "You were sort of evasive on the phone last night."

"I have a lot to tell you, and I didn't want to tell you over the phone."

I proceeded to tell Stellan about Wainright's devious plan to introduce beryllium powder into the house he had built, and how, with help from Ralph, Geraldine, Elaine, and Kajika, we'd been able to substitute a mixture of black iron powder and powdered sugar.

As we set down at the table for our breakfasts, Stellan asked, "So why did you substitute a powder mixture, instead of just arresting George Callaway?"

"Geraldine and Ralph decided Wainright was behind this, and Elaine got some evidence that's true from a wiretap on Callaway.

390

So, we all decided stopping Callaway could just provoke Wainright into trying something else."

"I see," Stellan said. He drummed his fingers on the table for moment and then asked, "What's happening now?"

"Yesterday," I said, "the District Court Judge voided the deed and mortgage on the house, so it now legally belongs to Ralph. He's going to let us use the house to accommodate our construction crews and for any other uses we might have for it."

"That's great!" Stellan said. "We can certainly use better housing for our help; our own inn or hostel. When can we get rid of your powder mixture, so they can move in?"

"That's what I wanted to talk about with you this morning. We may not be able to get rid of the powder, depending on Wainright's setup. He may have a way to monitor the system, and if he does, we'll need to leave it in place and operational. I'd like you to help me investigate it."

Stellan had stopped eating and laid down his fork. "Let me get this straight. You think Wainright might be able to tell if this system is operating, and you want to fool him into thinking it's working; killing us all slowly and painfully."

"That's right," I said, taking a sip of my orange juice.

Stellan shook his head and took another bite of scrambled eggs. We ate in silence for a time, then he said, "Okay, I think I understand what you're doing; you're trying to buy time. The quote by Jack Heath applies; 'Better the devil you know than the devil you don't.' Sometimes, John. . ." Stellan didn't finish his thought.

I broke in. "What I'd like you to help me with is investigating the house, our inn as you called it, to see exactly what we're dealing with."

Stellan thought about this for a while and then said, "Okay. When do we start and what do we do?"

"First," I said, "we should keep this to ourselves, because we don't want any word of our having thwarted his plan getting back to Wainright. We know he's in contact with Callaway, so we don't want any rumors getting to Callaway."

"Granted," Stellan said.

"Next, we should survey the house, I think I'll take your lead and call it Civalien Inn, from a distance to see if there's anything visible from the outside requiring attention. Then we go inside and see what Callaway's done. We'll plan from there."

Stellan mulled over my plan. "This may take some time."

"Yes, it might."

Stellan got up and started cleaning up our breakfast mess. "Let me get the crew started making Megos, and we'll work on this some more."

I took over the cleanup and Stellan went back to the shop. Sometime later, we gathered our binoculars and headed out for the Lazy HZ. When we arrived, we went to Geraldine's and talked with her about what she had observed on the nights Callaway had entered what I now thought of as Civalien Inn. She did not have too much to add to what we already knew, but she did show us a couple of short videos taken by one of the trail cams we had set up. These showed something moving around on the roof. Geraldine, her eyes sparkling, insisted on going with us to survey the building. Her presence with her camera and telephoto lenses was welcome.

We spent the afternoon slowly circling the building at a distance, keeping to the trees when we could. We examined the exterior carefully while Geraldine took pictures. When we were opposite Geraldine's place, looking toward the north, we noticed a section of the steep part of the mansard roof that looked slightly different from the rest of the roof. This section was next to a brick chimney that projected just past the break in the roof line.

"It looks like they used some shingles from a different batch," I said.

"Or patched the roof," Stellan added.

Geraldine took pictures from various angles. When she walked back to us, she said, "There's somethin' on that there chimmly."

"Where?" I asked.

"Stickin' up on the nor'east corner," she said.

Stellan and I both swung our binoculars toward the location Geraldine indicated, but we couldn't see anything.

Geraldine adjusted her camera and handed it to Stellan. "Look through this here view finder," she told him.

Stellan looked for a short time and then lowered the camera. "It looks like it might be an antenna," he said, "or a very short lightning rod."

I snorted. "A lightning rod? Not very likely, but an antenna I'll buy. That complicates things."

"Is sure does," Stellan said. "What're we going to do about it?"

"We'll have to try to figure out what it's doing," I said. "We'll need to get some help on this. Do you know anyone?"

"I don't," Geraldine said.

"Neither do I," Stellan said.

I sighed. "I'll see if I can find someone. I'll start with the IT division at the University. If I don't find anyone there, I'll head south."

We packed up and went our separate ways. The next day, I visited the University of Wyoming IT department and interviewed a number of people. No luck. I called Elaine, who also had no leads for me. I called a friend who was into home electronics, and a glimmer of hope came to light.

"I've got a radio frequency detector," he said. "You'd be welcome to borrow it, if you want."

"Is it portable?" I asked.

"Sure is. I got it to check out GPS emissions near my mountain cabin. What are you trying to detect?"

I told him I was trying to determine whether a particular antenna was active, and if so, what it might be communicating with.

"How close can you get to it?" he asked.

"A couple hundred yards," I told him.

"That might be a problem, depending on the configuration of the antenna. If it's directional and you're not in the right direction, you probably can't sort the signal out of the background at that distance."

I thought about what he'd said. "Can you block certain frequencies, and can you record or transmit the signals you're detecting?"

"It's been a while since I've used the detector, but I think you can block certain frequency ranges. It can save the data on a USB drive. Why do you ask?"

"I was wondering if I could fly the detector near the antenna with a drone."

"That's an interesting idea," my friend said. "Why don't you bring a drone over, and we can give it a try."

I had to go to Cheyenne to find a suitable drone, so it was late in the day before I finally had the drone unpacked, assembled, and charged. It took me a couple hours to learn to control it sufficiently so I might be able to fly it over to the antenna. I called my friend and made arrangements to meet in the morning.

By noon we had attached the frequency detector to the drone and blocked the frequencies used by the drone control system. With some more practice I was able to hover the drone around and over his ham radio antenna. He made some transmissions, and the frequency detector worked beautifully. My friend added a bluetooth transmitter so we were able to read the USB drive on the fly, and I hunted up some additional batteries. The next morning, Stellan and I drove to Civalien Inn.

The day was boring, flying the drone over to the building, parking it on the roof to save the battery, flying it back after a half hour or so, downloading data from the USB drive, and flying the drone back to the building. Around 4:00, we got some results. There was a period of approximately 30 seconds when there was a transmission from the antenna in the 1.6 gigahertz range.

Stellan fired up his lap top computer and searched to see what technology this transmission was using.

"It looks like it could be a sat phone," Stellan said. He used the calculator app and added, "And it might have transmitted about 3 megabits of data."

"That's not very much," I said, "and if it only transmits occasionally during the day, it probably isn't transmitting any video."

"Perhaps it's a demand system," Stellan said. "If something is happening, it might transmit more."

"How about if we test that," I said. "Wainright's seen me, so we'll put the drone back on the roof, and I'll go walk around the building, quietly for one circuit, and then making noise for a circuit."

We carried out my plan, and no new transmissions occurred.

"I think we can move on to the next step now," I said.

"What's that?" Stellan asked.

"Entering the building and checking out what's inside."

Stellan looked at his watch. "It's getting late, and I need to visit with the Mego workers tomorrow morning. How about if we head home?"

We retrieved the drone, packed up our equipment, and drove back to Laramie. Stellan left, and I called Elaine. I told her what we had discovered so far, and asked her to check with Callaway for a key to the building. We, of course, knew either he must have one or the building had not been locked. She said she would call him and let me know. I then asked if she knew of a locksmith around Saratoga. She gave me a name, and I thanked her and ended our call, but not before inviting her to meet us at Ralph's in the morning. I then called my friend, thanking him for his prior help and asking if he could help me further by adding a longer-range transmitter to the drone. It was 10:00 before we finished. I put all the drone's batteries on to charge and went to bed.

The next day, we were back at Civalien Inn. Stellan dropped me off with our equipment and returned to get Ralph, Elaine, Kajika, and Don, the locksmith. I attempted to fly the drone to the roof and park it next to the antenna, but the wind was too strong and seemed to be picking up as time went on. I waited. When the others arrived, I'm sure Don wondered what we were doing, but he was best left in the dark. Elaine pulled me aside and told me Callaway had denied having a key to the building. I gave the word to proceed.

Ralph, being the owner, opened the gate we had installed. I had Kajika scout the building first to see what he could determine. After carefully approaching the front door, he looked around for a short time and then walked around to the south side of the building, staying close to the fence as he went. I followed on the outside of the fence.

"Someone made several trips around this side of the building," he told me. "Their steps were irregular, so they were probably either tired or carrying something heavy."

"Maybe both," I said. Kajika nodded.

He stopped, approximately below where Stellan and I had observed the chimney with the antenna attached, and observed the ground closely.

"They set up something here," he said.

I examined the ground as best I could through the chain link fence, but I couldn't see anything. "What does it look like?" I asked.

"There're two depressions in the soil, about 18 inches apart."

"Parallel with the house?" I asked.

"Yes."

"Probably the feet of a ladder."

We both looked up at the edge of the roof, and now I was the one who detected some slight damage to the edge of the shingles, probably because I had a better viewing angle.

"Can you tell how recently this disturbance was done?" I asked.

Kajika considered my question for a moment and examined the ground carefully. "Given the mild weather conditions we've had recently and the fact there's not been any rain, I'd say several weeks ago. The plants have mostly recovered and both the footsteps and these indentations are pretty well filled in. With this wind, they may be gone before the day's over."

I went back to the front of the building while Kajika continued his circuit. I discussed the situation with Stellan, and we agreed we needed to be monitoring the sat phone transmission before entering the building. So, Stellan and I took the ladder we had brought from my shop and set it where Callaway had positioned his. Stellan climbed up to have a look. I steadied the ladder.

"You know those shingles we thought looked slightly off color?" he called down. "These are PV shingles, and there is an antenna mounted on the edge of the chimney. It looks like the cable from the antenna runs down the east side of the bricks."

"Interesting," I said. "Is there a place to fasten this drone up there next to the antenna?"

"Maybe, but how about just the frequency detector? I think I can tape it to the chimney cap."

Stellan came back down. The wind was pushing hard on the ladder, so Stellan held it while I made a trip to the truck for some tools and electrical tape, and to separate the frequency detector from the drone. After I'd accomplished that surgery, Stellan went back up the ladder while I steadied it. We laid the ladder on the ground when he was finished, and went back to the front of the building.

I tried the front door, but it was locked. I waved Don over, and he had the door unlocked in a surprisingly short time. I had the others move back, and I slowly turned the knob. Stepping to one side of the door opening, I pushed the door, and it swung open to an anticlimactic silence. Stellan was monitoring the RF signal detector, and when I looked inquiringly in his direction, he shrugged and shook his head. I stepped inside and looked around.

I was in a dim entry hall with walnut paneling, a brass coat rack, an umbrella stand, and some portrait paintings of 19th century mountain men. Nothing ominous was visible. I tried the light switch to verify the electric power was off and was not surprised when nothing happened. Kajika stepped in behind me.

"Did you see anything else?" I asked.

"This isn't the door the guy used to come into this place," he said. "There's a back entrance with a lot more disturbance."

"But didn't you find tracks from this front door going around the side?"

"Yes, but the guy probably came out this door with his ladder and whatever else he was carrying. He probably took this route because it was dark and this is a much shorter route to the chimney area."

I felt foolish for not considering this scenario; it was so logical, since we knew Callaway had come over the fence near the northwest corner. Furthermore, he would not have established his staging area outside in the dark.

"Why don't you start seeing what you can discover in the building?" I asked. "I'll get the others and we'll follow you." I handed him the flashlight I had been carrying.

Kajika began scanning the hallway, and I went out where the others were waiting impatiently.

Ralph turned from where he'd been talking with Elaine and ask, "How's it lookin'?"

"So far, everything seems to be in order. As soon as Kajika finishes checking it over, we can all go in and take a look." I dug out some more flashlights.

Stellan saw what I was doing and asked, "Is the electricity off?"

"Yes," I answered.

Stellan looked thoughtful and then said, "That explains the PV shingles. If the power is off, the phone needs either a lot of battery or another power source; probably both. That would make sense of why the sat phone transmission was late in the afternoon, after the batteries had time to charge. It's probably timed to transmit just once daily."

Stellan's observation gave me more confidence we weren't going to run into any unexpected booby traps, so I had Don begin changing the locks. Kajika came back with the news he had discovered where Callaway might have been working, so we all trooped in and he led us upstairs and down a central hall.

My impression of the building was somewhat as I expected. The entry and the immediate rooms beyond were lavish and ostentatious, all 19th century décor. But when we got to the top of the stairs, we were greeted with unfinished floors and walls. Kajika led us a short way down the hall and then turned into a south-facing room.

When I entered into the room, the hairs on the back of my neck stood on end and I stopped dead in my tracks. Ralph bumped into me, and I stepped aside. The sun was shining in the windows; windows which looked remarkably like the windows in my dream of the murderous bank robber. This room was not exactly like the attic room of the Federal-style building in that dream, but it was awfully close. There was the same unfinished sub-floor, the wood shavings and construction debris. I shivered.

The others were gathered around Kajika examining a section of floor. I tuned back in and heard Kajika saying, ". . . tried to cover this disturbance by sweeping some of the sawdust and dirt over it, but it still looks different." There were murmurs of assent. Stellan got down on his hands and knees, looking closely at the floor.

"The deck screws in this section of the floor have been taken out and put back," he said. "You can tell, because the wood around most of the screwheads is chipped."

"Has anyone got a screwdriver?" Elaine asked.

I was galvanized into action and went to get a couple of screwdrivers from the tool box I had brought. Stellan and Kajika removed the deck screws and pried up an edge of the sub-floor slab. What we saw was an apparatus with a hopper on top, nestled between two floor joists. There were wires running various directions, all leading to a box fastened to the side of one of the joists.

"We'll have to study this to see how it works," Stellan said.

"There's got to be another one like this somewhere else," I said.

We scattered, looking for the second installation. Elaine discovered it, not in the kitchen floor, but incorporated into a space above some cabinets. She had seen a slight misalignment of some cupboard doors, and upon opening them to investigate, had seen where the top of the cupboard had been taken out and replaced. The workmanship on this modification was not as good as on the floor of the upstairs room, but that was understandable given the working conditions. If we had not been specifically looking for something, the damage probably would have gone unnoticed before this top cupboard was filled with seldom-used kitchen wares.

We didn't immediately investigate this kitchen installation. Instead we trooped toward the front door and gathered in the hall. Don had finished the front door lock and gone to the back.

"I wonder," I said, "if there is any way to temporarily disable the transmission system until we have a chance to examine it carefully."

"Why would you want it to be temporary?" Kajika asked. "Why not just destroy it?"

Elaine answered him. "The man behind all this is out of the country and we can't reach him, so we're trying to keep the system operational so he won't try something else."

"It would be best if we could do it today, before there's another transmission, which might reveal we've been here and are on to him" Stellan said, "We don't really know what kind of data's being transmitted."

Stellan explained to the others what was on the roof, and a lively discussion of how to disable the transmitter ensued. Ralph was the one who supplied the key.

"Maybe this here wind could just blow 'er down," he said. "Wrecks a lot uh stuff around here."

"We don't want to totally wreck it," I said, "just put it out of commission for a while."

Stellan got a distant look and finally said, "What if the wind tore the chimney cap loose and banged it on the antenna or the antenna cable for a while?"

"That could certainly disable it," I said, "but how would we put it back in service?"

"How about having Callaway do that?" Stellan asked. "After all, he's the one who installed it, so he should be able to fix it."

"I like that," Elaine said. "Then Callaway could tell Wainright what happened and explain why the transmissions were interrupted."

Stellan and I, followed by Kajika, went back to the side of the building where we had left the ladder. We set up again, and with me holding the ladder, Stellan removed the frequency detector. Then he and Kajika, helped by the wind, loosened the chimney cap by taking out all but one screw, wrenched it over the side of the chimney, and pounded it on the antenna coaxial cable until it was cut in two. They then tore the cap loose from the remaining screw, and after warning the others to move out of the way, allowed the wind to carry it off the roof and lodge against the fence. We packed up our tools, removed the ladder, and Kajika carefully erased our tracks.

All of us returned to Ralph's, happy to get out of the wind. Elaine had a short talk with Don, cautioned him to keep quiet about what he had witnessed. She stressed we were engaged in an ongoing investigation. Ralph and Stellan thanked him for his help and had him cut a half dozen more keys for Civalien Inn. I wrote him a check on the Civalien, Inc., account. Ralph then talked him into taking a tour of the Civalia site, and roped Kajika into being a guide. The three of them left in Ralph's truck.

That left me with Stellan and Elaine. The three of us discussed a plan of action for Civalien Inn over the next few days. We agreed Stellan and I would come back the next day with the equipment necessary to figure out how Wainright's apparatus operated. When we'd done so, hopefully within a day or two, Ralph would contact George Callaway to repair the chimney cap. Meanwhile, the cap would be left where it had blown against the fence. Elaine asked us to document our work with a written log, including pictures, and to be sure to wear gloves when we touched any of the apparatus installed by Callaway. She then left for Rawlins.

Ralph returned with Don, having left Kajika to continue working with the Civalia construction crew. We spent an hour or so answering Don's questions about Civalia and telling him some of our future plans. He seemed to be deeply interested and had some penetrating questions. We invited him back from time to time to see our progress, and then he left. Stellan and I were the last to leave.

CHAPTER 20

I lay awake for a long time that night, thinking again and again about the parallels and differences between my dream of the murderous bank robber and the situation at Civalien Inn. The buildings were similar, both having projecting dormer windows, although those of the Mansard style at Civalien Inn were not as prominent as those of the Federal-style building in my dream. Also, there was no raised floor with a crawl space underneath in Civalien Inn, but there was something intended to be deadly under the floor. The room looked remarkably similar to what I'd dreamed; the unfinished floor and walls, the construction debris, the double-hung windows, the lack of furnishings.

And then there were the similarities between the personalities of Wainright and the bank robber; the seeming disregard for all other humans and the all-consuming greed; the seeming lack of any ethical standards or compassion. Sleep was long in coming, and when it did, it was not particularly deep and restful. I was up early and made sure Stellan got up early, too.

With our pre-dawn start on the day, Stellan and I were deeply immersed in analyzing the apparatus under the floor of the upstairs room in Civalien Inn by 8:00. Our first task was to make a wiring diagram of the system. The coaxial cable to the antenna was obvious, as was the power connection to the motor on the hopper unit. Using a voltmeter, we identified the leads from the PV shingles. After that, it became more difficult.

After hours of going up and down stairs, disassembling electrical fixtures and vents, and using a cable tracker to map out where the wires ran, we discovered the powder metering system didn't operate unless the building utility system was energized.

The upstairs unit we were investigating energized when the vent fan in the downstairs bathroom was turned on. The powder fed into a supply vent located in the toe-space of a cabinet. The powder would then circulate across and up through the room, carried on the air currents generated by the bathroom exhaust fan.

We tested the operation of that system by isolating the bathroom circuit at the breaker panel and powering only the bathroom with a portable generator we had brought. We learned the entire system continuously received line power, making the PV shingles only necessary when the line power was down. We also discovered the metering motor was timed and only ran for a short interval as long as the fan was switched on.

Some of the other wiring was more difficult to trace and understand. We finally found two sensors, one weighing the hopper, and the other, when we finally found it inside the inlet duct, we identified as a microphone.

We took the cover off the box, exposing a sat phone, a microcontroller board, and various electronic switching and interface components. Best of all, there was a USB memory stick.

"We need to cut off all power to this system," Stellan said, "and then take a look at what's on that USB drive."

"I agree." I reached out, disconnected the PV shingle leads, removed the memory stick and handed it to Stellan. "You're more knowledgeable than I am about these systems, so why don't you look this over?"

Stellan and I then went to the kitchen and took out the panel in the top of the cupboard. As expected, there was a metering system, which dumped powder into a toe-space supply vent below the cupboards. The trigger for this system was the switch for the range hood exhaust vent. The weighing system and the microphone were present, but all of these components were controlled by the box under the upstairs floor where we had already investigated.

Satisfied we understood the system as well as we could from examining the physical installation, we replaced the kitchen panel, but just temporarily laid the floor panel back in place in the upstairs room. On the trip back to Laramie, we speculated endlessly about what might be on the USB drive, and we talked about how to proceed from this point. Our final decision was to let the system run and try to ignore it, but we did agree installing filters on the toe-space vents would be a good idea. I offered to handle the filters while Stellan examined the memory stick.

———— ∞∞∞ ————

Early in the morning I began making vent filters and suppressing my desire to call Stellan to see what he was finding. As the morning wore on, my need to know made suppressing my desire to call Stellan increasingly more difficult. Finally, about lunch time, Stellan did call and asked me to call Ralph to initiate the repair of the chimney cap with Callaway. I had a zillion questions for him, but he put me off by telling me he'd update me on the drive back to Civalien Inn. I called Ralph. A short time later, he called me back, telling me Callaway would be out the next day to fix the vent cap.

On the way back to Civalien Inn, Stellan told me the software to operate Wainright's powder-metering system was on the USB drive, written in binary machine code. Fortunately, the program was not very long, so he was able to decode it. The microphones were sound-actuated, so little or no sound data was recorded until yesterday, when we were active in the building. Another section on the drive was data storage. Unfortunately, the data was not overwritten, and the storage capacity of the drive was large enough to last for years, probably selected for the length of time the powder supply would last. Stellan was able to decipher the data storage and modify the data for yesterday, substituting data from an earlier day when it appeared wind noise might have added some trivial data. Hopefully, we would have the system operational before the day was over, and all audio traces of our investigations would be gone.

We picked up Ralph and had him wait outside while Stellan and I carefully installed filters on the vents, plugged in the USB drive, connected the PV panels, and as quietly as possible replaced the box cover and the floor panel. We then tiptoed out of the house, easing the door shut. Then Stellan stood by while Ralph and I pounded on the front door, making sounds which could be interpreted as breaking our way in, while we really simply opened the door. We then entered, discussing what we saw, as if it were the first time we had seen it. After a clomping tour of the building, we ended up in the kitchen talking about our plans and the fact we needed to get the power turned back on and the locks changed. To complete our deception, we placed an unnecessary board across the front door frame and tied the door knob to it with a rope.

We left Ralph to deal with Callaway when he came to repair the chimney cap. When he later told us about Callaway's visit, we laughed at Ralph's imitation of Callaway's efforts at getting him to leave, and decided Callaway probably wanted to check out the entire system, including the antenna. Ralph was innocently non-cooperative, telling Callaway how we'd had to break in, since we didn't have any keys. Callaway claimed he needed to work over the chimney cap, and would be back in a couple of days to finish the job. We speculated the real reason for the delay was to obtain replacement antenna parts, so we agreed it was time to "change the locks." Ralph also told us he made certain he locked the gate while Callaway was watching.

The chimney cap got replaced, and Elaine reported some communications between Callaway and Wainright. Stellan and I inspected the antenna cable and found Callaway had spliced it. We began to freely use Civalien Inn. Ralph, Stellan, Kajika, and I avoided being inside the building as much as possible, so we wouldn't inadvertently disclose our knowledge of Wainright's powder scheme, but the rest of the Civalia construction team moved in. There was general agreement the facilities, although unfinished and crude for the most part, were far superior to living in RVs.

Several times I noticed Gyan looking over the unfinished foundation slab for the lodge. I finally approached him and asked about his interest.

"We're probably a year away from having any greenhouse structures built," he told me. "Then getting the soil and water systems operational will take more time, as will getting the plants into full growth. All that could take three or more years. I was just wondering if we could build a more conventional greenhouse here as a stop-gap measure."

"Your idea has merit," I said. "I've been wondering what we should do with this slab of concrete. Let's plan on getting everyone together and discuss your idea."

The entire core Civalia group assembled that evening, and our discussion began with a report on the progress of Civalia given by Stellan.

"We are racing against the weather now," he began. "The Mego walls are nearly complete; we expect the last of the blocks to be in place within the week. The hypocaust floor and the central column have been constructed, and the fabric roof is scheduled for delivery about the time the walls are finished. We still have significant work left on the permanent outer wall of the work area wedge. About half of us are currently switching to working on that wall. When the Mego wall team finishes, they will switch to installing the fabric roof. Thanks to John, we have a winter wood supply."

I took an exaggerated bow.

"A stove isn't in yet, but pipes for the flue and external air supply are in place. We have a 500-gallon water tank, and a composting toilet. With Ralph's acquisition of Civalien Inn, we are not going to include further living or cooking facilities, which will increase the available work space for this winter. Because the living conditions for our workforce have improved with the opening of Civalien Inn, several of our workers have decided to stay on this winter."

Gyan then told us about his idea for a conventional greenhouse on the Jim Baker's Retreat concrete pad. A lot of discussion ensued. The general consensus was the idea was good, but the question was asked: would this project take resources from the construction of Civalia? Stellan and I were charged with investigating plans and estimating the impact.

The next afternoon, when Stellan had some relatively free time, we met. I put forth another harebrained idea I'd had about greenhouses in a cold climate like Wyoming.

"The problem with greenhouses is they often have either too much energy going in or too much going out."

"You're right," Stellan said. "They get roasting hot in the summer and freeze in the winter. Your wet foam insulation might help."

"It's not enough though," I said. "Years ago, I calculated greenhouses would still freeze in the winter. There just isn't enough solar energy to make up for the heat conduction through the glazing, even if it is insulated with wet foam; and in the summer, there's too much solar insolation."

"There's always heat storage in a thermal mass," Stellan countered. "That's what we'll essentially be doing in Civalia."

"True. But Civalia has a lot of mass besides the earth-sheltering mass; the water tanks, the greenhouse soil blocks, and the geopolymer mass of the structure. A standalone greenhouse won't have all of those."

"I have a sneaking suspicion you have an answer for that problem," Stellan said, "so cough it up."

"Well-1-1," I said, "suppose you start with a giant culvert arch, you know, like the ones used for tunnels with a road going through them, oriented north to south. Then block up the south end, and . . ."

"Wait a minute," Stellan said. "Don't you mean block up the north end? That's the shady end."

"No, I mean block up the south end. The north end gets a wall with something that looks like a picture window, and there is a heliostat field spread out to the north of the structure."

"I see," Stellan said. "Interesting. You plan to reflect light into the green house."

"Yes, and if it's night or the light levels are too low, the window can be easily super insulated. The heliostat field can be sized to provide adequate light energy, even at the winter solstice."

Stellan rubbed his jaw. "Clever, and I suppose you will insulate the hell out of the rest of the structure."

"Certainly," I said. "Actually, I've always thought it should be earth-sheltered. Another side benefit would be various solar collectors could be deployed in the window area if more than enough solar energy for the plants was available. Since the solar energy would be concentrated at the window, you could heat water, generate electricity, run absorption refrigeration, distill things, even cook things."

"Interesting." Stellan said again.

"And," I continued, "I haven't pursued this idea very hard in the past, because exporting entropy out of the greenhouse in really hot weather was a problem and distributing the light energy in the structure was another one. But your long-wave refrigerator and the light distribution panels you and Manjinder have developed might solve those two problems."

"This could solve another problem," Stellan said, thinking out loud. "We're going to have a significant amount of soil stockpiled after we get even this portion of Civalia constructed. True, we'll eventually use a fair amount of it for earth-sheltering the structure, but Civalia has such a large volume-to-surface area ratio, a lot will still be left over."

Stellan and I fell to work trying to estimate the cost of such a structure sized to fit the available foundation. With the help of the internet, we found the cost was around $¼ million. The heliostat field could conceivably double that. Alternatively, we could cut the size of the all-weather greenhouse in half, since adding on to it in the future would be relatively easy. The other half of the foundation could be covered with a more conventional hot-house type greenhouse, perhaps plastic film covered, although neither of us liked using plastic film, even if it was temporary. To augment food production, we considered turning the area around Civalien Inn into garden space, since it was already fenced. However, we weren't certain about the availability of irrigation water. I resolved to look into that.

A few phone calls got me a copy of the State Engineer's permit for the well at Civalien Inn, and some more calls located the well driller. He told me the well capacity, and that the water was acceptable for irrigation, so at least some conventional gardening was possible on the site. Stellan and I talked with Ralph and asked for his views, since he was the owner and knew the land better than anyone else. Ralph was intrigued by this new greenhouse concept, but he agreed we should not put all of our food eggs, so to speak, in one basket. A full meeting of the Civalia members generated the same results.

I began seriously designing and planning for the greenhouse project. Of course, this planning included financial planning. When I examined my finances and budgeted for this new greenhouse initiative, as well as the completion of the keyhole stage of Civalia, I came up short in my liquid assets. After much soul searching, internal debate, long walks, and some sleepless nights, I finally faced the fork in the road I'd come to. I could turn my back on the truth Stellan and I had found, that minimizing entropy production is the true basis of life and happiness, or I could maintain my current lifestyle, my shop, my antique cars, my continued life among my things. I decided to liquidate my antique car collection and my home/shop to finance this interim greenhouse, thereby supporting the construction of Civalia. Furthermore, to get maximum benefit, the interim greenhouse construction needed to start immediately.

I talked to Stellan, not telling him of my plans to sell my home/shop, but asking what the short-term plans for Mego productions were, and what his schedule was for moving the Mego production to the Civalia workspace. Armed with that information, I visited my bank and began discussions for a loan to "expand production." I arranged for the bankers to tour my home/shop on a day when the Mego production would be hectic, and arranged as large a loan as I could negotiate using my home/shop as collateral. I could tell the bankers were impressed with what was going on in my shop, and I'm sure they envisioned a whole new industry.

The loan was significantly more than the building was worth, but the bankers were "betting on the come," as they say. I used the loan money to start the greenhouse project, to move the Mego production to Civalia after a couple of months, to make some improvements on Civalien Inn, making it more hospitable for our workforce, and to pay back 10% of the loan plus some interest, the same formula I had used with the Amalgamated Bank of Omaha.

During the two months before the Mego production was moved, I also quietly liquidated my antique car collection, all of my retirement accounts, and most of my other possessions. I gave my Cadillac to Ralph, my truck and trailers to Civalien, Inc. Most of my shop tools and supplies also went to Civalien, Inc. When I told Stellan what I was doing, he didn't say much, just hugged me and told me he'd always be there for me. That was a comfort in otherwise turbulent and stressful times. Ralph and Geraldine were also very supportive, and Ralph told me I'd always have a place to live on the Lazy HZ.

"You know," I told him, "when I first thought about this greenhouse idea we're building, I thought it might be kind of interesting to live in a greenhouse instead of a conventional home. I just might try it out."

"Why'd ya wanna do that?" Geraldine asked.

"I was thinking," I said, "in a greenhouse, I'd have at least two of the most basic needs in life, food and shelter. You could probably add oxygen and water to those two. A greenhouse could probably also supply clothing, especially if I'd settle for a fig leaf."

Geraldine laughed and Ralph smiled.

"A greenhouse could also take care of all of my wastes, and export my entropy into outer space as heat. I also wouldn't have any of the traditional house maintenance; things like vacuuming, dusting, painting walls, grocery shopping, and paying utilities. I could have grass instead of carpet, plants instead of walls."

"Ya'd have a few more bugs and critters," Geraldine commented.

"You're right about that. I'd have to learn to live in harmony with a lot more living things, but I'd like to try."

"If'n ya get that there thing built, you'll have yer chance." Ralph observed.

The fall was setting in and we'd had a couple of hard frosts by the time we cleared the greenhouse construction with the planning office and the multi-plate greenhouse materials arrived. Fortunately, the first milestone of Civalia, the common workspace, had been completed and the roof installed. I drafted the Civalia workforce to help first build a Mego Wall on the northern end of the foundation, and then to bolt the multi-plate arch together, the legs of the arch resting in geopolymer troughs we had cast shortly after we'd committed to building the greenhouse. Since we were moving into the fall season when winds increase, we anchored and grouted the arch in place as we went along. We also started moving soil from the Civalia site to earth-shelter the greenhouse.

Stellan and I left a lot of the greenhouse construction work for Gyan to supervise, while I began building and installing heliostats. I used PV solar tracking units and built mirrors with aluminized Mylar film. Stellan and I had discussed how to make the heliostats, and this seemed like a reasonable short-term solution. Eventually, Stellan and Manjinder worked on making more durable mirrors and began developing large-scale entropy export panels.

In December, after more than one snow storm and many long days of struggle to beat the weather, the last multi-plate sections were bolted in place and the rear wall was installed. We celebrated with a dance in the newly completed greenhouse structure. It was a cool party, to say the least, so we danced with our coats on.

In early January, I officially filed for bankruptcy. As a settlement gesture, I willingly signed over my home/shop deed to the bankers, an unhappy lot. As the New Year started, I began my new life as a resident of Civalien Inn, helping wherever I could to further the construction of Civalia and the development of the interim greenhouse, coming to be known as John's Folly.

I have to say this turned out to be a highly satisfying phase in my life. Both Ralph and Geraldine began spending more and more time at Civalien Inn, ultimately moving in. The three of us became the hostelers for the inn, providing cooking, cleaning, and entertainment for the construction crew, Ralph and Geraldine being consummate story tellers. I joined them with their daily ranch chores, eventually suggesting we build a barn and some corrals within the inn fence. We did so in the spring, utilizing traditional log construction.

I also worked with Gyan on John's Folly to begin its life as an actual greenhouse. We rigged an insulating curtain partition at the point where the incomplete earth-sheltering ended, and proceeded to shake down the heliostat and entropy-export systems. Even when these were operational, it took a month to stabilize the temperature of the thermal mass. We then began growing plants in raised beds, which stepped upwards toward the back of the greenhouse to compensate some for the reflected sunlight entering almost horizontally. The light distribution panels did the rest.

Gyan's interest in indeterminate, edible plants grew, and he began acquiring existing specimens of these types of plants and planting them in John's Folly. Among them were several varieties of indeterminate tomato vines and a couple of fig tree varieties. I kidded him about fulfilling the prophecy in Micah 4:4 KJV

> But they shall sit every man under his vine and
> under his fig tree; and none shall make them afraid . . .

My kidding did not deter Gyan from pursuing his vision of developing a significant array of indeterminate edible plants, allowing Civalia residents to graze for a significant part of their diets. I helped him with this work. In late spring, we began serving a few indeterminate tomatoes, peas, green beans, and small potatoes. To facilitate these greenhouse experiments, I worked with Stellan and Manjinder to develop even larger-scale light distribution panels.

Construction on Civalia accelerated in the spring. Some work had proceeded through the winter; hypocaust flooring had been extended out for the common area of the wedge, and pillars for supporting the arched ceiling had been cast, as had been many more Megos. Excavation for the greenhouse soil tank was progressing, which allowed the remainder of John's Folly to be earth-sheltered. Gyan carefully harvested the top soil, including the plants with their roots, to start the reclamation process on John's Folly's earth cover.

With spring came a realization I'd been missing something. I asked Ralph, "Where's Gerald? I haven't seen him this winter or yet this spring."

Ralph pushed up his hat with his left hand and looked down. "I don't rightly know," he said, raising his gaze to mine. "One day last fall he just weren't there no more."

I was saddened, but soon was caught up in other opportunities for me to assist the development of Civalia. One of these was a project from Cindy. Once she was out of school, she decided, I'm sure with a little help and guidance from her dad and grandpa, to begin raising chickens in a greenhouse environment. This project matched well with her love of animals. I got to oversee and help in this grand experiment.

Cindy and I quarantined a portion of John's Folly and stocked it with a home-built incubator and brooder. I tasked Cindy with making the feeders and waterers, since those would not be needed for a while. We stocked the incubator with fertilized eggs, and her project was underway.

Two other projects I became involved with were instigated by Anand. The first was to add a sail to the Bruck, turning it into a wind wagon. That sort of project was right up my alley, so I had a great time with him sailing a Bruck up and down the road. His second project was a little bit more questionable. In his science class at school, he'd learned about dung beetles. He thought these creatures, epitomized by scarab beetles, those beetles revered by the ancient Egyptians, might be employed in place of the more mechanically-complicated, flush toilet system Stellan and I had specified for Civalia. He argued the scarab beetles disposing of our feces by dispersal and shallow burying would help improve the greenhouse soil far better than our deeper injection into the soil blocks.

The young man was persuasive, and when I brought up the issue of most of the diet of the dung beetles being herbivore feces, he corrected me by telling me the scarab beetles preferred the feces of omnivores; that was us.

I somewhat reluctantly agreed to help him with an experiment, so we set up a beetle enclosure in John's Folly. Since Anand was not yet living full-time at Civalia, I became the designated donor of beetle food. This, along with helping Cindy with her chickens, Gyan's horticultural experiments, and my own efforts to improve the operation of John's Folly, led me to spending considerable time there. So, I arranged some living quarters, and moved in.

Other things began stirring. Cass and Kajika called a meeting one evening with the Civalia team and the Civalien, Inc., Board. The subject was Kajika's desire to have us hire some of his fellow tribe members, so they could learn not only about the construction methods we were employing, but also about the underlying concepts of minimizing entropy change and cooperative community organization. He also wanted to arrange for some of the tribal elders to visit and learn for themselves what the Civalien Project was about.

"As far as I'm concerned," Stellan said, "If your fellow tribe members are anything like you, we'd be happy to have their help."

All of the other Civalia team immediately agreed, and Kajika beamed.

Geraldine then said, "An' we'd be happy to have yer elders visit, but I'd like to see us put 'em off fer a while."

Kajika lost his smile, and I asked, "Why is that, Geraldine?"

"We don't know spit 'bout their culture, an' havin' them workers 'round fer a time'll give us a chance to learn somethin' 'bout 'em. I'm bettin' they's had their fill a white men tellin' em what to do."

"That's an excellent idea," Cass said. "Working side-by-side, plus having formal and informal meetings, should help us learn a lot about each other. I'm looking forward to this."

Kajika smiled again.

"Will you be going home soon to begin arranging for more construction workers?" I asked him.

"Yes," he said. "It might take me a while to talk with the others and convince them they should come and work."

Stellan asked him, "Would it help if we made up a kit of some of the materials and features, like the light distribution panels, to show your friends?"

"Yes," Kajika said. "That would help, and the game, if I can take it."

"I can make a new game set," I said, "and perhaps, we can combine those two things a little by making some of the game pieces out of geopolymer and artificial shell."

About a week later, Kajika left for home, driving the Cadillac, which Ralph lent him, carrying an N-Trō-P game I made for him, and packing a variety of show-and-tell items from Stellan and Manjinder.

Construction on Civalia continued with setting up the Mego temporary walls for the extension wedges on both sides of the workspace, and the new additions to the central common ring. The walls for the common ring included Mego buttress walls to support side-loading from the arched roof.

Excavation continued for the greenhouse soil tank, speeded up somewhat by the acquisition of an ancient Cleveland wheel trencher, which Stellan and I worked on for almost a week to get it running and modified for our purposes. From the beginning, we had sought sources of bio-diesel for our equipment to lessen our entropic impact. The use of older, well-used equipment was another entropy reduction tactic. We monitored our energy usage and entropy production to help reach our goal of lifetime power consumption of one kilowatt. So far, we were on schedule to achieve our goal. If we could keep the embodied energy to these low levels and still achieve our 500-year design life, the contribution from shelter would be even less for those of the next six or seven generations.

In the middle of summer, Ralph and I got tired of having to monitor our words whenever we were in Civalien Inn. The thought of Wainright being privy to our conversations rankled. We began to discuss what we might be able to do to cut off his access without him suspecting us of doing so. The inspiration for our final plan came one day when a thunderstorm was passing by. Ralph said, "I wish lightnin'd strike that there antenna."

"Perhaps it can," I replied, and began to think about how we would simulate a lightning strike. I got Stellan to brainstorm with me, and we decided a good shot with a welder would do the trick. I called Elaine and talked over our plan with her. She gave us the green light, and also had some news for us. Tracing Wainright's communications might have located him in Antigua. Extradition might be possible, but it would be a long, drawn out, expensive project. We agreed our best course of action was to keep him thinking he was succeeding in killing us. What a happy thought.

To implement our plan, Ralph and I rigged a couple of welder leads where we could toss them out the window when the time came. One was attached to the chimney cap with some fine wires running over to the antenna; the other we prepared to clip into the ground of the metering system under the floor. We wrestled an engine-driven welder from Ralph's shop, which we located below the window. We then placed some pieces of scrap metal in the yard beyond the welder, telling the construction crew we were planning on building some yard art. A sizeable piece of sheet metal near the scrap metal, a ladder in back of the house, and a CO_2 fire extinguisher completed our preparations. We then waited for stormy weather.

In the mean time, we primed Wainright by two actions. Ralph and I began coughing some and complaining about feeling out of breath. We did this around some of the construction crew and when we were near the microphones. We figured Wainright might hear us directly, but he also might hear some of the others discussing our health. Then on two occasions, when no one else was around, I went outside and shook the sheet metal to simulate thunder, while Ralph started commenting on how lots of thunderstorms seemed to be forming, and how close some of them seemed to be. I'd quietly hurry back in and joined in the conversation, bolstering Ralph's observations.

Then a day came when a thunderstorm did approach. Ralph and I sprang into action. I set up the ladder, while Ralph went upstairs, pried up the floor panel, connected one of the welder-leads to the ground of the metering system, and dropped the ends of the welder-leads out the window to me. I hooked up the leads, started the welder, set it for maximum amperage, and headed up the ladder. Ralph handed me the stinger of the welder as I climbed by, and I dragged the cable onto the roof. The fun began when I clamped the electrode holder onto the antenna, which immediately turned red, began to melt, and the insulation began to burn off the coaxial cable.

"That's good," Ralph shouted from inside the room. I heard a whoosh as Ralph deployed the fire extinguisher.

I climbed back down to the window level and Ralph handed me the welder ground lead. I climbed back up and proceeded to severely damage the chimney cap again, this time making it look like it could have been struck by lightning. I also burned the fine wires we had laid between chimney cap and the antenna, leaving jagged burn marks on the bricks.

I checked the PV shingles on my way down to make sure they weren't burning, and when I was on the ground, I shut down the welder and removed the ladder. Ralph leaned out the window and gave me a thumbs-up.

I went in to inspect the damage. It was impressive. A lot of the wire insulation was burned away or melted around the control box, and the box itself was distorted, burned, and cracked where some of the wiring went through the side. Smoke was leaking out, and the smell of burned plastic and wiring was pretty strong. There was no chance the system was still operational.

Ralph and I cleaned up our mess, returned his welder, the scrap metal, and the ladder to his shop, and after waiting a sufficiently long time to make sure no fire was still smoldering, replaced the floor panel. I checked all the connected house wiring with a megger to make certain we had not damaged any of it. I wiped out traces of our presence in the area below the window as best I could, wishing Kajika was back to help me.

The next morning, Ralph called Callaway and told him the chimney cap needed attention again, having been struck by lightning. He told him he'd better bring a new cap, since the old one looked burned beyond salvage. He added a few coughs while he was talking to help convince Callaway their plot was still working. Callaway wasted no time getting out to Civalien Inn, arriving mid-afternoon. Ralph again met him and chaperoned him while he placed his ladder and climbed up to assess the damage and make repairs.

Ralph reported, "He 'peared ta be a might agitated, an' he 'mediately wanted ta check out all the wirin' inside. Said there's probably insulation damage. I told 'im it weren't necessary. While we smelled burnin' insulation, an' it did blow the breaker fer the downstairs bathroom, you done checked things with somethin' ya called a megger, an' it's all okay. He didn't like takin' no for an answer, but he finally got on with the job."

"I'd have liked to have seen his face," I said.

"It were classic. When I talked about climbin' up ta see the damage, he 'bout had a fit telling me how dangerous it were, and how he'd take care of everythin'. I coughed a few times fer 'im, an' told 'im how's I'm having trouble gettin' rid of this here cough."

Ralph grinned broadly. We both faked a cough and then laughed.

"Anyways when he carried his tool bag back down, there's a little piece a burned wire showin' 'midst all his tools. He stuck his tool bag in the back of his truck, and shut the camper door real fast; I 'spose so I couldn't snoop, an' then he went back up with some caulk. I 'spose ta hide where the wire'd gone through the roof."

"I hope he did a good job," I said. "Otherwise we'll have a leak. How'd he explain caulking a chimney cap?"

"Oh, he claimed he were just touchin' up the caulk around that there chimney; just preventive maintenance 'e says. I then invited him into the kitchen fer a cup a coffee before 'e went home. Yu should uh heard them excuses fly then."

Those of us knowing about Wainright's attempt to harm us felt much freer after disabling his system. Elaine reported a flurry of communications between Callaway and Wainright shortly after Callaway's last trip to Civalien Inn. After things quieted down, and at a time when all of the Civalia workforce were busy elsewhere, Elaine and Melvin supervised us in removing the hardware from under the floor and over the kitchen cupboard. Elaine bagged and tagged it all as evidence, making certain we protected it from contamination. She was obviously enjoying herself.

"This is the most interesting case I've ever worked on," she told us, "not only from the policing standpoint, but also from what all of you are trying to do. Even if this investigation winds down, I'd like to drop in once in a while to check on you."

"You'll be very welcome," I said.

Elaine did drop in from time to time, and we had begun having drop-in visits from various other people we had encountered, including both Sally and Al from the Saratoga Sun, Jeremy from the Forest Service, Alan from the planning office, Maggie and her family, and even Don, the locksmith. Various locals also dropped in occasionally to see what was going on. Some left shaking their heads at our unorthodox building methods, but curiosity brought them back occasionally. A few strangers arrived, and at first we didn't know how to deal with these visitors. Then, as Gyan began to get more and more produce from John's Folly, which began supplying an ever-increasing percentage of our daily food, Cass came up with an excellent plan for community outreach.

We modified the dining room at Civalien Inn by taking out the kitchen walls and extending the room along the entire south side of the building. We ended up having a long room with an open, semi-circular kitchen in the middle on the south side extending about half-way across the room. There was a counter around the kitchen area with several bar stools. The west third of the room became an auditorium/meeting room and the east two thirds a combination dining room/library with family style seating at tables for four or five people. A couple of small tables were set up with permanent copies of the N-Trō-P game mounted on them. The library shelves, instead of being in rows around the edge of the room, were placed randomly throughout the room at varying angles. The effect was to create more intimate spaces and reduce the institutional effect of a fairly large room. Lighting came from light distribution panels.

The book shelves were stocked with books relating to entropy, environmental awareness, collective living, cooperativeness, alternative economics, and paradigm shifts. We also put various trinkets and models made from artificial shell and geopolymer materials on the shelves, along with pictures, puzzles, and other interesting items. Some shelves had plants, as did the tops of the bookcases. The overall effect was a friendly space conducive for conversations, fellowship, and stimulating curiosity.

We then began opening our dining room to guests for a couple of meals each week. We quickly learned we needed to control guest numbers since large numbers of people were showing up, attracted by curiosity and free food. Lively discussions on improving our community outreach ensued at more than one of the regular Civalia group discussions. The suggestion was made to turn Civalien Inn into a conventional restaurant and charge people for the meals. This was hotly debated, but eventually rejected, since then we would be subject to the myriad of regulations and inspections as part of the food service industry, as well as raising problems of dealing with taxes and other financial issues. Besides, as Stellan noted, a money-based business was contrary to the basic tenants of Civalia.

Diane offered what became our agreed upon solution. Visitors were fed, if they would accept X number of OUs, depending on the quality and quantity of their meal. OUs were the name we decided upon for our debt instruments, and they could be discharge by the holder doing specific tasks for Civalia. We kept track of OUs in a ledger on one of the bookshelves. This system became our introductory course for outsiders on Civalien economics, and also gave us some insight into the temperament and personality of our guests. Some racked up a few OUs, and, when we asked them to work, were never heard from again. Others reveled in the novelty of this approach and wanted to perform some work immediately. Many came back for more. This approach did, for a time, successfully limited the number of guests dining at Civalien Inn.

However, in a surprisingly short time, we were again overwhelmed. I believe there were many factors for this, but the main one seemed to be curiosity about our project. The fact we were serving tasty, homegrown food, fresh from the greenhouse, didn't hurt. We instituted a reservation system to try to control the numbers. A few people became regulars, and in so doing, became a significant source of labor for Civalia. Some of these eventually became candidates for joining.

Other enhancements to Civalien Inn made during this time were both outdoor and indoor play spaces for the children of guests who were working off their OUs or dining with us. We made a batch of tenth scale Megos for them to build with, built some geopolymer structures and some cooperative playground equipment, i.e. equipment requiring more than one person for successful operation. Cindy and Anand became our playground supervisors. One piece of playground equipment became vitally significant for Civalia, a zip line.

While all of this development of our guest accommodations had been going on, construction on Civalia had progressed. By late August, both the common area wedge and the green house wedge were nearing completion. Kajika had returned with a crew of eight, and their contributions helped immensely. Traffic between Civalia and Civalien Inn became a problem, taking a significant amount of time and effort, and causing too much damage to the land from the foot traffic.

When we began to discuss this problem with the whole group, I mentioned that, given zero friction, the energy required for a round trip was zero. One of the Dancers who'd been playing on the zip line said, in jest, we should just install long zip lines. This brought to my mind a 13-mile long aerial tram line built in the early 1900's and now gone. The tram transported copper ore mined at the Ferris-Haggerty Mine on the western slope of the Sierra Madre Range in southern Wyoming to the Penn-Wyo Smelter located in Encampment, Wyoming. Much of the energy to operate the tramway came from the elevation difference between the mine and the smelter. To go to town, the miners rode the loaded ore buckets from the mine to Encampment and rode empties back to the mine.

Since Civalia was uphill from Civalien Inn, tram transportation from Civalia to Civalien Inn could be established with a gravity tram. Going back to Civalia would require considerable work. Stellan and I began to dream and scheme. With multiple transport buckets, the issue of local energy minima and maxima caused by sagging of the tram support cables between towers could be minimized by careful spacing.

To compensate for the differences in elevation between the two destinations, ballast could be added on the return side to balance the overall loop. We figured water would be used as ballast and would be readily available, easy to handle, and environmentally friendly. In the winter, to prevent freezing, any water ballast would be immediately dumped from a tram car ballast tank into a suitably protected storage tank when a tram car arrived at one of the terminals. I expected the ballast system, while initially operated by hand, would eventually be automated.

For a reasonable transit speed, our preliminary calculations indicated four or more people could provide sufficient operating power. This transportation system could be pedal-powered. With enough gear reduction, one person could even do the job, if they were willing to travel significantly slower than a casual walk.

With Stellan's focus on the construction of Civalia, the tram project became mine; I worked on it throughout the winter and well into the next summer. Stellan helped me a lot during the winter. To reduce travel impact on the land before the tram was operational, with the help of Ralph and Geraldine, I built several more Brucks to shift travel from the developing trails to the existing roads. The inaugural trip of the tram between Civalia and Civalien Inn occurred on July 25th that next summer.

Other things of note took place that first summer. One was a regular evening session, held a couple times each week, that Cass arranged for meeting with Kajika and his construction team made up of five men and three women. With Cass's guidance, deep bonds and mutual respect developed among all of us. Kajika, having kept in contact with one of the elders of his tribe, decided the time had come for us to meet with the tribal elders and tell them about Civalia. He arranged a meeting, and late on a rainy Monday morning, Kajika and three of his team led Cass, Ralph, Geraldine, and I to Ethete.

We arrived late in the afternoon, and Kajika made arrangements for us in a location with cooking facilities. The eight of us prepared a meal for the tribal elders from greenhouse food stocks we had brought. That evening, we became informally acquainted with the elders from both of the tribes on the Wind River Indian Reservation, the Eastern Shoshone and the Northern Arapahoe.

The next day, Kajika had arranged for us to formally meet with of the elders, but not all were there, since some had jobs to attend to. Kajika began telling them his observations of Civalia. First he told them how Civalia was designed to provide the basic needs of food and shelter for many people. He emphasized the food they had eaten last night, while maybe not familiar to them, was produced in a greenhouse similar to the one being constructed at Civalia.

He told them how he had been working on the structure for more than two months, and it was unlike any structure he had ever seen, but it was designed to last and it was designed for easy construction in stages. His fellow construction workers then backed up his assessment of the construction work.

Kajika called on me to explain the entropy basis of Civalia, but shortly after I started in, I could tell I was losing the audience. I deferred to Ralph, who began by telling some yarns about his early days in the Saratoga area, including some about a couple of Natives he'd met back in the "good ol' days" on a cattle drive. He then took a turn I wasn't expecting.

"You heard 'bout Johnny Appleseed back in them there early days?" he asked.

There were nods and murmurs of assent from his audience.

"Well," he said, "ol' Johnny Appleseed, if'n the tales is true, planted apple seeds all over, and it's my un'erstandin' most all uh 'em that growed were bad apples fer eatin'; only good fer makin' licker. An' that firewater weren't good fer any uh ya, not fer us neither." There were again nods and murmurs of assent. Ralph continued, "There's been lots uh others comin' along sellin' other won'erful seed an' things, tellin' us they'd make life better an' easier. Them Soil Conservation guys in the fifties came tellin' me ta rip out all my sage an' plant that there crested wheat. Fortunately, I didn't listen. My neighbor did, an' now he's payin' the price."

Geraldine got up and handed a couple of photographs to the elders, which they passed around as Ralph continued.

"An' here we are, an' another Johnny here," Ralph gestured at me, "is tellin' ya somethin' ya don't un'erstand. Sounds like a bunch a malarkey, don't it?" More nods and murmurs of assent. "Well, we don't know spit about what yer doin' an' the problems facing ya, an' if'n what Johnny here's talkin' 'bout'll do ya a lick uh good. So, what I'd suggest is ya show us around. Tell us what works an' what don't fer ya. An' then together we kin decide if'n anything we got ta say'll be uh any interest an' help ta ya."

The last elder to look at Geraldine's photos made a move to get up to return them, so I, being curious, stood up and walked over to retrieve them. They were "before" and "after" pictures of Ralph's neighbor Tom's field. The difference was stark and a little appalling. The before picture was dated in the 1940's, and I wondered about its history.

There was some general stirring, and Kajika had come forward to confer with the elders. Ralph had stepped aside and was patiently waiting. Some of the elders began drifting out and mingling with our group. One was talking with Geraldine and another with Cass. I was again astounded at Ralph's ability to handle and integrate disparate groups. One of the elders, apparently younger than me, approached and we struck up a conversation. She told me her name was Molly, and she was an aunt of Kajika. He had been telling her about entropy, and she was interested in learning more since she was teaching science classes in the local high school. Our conversation ranged over a variety of topics while we explored each other's thinking and knowledge.

Meanwhile a group of elders, along with Kajika, Ralph, and Geraldine, left the room. Cass was deep in conversation with another of the elders, an older woman. The three construction workers who had come with Kajika drifted over to Molly and me. She had had each of them in class at one time or another. After a while, at the suggestion of one of the constructions workers, the five of us sat down and began playing the N-Trō-P game. A couple of hours drifted by, and the tour group returned and our game broke up. The entire group disintegrated into small, slowly changing conversational groups.

When I later caught Kajika alone, I asked, "Is this meeting going like you wanted it to?"

"Not exactly," he answered, but he looked pleased. "Better. Ralph and Geraldine have made many friends."

It was true. Several of the elders gathered near Ralph and Geraldine, talking animatedly to them. Both were listening gravely, occasional offering what I imaged must be short, pithy comments.

Kajika said, "One of the elders asked Ralph what was in this for him. Our people are used to various people coming to us with grandiose schemes, most designed to take rather than give. His answer struck a chord with my people."

"What did he say?" I asked.

"He told them when white men first came to North America, they encountered our people who did not have the same concept of land ownership and property rights. The Natives also had little understanding of trade as the white interlopers understood it, so they were easily, from the stand point of the whites, taken advantage of. He used the word 'snookered.' He said from his readings he thinks the Native Americans' ideas of trade were closer to your Civalien economics than to capitalism. He didn't use those words exactly, but that's how I understood him. He then said some of you whites now think you might owe some debt for some of the lands taken from us in those colonial days. He showed them some of your OUs, and explained a little how Civalien economics work."

"Wow!" I said.

"Geraldine then said we, I think she meant all of you white people, were just trying to make a little payment on a long over-due debt. I think that's when the elders really began to thaw."

A while later we had lunch furnished by the tribal elders. After lunch we said our goodbyes and headed back for Civalia, but not before the elders gave us a commitment to send delegations to Civalia to investigate thoroughly what we had to offer.

Back on the road, Cass had some electrifying news for us. In her discussions with Lydia, the elder she had been talking to, she found out that Lydia was not only an Indian herbalist, but also a DO. They had discussed the medical implications of Civalia, and Lydia expressed an interest in not only visiting Civalia, but maybe staying there for at least a little time. She wanted to experiment with growing medicinal herbs in the Civalia greenhouse, and said she could, at the same time, provide medical care for Civalia residents.

In August, Gyan started planting in the Civalia greenhouse, even before all the glazing was in place. By the time it was en-closed, there was significant greenery. However, the greenhouse could not begin producing food for some time, so John's Folly continued to be the primary food source for the initial residents of Civalia and the construction work force. In late September, the first seven Civaliens, Stellan, Gyan, Cindy, Cass, Manjinder, Anand, and Diane, officially took up residence in Civalia. We held a house warming party that started after lunch at 1:00 and continued till after midnight. There was a ribbon cutting ceremo-ny, feasting, dancing, singing, tours for invited guests, speeches, laughing, crying for joy, and exclamations of wonder.

PART IV

THE CALLING
OF CIVALIA

CHAPTER 21

That first winter in Civalia was undoubtedly the most difficult. Getting enough systems to work to sustain the residents, providing home schooling for Cindy and Anand, keeping the greenhouse alive, and in what little spare time was available, continuing work on expanding Civalia. The number of visitors fell, to the relief of all, and John's Folly continued to feed us reasonably well.

We did have some visitors, the tribal elders; three different groups of four visiting at approximately one month intervals. Lydia was in the last group, and she stayed on when her group left for the reservation. Through Kajika, we learned the elders had decided there was merit in the concepts of our *Declaration of Life* and Civalia. They were working on plans to implement two similar structures within the next couple of years, one for the Eastern Shoshone and one for the Arapahoe tribes. We were awed they were contemplating an expansion of the Civalien concept.

Since engineering knowledge would be invaluable for Native projects, Ralph and Geraldine offered to help Kajika and one of the other Native construction workers, both of them having expressed an interest in attending the College of Engineering at the University. Arrangements were made for these youngsters to enter the University the next fall.

Some potential future residents for the next construction phase of Civalia began to surface. The most surprising of these was Maggie. Her kids were aging out of high school, beginning to go away to college and to marriages, and her husband, Earl, had been struck with a mid-life crisis, having taken off with his secretary.

"You've ruined me," Maggie told me. "The more I've come to understand and realize the truth of your *Declaration of Life*, the less I can stand to practice law and seek results for my clients, which I know are contrary to your Declaration."

Maggie continued, "I've been thinking, John, you should buy yourself a domain."

"Why?" I asked, genuinely puzzled.

"You know, of course," she said, "if you don't pay your property taxes, your land can be taken and sold for back taxes."

"Yes, that's why we formed Civalien, Inc.; to protect our domains."

"Right," she said, "but in the long run, you could still lose them, if Civalien, Inc. fails, or the State decides to build a road through it, or someone sues and wins a judgment, you're history. The law needs to be changed, and that means a lawsuit. To initiate a lawsuit, you need to be harmed. So, you need to buy a domain, fail to pay your taxes, and when they sell it out from under you, sue the bastards."

I talked this over with Ralph and Geraldine, and eventually the three of us agreed with Maggie. We purchased 125 acres of Tom's Foolery across the county road from Ralph's in my name, and with the help of the Civalia construction crew, we built a little Mego bungalow with a composting outhouse. I spent enough time there to legally call it my official residence. I got my mail there, including property tax notices which I failed to pay. The clock started ticking.

However, as much time as possible, I was in John's Folly. I'd come to really enjoy living in a greenhouse. When I visited with the Civalia crew, they also commented on how much time they were spending in theirs and how much they were enjoying it. We decided we are genetically programmed, with good reason of course, to live among plants.

The clock needed to tick for three years before the land could be sold for delinquent taxes, and besides all of us becoming three years older, a lot happened during that time. I worked out an agreement with the Forest Service, and the residents of Civalia began looking after tracts of the National Forest. Civalia was almost finished. Construction had accelerated exponentially as the population increased. There were 43 residents, down from a high of 48. All five people had left to work on similar communal structures elsewhere. Among the five was Lydia, who returned to the reservation to help her tribe build their own similar settlement. Two more had left to help begin other settlements on Ralph's land, one was working with Alan on a settlement near Rawlins, and the fifth one was near Lusk in Niobrara County helping to start a settlement with Stellan's cousin.

The two on Ralph's land, Civalia II and Civalia III, were located east of Civalien Inn, much closer to Highway 230 and the river. Those locations had been chosen because one of the founders had developed an apparatus to mine silt from the North Platte River. Their mining machine consisted of a semi-porous conveyor belt oriented perpendicular to, and driven by, the river current. The belt trapped silt that was suspended in the water and carried it out over the river bank, where it was scraped off. This silt became the base substance for their geopolymer material, replacing the fly ash we had been using to build Civalia.

Stellan was in great demand as a consultant on these and other startups; he was in and out a lot, effectively, but not officially, being the sixth to leave. He still spent as many nights at Civalia as he could. Cass was spending a considerable time with me; touring, speaking at workshops, in churches, and in lecture halls at various schools and universities. This work kept her from putting much time in Civalia, so she selected her replacement from the waiting list of people wishing to join the settlement and became the seventh to leave, taking up residence in Civalien Inn. Together we plotted the expansion of the Civalien concept across the United States and around the world.

On a more realistic level, Cass and I worked hard to build a positive reputation for Civalia within Carbon County, and tried to gain influence within the County government. By the end of the three years, we were more successful than I ever thought possible. The Civalien revolution became attractive to many local, ranch families squeezed by ever increasing competition from corporate ranches, low prices from the massive packing plants, high operational costs, lack of skilled help, and the ever-increasing load of regulatory requirements.

Ralph, personally knowing most of these ranch families, became the point-man in talking with them. One after another, they began to leave traditional ranching and join our project. The most common reason for their joining was the fact they were aging, but had no heirs; or at least no heirs wanting to carry on the ranching business. In one case, we provided knowledge, help, and resources to a rancher to build a Civalia type family home. Despite having a large extended family, none of them wanted to take over the ranch. He then turned his deeded lands over to Civalien, Inc. to preserve these lands as domains for his family.

Others, who were deeply in debt to the banks, simply declared bankruptcy and joined one of the new settlements being launched. We were then sometimes able to acquire their lands from the banks at rock bottom prices, since our domains were beginning to depress real estate prices. The reason was simple: we were taking land out of agricultural production and making the agricultural support services in the area increasingly scarce and more expensive. The fact we were making some of these tracts essentially landlocked also contributed to the decline of the local agricultural industry.

We also became politically active, led by Cass and Maggie. One of our Civalia members became a County Commissioner from the Encampment area. Alan, becoming ever more interested in Civalia, had successfully run for County Commissioner from Rawlins, and another person sympathetic to our cause had been elected from Saratoga. So, we had a three-to-two majority for reforms we wanted to make in the county.

The opposition largely stemmed from absentee land owners

and corporate business interests. Cass and I kept busy trying to promote our *Declaration of Life* philosophy in the wider community and to counter opposition from critics, disbelievers, and vested interests. Sometimes we were forced to stand up to intimidation and sometimes to quash outright bribery. Maggie worked hard to defend us from lawsuits designed to bankrupt and crush us. What saved us was the fact we were becoming ever more independent of the moneyed economic system. They could not starve us out or shut off our water or turn off our power and heat.

In fact these battles worked in our favor. Besides demonstrating to the lower and middle class residents of Carbon County the grasping, rapacious nature of some of the corporations and wealthy absentee owners, these battles demonstrated the advantages of controlling our own basic necessities. Thus, just before I lost my domain to delinquent taxes, we were able to collect enough political power to get the Carbon County zoning laws amended. This amendment recognized individual domains and, more importantly, required any planned "development" on lands adjacent to a domain tract to show the development would not make an unauthorized alteration of the adjacent domain.

I don't think the entities fighting us fully understood the concept of a domain, because when my domain was auctioned on the steps of the Court House in Rawlins, there were several individuals and companies bidding for it. Ralph and Geraldine had thought they might buy it back for little to nothing, just the back taxes, but the final bid was astronomical. We understood why a short time later when plans for converting nearly the entire 125 acres to a hog production facility were filed with the planning office. The plans showed confinement buildings, sewage lagoons, feed storage silos, a slaughter house, refrigerated meat storage lockers, and worker housing. I think they planned to overwhelm and stink us out. The fight was on; David against Goliath.

About the same time, Maggie filed suit in the Second District Court on my behalf for damages caused by the County seizing my domain for back taxes. When our day in court arrived, Maggie began presenting our case by summarizing the events to date. Then, as we had agreed, she called Ralph as a witness instead of me, both of us knowing he connected with audiences much better than I ever could.

Ralph laid his hat on the plaintiffs' table and stood up. As he walked to the witness stand and was sworn in, he was the epitome of the frontiersman; black pants tucked into cowboy boots, suspenders, a white shirt, a handlebar mustache. He began his testimony.

"Yer Honor, I've lived many years on my ranch, an' back in the 60s I come ta think 'bout how, if'n I had a pantry full uh food, an' maybe a house plant or two, but the house was sealed up where sunshine could get in an' heat get out, but couldn't no air or water get in or out, an' no sewage get out, breathin'd get tough an' I'd not last long. Maybe a day or two, an' it wouldn't be pleasant with all that there sewage pilin' up."

The Judge smiled at Ralph's last remark.

"An' when I croaked, I'd still have plenty ta eat. Then I thought if'n I had more plants, probably a lot more plants, I'd last longer. Water'd still be a problem. When I met John, here," Ralph gestured toward me, "he told me my thoughts was right. Energy in that there food don't go away, it just changes into forms don't do me no good, bad air an' sewage; same amount uh energy, just lower potential, John says. But plants usin' sun energy can change that there bad air an' sewage back ta food an' good air. But with all that sun energy coming in ta that there house, there's even more uh that there energy buildin' up what neither me nor them plants can use. John told me it's got a high falutin' name, entropy. This entropy's gotta get out uh the house somehow or it'll kill me an' the plants too. John told me it'd have ta get out as heat. Ya can't see it, but it's gotta get out. He said these things keepin' me living, them plants changin' bad ta good an' shipping that there bad energy out as heat, is called 'environmental services,' an' he called the area ya need for plants ta get 'er done a 'domain.'"

Ralph looked contemplative for a moment and twisted the left side of his mustache. He resumed.

"John run some figgers an' told me in Wyoming here, takin' in ta account all the plants in this here state, 'bout an average uh

125 acres is needed ta take care uh me, an' that's only if'n I use energy, my lights an' pickup an' stove an' other things, at a rate uh 'bout a thousand Watts. Most uh us, you an' me, use 'bout eleven killa'Watts, so's we'd need 'bout fourteen hun'rt acres."

Ralph again paused and gazed at the Justice.

"John was livin' simple, ain't got no car, no 'lectricity, had a privy, an now got no plants ta change his bad air an' sewage back ta food an' good air, 'an' get that heat energy out uh his way. That there tax man done take away his environmental services an' put ol' John back in a small box. Ain't done him no harm, ya might claim, he ain't died. But now he's gotta live on his neighbors, takin' a little here an' a little there, making all their lives just a little harder, an' a little shorter, damaging the plants, an' not getting that there energy he can't use out as heat. I say it ain't right."

He took a deep breath.

"An' we're seein' the results uh the energy we can't use buildin' up in our whole house; this here Earth. Heat's buildin' up in oceans; our breath's buildin' up in the air, more uh that there carbon dioxide; trash an' sewage's buildin' up on our land an' in our streams, lakes, an' oceans; all energy we can't use an' there's not enough plants ta convert it and send it out uh our house; out ta the stars. I say it ain't right."

The defense declined to cross examine Ralph, so he sat down and Maggie continued her argument. She told the Judge we were asking for a personal area required to provide minimum environmental services be designated a domain, and be exempt from property taxation. She argued if individuals do not have a right to the environmental services necessary to support their life, they do not have a right to life, as set forth in the Declaration of Independence. She gave the Judge an exhibit of my calculations of domain size, scientific data on net photosynthetic production, and a paper I had written giving the mathematical, theoretical basis of our arguments.

The Carbon County Attorney presented his defense, largely relying on Wyoming Constitutional and economic arguments, emphasizing the economic loss if domains were to be exempted.

Our day in court was fairly short and to the point. When we

left, I complemented Ralph on his testimony and told him it was a vivid and compelling description of the entropy process on Earth.

"It weren't me what thought it up," Ralph said.

"No, kidding? Who did?" I asked.

"Geraldine done come up with that. She's one smart lady," he said.

"I couldn't agree more," I replied.

The court did not deliberate long, and within the week they returned their verdict. The Wyoming Constitution authorizes local governments to collect property taxes and, when they are not paid, to seize the property. The court found in favor of the defendant. We had expected this ruling and decided to immediately appeal to the Wyoming Supreme Court.

All of this political and legal activity required communications between all of us, and we started out relying on the existing land-line and cellular telephone networks. Since we could not control these, we decided to begin constructing our own communication channels. Our first one was running a fiber optic cable between Civalia and Civalien Inn. We used the tram towers to support the cable. Ultimately, each settlement became a relay station in our network. Judging by the standards of the World Wide Web, ours was primitive and slow, but without advertising, social media, and other commercial traffic, it was more than adequate. We did keep very limited access to the existing communication infrastructure.

Crafting our Supreme Court appeal took long hours of re-search, careful wording, arguing, and rehearsing. Our first hurdle was to get our appeal heard. We sweated it out for several weeks after our submittal, the Court taking significantly longer than usual to decide whether or not to hear our case. In the end, they did. We learned later we had barely scraped through that door. The Supreme Court hears oral arguments on the University of Wyoming campus in the fall, and we were fortunate to be sched-uled to present our arguments there.

When our day in court arrived, Maggie presented our case beautifully. She emphasized we were not seeking to overturn the entire property tax provision as embodied in the Wyoming Constitution. We were only seeking to exempt domains of such size and composition to supply minimum environmental services for an individual person. "Surely," she told the Justices, "an exemption supporting—no, necessary for—the most basic right, the right to life, the first right listed in the *Declaration of Independence*, must carry more weight than the subsequent rights. Liberty and the pursuit of happiness are meaningless without life. Domains, being essential for life, are inherent to the right to life, and must, therefore, be exempt from taxation."

She then pointed out property tax exemptions already exist for churches and non-profit corporations. However, the roles of these organizations serve the subsequent rights of liberty and the pursuit of happiness, not the basic right to life itself. Therefore, exempting domains serving the right to life is not only reasonable, but is a foregone conclusion.

The Justices questioned Maggie on how such a domain might be measured, and she told them our reasoning was based on food calories; an average 2,000 calories per day for a woman and 2,500 for a man, all of which must ultimately be supplied by fixed photosynthetic energy. However, not many individuals are average, and not all calories are created equal. A mixture of carbohydrate, fat, and protein calories are all necessary for physical health. Similarly, the carrying capacity of land might well vary from year to year, and for long term health of the biome, various other animal, insect, bird, microbial, and other living species must be included and allowed to exist. A reasonable safety factor must also be included to accommodate natural variation. With all of this in mind, the net photosynthetic production of an area, scientifically measureable, could be used to establish the size of a domain using factors established by scientific research.

Furthermore, since man does not live by bread alone, an extra measure of energy flow is needed for a satisfying life. Maggie then presented the research showing 1,000 to 1,200 Watts is an adequate energy flow for this purpose.

As an initial starting point, Maggie offered my overall estimate for Wyoming of 125 acres for a domain size. Maggie continued, "In average Wyoming terrain, an average person should be able to exist on a tract this size without degrading it or interfering in any way with the biome another person might have on an adjacent tract. This size of tract also has the capacity for an individual to experience a satisfying life, as well as supply their basic sustenance."

A couple of the Justices looked decidedly unbelieving and shook their heads slightly. When Maggie sat down, there was a rustling and whispering in the court room, and then the Carbon County Attorney rose to present his oral arguments, which paralleled the arguments he had given in the Second District Court. He had a few more economic numbers, including a dire projection of the catastrophe awaiting Carbon County if domains were to be exempted. He also emphasized the Constitutional basis for and cited some other legal precedents for property taxes.

I was feeling somewhat glum until one of the Justices asked the Attorney how the County compensated for the lack of taxes from the exempt churches and non-profits. The County Attorney appeared flustered for a moment and then stated the county set the tax rate based on the County budget and a voter-approved tax rate.

"So," the Justice asked, "it appears voters have approved a tax rate allowing the County to exempt churches and non-profits. Assuming the required tax rate would rise if domains were exempted, could such a tax rise be passed by the voters?"

The Attorney was flustered. "Perhaps," he said, "but if everyone has a domain, there wouldn't be any tax payers left."

"I beg your pardon," the Justice said. "There would still be for-profit corporations and, if my understanding is correct, some tracts of land are much larger than domains and owned by individuals."

"If it pleases Your Honor," the Attorney said, beads of sweat beginning to break out on his forehead, "I misspoke. I should have said the tax rate could go so high it could not get approval by the voters."

The Justice looked amused. "Do you think, if the majority of voters had a domain, they would refuse to vote for a higher property tax rate?"

"Uh, no, Your Honor." The Attorney wilted and stepped down from the podium.

We waited for the Supreme Court's decision, and while we waited, we fought the hog farm. Fortunately, we had the revised zoning laws to help us. These gave the County the power to deny the application on the basis of unauthorized alterations of the neighbors' domains. The company, which had been formed to build the hog facilities, appealed the rejection to the County Commissioners. In a three-to-two vote they were denied. They sued, and the case went to the Second District Court. The Court procrastinated, since they knew our case on the issue of domains was in the hands of the Supreme Court, and a decision had not yet been handed down. This gave us a little breathing room.

I hadn't been to Civalia for upwards of a year and a half, having been closeted with Maggie about the court cases, and in Rawlins and Laramie for the court hearings, caring for John's Folly, working with political candidates, and spending my obligatory time on my now appropriated domain. So when Stellan stopped by John's Folly and asked if I wanted to see how Civalia was coming, I jumped at the chance. We rode the tram from Civalien Inn to Civalia and were greeted at the station by Gyan and Cindy. Since I hadn't seen her for a time, I was shocked to see how much Cindy had grown and matured. She took my arm and started pulling me off to see her chickens, but Stellan intervened.

He pointed toward the edge of the meadow and asked, "Have you noticed the changes in the ephemeral stream on the north side of the meadow?"

"I've been too busy to pay much attention," I answered, "but now you mention it, I do see the brush and willows have grown considerably."

"There's a reason for that," Stellan said. "We've reintroduced beavers in the water shed on the forest, and they first turned this into an intermittent stream, and this year it looks like it'll be perennial. We're getting a new beaver pond near the lower end of the meadow. A lot of plants, birds, insects, and other critters are coming with it"

I was awed as I swept my gaze along the former watercourse, thinking back on what this meadow looked like when I had first been here with Ralph and now seeing the increased biological growth and activity in the region. I was pulled from my reverie by Cindy impatiently tugging my arm.

On the way to see Cindy's chickens, Gyan showed us some of his experimental plantings, and we grazed on some indeterminate peas he had been developing. Dehumidifier wheels slowly revolved on the inside wall of the greenhouse, and some of the residents, most of whom I had met at one time or another but was not particularly familiar with, were busy at various gardening tasks. Some bees buzzed around plants that were flowering. Gyan told me that since there were not enough flowering plants in the greenhouse to support a bee hive, they had developed a hive allowing the bees to roam both outside and inside.

"The chickens like to eat 'em," Cindy said, and tugged on my arm again.

We went on to where Cindy's chickens were grazing in a section of the greenhouse. We approached a glass wall, which I assumed was installed to limit the range of the chickens. However, when we came to the entrance to this wall, it was an airlock. I asked Gyan about this feature.

"We're experimenting with segmenting the greenhouse into different biomes with different temperature, humidity, and lighting conditions. We think this will give us more diversity of edible plants and more resilience against possible plant disease and insect infestations."

When Cindy stepped into the enclosure, several hens came running. The chickens gathered around her, crowding, clucking, and scrapping with each other. Then, when she scattered some grain, each hen immediately focused on pecking up as many grains as possible. Cindy told me how they were rotating the hens through the greenhouse to control insects and prune some of the lower foliage. She showed me the mobile hen coop she had built to move them and house the hens at night and told me the hens also provided eggs for the residents.

Cindy's hens were in one of the latest greenhouse sections constructed. Stellan asked, "Do you see anything different?"

I looked around but didn't immediately see anything.

"Look at the outside wall," he said.

I did so and immediately saw through the already head-high foliage that the outside greenhouse wall resembled, in some respects, an Indian cliff dwelling. In particular, it was elevated compared to private areas built when the first few Civalia wedges were constructed.

"We learned as we went," Stellan said. "Most people wanted to have a view out over the top of the greenhouse foliage instead of looking at a wall of plants. Access is by either ramps or stairs, so we elders can still get about. We have plans to rebuild some of the earlier private spaces. A few, very few, people like the hidden-away feel of the original ones, but we'll probably convert most of them to storage spaces."

"What other changes have you made?" I asked.

"You know about the change we made to the overall shape; making Civalia a Nautilus spiral, so we could have a south facing entrance on the west side."

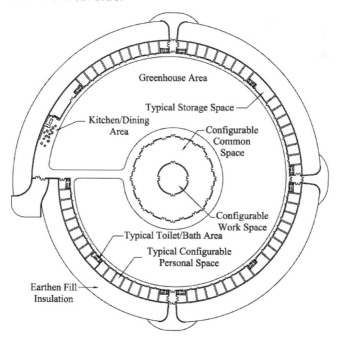

"Yes," I said.

"But there is something else I want to show you."

Stellan led us to the inner side of the greenhouse and began walking along the arcade around the outer edge of the communal space. Up ahead, I saw a grand portico forming an entrance to a section. The portico had fluted Ionic columns and a pediment over the doorway.

"That's new," I said.

"Yes, it is," Stellan answered.

We stopped in front of this architectural item, and I looked inside. I was expecting a grand hall or something, but there wasn't really anything of note to see; just an ordinary common room, probably being used as a classroom, judging by the furnishings, equipment, and occupants. I turned to Stellan with what I'm certain was a puzzled expression.

He grinned and told me to feel one of the columns. I did so, and was surprised to find it warm to the touch.

Stellan then said, "If you listen carefully, you will hear a swishing sound. These two columns contain the cylinders of one of your liquid piston engines. The turbine is under the hypocaust floor, and the fluid injection equipment is in the pediment. This is the first prototype, but I'm sure we'll be making more. Other settlements have already inquired about us building them some."

After some time, I reluctantly moved on and saw more of Civalia. As I paid more attention to my surroundings, I noticed a proliferation of art works.

When I commented on this, Stellan said, "Even though constructing an edifice of this size and complexity takes a lot of hard work and time, I'm amazed at how much time and energy we've all had for other things in our lives; socializing, hobbies, reading, research, music, you name it. Now that construction is coming to an end, there is even more time. Let me show you something else."

Stellan led me farther around the arcade and we pushed through some heavy, double doors. The music I now realized I had been hearing on a subliminal level was immediately louder.

"This is our auditorium and practice area," Stellan said.

"There's almost always at least one person in here practicing. Occasionally we have a concert, but they tend to be short and informal, much like Skinner suggested they would be in *Walden Two*."

We listened for a short time to a range of playing, some obviously beginners, and some quite accomplished. It was all fairly faint. When I asked Stellan about the sound levels, he told me, "We've made massive walls in this section, so it's fairly soundproof. Some residents expressed an aversion to loud music, so we've designed this section to be isolated. For some of the concerts, we open these outer doors and the music drifts into the greenhouse area. The private areas are also all sound-isolated. This auditorium is where we have our group meetings." We walked out to the arcade, and the music sounds were almost shut off as the double doors closed behind us.

We began walking back along the arcade when I observed, "Your residents seem to be engaged in a wide variety of activities. What's an average day like?"

"Roughly speaking," Stellan said, "we're moving toward the Nearing's three fours. We still have to work about six hours a day five days a week to feed ourselves and keep up with all the other chores, including taking care of our domains. But I expect that will decline with our construction phase ending and the forest getting into better shape. The rest of our time, we either follow personal pursuits or get together in groups of various sizes to do a wide range of social activities."

Stellan stopped and turned to me. "John," he said, "I've never been so content and been so fulfilled before in my life. I've heard others of us say the same thing. What we've done is . . . is. Well, I think it is beyond words."

I got a lump in my throat and my eyes became teary. We began walking again.

"What happened with the television issue?" I asked. "I re-member we agreed that issue should be decided by the entire Civalia membership." I paused, "I don't like the word membership. It sounds like a club, but I can't think of anything better."

Stellan smiled. "With Kajika's help, we've come to refer to ourselves as a tribe, the Civalia Tribe, and the consensus was to not introduce television into Civalia. So far, nobody seems to have missed it. Creativity has blossomed. Besides the artworks and the musical repertoire, our library has grown with works written by the residents themselves. Diane is writing a history of Civalia."

We walked outside through the west entrance. When I stepped out the door, I was greeted by a sight that seemed to belie what

Stellan had just told me. A young man was working on what was presumably a sculpture, but to me it was hideously appalling. The young man looked up and saw us, put down his tools, and came over wiping his hands on a rag.

"Hi, Sean," Stellan said. "Are you making progress?"

"You bet," Sean said.

Stellan introduced us.

"What do think of my sculpture?" Sean asked.

I was flummoxed and stammered for a moment trying to think of something nice to say, but finally broke down and said, "It looks like a pile of shit!"

Sean beamed and Stellan smiled.

"What's going on here?" I asked, looking from one to the other.

Stellan drew me over to an easel with a drawing on it, and showed me a sketch of what the completed sculpture would look like. "Sean calls his sculpture *Civalia Groks Entropy*, and you have just validated his work. The base is supposed to look just like what you labeled it. As you can see from his sketch, eventually you'll see plants and creatures of all types rising up, out of and above this base, intertwining into intricate, graceful shapes, and culminating in some clear, calcite, artificial shell that tapers off into filaments. Sean intends it to show entropy being radiated into space. I don't know exactly how he's going to do it, but I'm confident he'll get the job done. We're all awed by what he's done so far, not just this, but his other artwork in Civalia."

We talked for a while longer, Sean expressing how nice it was to work with geopolymer and artificial shell material. He was particularly pleased to be able to build his sculpture by completing a section and then pouring more geopolymer on top to add height. Most sculpting, he told me, was done from the top down, but these materials allowed him to work from the bottom up. As Stellan and I prepared to leave, Sean looked at me rather intently and said he had heard a lot about me and was please to finally meet me.

Stellan and I wrapped up our tour, and I departed with more than a little feeling of longing for the dynamic social cohesion I had detected in the Civalia Tribe. I drowned this longing in the continued battle of promoting Civalien philosophy and economics.

Elaine called me and asked if I had been listening to the news. I had not. "Well," she said, "a Category 5 hurricane went across Antigua two weeks ago. Callaway has been trying to call and e-mail Wainright ever since, without any response. I think Wainright must have been injured, killed, or gone somewhere else. I've decided this is a good time to bring in Callaway."

I agreed and spent some time contemplating my dream about being a bank robber. As the raptor, I had watched the robber stagger into a rain storm and disappear. I don't know what happened to him, and I still don't know what happened to Wainright. I hope he disappeared as completely and permanently as the robber in my dream.

When Elaine picked up Callaway, he was shocked to learn we had known about his putting the beryllium powder apparatus into Civalien Inn. He confessed to doing it for Wainright after Elaine threatened him with aggravated battery. In the end, because no one had been hurt and we weren't eager to press charges, Callaway settled for having his contractor's license revoked. He left Rawlins for parts unknown.

The opinion of the Wyoming Supreme Court was finally released, and it was a bomb shell! They agreed that domains should not be taxed. However, they stated the definition of a domain should be established by scientific criteria and then set forth in law; they referenced the paper I had written on the mathematical basis for domains. We immediately contacted our legislators, the Governor, and the University of Wyoming to try to establish the University as the agency for scientifically defining domains.

I'm certain the opposition also began an immediate lobbying campaign. Cass, Maggie, and I began crisscrossing Wyoming giving lectures and presentations, and handing out flyers we had written. We arranged even more tours of Civalia, concentrating on legislators and University faculty and administrators.

But we did not ignore the citizens of Carbon County. We held a massive ice cream social on National Ice Cream Day, increased the number of people we invited to Civalien Inn for meals, and held concerts specifically for local residents.

We reached some of the business owners in Carbon County, particularly those having considerable debt. The number of declared business bankruptcies increased markedly during this time. However, some of the business owners grew angry as demand for their products and services began to decline. Multi-state corporate businesses began closing because of falling revenues. We tried to support the local business owners as best we could, but at the same time, hasten the demise of the corporate businesses and franchises.

When the legislature met the next spring, there were droves of lobbyists camped out in Cheyenne; Maggie, Cass, and I were among them. We had worked with our Carbon County representatives and the Albany County legislators to craft legislation funding the University to perform the required research and develop a procedure to establish domains. In addition, our proposed legislation would make the resulting domains lawful throughout the state. The political battle was fierce. Amendments were added and ripped away, vested interests attempted to kill the bill outright, there were demonstrations for and against it on the capitol lawn, impassioned speeches were made on the floor, ink flowed in newspaper editorial, and the amount of money spent on advertising against the bill would have floated a battleship.

We judged this negative advertising backfired, because inquiries to existing settlements increased significantly. When we asked some of these inquirers what had motivated them to make contact with a settlement, they told us they had first heard of us through the flood of negative advertising. Because they had never heard of us before, they were curious to know what we were really about. A significant number of them eventually signed on, and Civalien Project settlements began springing up all across the State.

In the end, the legislature figured they had to do something in response to the Supreme Court ruling, so they kicked the can down the road. Monies were authorized for the University to research and study domains, but they did not go so far as to protect them from seizure and eminent domain.

We went to Laramie and began working with the University to have a hand in setting up the research and study programs. That was exhausting work, and we felt like we spent most of our time spinning our wheels. When the semester ended, we headed back to Civalia with a multi-disciplinary University research team that included members from eleven different departments within five different colleges. We put them up as well as we could, taking over the Hotel Wolf in Saratoga.

As the summer dragged on, three significant things happened. The Second District Court ruled in our favor in the suit brought by the hog farm company, stating the Supreme Court had upheld the validity of domains, even if the exact size and composition of the domains were yet to be determined. Therefore, rejection of the hog farms permit was sustained. Next, we got a tax change through the County Commissioners to exempt domains from taxation and to compensate by increasing property taxes on all corporate and large private land holders. Lastly, a significant number of the UW researchers began to sympathize and identify with us; several going so far as to inquire into joining one of the growing number of settlements. As per their charge, the research team began to converge on consensus of how to measure and size domains.

A researcher from the Department of Sociology, Ingrid Cleary, became intrigued with the fact the vast majority of residents in Civalia were not married. She formed hypotheses, interviewed residents, formed new hypotheses, designed some experiments, and finally came to the conclusion that having a domain freeing them from dependence on others reduced the attraction for marriage for all individuals, both female and male. Although most of the residents of Civalia did not use their freedom to get away from everyone else, the knowledge they could, coupled with a handful of emergency camping kits available to any Civalia resident who wanted to use one, appeared to reinforce their independence. Individual private quarters for everyone also helped.

Ingrid also attributed some of the lack of interest in marriage to the community structure where individuals were not isolated, so not lonely. Furthermore, they were engaged in meaningful work, so not feeling useless, and challenged with creative endeavors, so not feeling stifled. That summer also saw the first baby born in Civalia, and Ingrid observed the more common burdens and woes of motherhood were missing. The new mother, instead of feeling trapped by the demands of her new baby, had to turn away help and interest in her newborn from the entire community, which, along with the her, had planned for this new arrival.

Another facet of Civalia that intrigued Ingrid was the relative lack of disputes and aggression compared to "normal" American society. We had noticed this also. Again, the possibility of getting away from everyone and thinking about things seemed like a critical factor in defusing anger. No one in Civalia had yet invoked the option of calling for a jury of their peers to settle a dispute.

"You know," Ingrid told me, "when I was in grade school, some representatives from a kibbutz in Israel visited my school and talked with us about life in their kibbutz. I was struck by how open and guileless their faces were. I trusted them implicitly. I think that experience started me on the road to becoming a sociologist. I'm seeing this same thing here in Civalia."

However, not all was as Ingrid observed in Civalia. A settlement had started up near Encampment with some extremely controlling founders. They shortly came in conflict with a neighboring settlement when they tried to take over a very large swatch of land. They refused to communicate with any outside people, and a number of their original members deserted. They seemed to me more of a cult than anything else. The question was what to do? The County assessor had been designated as the official responsible for administering domains, and she, in this case, had determined the settlement had excess lands, so their non-domain tracts were taxed heavily.

They either could not, or would not, pay those taxes, so these holdings were seized and sold at auction. Elaine and Melvin had the unenviable chore of evicting them and selling the property. Eventually, the founders abandoned their structure and left the area. A number of the former residents moved to other settlements. Most of these people needed significant time and counseling to adapt to a Civalien settlement. Some never did and moved away or became reclusive. Civalien, Inc. bought the structure, but it was so poorly done, and contained so many undesirable features, such as prison cells and a throne room, that we simply tore it down. The planning office tightened their review procedures, requesting more detailed design and use information.

Cass's Satisfaction with Life Index impressed Ingrid. With Cass's help, she initiated a research project comparing non-Civalien Project individuals with those living in Civalien settlements. The Index values for Civalien residents were significantly higher than those of the control group selected from the general population in the surrounding communities. Ingrid was one of the researchers who joined Civalia.

During the summer, Sean added statues of the important contributors and principle pioneers and founders of Civalia to his *Civalia Groks Entropy* sculpture. These included Stellan, Gyan, Cindy, Ralph, Geraldine, Manjinder, Anand, Diane, Elaine, Maggie, Wainright, and me. I argued with him about including me and Wainright, but he insisted much of what had been built would not have happened if it hadn't been for both of us. His sculpture was a striking sight when approaching Civalia from the County Road.

And Sean had done more. Somehow he had integrated light collection features and light pipes into the sculpture, so during a sunny day, the faces of the various statues were successively illuminated throughout the day. Not only that, but he'd integrated some of Stellan and Manjinder's optical film technology, so the colors of illumination for each individual statue were different, and the color on each face subtly changed with the seasons. Watching these changes was mesmerizing.

Looking back, that summer was clearly a turning point for the Civalien Project. Raising property taxes for lands not designated as domains began to drive corporate business and large absentee land holders out of the County. Having at least a preliminary means of defining domains in a variety of environs opened the floodgates for individuals seeking domains. The planning office became overwhelmed, so we worked with the County Commissioners to add staff, and worked to contain and organize the chaos. In the fall elections, Civalien Project sympathizers swept the County Commissioners seats. Further County reforms became easier and accelerated the exodus of the highly taxed land owners and corporations.

That summer another event occurred that was a second major turning point. One day when I happened to be there, a stranger came into John's Folly without knocking. I'd never met him before, and he began berating me for raising the taxes to "astronomical levels," as he put it. He was shaking his finger in my face and his eyes were blazing. I happened to have been harvesting some bananas from a dwarf banana tree Gyan had been experimenting with. The bananas I'd cut down were lying on a small table beside me. I tore one off, never taking my eyes off him, scored the base of the stem with my thumb nail, and pushed it against the hand he was using to shake his finger at me. He reflexively took the banana and began shaking it at me, continuing to tell me off, spittle flying from his mouth. I tore off a second banana, stripped the peel halfway down, and took a bite of the banana. The man followed suit, never taking his eyes off of mine and never stopping his harangue, but he pulled the banana back and peeled it halfway down. When he took a bite, he seemed to come out of a trance.

He looked down at the banana, looked back at me, and said, "Awe, shit. What've I been saying?"

"You were telling me what a shithead I am, and worse, for getting your taxes raised," I said, still looking at him.

He looked at the banana tree. "How in hell do you raise bananas in Wyoming?" He swept his gaze slowly from left to right, taking in the extent of John's Folly. Then he looked up at the ceiling where our light panels were distributing the sunlight from the heliostats throughout the greenhouse. "Where in hell is the light coming from? This looked like a pile of dirt from the outside." He gave me a strange look, turned, and went out the door, taking another bite of the banana as he went. He never looked back.

I was more than a little shaken after this encounter, and it was a while before I felt grounded enough to go look for Ralph. I didn't find him, but I found Geraldine. When I described the man to her; medium height, dark brown hair and brown eyes, athletic build, dressed like he was headed out to the golf course; she said she didn't know who it might be, but she told me Ralph could be found at his house by the County Road. I snagged a Bruck, the one Anand had modified by adding a sail. The wind happened to be favorable, so I sailed, instead of pedaled, to Ralph's. The combination of concentrating on controlling this wind wagon and the thrill of its speed somewhat calmed me.

When I started describing my visitor, Ralph said, "Sure, I know 'im. That there's Malcolm Russell. He stopped by here earlier today an' asked where 'e might find ya."

"Tell me about him," I said.

"He's the manager uh that there Ol' Baldy place. Been there fer years. What'd 'e want from ya?"

I described my encounter with Malcolm to Ralph. He rubbed his chin and said, "He's got money an' interest in that place, an' ya've probably hit 'im hard. Far's I know he's a good guy."

Over the next few weeks, I never saw Malcolm again, but other people told me he'd been around. He'd made reservations for dinner and worked off his OUs at Civalia several times. He'd also struck up conversations with some of the Civalia Tribe and got them to give him tours of the common areas of Civalia. He appeared particularly interested in the work area and our liquid piston engine designed to look like a portico, but he also had many questions about the greenhouse and Civalien economics. I also learned he had shown up at some of the other settlements and talked with their residents.

I became worried Malcolm was casing Civalia to find some way to exact revenge for our role in raising his taxes. I consulted with Elaine about this situation; she did a background check on Malcolm, which came up empty. Furthermore, her discrete inquiries gave the picture of an outstanding citizen. She advised me to begin adding security to Civalia and all of our associated structures, a move I was loathe taking, since there was almost always someone around. I procrastinated on even bringing that issue up with the Civalia tribe.

Ralph told me Malcolm had stopped by and talked with him

two or three more times. When I asked what they'd talked about, Ralph told me Malcolm had asked how we'd financed all of this construction, and the story came out about how I'd gotten his, Ralph's, land back for a fraction of what Wainright had borrowed from the Amalgamated Bank of Omaha and how I'd borrowed against my shop and then declared bankruptcy. Malcolm commented about how that sounded like a certain President. Ralph recalled they had both chuckled at that quip. Ralph, concerned Malcolm might get the wrong impression of me, then told him about how I'd told him about banks bringing money into existence with a stroke of a pen, so to speak, and then charging interest on it or getting real property by foreclosure.

Hearing this information about Malcolm's investigations, I became even more fearful he was planning something nasty, so I resolved to increase Civalia security. However, before I got around to taking any concrete action, a tragedy occurred. According to witnesses at the Old Baldy Club, at about eight in the morning, Malcolm had taken the tractor/backhoe out, something he did quite often, to work on the irrigation system near the southern end of the golf course. He hit a high pressure gas line. The resulting fire raged for over three hours before the gas could be shut off, and it incinerated the back half of the tractor. Pictures of the scene in the Saratoga Sun showed the cab of the backhoe had been literally melted into a puddle. Some human remains were found, mostly the residue of incinerated bone, but some remnants of Malcolm's stainless steel watch were found when the site cooled enough to search. The community was stunned, but I have to admit I was a little relieved.

Two days later, I received an ordinary looking envelope with no return address in the mail. I expected it to be junk mail, but when I opened it, I was astonished to find a cashiers' check in the amount of $314,722,034.00, made out to Civalien, Inc. Certain this had to be some sort of scam, I turned it over, expecting to find some sort of pitch on the back designed to make me part with a significant amount of money. There was nothing there but the usual signature line and all of the usual disclaimers. When I examined the front side again, I saw the purchaser had been none other than Malcolm Russell. The letter was postmarked in Denver the day before the fire. I called Elaine, asking her for an escort to Rawlins. I would have liked to have had an armored car, but an escort was the next best thing.

In Rawlins, I poured out my story to Elaine, and showed her the envelope and the check. She treated them as evidence, examining them carefully and dusting them for prints.

"Did you know there is a message written on the inside of the envelope?" she asked.

"There is?" I said.

"Is says, 'Sorry I yelled at you. You are right in so many ways.' That's followed by the initials MR."

"Do you suppose this is any good?" I asked.

"There's one way to find out," Elaine said.

Elaine escorted me to the Rawlins National Bank, where I presented the check to the teller for deposit into the Civalien, Inc., account. You'd have thought we'd stuck a stick into a hornets' nest. First there was a succession of ever more senior bank representatives, then there were calls to ever increasingly higher levels of governmental agencies, then there were return calls from ever increasingly higher levels of law enforcement agencies, and finally there began to be the appearance of representatives of ever larger news networks. All this took place over the next five hours while we were in the bank.

I was exhausted, and it took Elaine's police powers to even get us back to the Sherriff's Office. I holed up at Elaine's house for about a week until the furor had died down. The check turned out to be good, but the funds were being withheld until a full investigation could be done. Elaine was my conduit into what was happening, and when they finally released the funds to Civalien, Inc., she told me what had happened.

Apparently, Malcolm had contacted a number of bankers and Wall Street members of the Old Baldy Club, telling them the Civalien movement in the area was threatening the Club in many ways. He said the most immediate threat was the defection of hired help, which was true, and the longer-term threat was closing or restricting the airport from lack of help, which also had a grain of truth. These events, if allowed to mature, would prevent them from flying into the Club in their personal jets.

Funds were needed to stave off these threats, and although, he never said it in so many words, the bankers and Wall Street tycoons understood the funds would be used to "exhort and convince" local officials to curb the Civalien movement and to not only maintain the airport, but to expand it to accommodate ever larger jets. Hence they sent funds directly to Malcolm, a trusted employee. The bulk of these funds were to find their way into the airport expansion. Still, the amount seemed exorbitant. Elaine wondered how Malcolm had gotten so much. So did I. Elaine's investigations revealed these types of transactions for other causes had occurred in the past.

A lot of these funds, come to find out, being "off the books," were not totally by the book. Banks made loans without proper vetting, Wall Street tycoons used slight-of-hand tactics, and overall the funds were what Elaine called "dodgy." Since there was no contractual obligation for these funds to be used in specific ways, there were no legal handles for them to be retracted. I also learned the amount he had actually received from these people was closer to $400 million, but most of the difference was still in Malcolm's estate and was being fought over by a hoard of lawyers. I suspected there would be little left for the litigants when the smoke cleared from the battle. There had already been multiple bankruptcies and suicides.

I did the calculations and arrived at the conclusion Malcolm had left 20 percent of the amount he collected for the donors to fight over, similar to the 20 percent I'd allotted for the Amalgamated Bank of Omaha. He'd also targeted the bankers and tycoons who feed off the spoils of money created out of thin air. While I had not personally made all the moves and decisions which dumped over $300 million in the Civalien, Inc. bank account, I was still responsible in a significant way for them. When I added up all the amounts that have flowed into the Civalien Project, the first shot from the Amalgamated Bank, several hundred smaller shots from individuals joining the various Civalia-like communities and financing construction by using my formula, and now this massive infusion from Malcolm, the total was more than $370 million.

Elaine also told me Malcolm had spent a significant amount of time in Denver prior to his death, probably dealing with financial matters, since the cashiers' check came from there. However, he had been spotted a couple of times in the Civic Center Park on East Colfax by surveillance cameras. He didn't appear to be doing anything except loitering, so maybe he was just killing time before some other meeting. However, I've been in that park, and one of the salient features is the homeless population. I wondered whether Malcolm had some other objective being in the park. Was the body destroyed in the backhoe really Malcolm's? I'll never know.

What I do know is the monies he gave helped thrust the expansion of the Civalien movement into high gear. Significant expansion has occurred throughout Wyoming, eastward into Nebraska and South Dakota, southward into Colorado, northward into southern Montana, and westward into Utah and Idaho. Isolated locations have sprung up throughout the United States and also in a handful of other countries.

Settlement size and architecture have varied from our classical Civalia model, understandably, because each must be compatible with the local biomes and the people who inhabit it. A scattering of individual domains has appeared, also understandable, since some people are reclusive. Specialized manufacturing has appeared at most of the settlements. For example, Civalia became the source of LPE generators and solar powered dehumidifiers, while Civalia II was known for manufacturing high quality artificial shell. Other settlements specialized in glass, musical instruments, Brucks, organic electronics, light guides, leather, wool fabric and clothing, wood products, and a whole host of other items that have the capacity to make life easier and more enjoyable while minimizing entropy production. One specialty specifically interested me. Using research carried out at the University, Civalia II began making various types of cordage from spider silk. I used this technology to replace the metallic tram cables between Civalia and Civalien Inn.

Much of this expansion of settlements and diversification of manufacturing can be traced to the money Malcolm gave to Civalien, Inc. Sean, recognizing Malcolm's contribution, added a statue of Malcolm to his *Civalia Groks Entropy* sculpture.

As the Civalien Project expanded, the local city governments and then the county governments began to shrink. In part, this was due to a reduction in demand for their utility and trash collection services. The reasons for this were obvious, citizens moving out of the towns and cities for Civalien settlements, and these settlements providing these services for themselves. However, other reasons also existed. Theft declined, since wealth began to shift from what one owned to what skills and knowledge one possessed, and personal satisfaction began to rise as remarked by Ingrid. Some small changes in Wyoming government toward more Civalien Project values also began appearing, driven by the Wyoming Supreme Court decision. Geraldine, Ralph, and I looked forward to the day we could dissolve Civalien, Inc.

What remained sacrosanct and gained robustness at all settlements was the production of the basic necessities of life, Maslow's bottom two Physiological and Safety Levels. Our lives were made easier and richer by debt mediated trade, reducing our entropy footprint at the same time, and allowing Civaliens everywhere to seek the upper three levels of Maslow's pyramid. Domains to supply environmental services and the basic tenant of self-sufficiency are key.

This revolution, generated by many thoughtful caring people, is well beyond any that just my feeble efforts could have achieved. Even now, when I step out at night and look up at the stars, realizing the time is approaching when I'll disappear as Gerald did several years ago, I can't help but wonder whether this avalanche of change, which I at least had a hand in initiating, will prove to be positive, negative, or neutral when viewed in geologic time. I have confidence this change is more aligned with the physical laws of the Universe, so I trust it will be positive.

APPENDIX I

THE PHYSICS OF CIVALIA

The Science of Energy Transformations and Entropy

An understanding of energy transformations and entropy requires an understanding of thermodynamic systems and the first and second laws of thermodynamics. In the 1850's Rudolf Clausius, a German physicist, working in the theoretical realm of the heat engines of the day, envisioned volumes of space containing matter and radiant energy, which he termed systems. Each system is surrounded by an imaginary boundary, these boundaries being infinitely flexible and stretchable. They are one of three types; an open system boundary allowing mass, heat, and work to freely cross; a closed boundary allowing heat and work to freely cross but not matter; and an isolated boundary allowing no matter, heat, or work to cross.

When a system is considered relative to the First Law of Thermodynamics which states **energy cannot be created or destroyed, only transformed**, a more succinct statement being **energy is conserved**, the general energy balance equation for a system is:

$$E_{final} - E_{init} = Q_{in} - Q_{out} + W_{in} - W_{out} + E_{mass-in} - E_{mas-out}$$

Where $E_{final} - E_{init}$ is the net change in the system energy; $Q_{in} - Q_{out}$ is the net heat into the system; $W_{in} - W_{out}$ is net work into the system; and $E_{mass-in} - E_{mas-out}$ is the change in energy within the system associated with mass flows into and out of the system. This general equation describes an open thermodynamic system.

In a closed system no mass crosses the system boundary, and the equation becomes:

$$E_{final} - E_{init} = Q_{in} - Q_{out} + W_{in} - W_{out}$$

In an isolated system no mass, heat, or work crosses the system boundary, so the energy change in such a system is always zero:

$$E_{final} - E_{init} = 0$$

Even though the change in total energy of an isolated system is zero, energy transformations can take place within the system. For these or any energy transformations a <u>source</u> of energy at a given potential must be present, and there must be one or more <u>sinks</u> at lower potential, i.e. places for the energy to go in its altered forms.

All energy transformations occur with varying levels of friction from zero, a purely hypothetical situation, to 100 percent. Transformations with zero friction are termed reversible, and the portion of transformations attributed to any friction greater than zero is termed irreversibility. These portions of the transformations leave a significant amount of energy unavailable for doing useful work, and some friction, irreversibility, is always present.

Clausius showed heat losses from the engines he was experimenting with prevented the engines from being 100 percent reversible. Building on Sadi Carnot's thermodynamic work describing heat engine efficiency, Clausius found the heat lost from the engines divided by the absolute temperature was a quantifiable property of the engine systems. He coined the word "entropy," from the Greek word entropia, which means "turning toward" or "transformation," to describe this newly recognized measure of the unavailable energy produced by any energy transformation.

This work led to the Second Law of Thermodynamics, which states **the sum of entropies in energy sources and sinks will increase with any energy transformation, the limit being no change for a perfectly reversible transformation.**

A closer examination of energy transformations gives insight into the ramifications of the Second Law. Suppose a simple energy transformation occurs; a rock rolls down a hill. The rock initially has gravitational energy equivalent to the weight of the rock times the vertical elevation difference between the top and the bottom of the hill. As the rock begins rolling, some of the gravitational energy is converted into kinetic energy in both the linear motion and angular rotation of the rock. Some of this kinetic energy is transformed into displacements of the soil, vibrations in the ground, sound waves, and other frictional, displacement, and vibrational energies, all of which dissipate into the environment and become unavailable. Most ends up converted into increased temperature in the environment.

When the rock finally comes to rest, all of the initial gravitational energy can be accounted for, but it has been transformed into a myriad of different energy forms which cannot be utilized again. This is an irreversible energy transformation. But wait. Can't Sisyphus roll the rock back up the hill and make it a reversible transformation?

Sisyphus can indeed roll the rock back up the hill, but he will have to transform energy from another source to raise the rock, plus the energy to move his own body up the hill, plus the energy to keep his body going, plus the energy to overcome any friction he might encounter. His work does not make the original transformation reversible. The sum of entropies in the energy sources and sinks has increased markedly.

With these ideas in mind examining the entropy balance for thermodynamic systems leads to new insights. If the boulder on the hill of this example exists within an isolated thermodynamic system where mass, radiant energy, and work do not cross the boundary, Sisyphus, having mass, could not come to its rescue and return it to the top of the hill. Neither could he use a long pole to push it to the top of the hill, applying work to the rock through the system boundary. Nor could he use a radiant energy tractor beam, if such a device existed, passing through the system boundary to reposition it.

For all energy transformations in an isolated system the differential entropy balance equation with respect to time is then:

$$\frac{dS_{cv}}{dt} > 0$$

where S_{cv} is the entropy within the system, and dt is an infinitesimal time interval. If an energy transformation could be perfectly reversible, the entropy change would be zero. Otherwise, for any real energy transformation there is a positve increase in entropy within the closed system.

To the best of current knowledge and observation the Universe is an isolated system. Myriads of energy transformations are taking place throughout the observable Universe, and the entropy of the Universe is increasing. This is evidenced by star deaths, collisions of galaxies, and a host of other cosmic events. Astronomers tell us how some of the events caused by this increase in the entropy of the Universe will affect the Earth. The time will come when total solar eclipses will no longer happen on the Earth as the moon moves farther away and the sun consumes its hydrogen fuel and grows larger.

In the even more distant future the time will come when no stars outside our galaxy will be visible from the Earth, since the Universe is expanding and all of the stars are dimming as they accelerate away from us with the expansion of the universe. Although it's a long time in the future, the visible light from the stars outside of our galaxy will wink out one by one as the Doppler shift moves the light out of the visible spectrum. It will be star light, star dim, the last star ever visible.

The winking out of all these stars will take trillions of years, and long before, about another five and half billion years, the sun will have turned into a red giant and swallowed up the Earth. None of us alive today will have to worry about any of these events, nor will we have any control over them.

The fact the Universe is an isolated system gives some idea of what constitutes the allegorical top and bottom of the energy hill. The greatest energy potential appears to be mass, which has the

Einsteinian energy equivalency $E = mc^2$. The lowest potential is the background, longwave, cosmic radiation at a temperature of 2.7 degrees Kelvin. All energy transformations take place in this theater, dancing and swirling their way from the top of the hill to the bottom. Even though some transformations go up the potential hill, there are always countervailing transformations of greater magnitude headed down, so the overall trend is down the hill.

The Thermodynamics of the Earth

The Earth, essentially a closed thermodynamic system, exists within this cosmic theater. Radiant energy crosses the boundary of the Earth system as does some work. Usually a negligible amount of mass crosses the boundary, but occasionally there is a significant event such as the Tunguska Event in Russia on June 30, 1908. Another is the formation of the Yucatan peninsula, thought to be formed by an asteroid impact. Nevertheless, for the vast majority of the people and the majority of the time, the Earth is a closed system. An estimated 40,000 metric tons of space dust falls on the Earth annually, but an estimated 95,000 metric tons of the lighter elements in the atmosphere, mainly hydrogen and helium, escape into outer space. These decrease the mass of the Earth by an estimated 0.000,000,000,000,001% annually. This miniscule mass transfer indicates for practical purposes the Earth can be considered a closed system.

The path of most energy chains on Earth starts with mass being converted into shortwave radiant energy in the Sun. Some of this transformed solar radiation enters the Earth's system through the boundary around the Earth. The rate of this energy flow is 172,500 terawatts at 5,800 degrees Kelvin. 50,000 terawatts are reflected without being transformed. Three terawatts of gravitational work driving the tides also flows across the Earth's boundary into the Earth system. These two energy flows are the only two significant sources of external energy and carry about 21 terawatt-seconds per degree Kevin per second of entropy into the Earth system.

The First Law of Thermodynamics requires a corresponding flow of energy must be exiting the Earth system, equal to the rate of energy entering, i.e., it must be balanced. If this is not true, the

Earth would either heat up or cool down until the balance was restored. In Geologic time an average 122,500 terawatts of heat have radiated from the Earth. Currently this energy radiates at a temperature of 283 degrees Kevin, the average temperature of the Earth as seen from space, and carries with it 433 terawatt-seconds per degree Kevin per second of entropy out of the Earth system. The extra entropy being carried out is entropy produced by the energy transformation chains taking place within the Earth system. Radiating heat into outer space is the only means for exporting entropy.

The entropy balance equation for a closed system is:

$$\frac{dS_{cv}}{dt} = \sum \frac{\dot{Q}_j}{T_j} + \dot{\sigma}_{cv}$$

Where Q_j is the change in the jth heat energy component in infinitesimal time t, T_j is the absolute temperature of Q_j, and $\dot{\sigma}_{cv}$ is the additional produced entropy within the closed system in time t. One clear conclusion from the last term of this equation is any transformation of internal stored energy within a closed system will increase the entropy of the system. The Earth is no exception; transforming energy stored within the Earth produces entropy. Some of these are natural transformations, for example, gravitational shrinkage, cooling of the core, natural transformation of radioactive materials, and other natural geologic phenomenon. All of these have a total energy flow of about 30 terawatts. The entropy produced by these transformations is responsible for raising the temperature of the Earth enough to export this additional produced entropy with radiant heat.

The vast majority of the solar energy entering the Earth system drives the gigantic heat engines of the weather, ocean movements, and the hydrologic cycles. These elemental transformations move air and water around and evaporate water, depositing some of the water as stored gravitational energy in snow, ice, and liquid water elevated above sea level, and the salinity gradient energy from purified water. A small fraction, 133 terawatts, of solar energy goes into the biome, 67 terawatts of that becoming net photosynthetic production. The collection of energy transformation chains within the biome is of particular interest, because these chains are the basis of all life, ours included.

All living creatures, if considered as thermodynamic systems, are open systems. Such systems exchange radiant energy, mass, and work with their environment, and they produce entropy within their systems. The entropy balance equation for an open system is:

$$\frac{dS_{cv}}{dt} = \sum_j \frac{\dot{Q}_j}{T_j} + \sum_i \dot{m}_i = s_i - \sum_e \dot{m}_e s_e + \dot{\sigma}_{cv}$$

Where $\dot{m}_i$ is the rate of the ith mass stream entering the system, s_i is the specific entropy content of that incoming mass, $\dot{m}_e$ is the rate of the eth mass stream exiting the system, and s_e is the specific entropy content of that exiting mass, and $\dot{\sigma}_{cv}$ is again the produced entropy within the open system, in this case any animate or inanimate system within the closed system of the Earth.

Why Entropy Matters

Entropy, the measure of the quantity of unavailable energy in a system, is perhaps best thought of as a measure of waste. This unavailable energy does not just disappear, but remains present and degrades the sinks into which it flows. It's embodied in the trash we throw out, the sewage we create, the CO_2 we breathe out, the exhaust and wastes we send into the atmosphere from our vehicles, homes, factories, farms, toys, and from every energy transformation, no matter how small or how large. This unavailable energy enters one or more of the three intermediate sinks we have on the Earth, the air, water, and soil.

Just as your home, vehicle, factory, etc. become uninhabitable, lethal in fact, in short order if entropy produced in them is not rejected into the intermediate sinks and builds up in their systems, combustion products, sewage, and manufacturing wastes, for example, so will the Earth become uninhabitable if the entropy in the intermediate sinks cannot be rejected into outer space, and radiant heat is the only vector to do so. Obviously, any waste energy in a form other than radiant heat must be transformed into radiant heat to be exported out of the Earth system. Solar and tidal energy can be used to transform waste energy for export, but internal stored energy generally cannot, since it contributes to the entropy load in the intermediate sinks.

The factors governing how entropy in the form of heat is carried out of the closed Earth system are found in the Stefan-Boltzmann Equation for thermal radiation:

$$\Delta P = e\sigma A (T_1^4 - T_2^4)$$

Where ΔP is the net power flow in Watts, σ is the Stefan-Boltzmann constant, $5.67 \times 10^{-18} W\ m^{-2}\ K^{-4}$, A is the area of the radiator, e is the emissivity of the emitting surface (unit less), and T_1 and T_2 are the emitter and receiver absolute temperatures, degrees Kelvin, respectively. When considering the Earth the area is constant as is the receiver temperature, so the two variable factors are the emissivity and the temperature of the Earth as seen from space.

Major factors affecting emissivity are texture and color, which change with human activity; building, paving, logging, mining, desertification, plowing, summer fallow, clearing, burning, contrails, and grazing, particularly overgrazing, to name a few. Some natural factors are cloudiness, ground cover, snow and ice cover, and atmospheric gases. Emissivity is related to absorptivity, so changing the emissivity will likely directly change absorptivity. Therefore, increasing emissivity will not only increase the radiant energy leaving the Earth, but will also likely increase absorptivity, hence the amount of incoming radiant energy needing to be exported.

The Biome

The operation of the biome has some unusual features when compared to the inanimate energy flows on the Earth. In the biome solar energy is captured by photosynthetic autotrophs, and they extract relatively higher entropy substances, carbon dioxide, water and other simple substances from the intermediate sinks of the air, water, and soil, transforming them into oxygen and complex carbohydrates. In doing so, plants transform the entropy associated with these high entropy materials and transfer it as heat into the environment along with the entropy produced in the chemical reactions and their respiration. This waste energy is then radiated into outer space. Heterotrophs feed directly or indirectly on the plant material, and their entropy is rejected back into the intermediate sinks as carbon dioxide, urine, feces, sweat, heat, and other minor detritus. These high entropy substances are further broken down by decomposers adding more entropy to the intermediate sinks. The autotrophs then begin the cycle again.

Human Impacts on the Biome

Thus far this discussion presents the action of the energetic systems on the Earth as they largely existed prior to the Industrial Revolution in the 1800's. Since that time humans have added six new, significant factors to the natural energy chains on the Earth:

- extracting and transforming vast quantities of internal stored energy,
- decimating significant areas of the plant community,
- reproducing beyond the human carrying capacity of the Earth,
- appropriating about 40 percent of the net photosynthetic production on the Earth,
- developing and distributing vast quantities of materials which decomposers and photosynthetic autotrophs cannot convert,
- and learning to transform orders of magnitude more energy than our human ancestors prior to the industrial revolution were capable of doing.

The roster of internal energy transformations include geothermal, nuclear, and the most significant, fossil fuels. Fossil fuel energy use in the last century has been about 6,830,000 terawatt hours, having an entropy production of approximately 1,410,000 terawatt-seconds per degree Kelvin. If the entirety of this entropy production had been heat, a very minor temperature rise would have occurred to export this entropy. However, a significant percentage of the entropy produced in the combustion of fossil fuels is rejected into the intermediate sink of the air as CO_2.

NASA records the CO_2 content of the atmosphere cycling between 170 and 302 ppm for the last 800,000 years until 1950 when it was about 310 ppm. Since then it has shot up until it is currently 410 ppm. The fossil fuel use in 1950 was about 20,000 terawatts hours, and the usage has increased to over 133,000 terawatt hours in 2017, an energy flow rate of around 16 terawatts, a significant percentage of the 67 terawatt flow through the biome. The annual usage continues to increase and the CO_2 concentration with it. The biome, originally sized to handle the CO_2 production for terrestrial energy transformations is overwhelmed by this added production.

The insulating effect of CO_2 and other greenhouse gases is increasing the surface temperature of the Earth, as a higher temperature differential is required to transport heat through the insulating layer to maintain the 122,500 terawatt energy flow out of the Earth. This increased CO_2 in the atmosphere has stored an additional 24 million terawatt-seconds per degree Kelvin of entropy since 1950. In the last 55 years the top 2,000 meters of the ocean has also increased in temperature to store an additional 1.2 billion terawatt-seconds per degree Kelvin of entropy.

Compounding the problem of internal energy transformation use is the physical reduction of the photosynthetic autotrophs on a global scale. The forest areas of the Earth are estimated to be reduced by 80% from pre-historic coverage. One example of this is the Cedars of Lebanon, which were reduced to tiny remnants of the original forests. A current example is the destruction of the Amazon Forest in Brazil. Farming also reduces overall autotroph activity by laying the soil bare for extended periods and destroying the soil biome necessary for vigorous, healthy autotroph growth. Another avenue of autotroph destruction is land "development" with building, paving, mining, and other human activities that destroy autotroph habitat.

Much of these autotroph habitat destroying activities are driven by the increase in the human population on the Earth. The population, now exceeding 7.7 billion people has reduced the per capita surface area to around 16.3 acres, an area slightly smaller than four, average-sized, Wal-Mart Supercenters. Of these

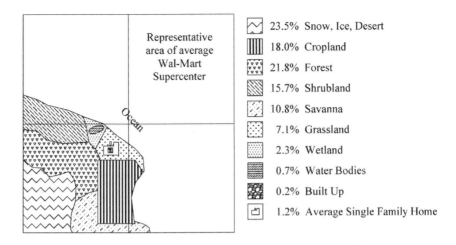

	23.5%	Snow, Ice, Desert
	18.0%	Cropland
	21.8%	Forest
	15.7%	Shrubland
	10.8%	Savanna
	7.1%	Grassland
	2.3%	Wetland
	0.7%	Water Bodies
	0.2%	Built Up
	1.2%	Average Single Family Home

four Supercenters, 1.15 of them are land, and the rest are ocean. Snow, ice, and desert cover 23.5% of the land, and humans utilize another 37.6% of the land, 18% for cropland, 19.4% for pasture, and 0.2% developed. An averaged sized single family home being built in the United States today, 2,400 square feet, will cover 1.2% of the land.

These numbers show an overwhelming presence of Homo sapiens leading to humans appropriating, either directly or indirectly, around 40% of all fixed photosynthetic energy. This taking of the source of life has increased the extinction rate for animals, insects, and birds by 1,000 to 10,000 times. Plant extinctions are also now beginning to appear.

The fifth new factor humans have introduced into the world is the development of many new materials which the natural processes, decomposers, and autotrophs cannot break down and utilize. A couple of the more visible of these are such things as rubber tires and plastics, although many chemicals, such as tri-chloroethylene, PCBs, dioxin, and DDT, all known a POPs, Persistent Organic Pollutants, exist and are widely scattered. Around 8.3 billion tons of plastics have been manufactured since the 1950's. The overwhelming fraction of these is still in existence, a significant part of them floating in the oceans. Damage to all wild life and particularly marine life is extensive. Humans are also not impervious to this damage, and studies have shown we may eat as many as a 100 micro-particles of plastic with every meal.

The sixth factor humans have added to the natural energy transfer chains on the Earth is the knowledge of how to transform prodigious amounts of energy. In everyday life individual people commonly release and control energy flows which may be up to hundreds of thousands times greater than their own. This transforming of large amounts of energy in relatively small geographical areas produces the heat island effect of cities, which has been known for decades. The temperature in a city of a million people can be one to three degrees Celsius higher on the average than the surrounding countryside. Variations throughout the day can be as high as 12 degrees. The release of heat and aerosols from large cities can also change the wind and precipitation patterns around the cities, turning humans into unwitting, incompetent, weather gods.

We've come to expect such power, but what we are doing is generating tremendously more entropy, which if the Earth is to remain habitable, must be exported into outer space and most often times is not. The real issue with Homo sapiens seems to be we do not recognize we are not energy source limited, we are energy sink limited.

An Exordium

The current situation seems apocalyptic and hopeless, but only if viewed from the trajectory of the current paradigm of endless economic growth, unlimited energy transformations, and unbounded population increase. While the situation is dire and significant change cannot now be avoided, by changing our paradigm and creating a society based on the physical laws of thermodynamics and entropy, a way to a realistic, pragmatic future is possible. The fork in the road is before us, and we must choose between the paths to perish in our own flood of entropy or radically reduce our entropy production. Entropy, the actual foundation of time, will not wait for us to contemplate this choice for long.

APPENDIX II

CIVALIA ECONOMICS

The performance of modern, western, market-economic systems is measured by Gross Domestic Product, *GDP*, which is all the goods and services produced within a specific geographical area, usually a country, in a given time period, usually a year. Given the broad scope of this measurement, it represents the basic functioning of these economic systems. The equation for *GDP* is given as:

$$GDP = C + I + G + X$$

where *C* is the Consumption Function, *I*, is the Investment Function, *G* is Governmental Purchases, and *X* is the Net Export Function. The Consumption Function, *C*, is given by the equation:

$$C = a + MPC \times DI$$

where *a* is Autonomous Consumption, i.e., the minimum level of consumption, spending, necessary to remain alive, *MPC* is the Marginal Propensity to Consume, and *DI* is Disposable Income *DI* is given by the equation:

$$DI = GDP - T$$

where *T* is the Tax Function given by the equation:

$$T = FT + t \times GDP$$

where *FT* is Fixed Taxes, and *t* is the Effective Tax Rate.
The Investment Function, *I*, is given by the equation:

$$I=i+MPI\times DI$$

where *i* is Fixed Investment, i.e. the minimum level of investment, spending, necessary to keep infrastructure and durable goods habitable and operational respectively, *MPI* is the Marginal Propensity to Invest, and *DI* is again Disposable Income.

The Net Export Function, *X*, is given by the equation:

$$X=x-MPm\times GDP$$

where *x* is Exports, and *MPm* is the Marginal Propensity to Import.

Examining these equations shows *GDP* appears on both sides of the *GDP* equation, and the traditional means of solving this equation is by iterative calculations. However, an equation can be derived from this collection of related equations which has the single *GDP* variable on the left hand side of the equation and reveals the true nature of the economic systems based upon it.

Although a single *GDP* variable can be isolated from the complete *GDP* equation, to investigate the fundamental nature of economic systems based on *GDP*, some confounding factors, which presumably give a modicum of control to the basic systems, can be removed. Assuming imports and exports balance makes *X* zero, an idealized situation, and assuming government is neither spending nor taxing removes the arbitrary machinations of government. The *GDP* equation then becomes:

$$GDP=C+I$$

Substituting for *C* and *I* gives:

$$GDP=a+MPC\times DI+i+MPI\times DI$$

Substituting for *DI* gives:

$$GDP=a+MPC \times (GDP\text{-}T)+i+MPI \times (GDP\text{-}T)$$

Since taxes are assumed to be zero and imports and exports are assumed balanced, the equation no longer calculates *GDP*, but merely represents money flowing through these economic systems, so setting *T* to zero and substituting *$* to represent money flow for *GDP* produces the equation:

$$\$=a+MPC \times \$+i+MPI \times \$$$

Rearranging the equation gives:

$$\$=a+i+\$(MPC+MPI)$$

Subtracting *$(MPC+MPI)* from both sides of the equation yields:

$$\$\text{-}\$(MPC+MPI)=a+i$$

Rearranging provides an equation with a single *$* variable:

$$\$(1\text{-}(MPC+MPI))=a+i$$

Finally, dividing both sides of the equation by *(1-(MPC+MPI))* isolates *$*:

$$\$= \frac{(a+i)}{(1\text{-}(MPC+MPI))}$$

Both *MPC* and *MPI* are fractions between zero and one, but precise equations are not possible for them, because they depend on consumer confidence and a host of other factors such as weather, international relations, the political climate, and the latest fads. However, their general trends are known. They will obviously be zero if *$* falls to or below the minimum spending, *(a+i)*, and they will increase as *$* rises above *(a+i)*. This means they are positive slope functions of $\$$, and increase as $\$$ increases and decrease as $\$$ decreases. If $\$$ increases, the denominator of the fraction on the right hand side of the $\$$ equation decreases, thereby further increasing $\$$ over time. Conversely, decreasing $\$$ increases the denominator and further decreases $\$$. Also obviously the sum of *MPC* and *MPI* cannot be equal to or greater than one without this equation becoming undefined or meaningless.

This action of this equation is a classic instance of a positive feedback system, and explains why modern, western, market-economic systems are prone to wild oscillations, i.e. bubbles and crashes, irrational exuberance and recession, wild speculation and depression, bull and bear markets. In economic systems based on *GDP* a deviation towards a bubble causes more impetus to increase money flow, and a deviation toward a crash applies force to decrease the flow. A common positive feedback system most everyone has experienced is the screech of a PA system when sound waves from the speakers feed back to the microphone. The same phenomenon occurs in these economic systems.

Understanding the positive feedback nature of our economic system leads to an understanding of why the Federal Reserve attempts to maintain a two percent inflation rate along with a commensurate percentage *GDP* growth rate. Why these positive growth rates?

Obviously, maintaining a negative trend would insure the greatest depression ever with no possibility of recovery as everything spiraled down, pushed by the positive feedback. If a zero growth rate is attempted, history has shown, via the Dow Jones Industrial Average, the growth of US stocks, and other financial indicators, negative movements in the *GDP* are generally steeper in negative than in positive movements. Therefore, recovering from a slight downturn, a decidedly negative deviation in this scenario, would be more difficult to recover from than if a small positive growth rate is maintained, In this case a slight downturn might just be a slowing of the growth rate and not a negative trend. Maintaining a positive trend minimizes the probability of falling into a recession or depression, but it does not prevent such a scenario.

Why not go for even higher inflation and *GDP* growth rates, avoiding negative inflation and growth even more? The answer to this question lies in human psychology and perception. Like the proverbial frog in a pan of slowly heating water not recognizing a fatal situation, people tend to not recognize the slow decrease in their purchasing power at a two percent inflation rate. This slow rate takes approximately 35 years for prices to double, the majority of the working life of many people. If it were higher, say ten percent, prices would double about every seven years, a very noticeable time frame.

The problem with continuous growth is it's impossible. Nothing can grow forever; as anyone who has, or have known someone with, cancer can attest. The question then becomes: what can be done?

There is no physical reason why an economic system cannot be designed to be a negative feedback system, a system similar to home heating and cooling systems. In a negative feedback system a deviation from the set point causes a correction in the opposite direction to the deviation. This is what the Federal Reserve Bank attempts to do after the fact by jiggering the interest rate, and the Federal Government does by "stimulating" the economy with massive amounts of deficit spending. The fragility of this system was apparent in the latest crash of the 2008 financial system. What's needed is a robust, inherently-negative, feedback system.

Changing the sign in the denominator of the equation derived from the existing economic system:

$$\$ = \frac{(a+i)}{(1+(MPC+MPI))}$$

converts the economic system into a negative feedback system. With this change, when $\$$ increases, the denominator on the right hand side of the equation increases, driving $\$$ down and corrects the increase. The opposite is true for decreases in $\$$, thus providing corrective negative feedback.

There may be other ways to convert to a negative feedback economic system, either some other modification of the existing system or perhaps some totally different economic system formulations incorporating negative feedback. This is an area which begs for study, experimentation, and application. However, changing from a positive feedback system to a negative feedback system is imperative to prevent the current positive feedback economic systems from destroying the Earth as surely as cancer destroys individuals. One way to make this change is given in this book, and I leave it to the reader to ponder the question: why have positive feedback economic systems based on *GDP* been allowed to continue for millennia?

READING LIST

An understanding of energy and entropy must be based on clear, accurate scientific concepts. Some works I have found meetings these criteria are:

Ashby, Michael F. *Materials and the Environment–Eco-Informed Material Choice*, Elsevier, 2009

Jensen, Johannes, Sørensen, Bent *Fundamentals of Energy Storage*, John Wiley & Sons, Wiley Interscience Publications, 1984

Schmidt, Philip S., Ofodike, A. Ezekoye, Howell, John R., and Baker, Derek K. *Thermodynamics–An Integrated Learning System*, John Wiley & Sons, Inc., 2006

Smil, Vaclav *General Energetics–Energy in the Biosphere and Civilization*, John Wiley & Sons, Wiley Interscience

Sørensen, Bent *Renewable Energy–Its physics, engineering, environmental impacts, economics & planning*, Third Edition, Elsevier Academic Press, 2004

Many authors have applied some of the basic physics knowledge and existing data to various aspects of the transformation of energy, but primarily to the dominant energy source, fossil fuels, within human societies on Earth. These include:

Butler, Tom, Wuerthner, George and Heinberg, Richard *Energy –Overdevelopment and the Delusion of Endless Growth*, Post Carbon Institute, 2012

Daniels, Farrington *Direct Use of the Sun's Energy*, Ballantine Books, New York 1964

Deffeyes, Kenneth S. *Beyond Oil–The View from Hubbert's Peak*, Hill and Wang, New York, 2005

Gever, John, Kaufmann, Robert, Skole, David, Vörösmarty, Charles *Beyond Oil–The Threat to Food and Fuel in the Coming Decades*, University Press of Colorado, 1991

Heinberg, Richard *The Party's Over–Oil, War and the Fate of Industrial Societies*, New Society Publishers, 2003

Juhasz, Antonia *The Tyranny of Oil–The World's Most Powerful Industry—and What We Must Do to Stop It*, William Morrow/ Harper Collins, 2008

Rifkin, Jeremy *Entropy–A New World View*, Bantam Books, 1980

Roberts, Paul *The End of Oil–On the Edge of a Perilous New World*, Mariner Books, 2004

The results of the massive energy transformations of the industrial age; a partial list is over population, pollution (another name for entropy buildup), deforestation, desertification, and water scarcity; have been documented by numerous authors:

Catton, William R., Jr. *Bottleneck–Humanity's Impending Impasse*, Xlibris, 2009

Catton, William R., Jr. *Overshoot–The Ecological Basis of Revolutionary Change*, University of Illinois Press, 1980

Cohen, Joel E. *How Many People Can the Earth Support?*, W. W. Norton & Company, New York, 1995

Ehrlich, Paul and Ehrlich, Anne *Extinction–The Causes and Consequences of the Disappearance of Species*, Random House, 1981

Ehrlich, Paul *The Population Bomb–Population Control or Race to Oblivion?*, Ballantine Books, 1970

Erickson, Jon *Dying Planet–The Extinction of Species*, Tab Books, 1991

Gore, Al *Earth in the Balance–Ecology and the Human Spirit*, Plume/The Penguin Group, 1993

Graham, Frank, Jr. *Where the Place Called Morning Lies–A Personal View of the American Environment*, The Viking Press, New York, 1973

Kay, Jane Holtz *Asphalt Nation–How the Automobile Took Over America and How We Can Take It Back*, University of California Press, Berkley, 1997

Mann, Michael E. and Kump, Lee R. *Dire Predictions–Understanding Global Warming*, Pearson Education, DK, 2009

McHarg, Ian L. *Man: Planetary Disease*, ED 061 052, Transcript of 1971 B. Y. Morrison Memorial Lecture, Agricultural Research Service (DOA), Washington, D.C.

Navarra, John Gabriel *The World You Inherit–A Story of Pollution*, The Natural History Press, Garden City, New York, 1970

Meadows, Donella, Randers, Jorgen and Meadows, Dennis *Limits to Growth–The 30-year Update*, Chelsea Green Publishing Company, White River Junction, Vermont, 2004

Reisner, Marc *Cadillac Desert–The American West and Its Disappearing Water*, Penguin Books, 1986

Schell, Jonathan *The Fate of the Earth*, Alfred A. Knopf, New York, 1982

The Environmental Defense Fund and Boyle, Robert H. *Malignant Neglect*, Alfred A. Knopf, New York, 1979

Westphall, Victor *What are THEY Doing to MY World?*, Corwall Books, New York, 1981

Other authors have described the interaction of the predominant, capitalistic economic system in the world with energy transformations:

De Graaf, John, Wann, David and Naylor, Thomas H. *Affluenza–The All-Consumming Epidemic*, Second Edition, Berrett-Koehler Publishers, Inc., San Francisco, 2005

Dietz, Rob and O'Neill, Dan *enough is ENOUGH–Building a Sustainable Economy in a World of Finite Resources*, Berrett-Koehler Publishers, Inc., 2013

Greider, William Secrets of the Temple–*How the Federal Reserve Runs the Country*, Simon and Schuster, 1987

Hartmann, Thom *Unequal Protection–The Rise of Corporate Dominance and the Theft of Human Rights*, Rodale, 2002

Klein, Naomi *This Changes Everything–Capitalism vs the Climate*, Simon & Schuster Paperbacks, 2014

Mayer, Jane *Dark Money–The Hidden History of the Billionaires Behind the Rise of the Radical Right*, Anchor Books, New York, 2016

Perkins, John *Confessions of an Economic Hit Man*, Berrett-Koehler Publishers, Inc., San Francisco, 2004

Scott, Rachel *Muscle & Blood–The massive, hidden agony of industrial slaughter in America*, E.P. Dutton & Co., Inc., New York, 1974

Taibbi, Matt *Griftopia–A Story of Bankers, Politicians, and the Most Audacious Power Grab in American History*, Spiegel & Grau Tade Paperbacks, New York, 2011

Wolman, William and Colamosca, Anne *The Judas Economy–The Triumph of Capital and the Betrayal of Work*, Addison-Wesley Publishing Company, Inc., Reading Massachusetts, 1997

Some authors have written about how to live and build in more compatible ways with the world we live in:

Alexander, Christopher, Ishikawa, Sara, Silverstein, Murray, Jacobson, Max, Fiksdahl-King, Ingrid and Angel Shlomo *A Pattern Language–Towns Building Construction*, Oxford University Press, New York, 1977

Babauta, Leo *The Power of Less–the fine art of limiting yourself to the essential . . . In business and in life*, Hyperion, New York, 2009

Brown, Lester R. *Eco-Economy–Building an Economy for the Earth*, W. W. Norton & Company, New York 2001

Hensley, Marcia Meredith, *Staking Her Claim–Women Homesteading the West*, High Plains Press, 2008

Jackson, Wes *New Roots for Agriculture*, UNP–Nebraska Paperbacks, 1985

Ludwig, Ma'ikwe *Together Resilient–Building Community in the Age of Climate Disruption*, Fellowship for Intentional Community, 2017

Mails, Thomas E. *The Hopi Survival Kit*, Stewart, Tabori & Chang, New York, 1997

Nearing, Helen and Scott *The Good Life–Helen and Scott Nearing's Sixty Years of Self-Sufficient Living*, Schocken Books, New York, 1970

Reich, Charles A. *The Greening of America*, Bantam Books, 1970

Sale, Kirkpatrick *Human Scale–Big government, big business, big everything–how the crises that imperial modern America are the inevitable result of giantism grown out of control and what can be done about it*, Coward, McCann & Geoghegan, New York 1980

Ward, Barbara and Dubos, René *Only One Earth–The Care and Maintenance of a Small Planet*, W. W. Norton & Company, New York. 1972

Weisman, Alan *Gaviotas–A Village to Reinvent the World*, Chelsea Green Publishing Company, White River Junction, Vermont, 1995

Worster, Donald *Natures Economy*, Sierra Club Books, San Francisco, 1977

To do something about the world we now find ourselves in it is imperative we learn to think in unaccustomed ways. Several authors I have found who challenge us to examine and modify our thinking are:

Adams, James L. *Conceptual Blockbusting–A Guide to Better Ideas*, W. H. Freeman and Company, San Francisco, 1974

Brams, Steven J. and Taylor, Alan D. *Fair Division–From cake-cutting to dispute resolution*, Cambridge University Press, 1996

Davidovits, Joseph *The Book of Stone–Volume 1 alchemy and pyramids*, Geopolymer Institute, 1983

Eisler, Riane *The Chalice & The Blade–Our History, Our Future*, HarperSanFrancisco, 1987

Gardner, Martin *aha Insight*, Scientific American/W. H. Freeman and Company, San Francisco, 1978

Hampden-Turner, Charles *Maps of the Mind–Charts and concepts of the mind and its labyrinths*, Collier Books, New York, 1982

Hughes, William, Critical *Thinking–An introduction to the basic skills*, broadview press, 1992

Kohn, Alfie *No Contest–The Case Against Competition–Why we lose in our race to win*, Houghton Mifflin, 1986/1992

Lehrer, Jonah *Imagine–How Creativity Works*, Houghton Mifflin Harcourt, Boston, 2012

Medina, John *Brain Rules–12 Principles for Surviving and Thriving at Work, Home, and School*, Second Edition, Pear Press, 2014

Neill, A. S. *Summerhill–A Radical Approach to Child Rearing*, A Wallaby Book by Pocket Books, New York, 1977

Orbanes, Philip E. *Monopoly®–The World's Most Famous Game & How It Got That Way*, Da Capo Press, 2006

Postman, Neil and Postman, Andrew *Amusing Ourselves to Death –Public Discourse in the Age of Show Business*, 20th Anniversary Edition, Penguin Books, 1985, 2005

Postman, Neil *Technopoly–The Surrender of Culture to Technology*, Vantage Books, New York, 1993

Sagan, Carl *The Demon-Haunted World–Science as a Candle in the Dark*, Ballantine Books, New York, 1996

Talbot, Michael *The Holographic Universe*, HarperPerennial, 1991

Velikovsky, Immanuel *Earth in Upheaval*, Doubleday & Company, Inc., Garden City, New York, 1955

Velikovsky, Immanuel *Worlds in Collision*, Dell Publishing Co., Inc., 1950

Some fiction can cause us to expand the boundaries of our thinking. A few authors who have done so for me are:

Abbott, Edwin A. *Flatland–A Romance of Many Dimensions*, Shambhala, Boston & London, 1999

Baker, Robert A., Editor *A Stress Analysis of a Strapless Evening Gown - and Other Essays for a Scientific Age*, Prentice Hall, 1963

Skinner, B. F. *Walden Two*, The MacMillan Company, New York, 1948

Quinn, Daniel, *Ishmael*, Bantam/Turner, New York, 1992

Heinlein, Robert A. *Stranger in a Strange Land*, Ace/Putnam, New York, 1991

Brunner, John *The Sheep Look Up*, Harper & Row, New York 1972

Forward, Robert L. *Dragon's Egg*, Del Rey/Ballantine Books, 1980

Forward, Robert L. *Starquake*, Del Rey/Ballantine Books, 1986

Niven, Larry *Ringworld*, Del Rey/Ballantine Books, 1980

Sherman, Alan *The Rape of the A*P*E*–The Official History of the Sex Revolution 1945-1973 The Obscening of America An R*S*V*P* Document American *** American Puritan Ethic **** Redeeming Social Value Pronography*, Playboy Press, 1973

ACKNOWLEDGMENTS

I wish to express my gratitude to my parents, Allen and Mildred Morton, for allowing me to think and explore as a child and providing me with the tools, extraordinary freedom, and challenges to do so. Then, as I entered the educational system, my teachers, both those I considered "good" and those I considered "bad," challenged me to think and introduced me to a wide range of ideas. I am grateful to all of those intrepid souls who helped me learn to use and develop my thinking, starting with my kindergarten teacher who was tasked with infusing knowledge into one girl and 26 boys. Only later can I appreciate the difficulty of her work that year.

When I entered college, one professor, Doctor Carl Cinnamon, stands out, since he started me on the path to exploring energy and entropy. I can still hear him say, "Anyone can scramble an egg, but where's the man who can unscramble an egg?" It was then I also met a lifelong friend, David Corthell, who challenged my thinking by introducing me to the recording artist Tom Lehrer and the author Allan Sherman. Their penetrating, perceptive satire helped open my eyes and begin to question the social mores and morays I'd been taught.

Toward the end of my college stint, I met a fellow student, Fred Hood, who became one of the most influential people in my life. Together we delved deeply into energy and entropy considerations. Without Fred's penetrating thinking and the support of him, his wife, Nicole, and their family, these ideas and this book might never have existed.

I also wish to thank the countless people over the centuries that have developed printing technology and written ideas into books so that I might read and consider them. What a wonderful gift! And I sincerely thank those who have helped me add the ideas in this book to the collection of books and ideas in the world. These include my editor, Catherine Cattarello; those who contributed art work, Eve Margo Withrow, Shannon Watts, Doc Thissen, and Pauline Verbest; and those who turned this book into reality, Robin Shukle and Liz Mrofka at What If Ideation and Publishing. Thank you, one and all.

ABOUT THE AUTHOR

 Scott Morton is a Wyoming native who has retired from an extremely varied career as a ranch hand, building contractor, inventor, mechanic, professional engineer, and mechanical engineering senior design instructor. Since retiring he has devoted his skills to "shopping" in his personal workshop, tinkering, restoring and displaying antique cars, building automated control systems, and writing creative instead of technical works.

Made in the USA
Middletown, DE
22 December 2019